"Are you sure we should do this?" she asked breathlessly.

"No. I'm never sure of anything with you."

They stared at each other, both aware that they were on a ledge from which there was no turning back. She willed him to make the first move. Without breaking eye contact, he slid his hand behind her neck, then his fingers tangled roughly in her hair. He pulled her close but didn't kiss her again. He seemed to be waiting for her permission. Lost in the storm of his eyes, she felt herself leaning forward slightly, her lips parting.

He needed no further invitation. His arm slid around her lower back, pulling her toward him as his other hand tugged her face roughly down to his. If the kiss in the park today had been unexpectedly steamy, she went into this kiss fully expecting the rush. And it delivered.

The kiss was every bit as hot as the one earlier, but this one had an extra layer of emotion. Somewhere under the burning haze of sexual desire she felt the pull of something else.

This kiss wasn't just about this moment. It held the promise of something more. Much more.

Only with You

LAUREN LAYNE

FOREVER

NEW YORK BOSTON

Forever
Hachette Book Group
237 Park Avenue
New York, NY 10017

www.HachetteBookGroup.com

Printed in the United States of America

First Edition: July 2014
10 9 8 7 6 5 4 3 2 1

OPM

Forever is an imprint of Grand Central Publishing.
The Forever name and logo are trademarks of Hachette Book Group, Inc.

For Allie.

I'm lucky to call you my sister;
luckier to call you my best friend.
There's a reason that the heroine of my
first book is a smart, sparkly,
irresistible little sister.

Acknowledgments

Only with You is not my first published book, but it *is* the first book I ever sold, and for that, I have a whole slew of thank-yous:

Anth: You were there since the very beginning when this book was little more than a gangly document written in the back of an airplane hangar. You never doubted that I'd get here. I love you.

To my agent, Nicole, who read the first five pages of this book from the slush pile and asked for more. Without you, I'd be lost.

To Lauren Plude and the entire Grand Central Publishing team: thank you for believing in this story from the start and making my dream of becoming a published author a reality.

And to all of my friends, families, and colleagues, who upon learning that I'd sold *Only with You*, said, "Well, of course!": your unwavering confidence was and is my rock.

Only with
You

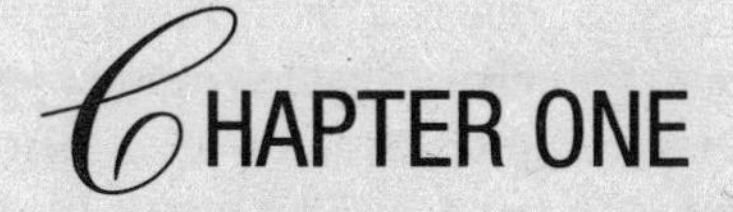

Chapter One

If only the boots had come with some sort of warning label.

Perhaps a succinct sticker reading, HOOKER.

Or even a tasteful note card indicating, "These shoes will change your life."

But the knee-high, rhinestone-covered boots said neither of these things, and so Sophie Claire Dalton made the most crucial decision of her life without having all the information.

Not that Sophie *realized* the magnitude of the choice she was about to make. If someone were to ask her about the important decision of her life, the feminine dilemma of shoe choice probably wouldn't have been on her radar.

She might have thought it was the tearful junior prom date decision between Adam and Gary.

(Adam. Way cuter. Less acne.)

Or perhaps the melodramatic soul-searching about whether to pursue soccer or cheerleading.

(Cheerleading, totally. Boxy athletic shorts hadn't stood a pubescent chance against a flippy little skirt.)

It could have been her long-deliberated college destination.

(Stanford. Yep, Sophie was one of *those* girls.)

Then there was the choice that had nearly ripped her heart out. Jon McHale had dropped to his knee their senior year of college with a diamond ring the size of her face and the promise of yuppie housewife security.

(Answer: No. Although *that* decision had been particularly rough. The ring had been Tiffany and the man had been sweet.)

Or perhaps most likely, Sophie might have guessed the proverbial fork was the debate over whether to finish her stint at Harvard Law or drop out and pursue a life of, well... aimlessness.

(Current occupation: cocktail waitress.)

And yet, none of these decisions would be as life-altering as the choice she was about to make.

Classic strappy black sandals, or... The Boots.

Clueless to the magnitude of what she was about to decide, Sophie teetered over to the full-length mirror of her Las Vegas hotel room, tugging at the hem of her black miniskirt. She extended the black sandal on her left foot for inspection and winced. Surely that white, flabby, and unshaven stump wasn't *her* leg.

Damn. The testicle-shaped birthmark above her left knee said the limb was definitely hers. And the pasty complexion looked just about right for a lazy Seattle native in the middle of January.

As for the shoes, the delicate high-heeled sandals had potential. Sexy but understated. Very Audrey Hepburn. Very Jackie Onassis.

But on the other hand…

Sophie pivoted awkwardly to extend her other leg and inspected the boot option. They'd been an impulse buy (okay fine, a slightly *tipsy* impulse buy) from the Lover's Package sex shop for last year's Halloween costume of Sexy Space Girl.

Alas, due to some unflattering Halloween-day bloating, the Sexy Space Girl had never made an appearance, and Sophie had tackled Halloween as the green M&M for the third year in a row.

The boots had sat abandoned and unworn in her closet, awaiting their destiny.

Sophie chewed on her lip and considered. The boots were certainly tacky, but wasn't that kind of the point of a bachelorette party in Vegas? Particularly a bachelorette party for which the slightly unhinged bride had declared a theme of Totally Trashy? These boots were practically the poster children for trashy.

Not to mention they'd cover the glow-in-the-dark-white shade of her calves.

Decision made, Sophie flipped off her old standby black sandal. There'd be plenty of time to channel first ladies and iconic movie stars at job interviews and bridal showers.

The bride's pouty voice echoed in Sophie's ear. *I want my bachelorette party to be hella skanky and memorable. If you're going to be on your period that weekend, fix it.*

Which was totally reasonable, since all women could *totally* just up and regulate their uteruses with a firm talking-to.

Sophie was a sucker for traditional wedding hoopla, bachelorette parties included. But she wasn't looking forward to this one. Had the bride not been her cousin, and the maid of honor not been Sophie's sister, she would have bailed. But family was family, so here she was in a hotel room she couldn't afford, dressed like some sort of space-station call girl.

Grabbing her cosmetic bag, Sophie teetered into the bathroom and eyed the multiple mirrors. She pulled the magnifying mirror away from the wall and stared at herself in rapt horror. No pasty American female in her late twenties would have thought it a good idea to zoom in on skin that had been maybe just a *tiny* bit free with the gin and lax on the sunscreen.

Sophie pushed the judgmental mirror away and gave it the bird. She didn't need a crappy little mirror calling attention to her flaws. She had a mother and a sister for that.

Turning toward the normal, less judgmental mirror, she began applying her makeup with a heavier hand than usual. And the last step in the transformation to tart?

Fake eyelashes.

They'd been deemed mandatory for all bridesmaids. A Totally Trashy uniform of sorts. Sophie squinted at the elaborate packaging. Not only were these things like an inch long, but they had little fake gemstones on them. She shrugged. At least they'd match her boots.

After twenty minutes and a good deal of cursing (Jackie O was long gone by this point), Sophie managed to attach something that looked akin to bedazzled pube clumps onto her normally pale, stubby lashes.

Lovely, she thought. *Really lovely and classy.*

Last, she wound her blonde hair around a curling iron to create a mass of showgirl curls. Stepping back, she surveyed the overall results in the mirror. Not bad, considering.

This was not the Sophie Dalton who'd been dumped over

the phone yesterday afternoon while standing in the airport security line as the TSA agents were disassembling her carefully packed bag.

A bag that contained The Boots. And a purple vibrator. Which the judgmental little security man had *sooooo* not believed was a gag gift for Trish.

But *that* loser version of herself wasn't here tonight.

No, the Sophie in the mirror had her shit together. Granted, it was trampy shit. And she would have to blame the slightly red, puffy eyes on the dry Las Vegas air. Still, she thought she was hiding the pathetic pretty damn well. At least she wasn't wallowing at home with a pint of Ben & Jerry's.

Sophie yanked the curling iron plug from the wall and blinked back the tears that would probably send her fake eyelashes sliding down her cheeks. She wasn't even sure why she was crying. It wasn't as though Brian had been The One. He was the fun guy, not the husband potential you brought home to Mom. They'd only been dating for eight months and Brian had switched jobs no fewer than three times.

For once, *Sophie* had been the stable one in the relationship.

Which was why it stung when he'd told her yesterday that she simply didn't have enough *drive*. That he needed a woman who knew what she wanted, whereas Sophie was just floating.

Floating, he'd said. Right before the Sea-Tac Airport TSA agents had loudly commanded her to hang up the phone and repack her "pleasure toys."

Whatever. His loss.

Slopping on a glittery lip gloss that claimed to "plump"

lips into a sexy pout with God only knew what kind of chemicals, Sophie took one final glance in the mirror.

Skirt the size of a Band-Aid? Check.

Scrappy halter top barely covering her nipples? Got it.

Pole dancer makeup? Definitely.

And the final touch: boots that belonged in a brothel.

Perfect. She looked like a girl looking for no-strings-attached sex.

Exactly what she needed.

CHAPTER TWO

As with most massive Vegas hotels, the trek from her room to the elevator was more exercise than Sophie got in the average month. Six wrong turns later, she found herself in the barely lit elevator lobby of the thirty-sixth floor.

Sophie had been secretly hoping for one of the themed Las Vegas hotels. A girl didn't have to bother with faking class when surrounded by gaudy imitations of New York City or the Eiffel Tower.

But Brynn hadn't asked Sophie for input, which meant they were staying at one of the newer, swanky resorts. Not a tacky fake pyramid in sight. It was all sleek furniture, mod décor, and shitty lighting.

On second thought, maybe the resort *did* have a theme: ostentatious. Perfect for Sophie's sister and cousin.

She pulled out her cell and sent a text message to her sister.

On my way. Where should I meet you?

Her phone beeped almost immediately with a return message.

Sapphire in the lobby. I'll let Trish know you'll be late.

Sophie dropped the phone back into her clutch with an eye roll. *Two minutes* late. She hadn't even made it to the bar yet, and already she was getting a lecture. The elevator arrived with a chime, and Sophie sighed. Naturally, out of the eight possible elevator doors, the one that opened was at the far end from where she was standing.

Sound the judgmental alarm, big sister, she thought. *I might be a whole* three *minutes late.*

Thanks to the painful boots, Sophie's gait was more of a constipated shuffle than an actual walk. She was barely two-thirds of the way toward the open elevator when the doors started to close again.

"Oh, come on!"

Really? Of all the cities, Las Vegas hadn't had high heels in mind when they'd set up the elevator timing? But the Vegas gods apparently heard her dismay, because, as if on command, the doors reopened just as she reached them.

Finally something going her way. She shuffled into the dimly lit elevator and stumbled.

Oh wow. Okay, so *two* things were going her way. It wasn't the Vegas gods who had held the elevator for her. It had been another type of god entirely.

The tall, handsome variety.

Sophie was vaguely aware that she was gaping, but some men were simply meant to be ogled.

The perfectly tailored suit was definitely designer, and the subtle cologne smelled like money. His body had broad shoulders and a lean torso—the hallmark of a well-used gym membership.

The short cut of his brown hair only emphasized the classic masculinity of the square jaw and straight nose.

The eyes were a startling pale gray. Scratch that. Silver. And cold.

Sophie stiffened as she realized the physical appreciation was all one-way. Far from being admiring, his gaze was downright icy, and the rest of his face was completely expressionless. She instinctively disliked men who couldn't muster a simple, polite smile for strangers, especially when she was drooling like Cujo.

Still, his indifference was nothing a little flash of leg couldn't fix.

Sophie slipped into one of her more appealing characters. The one that had elderly men calling her "little lady," and the younger generation buying her martinis and jewelry.

Slowly, she slid her hand down her side and fiddled with the hem of her skirt in shy modesty, as if, *Oops*, she just now realized her tiny skirt barely covered her lady bits.

Knowing that his eyes would have drifted down to her thighs before gentlemanly manners insisted he look back at her face, she let her lips turn upward into a bashful smile and pulled at the tip of her hair self-consciously.

It was all done in a split second, the movements perfectly manufactured to imply that she had absolutely *no* idea how darling she looked.

Sophie eyed her prey to see how he was reacting to her routine.

Her smile slipped.

He hadn't taken the bait. He wasn't even *looking* at her. He was staring at the elevator doors with a pinched expression as though he couldn't wait to be out of a small confined space with someone so unsavory.

She narrowed her eyes. *Fine, then.* So he wasn't a seduction candidate. There'd be plenty of horndogs prowling around the Vegas Strip who would be interested in a little harmless rebound sex.

This guy's idea of sex was probably the equivalent of a nap. Efficient missionary position. Bra on. Disdain for messy body fluids. Yawn.

He reminded her of Brynn. They had that same uptight *Oh crap, I lost a tree trunk up my ass* expression. Still, she couldn't leave him alone. Not completely. The man's rigid posture and sullen mouth just begged to be provoked. Sophie took a step closer, hiding a smile as he shifted farther away from her.

"Hi there!" she chirped, knowing that her chipper tone would irritate him.

Silence.

She tried again. "Thanks so much for holding the elevator for me. As you can see, these boots here aren't exactly made for walkin'—"

Sophie's sentence broke off.

The elevator jolted sharply and everything went pitch-black before lurching downward in a faster-than-normal descent.

Ohmigod ohmigod.

The narrow platform soles of her boots were no match for Armageddon, and Sophie was thrown off-balance.

Directly into the arms of the Gray Suit.

She buried her face against his chest, her nails clutching at his neck like a terrified kitten. *Please, God, if you make this death trap stop plummeting I swear I'll stop pestering this grumpy man.*

The elevator shuddered again and then stopped.

She remained attached to the stranger as he seemed the only secure thing in sight. She inhaled the reassuring scent of Rich Man and relished the way his breath ruffled her hair. Vaguely she became aware that her nails were still clenched around the back of his neck, but she couldn't bring herself to move away from his warmth just yet.

He finally cleared his throat and pushed her upright with a rough grip on her shoulders. She whimpered slightly at the withdrawal of physical support, her mind still blank with terror.

"What the hell?" he muttered.

Sophie leaned her shaking body against the wall of the elevator, wishing the irritable stranger would hold her again. Just until the trembling stopped.

"Are we stuck?" she asked in an unsteady voice.

"Looks that way," he said gruffly.

He pulled a phone out of his pocket and used its light to illuminate the elevator control panel.

"Shit."

"What's wrong?" she asked.

"The emergency button isn't working. Nothing will light up."

Sophie peered in the direction of the elevator controls. "Are you sure you're hitting the right button? It should be the red one with the little fireman's hat."

He turned away from the control panel to stare at her. "I know what button it is."

Sophie winced. This could not be happening. She could *not* be stuck in an elevator while wearing less than she would to the beach.

Cool under pressure wasn't exactly one of her specialties, but she gave it a shot. Pushing panic aside, she forced herself to think.

"Cell phone!" she said. "We can call from our cell phones."

But The Suit was way ahead of her, already pushing buttons on his fancy phone. The expression on his face said it all. No service.

"Check yours," he commanded.

"Yes, sir!" she grumbled, fumbling around for her clutch and pulling out her phone. The only benefit of the complete darkness was the fact that he didn't have to watch the way her miniskirt persistently climbed its way up her hips.

Please get a trillion service bars, she silently begged her phone. Even dealing with Trish in all of her holy Bridezilla horror beat being locked in a tiny black box with the human equivalent of dry ice. But all she saw was the sad little symbol of no service.

"Nothing," she moaned. "We're totally stuck. Shouldn't the elevators have emergency lights or something?"

"They're *supposed* to," her companion said darkly.

Realizing that her legs were still shaking, Sophie slid down the wall until she was sitting on the elevator floor. She wasn't claustrophobic. Not exactly. And she didn't have a fear of heights, but...

She was scared.

"Are you crying?" he asked.

"No." She sniffled.

"Oh Jesus. You are."

She heard a sigh followed by the sound of sliding fabric. Surprised, she realized he'd just settled on the floor beside her. He pressed something against her elbow.

A handkerchief. Not a rough paper tissue, but a soft, actual handkerchief. How perfectly cliché. What decade was he from? She accepted it reluctantly, knowing that she was bound to get black mascara streaks all over its pristine whiteness, which would only foster his grumpiness.

But it was either that or show up to the bar looking like a raccoon.

Wiping her watery eyes, she looked at him. So maybe she was a *tiny* bit grateful for his presence. Being stuck with a jerk beat being stuck alone.

"You should know I'm not going to save this as a memento," she said, waving the handkerchief defiantly in his face.

"What?"

"You know, like in the movies when the gentleman hands the distraught lady a handkerchief and he finds out at the end of the movie that she's saved it for like decades as a keepsake?"

"What movie is that? It sounds awful."

"Never mind," she said on a sigh. No imagination, this one. "So what do we do now?"

"We wait. It's a modern hotel; they'll have realized by now that something's wrong."

She nodded, knowing he was probably right.

"Christ," he muttered under his breath. "Of all the days, and of all the women."

Sophie stiffened at the scorn in his tone. "Oh, I'm sorry, would there be a more *convenient* time to get stuck in an elevator? Or a more preferable woman? A mute nun, perhaps?"

He didn't answer. Which was answer enough.

"What exactly is your problem?" she asked. "You can't so much as smile at a stranger, much less make standard small talk when stuck in a small, confined space?"

Nothing.

The elevator jerked suddenly, and her hand grabbed at his leg in panic. The movement stopped as suddenly as it began, and they once again jolted to a silent stop.

"Oh God," she whispered, biting her lip against the next round of terrified tears, her fingers still clenched on the irritable stranger.

He tensed, but didn't remove her hand from its viselike grip on his thigh.

"What's your name?" he asked.

"Sophie." She sniffed. "Yours?"

"Gray."

That briefly distracted her from her terror. "Like the color?"

Like your suit? Like your eyes? Like your personality?

"Yes. Like the color."

"That's a nice name." It was sorta sexy. Very manly. He said nothing, but his leg shifted slightly under her grip, and she wondered if her hand was making him uncomfortable. Probably. She left it where it was.

"How long until we're rescued?" she asked.

"Soon. This is Las Vegas. I'm sure they have an elevator maintenance service nearby."

"Do you come to Vegas often?" she asked.

He let out the smallest of pained sighs at her continued conversation. "Every couple weeks or so," Gray finally responded.

"That often?" she asked, surprised. He didn't seem like the gambling type. "What's your vice of choice? Slots? Texas Hold'em? Lap dances? A little Cirque du Soleil?"

This time he didn't bother to hide his sigh. "Listen, I get that you're nervous, but do we have to, you know... talk?"

"Yes, we have to *talk*. It helps take my mind off the fact that we're stuck in a dark death box. Plus your conversational skills clearly need some practice."

"Are you always this noisy?" he asked.

"It's not like I'm singing show tunes. It's just small talk. You know...safe topics. Weather, movies, careers...Let's start simple. Where are you from?"

More silence.

"Chicago," he said finally.

She waited. Nothing. No detail. No reciprocal question. Not even a full freaking sentence. Sophie gently rapped her skull against the elevator wall in exasperation. "You're killing me. Don't you ever put more than three words together at a time?"

"Now who's being rude?"

Sophie fought for calm, both over nerves and temper. Her fingers tightened reflexively on his leg. She belatedly realized exactly how high her hand had slid up his thigh. Her pinky was almost touching...

Oh God. She froze as she realized she was practically *fondling* the horrid man.

Gray turned his head sharply toward her, and she felt his breath against her cheek in the confined space. He looked away just as suddenly and studied the ceiling.

"I'm not interested in acquiring your services, so you can save yourself the effort," he said quietly.

She blinked at him, totally confused. "My services?"

"You know, I mean..." He shifted uncomfortably. "I'm not really the type to pay for sexual, um...attention."

Heat and disbelief swelled to Sophie's head. She slowly pulled her hand away from his thigh as she processed what he'd just said.

"You think I'm a prostitute?" Her voice sounded like a twelve-pack-a-day chain smoker's.

Something unfamiliar crept over Sophie's cheeks, and she realized she was feeling something she hadn't in years:

humiliation. She couldn't even remember the last time she'd bothered to care what someone else thought of her. Somewhere between her family's lectures and getting her first job carrying full martinis on a tiny little tray, Sophie had learned to let the looks and snide comments roll off her.

She'd thought herself immune to surprised disdain and friendly condescension. She'd learned to deal with the label of "law school dropout."

But this?

A prostitute? It was a whole other ball game of embarrassment.

It was worse than the time she'd seen her mother's golf instructor at the bachelor party where she'd been working as a bartender. Worse than the time she'd been uninvited from her former best friend's engagement party for being too "showy." Worse than Brian accusing her of *floating*.

Sophie was still reeling when the lights flickered on. The elevator gave another sharp jolt before it began a downward descent. A very slow, *normal* downward descent.

"Looks like they fixed it," Gray said.

He climbed to his feet, and although he avoided her eyes, he must have had some long-stifled seed of humanity floating around, because he extended a hand to help her up. But there was no way Sophie would let her *hooker* hands touch his saintly ones, so she ignored the hand and crawled to her feet, more conscious than ever that she wasn't wearing enough fabric to cover a Chihuahua.

His gaze was fixed once more on the door, and she realized that he wasn't going to discuss the misunderstanding. He hadn't even *asked* if she was a hooker. He'd just assumed.

"You think I'm a prostitute," she repeated, her voice stronger this time.

His silver gaze flicked to hers. Then away. "Look, it's not that I don't respect your choices. I've just never been in the market for an escort service," he said.

"An *escort service*, is it? At least have the balls to call us what we really are. Call girl. Hooker. *Whore.*"

He flinched but didn't refute her.

"You know what I think of you?" she hissed, humiliation sending her into attack mode.

"I can hardly wait to hear," he drawled in a bored voice.

But he never heard. The elevator gave a small beep as they arrived at the lobby level, and the doors opened. A flood of voices and faces swarmed toward them. Correction: they swarmed toward *him*.

"Mr. Wyatt!" A small man in a flashy striped suit rushed forward to greet her fellow captive. "I can't believe it was *you* on that elevator. I'm so sorry, sir. I assure you, it will *never* happen again. I'm Philip Clinksy; as manager of the hotel, I'm personally horrified. If there's anything I can do—"

"No matter," Gray interrupted. "I'd like to continue with my dinner plans as soon as possible."

Sophie rolled her eyes at the sheer injustice of it all. It figured that the world's biggest jerk was apparently some sort of VIP.

"Very good, sir," Mr. Clinksy said. The man was practically bowing. "Mr. Wyatt, *of course*, your dinner will be on the hotel after this harrowing experience. We don't know what happened, but rest assured we have every possible technician looking into what affected your elevator..."

Gray shot him a cold look, and the manager stopped his ass-kissing abruptly. Silver eyes shifted to Sophie, and for the briefest moment she thought she saw something slightly human. Regret? An apology? Pity?

Oh God, please don't let it be pity.

He held her gaze for a moment before nodding his head slightly in the barest form of acknowledgment. And then he walked away.

Without a word.

Without an apology.

Without giving her a chance to explain that she was not who he thought she was. Or *what* he thought she was.

She waited for him to look back. Waited for him to realize that at the very least, some verbal acknowledgment of their minicatastrophe was required. But he kept walking.

A gorgeous shithead in a beautiful suit.

"Will you be joining Mr. Wyatt tonight?"

It took Sophie a moment to realize that the ingratiating Mr. Clinksy was talking to her.

"Oh! No. Definitely not. We're not together." *Not even if he paid me.* "Just two strangers stuck in the wrong place at the wrong time."

"Ah, I see." Was it her imagination, or did the hotel manager look slightly disdainful? The skimpy attire that had seemed like a good-natured joke in her hotel room now felt horribly demeaning. She longed for a sweatshirt.

"Well, I'm very sorry about all this, Ms...."

"Dalton," she responded with a faint smile. "Sophie Dalton."

"Are you a guest here? If there's anything we can do..."

Ten minutes later, Sophie had a handful of complimentary drink vouchers in her clutch, but her pride was hanging on by a thread. As she numbly wandered toward the bar, she had the oddest sense that something extraordinary had just happened. Something beyond getting stuck in an elevator.

Sophie was no stranger to embarrassing herself. Hell, for

that matter, she was no stranger to embarrassing *others*. Just ask her family.

But Sophie had always been in charge of those perceptions. Always decided the when and the where of her impropriety.

Until now.

After years of carefully selected choices on the path of mediocrity, a stranger had just succeeded where her friends and family had failed.

Sophie had just been introduced to rock bottom.

And this time, she hadn't even been looking for it.

CHAPTER THREE

Two weeks later, Sophie was in an entirely different sort of hell. One commonly known as "dinner with the parents."

"William, stop eating all the shrimp. They're for the salad," Sophie's mom said, slapping at the hand of her favorite dinner guest.

Sophie raised an eyebrow at the uncharacteristic behavior. Not that Marnie Dalton wasn't the type to slap hands. She totally was. Sophie's career-focused, take-no-prisoners, cloth-napkins-only mother ran her home with the rigid precision of Fort Knox.

But Marnie usually made an exception for Will. Hell, *all* women made exceptions for William Thatcher III. It was sort of nauseating, but Sophie had gotten tired of dry-heaving over her best friend's manipulation of the female population somewhere around college. After all, it really wasn't his fault that all women turned to simpering puddles of swoon around him.

All women except for Sophie.

Sophie's mother scurried out of the kitchen, muttering something about crass fingerprints on the napkin rings.

"What's up with your mom? She's high-strung tonight," Will said, busying himself once again with the shrimp.

"Just tonight?" Sophie asked with a snort.

"You know what I mean. More than usual," he corrected, snagging another shrimp.

Sophie shrugged. She'd stopped trying to figure out what made her mother tick. Other than lecturing her daughters and spying on the neighbors, of course.

"Have you told your parents you quit your job yet?" Will asked as he tossed a shrimp tail in the garbage disposal.

Sophie winced. "Eh...not exactly."

Will shook his head and reached for the croutons. "Well, warn me before you do so I can clear out. Having an unemployed daughter in the house is going to go over about as well as a zit before prom."

Sophie made a grab for the wine bottle and topped off her glass. "Best friends are supposed to be encouraging."

"They're also supposed to be *honest*," Will replied. "But if you need a little 'bright side,' how about this: your parents are going to be thrilled that you're not serving up Irish car bombs at Stump's anymore. Once they get over the whole lack of health insurance and 401(k), that is. Oh wait, you never had either of those in the first place."

Sophie groaned. "They're going to kill me."

"Pretty much," Will agreed. "I know you're all for spontaneity and shit, but quitting a job without having another lined up? Ballsy. What brought it on?"

Oh, now, let me see, what's changed?...I got mistaken for a freaking streetwalker, that's what.

But Sophie hadn't even told Will about the Las Vegas incident. Not that he'd judge her for it, but the whole episode still felt too fresh. Talking about it would be like rubbing lemon juice in the wound and then adding a little salt for good measure.

"Just needed a fresh start," she replied. *One that doesn't involve stinging humiliation and pleather boots.*

It wouldn't make sense if she tried to explain it, but after the sting of Las Vegas, Sophie needed this change. It was as though that uptight asshole in the elevator had held up a mirror and forced Sophie to face her life.

She wasn't twenty-two anymore. Being a cocktail waitress and every-night party girl wasn't just a rebellious phase. It had become a career.

A career as a waitress was fine.

A career as an aging sorority girl in thigh-high boots and with no goals? Not so much.

So...she'd quit.

"You need money?" Will asked quietly.

Sophie melted just a little at the support in his familiar blue eyes. She *did* need money. "Savings account" had not exactly been her middle name over the past few years. But she wouldn't take it from Will. She'd just have to find a job. A respectable one. ASAP.

"Not taking your money," she said with a wave of her hand. "But I don't suppose you'd want to hire me?"

Will gave an apologetic grin. "Uh-uh. You know how I roll. No employees, no overhead."

"I know, I know," she grumbled. Will was a wildly successful entrepreneur, but he operated completely on his own. Being a boss wasn't in the cards for him.

"Sophie, don't slouch," her mother scolded, returning to the kitchen. "Men don't find poor posture attractive."

"What *do* they find attractive, Mom?" Sophie propped her chin on her hands and pretended to look fascinated. "I mean other than Mary Janes, corsets, homemade jam, and the ability to sew dust ruffles."

"What's a dust ruffle?" Will asked.

Marnie hesitated, clearly torn between wanting to explain dust ruffles to her favorite pseudo-son, or lecture her least-favorite daughter about being single.

Since Sophie was related by blood, she got the short end of the stick.

"Honestly, Sophie," her mother said with a sniff. "When will you learn that the marrying kind of men aren't going to be attracted to your caustic humor and..."

"And what, Mom? I'm learning so much tonight!" Sophie said as her mother broke off and began furiously chopping a cucumber. "What else won't men be attracted to? My foul mouth? Big hair? Lack of savings account? The fact that I don't have a dust ruffle?"

"Dust ruffle," Will muttered around a crouton, still sounding mystified. "I've gotta look that up." He pulled out his phone and started typing.

"Sophie, I don't want to fight," her mother said with a long sigh. "You know I do my best not to pester..."

Will snorted.

"...but sometimes I just don't understand your choices. For example, what are you wearing? Did you intentionally pull out your oldest clothes for our nice family dinner?"

"Let me know when the 'nice' part starts," Sophie muttered as she dug her finger into the hole in her jeans.

"I think Sophie looks great," Will said loyally. "Some men like the unfussy look."

Marnie perked up slightly at the prospect of Will finding

Sophie attractive. It was her lifelong mission to see Sophie married off to her oldest friend. And Marnie was impervious to Sophie's constant assurances that she and Will were so never going to happen. Ever.

Not that they hadn't tried way back when.

On paper, Sophie and Will should have had the typical high school puppy-love story. He'd been the cocky, senior football star. His perfectly messy hair and blue eyes had sent many a teenage girl's virtue out the window.

As for Sophie's part, she'd been the dewy underclassman princess who'd blossomed over the summer, getting boobs *and* highlights. (To this day, she wasn't sure which she was more grateful for.)

Dating had seemed like a logical step, and it had been mutually beneficial. Will had gotten obligatory high fives for "nailing" the newest cheerleading recruit. And for Sophie, everyone knew that getting asked to prom by a *senior* was the high school equivalent of the Holy Grail.

The rest should have been yearbook history.

But the oddest thing had happened. They'd been two attractive, horny high schoolers without a speck of sizzle.

Sophie and Will had tried to pretend that the boring, clumsy first kiss beneath the bleachers was just a fluke. He'd blamed his distraction on the C he'd gotten in physics, and Sophie had claimed PMS. But after prom night had ended with a platonic game of Go Fish instead of dry humping in his Lexus, they'd been forced to admit it: no physical chemistry. Not even butterflies. They could talk for hours, laugh at the same jokes, and had dozens of mutual friends. But the hand-holding was merely tolerable, and the kissing was downright awkward.

So they'd done the teenage unthinkable. They'd become friends. *Real* friends, not like the usual high school friends of the opposite sex that claimed they were "best friends," but really were just stalling until one of them finally admitted their true feelings.

And perhaps because Will and Sophie had become friends without any of the usual hormonal complications, their friendship had actually lasted. Despite Will going to college three years before her, he'd kept his promise to stay in touch. And when Sophie had headed off to Stanford, putting even *more* distance between them, they'd e-mailed regularly and been nearly inseparable over their Christmas breaks.

Everyone waited for the inevitable moment of romantic realization, but here they were several years later, still completely platonic as ever.

Will had practically become a part of the family after his own parents had moved out of state without much of a backward glance. As with the fledgling high school romance that had started it all, the dinner arrangement was mutually beneficial. Will got the chance to eat something other than takeout, and Sophie had someone to help distract her parents from their constant meddling.

The only person who *didn't* like the arrangement was Brynn.

Sophie's older sister wasn't exactly the forgive-and-forget type, and when Brynn had been a freshman in high school, Will had been responsible for her 32A bra finding its way up the football field's flagpole. At the homecoming game.

It had been the start of a beautiful hatred, and their dislike had only increased over the years. Even Sophie's knack for easing awkward situations hadn't been able to resolve their animosity.

Realizing that her sister still hadn't arrived, Sophie glanced at the clock. Brynn was late. Something that happened... never. "Where's Brynn?" Sophie asked her mother.

Dinner was always served precisely at seven, but Marnie encouraged (or mandated, depending who you asked) that everyone get there around five thirty for her aperitif hour.

"Oh, she won't be here until six," Marnie said cheerfully as she seasoned the chicken.

Had the tardy daughter been *Sophie*, a lecture would have been in order. But when perfect *Brynn* was late, there was always a good reason. Sophie took another sip of wine and tried not to care.

Sophie's dad wandered into the kitchen, having finished up his phone call. A recently retired doctor, Chris Dalton was struggling with what he interpreted as the "utter uselessness" of retirement, and was loving the fact that some of his former staff still called to ask for his opinion.

"Hey, Dad!" Sophie said brightly. She and her father weren't close, but he didn't pester her as much as her mother. In fact, he didn't pester her much at all. Or even really talk to her.

"Soph," her dad said, planting a distracted kiss near the side of her head as he plucked a wineglass from the shelf.

She turned to face him. "How's that golf handicap these days? Mom mentioned you'd—"

"Will!" Chris said, interrupting Sophie and shaking the hand of the closest thing he had to a son. "Just heard that the Ms signed two new pitchers. I think this will finally be their year, no?"

Ugh. Baseball. Not her thing.

"Can I help, Mom?" Sophie asked, watching her mom dredge the chicken breasts in flour.

"Oh, no thanks, dear. I've got it under control. Just some simple lemon chicken paillards, some truffled mushrooms, and a sherry-vinaigrette shrimp and caprese salad tonight."

Sophie raised an eyebrow at the complexity of the meal. Her mom must have gotten a new cookbook.

"What's Brynn up to?" Sophie asked, toying with the stem of the wineglass. "I haven't talked to her all week."

Marnie looked up, her eyes glowing with the opportunity to share Big News. "Oh, then you haven't heard? Brynn's got herself a boyfriend! She's bringing him to dinner."

Oh, yippee. The evening ahead was sure to be rife with yawns. Brynn had a knack for finding men that most closely resembled doorknobs and attempting to date them.

At least the unexpected company explained why they were having chicken "paillards" when they normally got overdone pork chops.

"Wow, that's great," Sophie said half-enthusiastically.

"A boyfriend?" Will asked. "What kind of loser is she bringing around this time?"

Sophie's dad snickered, which was a testament to how desperately he wanted Will's approval, because normally anything remotely close to insulting Brynn was off-limits.

Marnie shot Will a censorious look. "Now, William, you know that guy she brought last time was a nice fellow, he was just a little..."

"He was a *dentist*," Will said in disdain. "She's an orthodontist. What the hell do they talk about, plaque?"

"I don't actually think orthodontists deal much in plaque," Sophie mused while topping off her Chardonnay. "I think it's more about devising new ways to attach metal to teeth while destroying the confidence of middle schoolers everywhere."

"Just be *nice*, kids," Marnie said to Will and Sophie. "And you too," she added with a sidelong glance at her husband.

"Jeez, you'd think we were going to tar and feather the poor fellow," Chris muttered to Will.

The doorbell rang, and Will and Sophie exchanged puzzled looks.

"Please tell me my sister isn't ringing the doorbell to the house she grew up in," Sophie said. In the years since they started the Sunday dinner tradition, nobody had ever done anything more than wipe their feet on the mat as they hollered, *I'm here*.

Marnie was so excited she was practically levitating. "This must mean that he's an important one! That's her warning that we're all to be on our *best behavior*.

"Come on, Chris," Marnie hissed. "We should meet them at the door and make a good impression."

"I'm sure the five minutes of waiting on the front porch has already done that," Sophie called after them.

"Why does she have to ruin a family dinner by bringing another boyfriend?" Will said as he finished the last of his wine.

"What's the big deal?" Sophie asked, helping herself to more cheese and crackers. "You haven't even met the guy, and you already hate him?"

Will ignored the question. "I'll bet he'll be pasty-skinned, pale-eyed, and blond like the rest of you. It's like she only dates men who will fit in perfectly with the Dalton family portraits. All the Nordic features and pale coloring is a bit overwhelming."

Sophie didn't disagree. Their annual family portraits were a little bit...bland. Nobody ever bothered to ask where she and Brynn had gotten their matching blonde, blue-eyed looks. It was immediately obvious that it came from both parents.

Granted, her father's hair was more gray than blond, but it only added to his distinguished authority. Not that he needed help in that department. The man never wore jeans and didn't even own a shirt that didn't have a collar.

Marnie also was a fastidious dresser, believing that jeans were strictly for gardening and that unpolished nails were for "street people."

Sophie's mother's voice trilled from the hallway, "William and Sophie Claire, won't you please come join us in the *drawing room*?"

"You have a drawing room?" Will asked.

"She's probably been rereading Jane Austen and decided to rename the living room."

They grabbed their wineglasses and headed toward the sound of Brynn's smooth alto voice and the sharper squawk that generally meant Marnie was in full-out "impress" mode.

Sophie hoped her sister's new man-friend was adept at flattery and pleasant niceties, because he was going to need a hefty dose of social skills to maneuver his new girlfriend's overprotective father and eager-for-grandbabies mother.

She shuffled after Will into the "drawing room," mentally preparing herself for mind-numbing conversation with one of Brynn's adoring drones.

Sophie halted to a stop so suddenly that some of her wine sloshed over the edge of her glass and onto Marnie's pristine white carpet.

Her mother made an exasperated sound, but a little spilled Chardonnay was the least of Sophie's worries.

Oh.

My.

God.

It was him.

The man from the Las Vegas elevator standing in front of her like some sort of icy-eyed ghost. And he had an arm around her sister's waist.

Oh, holy crap.

The aged gouda she'd just swallowed began churning in the wine tsunami of her stomach.

Will pinched her upper arm none too gently, and Sophie belatedly realized that her sister had finished introductions.

Everybody was staring at her, including Mr. I'm Not Looking for an Escort Service. She had so not missed that deadly sexy gaze. Emphasis on the "deadly" part. Still, it was reassuring that he too looked a bit shell-shocked. He didn't say a word, but based on what she knew of him, she didn't really expect him to.

The ball was clearly in her court.

"Soph?" Her sister's perfectly symmetrical smile was looking a little strained around the edges. "Everything okay?"

"Sorry," Sophie said lamely. "Totally zoned out there for a minute."

"Awwwwkward..." Will muttered under his breath.

"Okay?" Brynn said, giving her a puzzled look. "Um, *again*, this is Grayson Wyatt. Gray, my sister, Sophie."

Sophie pushed a smile onto her face even as she felt the telltale tingle at the corners of her eyes.

Do not cry. Do. Not. Cry.

But the tears threatened to fall anyway. Her family was about to learn that Sophie's disdain for convention had reached new heights. Good Lord, her father was about to find out that his baby girl had been mistaken for a freaking prostitute.

Unless…

It was a long shot, but Sophie slowly lifted her gaze to Gray's impenetrable gray one.

Please.

If he heard her silent request, he didn't respond. There wasn't so much as a twitch of his hard features or a hint of understanding in his eyes. And then…

"It's a pleasure to meet you, Ms. Dalton," Gray said, stepping forward and extending a hand. "I can certainly see the sibling resemblance."

It took Sophie a moment to register what had just happened. Not only had he correctly interpreted her silent plea to keep their first meeting a secret, but he had actually granted her request.

Granted, the man was still wretched. What was with the "Ms. Dalton" crap? And he hadn't smiled once. Stiff.

But he'd passed on the chance to humiliate her. And for that, she could have kissed him.

Except, not. Of course. Bad idea. Not only because he was still on her list of Horrible Human Beings, but also because he was dating her sister.

Oh God, my sister is dating this jerk. How had that not fully registered until now? She'd been so busy reeling from seeing him again that she hadn't even comprehended the implications. This wasn't just a chance meeting. The enemy was in her childhood home.

"What is with you?" Will whispered as Marnie captured Gray and Brynn's attention with a description of her closet remodel. "How much wine have you had?"

"I must have had too much too fast," Sophie said quietly. It felt wrong to lie to Will. She *never* lied to Will. Never had to. But there were some things she wasn't ready to share, even with her best friend. He'd just laugh and tell her it was no big deal.

And that was the real kicker.

She was scared to tell Will that it *was* a big deal. After years of acting like her flighty reputation didn't matter, a gray-eyed stiff had picked at a scab she didn't even know she had.

He'd made her bleed.

Sophie took a sip of wine and tried to still her too-fast pounding in her chest. She tried to keep her eyes focused on her mom, but they kept straying to Gray.

She sucked in a quick breath when she saw he'd been watching her. His eyes quickly moved back to Marnie, but she saw the tension in his jaw.

He didn't like this any more than she did.

"...And I think you should know, my Brynny doesn't bring just any boyfriend home to meet her parents," Marnie was saying.

"Oh, he's not quite my boyfriend," Brynn said quickly. "We've only been on a few dates. I know it's a bit soon to bring him to meet the family, but he just moved to the area, and I knew he'd appreciate a home-cooked meal and a chance to get the scoop on Seattle sports!"

Brynn flashed a winning smile at her parents, who puffed up at the praise, but Sophie winced. She didn't know *how* she knew it, but she instinctively understood that a man like Gray would hate feeling like a friendless charity case. She cast another glance in his direction, and sure enough, his clenched jaw looked like it could shatter his molars. Good thing he was dating an orthodontist.

Looking to distract the conversation before her mother and Brynn started stuffing baked goods in Gray's pockets while discussing baby names, Sophie jerked Will forward as buffer. She couldn't remember if Brynn had already introduced Will while she'd been having a mental and emotional breakdown, but it couldn't hurt to put her own spin on things.

"Mr. Wyatt, this is Will Thatcher. My date."

Will let out a derisive snort, but took pity on her, because he didn't bother to correct the implication that they were more than friends. The two men shook hands.

"A pleasure to meet you," Gray said politely.

Will said nothing. Sophie tossed back the rest of her wine.

"Mom!" she said sharply, pulling her mother out of a hushed conversation with Brynn. "I think we've all adequately enjoyed the *drawing room*."

"Of course!" Marnie said, realizing that standing in their rarely used living room was hardly the way to make her potential future son-in-law feel more at home. "Come into the kitchen; it's far more cozy!"

Will and Sophie exchanged a look. Her mom had recently hired an interior designer to make over their house in "industrial mod." "Cozy" it was not.

Marnie linked arms with Brynn and they left the room in a flurry of whispers. Will followed them, making soft mimicking noises behind Brynn's back.

"So what do you know about the Mariners?" Sophie's father said to Gray, as he led him toward the kitchen. Sophie trailed after them, trying to keep her eyes pinned on the back of her father's head so her gaze didn't drift to Gray's back. She hadn't seen him from this angle before, and it was every bit as yummy as the front.

Stop. It.

"Um, I'm not as familiar with Seattle pro sports teams as I'd like," Gray was saying stiffly. Sophie rolled her eyes. At least his horrible conversation skills weren't limited to her.

Gray stopped abruptly in the hallway and turned back toward Sophie. "Miss Dalton, I was wondering if you might show me to the restroom?"

She jolted slightly as she realized he was addressing her, and she swallowed dryly. "Um, sure, it's just down the hall on the right—"

He grabbed her arm and pulled her in that direction, while an oblivious Chris continued to the kitchen, still rambling about ERAs and RBIs.

Gray shoved Sophie roughly into the tiny powder room and shut the door behind them.

"Well this is familiar," Sophie said. "You, me, small dark spaces. Animosity. The sister element is new, though. Quite the twist—"

The light flickered on, and she found Gray glaring down at her.

"I think I liked the dark better," she muttered. "I certainly haven't missed your scowl."

"What are you doing here?" he demanded. His lips were pressed together so tightly it was a wonder any sound came out.

"What do you mean what am *I* doing here? You're in *my* parents' house. Sunday dinners have been a weekly occurrence for a couple decades now. *You're* the newcomer."

His jaw twitched as though irritated to be caught asking the obvious. "You never said you were from Seattle," he accused.

Sophie's temper spiked. How was this horrible coincidence her fault? "You never asked! I was merely playing dress-up at my cousin's bachelorette party, but you were too busy assuming I was a hooker," she hissed. "Which I'm not. Obviously."

"Obviously," he snarled. Gray glanced down at her worn jeans and seriously ancient Stanford T-shirt. His gaze seemed to linger on her midriff, and Sophie resisted the urge to tug at the hem of her shirt. She was well covered compared to the last time she'd seen him, but something about the way this man looked at her made her feel… naked.

"I knew my sister had horrible taste in men, but you're a new low. You're judgmental, cruel, heartless—"

Gray took a step closer until her back pressed against the bathroom door. Dimly she realized they were both breathing hard, and the sound of their panting in the tiny room felt entirely too erotic given that she *did not like this man*.

"I find it difficult to believe that you can be related to someone like Brynn," he said, his eyes moving over her once more.

"Why, because she's so proper and I'm so slutty?"

Gray growled. "No, it's just…Look, I obviously made a mistake about the prostitute thing, and I'm sorry. But we can't just fake our way through the evening. Is there any excuse you can give to leave?"

She pushed at his shoulders in outrage, but he didn't budge. "You want me to weasel out of my own family's dinner so you're more comfortable? You're the interloper. You leave!"

"I'm a guest; that would be rude."

Sophie gave an indelicate snort. "I'm sure it wouldn't be the first time."

Gray's eyes closed briefly, and for a minute he looked almost weary. "This is what I get for agreeing to come to a woman's house who I barely know."

Something twisted in Sophie's stomach. "So you and my sister aren't serious?"

She didn't know why she asked. Or why the answer was somehow important.

His eyes opened and they locked with hers before drifting to her mouth. "No. A couple of casual dates. More companionship than romance."

"Oh," Sophie said, licking her dry lips. "I don't like you," she blurted out, feeling very much like a fourth grader. But she'd had to say something. He was just so close.

"I don't like you much either," he said.

But the way their bodies leaned toward each other made liars out of both of them.

What is this? Sophie thought with panic. *This man is everything you despise.*

And yet, she wanted...

Brynn's voice calling Gray's name had them both jerking back. Unfortunately for Sophie, jerking back meant slamming her head against the back of the door.

"Ouch," she yelped.

His expression turned almost gentle as he reached out a hand toward the spot she was rubbing, but again, Brynn's voice had him pulling back.

"Gray? Did you get lost?" Brynn called.

"Shit," he muttered.

"Shit," Sophie echoed.

"You go," she whispered. "I'll stay here and follow in a minute. I'll pretend I was upstairs or something."

He hesitated for the briefest of moments. "Maybe we shouldn't mention..."

"Oh, please," Sophie interrupted. "As if I want my family to know about our little history."

Gray gave one last nod before opening the bathroom door and slipping out. Sophie leaned back against the door as she heard Gray greet her sister. "Sorry about that. I took a few wrong turns before finding the bathroom."

Brynn laughed softly. "That's what you get for asking Sophie for directions."

Sophie rolled her eyes, although the light insult didn't really sting. Brynn could be uptight and condescending at times, but she wasn't as difficult as their parents. Most of the time she and Sophie got along pretty well, which was saying something for sisters who'd grown up fighting over car keys, prom dates, and too-tight sweaters.

Sophie stayed in the bathroom for several minutes trying to gather her thoughts. In all the time she'd spent replaying the Las Vegas incident in her head, she'd never once imagined having to see Gray again.

On one hand, it was a relief that there was no longer someone out there thinking she was a prostitute.

But on the other hand, the man made her uncomfortable.

And angry.

And, most annoying of all, he made her feel a little... tingly.

Hearing her mother yelling for her, Sophie reluctantly shuffled into the kitchen and reclaimed her spot at the bar stool next to Will. Nobody acknowledged her return.

Sophie risked a glance at Gray. But he'd apparently decided the best course of action was to pretend she didn't exist, and didn't once look her way. Which suited Sophie just fine—she'd happily let Brynn absorb all of that surly, scowling attention.

Didn't mean she couldn't study him, though. It was somewhat reassuring to realize that he looked exactly the same as she remembered. Fastidious and boring. The suit had been replaced by khakis and a button-down, but the military-cut dark hair, tense jaw, and piercing gaze were all familiar.

Sophie's eyes moved to her sister. As usual, Brynn's light blonde hair fell in a sleek, straight swish around her shoulders. Her light blue sweater set was the perfect color for her gray-blue eyes, and her conservative silk skirt didn't have a single wrinkle.

Gray had said they'd only been on a couple casual dates. Did that mean…sex? Sophie glanced between the two of them, considering. Instinct told her no. There was too much pretense. Brynn hadn't once let her orthodontist smile waver, and Gray was hardly staring at Brynn with besotted adoration.

His knuckles were clenched around his wineglass, and his posture held all the approachability of an army general. Sophie had to admit that his tension was perhaps warranted for once. Marnie was currently trying to convince him of the merits of buying a home in the suburbs.

"There's just so much more room away from the city to start a family!" Marnie was saying to a stricken-looking Gray.

Sophie couldn't help it. She felt sorry for the guy. There were some things you protected even your worst enemy from. Marnie Dalton was one of them.

She dug her tennis shoe into Will's shin, trying not to think about how scrubby she must seem in comparison with Brynn's country-club attire. At least she wasn't wearing her hooker boots.

Will shot her an irritated glance. *What?*

Do something! She flicked her eyes obviously in Gray's direction.

His lip curled. *No.*

Her toe hit his shin again with more force.

He cut her a glare. *You owe me.*

"So, Gray," Will interrupted grudgingly, "how did you and Brynn meet?"

Marnie gasped. "Of course! I didn't even think to ask. How considerate, William."

Sophie rolled her eyes. *Easy, Mom. Take on one dinner guest at a time.* And she'd have bet her nonexistent life savings that Brynn had already told her mother exactly how they'd met. Marnie probably had an entire scrapbook dedicated to it.

"We met at the gym, actually," Brynn said, setting her hand on Gray's overworked bicep. "He was at the treadmill next to me, and when I dropped my iPod, he picked it up."

"Naturally, I had to ask her to dinner," Gray said with all the emotion of a cyborg.

"Oh, *naturally*," Sophie said around a piece of bread. Her mother gave her a warning glare.

"Honey, is dinner ready? I'm starving," Sophie's dad said distractedly, tearing himself away from the kitchen TV.

"Let me just plate this chicken and we're all set. Sophie, dear, if you could grab the wine, and, Brynn, take that salad to the table with you..."

"May I carry anything for you?" Gray asked.

Sophie rolled her eyes. Where were all these pretty manners when he'd left her standing like a cheap whore in a Las Vegas elevator lobby?

Marnie's hand fluttered to her chest. "Oh, goodness, no.

You just make yourself comfortable for our cozy little family meal. Will, show Gray into the dining room, would you?"

Sophie was so busy trying not to sit *next* to Gray, that she somehow ended up sitting *across* from him. Much worse. Now she had no way of not looking at him.

He gave her a tense glare. She responded with a cheery smile.

Sophie was just reaching for the salad bowl when her mother loudly cleared her throat and bowed her head. Brynn and Sophie exchanged a puzzled glance. They had never been a religious family. Marnie launched into a horribly maligned grace.

Sophie's mother shot Gray a pious look after she'd finished. "Thanks for humoring me, Gray. That's a pre-meal prayer that's been passed down from my great-great grandmother."

"Interesting..." Sophie said. "I wouldn't say it's familiar, would you guys? Brynn? Dad?"

Brynn quickly hid a smirk behind her napkin, and even Chris seemed to be struggling not to laugh.

Marnie studiously ignored them and gave her white napkin a snap before letting it flutter to her lap. "So, Gray, Brynn mentioned you're from Chicago. Do you have family there?"

Gray paused briefly before responding, and Sophie could have sworn she saw something raw flash across his face. "My brother actually lives here in Seattle. He's in law school at the University of Washington. And my sister lives in New York."

"What about your parents?" Sophie asked. She realized she had yet to speak directly to Gray, and the last thing she wanted was for her family to take note of her odd behavior.

"My parents are dead," he replied flatly.

Whoops. Sophie's family glared at her and she stared guiltily at her plate. As if she'd *meant* to hit on a painful topic.

"Tell me, how is it that a fine, successful fellow like yourself isn't married yet?" Will asked with sham interest.

The silence around the table became even more pronounced. Sophie could have strangled Will. Sure, he'd distracted everyone from her faux pas over Gray's dead parents, but her best friend knew full well that the topic of marriage at Sunday dinner was off-limits. Especially since Marnie was already mentally selecting wedding colors.

Gray stared at Will.

A welcome break from him staring at Sophie, but awkward nonetheless. The man really had to learn the art of fake smiling if he was going to survive in this family.

"I was engaged once. It didn't work out," Gray said finally.

Sophie jerked in surprise, her knee hitting the bottom of the table and sending her water glass sloshing onto the ivory tablecloth. Her mother shot her a death glare, but Sophie barely noticed. He'd been *engaged*? The thought of him proposing to anyone strained all of Sophie's brainpower. And the thought of him being in love? Well, *that* simply did not compute.

The man couldn't even make it through *dinner* with adequate conversation; how had he thought he'd survive marriage?

No wonder it hadn't worked out.

With the awkwardness at the table reaching DEFCON ten, Brynn shot her a beseeching look, which Sophie tried to ignore. She knew what her sister wanted, and she wasn't in the mood. Brynn wanted Sophie to sprinkle some ditzy conversation over the group—making everyone else comfortable by making herself into a clown.

Such antics had sort of become Sophie's shtick over the past few years. While nobody in the family seemed to expect Sophie to be impressive, they'd come to rely on her as a sort of social wizard. At the awkward wedding when Uncle Abe had too much to drink? Here comes Sophie starting the conga line. Or at the fund-raising gala where Brynn slipped on a stuffed mushroom and tore her dress clear up to her hoo-ha? Enter Sophie with spontaneous karaoke.

But Sophie didn't want to play that part tonight. Not in front of Gray. She was still reeling from the fact that the one man she'd hoped never to see again had infiltrated her personal life. She caught Brynn's eye and shook her head. *Not this time.*

But then Sophie's eyes fell on Gray and she felt a twinge of empathy. His face looked strained, and his knuckles were white around his fork. He was obviously out of his element.

And he *had* done her a favor by not outing her in front of her parents. Perhaps she could return the favor and make them even.

She sighed and gave in. It wasn't like Gray's opinion of her could slip any lower. Sophie took a bracing sip of wine and slipped into her flighty, charming mode.

"So, Gray," Sophie said with an easy grin, "I don't suppose Brynn has told you about the time that the two of us decided to camp in the backyard and got so scared by a raccoon that we both wet our pants?"

Brynn looked slightly ruffled, likely wishing Sophie hadn't selected a story that involved her peeing in her Rainbow Brite panties. But, hey, if Sophie was taking one for the team, she was bringing Brynn down with her.

Sophie moved easily from story to story, carefully keeping the conversation light and substance-free.

By the time they'd finished dessert, Sophie had exhausted her arsenal of childhood memories, but her sister had relaxed and even Gray seemed to have temporarily released his shoulders from their military pose.

Marnie returned to the dining room carrying her grandmother's silver coffee set.

Something she dusted off about once every...never. Not because Marnie wasn't the silver set type. She totally was. The fancier and more antique, the better. But actually using the set meant getting it *dirty*. And dirty was not Marnie's thing.

As Marnie poured the coffee and sliced an apple tart that was too perfect to be homemade, Sophie's gaze caught on her father.

Oh no. Sophie knew her father's "serious face" too well. Chris Dalton had apparently realized he was letting his daughter's suitor off too easily.

"Uh-oh. Here we go," Will whispered.

"Gray, what is it you do for a living?" Chris asked.

Gray cut a very precise bite of Marnie's apple tart before responding, "I'm in the hospitality business. Hotel acquisitions, specifically."

Chris leaned back in his chair and studied him. "So you're a sales guy?" This was not a compliment.

"Sort of," Gray replied.

Brynn set a hand on Gray's arm. "He's being modest. He's the CEO and president of the company."

"President, that's not bad," Chris said. "You must have a decent education behind you, then?"

"Dad," Brynn said warningly.

"Yes, sir, I got both my bachelor's degree and my MBA from Northwestern."

"Mmm. Adequate. You probably got all the 'wild' out of your system in school? Ready to settle down and be a man?"

"Oh my God," Sophie muttered into her coffee.

Gray set his coffee aside. "I'm not sure I was ever the 'wild' type, Mr. Dalton."

"Shocker," Will said as he helped himself to the rest of Sophie's tart.

The table fell silent for several moments until Brynn broke the awkward quiet.

"Hey, Soph, how's the job hunt going?"

Sophie closed her eyes briefly. *Crraaaappp.*

When she opened them, she wasn't surprised to see her parents staring at her.

Brynn let out a distressed sigh as she read the situation. "They didn't know."

Sophie gave a sharp shake of her head.

"Sorry," Brynn muttered. But the damage was done.

"Job hunt?" Marnie said, her voice two octaves above normal.

"Oh, Sophie," her father said wearily. "You didn't get let go, did you? In this economy, dive bars like Stimp's..."

"It was *Stump's*, Dad. I worked there for four years, how do you not know this? And no, I didn't get fired. I quit."

Somehow Marnie and Chris looked even more dismayed than when they thought she'd been fired.

"Well...okay," Marnie said slowly. "I can't say I'm not relieved that you won't be working at that...dump any longer."

Marnie turned to Gray, whom Sophie had been carefully avoiding. She could imagine what she'd read in his eyes: *Wow, whorish* and *unemployed.*

"Sorry to drag you into family business, Gray," Marnie said with embarrassment. "It's just that we worry about our Sophie here. Always a free spirit. She's spent the past few years being a barfly and giving us heart palpitations worrying about her getting shot up by some alcoholic motorcycle ruffians."

Will caught Sophie's eye and mouthed, *Motorcycle ruffians?*

"It wasn't that bad, Mom," Sophie ground out. "Can we talk about this later?"

But Sophie's father wasn't ready to drop it. "Your sister said you were job hunting. Surely you didn't quit one job before you had another lined up?"

Sophie took a gulp of her wine.

"Oh, Sophie," her mother breathed in the tone known as Great Disappointment.

"I think it's great," Will said loyally. "Soph'll find something in no time."

"Says the man who's been self-employed since age sixteen and only has to worry about himself," Brynn muttered.

"Not everyone needs a laminated life plan to tell them what underwear to wear and what job to take," Will snapped back.

"At least I *wear* underwear," Brynn swiped back.

Gray looked puzzled at the vehemence of Brynn and Will's snapping. *Don't try to make sense of it*, Sophie thought. *They hate each other just for breathing.*

"More dessert?" Sophie asked the group brightly. All she wanted to do was head home and cry into a bubble bath. It was an especially practical idea since she probably couldn't afford tissues or her water bill. Her tears could just fill the tub.

"Hey, Gray," Brynn was saying in a thoughtful voice.

"Didn't you say your new secretary backed out at the last minute?"

Sophie's eyes flew to her sister at the random change in subject. Nothing about Brynn was ever random. Sophie went on high alert, and allowed herself a brief look at Gray. He too looked wary.

Well...*more* wary, anyway.

"Yes," he replied stiffly. "Laura was supposed to start tomorrow, but her fiancé received a job offer in Atlanta that they couldn't pass up."

"So you're short a staff member," Brynn pressed. "Going to be pretty tough to be CEO if you're trying to answer your own phone."

Oh no. No no no. Fire alarms started blaring in Sophie's head.

"Brynn," she began in a warning tone.

But her sister ignored her and remained fixed on Gray. "Well, I was just thinking...you're short an assistant, and Sophie's short a job."

Sophie saw the moment Gray realized what Brynn was up to. His eyes widened in horror.

Yeah. Exactly.

"Brynn..." she said again.

Again, her sister ignored her plea. "Sophie can easily adapt to the professional world. Sure she's done mostly restaurant stuff for a few years, but back in college she spent a couple years as a temp receptionist, and she had a great internship during law school."

Gray's eyes flew to hers. "You went to law school?"

"Dropout," Sophie said sweetly.

"But still," Brynn pressed. "She would be a *fantastic* assistant."

Gray continued to look a little dazed by Brynn's suggestion. Even Sophie's parents were staring at their oldest daughter in puzzlement, no doubt wondering why Brynn was trying to push Sophie's mediocrity onto her new perfect boyfriend.

"You're being a control freak," Will told Brynn.

"I'm being helpful," Brynn corrected, before leaning expectantly toward Gray. "So what do you think? You can at least give her a chance, right?"

"I, um... I don't think... I suppose..."

Sophie realized in sudden horror what was about to happen. This man's complete social ineptitude was about to land them both in an intolerable situation.

The pinched expression on Gray's face said that having Sophie for an employee was the last thing he wanted. But the fumbling look of panic in his eyes was even more alarming; he didn't know how to say no. He was about to make things worse.

"I am not working for your *boyfriend*," Sophie said harshly, cutting off Gray's babbling. "And I'm not working in a godforsaken office."

"Now, Sophie," her mother said, apparently coming around to the idea, "it could be a great opportunity..."

"An opportunity to what, learn how to staple?"

"You don't know how to staple?" Will asked.

"It could get your foot in the door, Soph," Chris said, looking thoughtful.

Great. Just great. Now her whole family was warming up to this ridiculous plot. Sophie looked at Will in desperation, but he just shrugged and rubbed his fingers together meaningfully.

Right.

Money.

Something she had none of. And something she'd need soon if she wanted to be able to pay her bills and eat something other than rice cakes. *Shoulda thought of that before giving your two weeks' notice*, she reminded herself.

Gray cleared his throat roughly. "Ms. Dalton, it doesn't sound like a career in hotel hospitality holds much interest for you, but I'd be happy to discuss the possibility of employment with you should you change your mind."

Sophie was so startled to hear Gray addressing her directly that it took a few moments for the actual words to sink in.

She stared at him. "You want *me* to come work for you?"

His wince said it all. *No.*

"If you would like," he replied, giving her an intent look with a hidden message.

Ah. *There* it was. He wanted *her* to get them out of this mess so he could save face. Here the perfect CEO was, throwing a bone at the pathetic, loser sister.

And his expression made it clear that as the poor loser sister, Sophie was supposed to do what her family was expecting her to do: refuse the responsible option.

For once, they were in agreement. Refusal had been on the tip of her tongue from the moment she'd realized where Brynn was going with her well-meaning interference.

The whole point of quitting Stump's was to regain some self-respect. And working for a man who despised her was not the path to emotional validation.

Except...

"I accept," she heard herself say.

Five pairs of startled eyes stared at her. Even Brynn looked surprised, and she was the one who'd engineered this whole disaster.

"Are you sure, Soph?" Will asked, looking uncharacteristically somber.

Not at all.

"Mr. Wyatt here offered me a great opportunity," she said with a calm she didn't feel. "As my parents so gently pointed out, I'd be a fool not to take it."

She met Gray's eyes as she said this, and the stormy disbelief she read there made her realize *exactly* why she'd done it.

Revenge.

CHAPTER FOUR

Gray told himself he wasn't watching the clock.

But when the knock came at his door, he was prepared.

Hell, he *should* be prepared. He'd been up half the night trying to decide exactly how to play this moment.

"Come in," he called, only after carefully schooling his face into a mask of cool indifference. No doubt his new "assistant" thought she could stroll in whenever she pleased because her sister was dating the boss.

Gray knew women like Sophie Dalton. Women whose middle names were "manipulation." They manipulated the system, their careers. Men.

Especially men.

And Gray had no intention of being played. Certainly not by a troublesome ditz who dressed like a hooker in her spare time and went out of her way to stand out like a sore thumb in an otherwise impeccably mannered family.

He needed to put distance between them. Immediately.

But the woman standing at his doorway was not the too-sexy blonde he'd been waiting for.

It was Ms. Jennings, the company's HR manager. He stifled a groan. Not that there was anything wrong with her. It was just employees in general. Not exactly his strong suit.

Ms. Jennings... Beth, if he remembered correctly... was not a particularly attractive woman. She didn't try to be. He liked that about her. It kept everything simpler. Her ink-black hair was too dark against pale skin, and the choppy, chin-length cut did nothing to soften her broad features.

Like most men, Gray knew little about women's fashion, but it was obvious that her army-green slacks and boxy blue blazer would never be featured in any fashion magazine.

But all interactions with Ms. Jennings so far had pointed to efficiency. And that was all he cared about.

Gray realized he'd been staring at her, and as a result her welcoming smile had faded slightly as she shuffled her feet nervously.

"Ms. Jennings, come in," he said, realizing that they'd been working together for a few days now and he'd barely spoken to her. He racked his brain for idle chatter. The book he'd bought on being a relatable manager had said something about expressing interest in employees themselves, as well as in their work.

Which really was just another way of promoting small talk. His Achilles' heel.

Gray desperately grasped for a topic that would say *I'm interested* rather than *I'm prying*.

Are you married? Any children?

No way. Too personal.

Any cats?

Too stereotyping.

Can you recommend a dentist?

Ugh. Then she'd think he'd been studying her teeth.

"How was traffic?" he asked finally. He immediately winced. Was this the best he could do? There were probably species of ferns that would make better company than him.

"Traffic was fine, thanks," she said, her brow furrowing.

"For me too," he said with a curt nod. *Jesus, Gray.*

Ms. Jennings' face relaxed slightly at his awkward response. Clearly she'd realized he wasn't intimidating so much as pathetic. He wasn't sure which was worse.

"I made a fresh pot of coffee," she said, approaching his desk and extending a cup toward him. "I took a guess. Black?"

He preferred a splash of cream, actually. And he'd already gotten his coffee. But he surreptitiously passed his old cup aside and accepted the company mug with a curt thank-you.

"Ms. Jennings, do you happen to know anything about the..." Gray broke off and gestured at the walls surrounding his desk.

"Ah yes," she said with a resigned sigh. "The trophies."

"Is that what you call them?"

"It's what *Martin* called them. I call them atrocities."

Gray was inclined to agree with Ms. Jennings' assessment. His successor had failed to mention that he'd be leaving his wall decorations behind. The CEO office of Brayburn Luxuries looked like a menagerie. No matter which direction he looked, Gray found himself staring at an elk, a moose, a bear, and some animal he didn't even recognize.

Between the hunting trophies, the rocking chair–style

desk chair, and the fact that he was pretty certain there were occasional safari noises coming from somewhere, Gray's nerves were starting to fray.

The first day on a new job was stressful enough without having to work in the middle of a zoo in an unfamiliar city.

With an assistant he'd accused of being a damn street-walker.

As if reading his thoughts, Ms. Jennings brightened. "Perhaps your new assistant can take care removing Martin's decor and finding something more your style. She starts today, right?"

"Yes."

"Well I'm just glad you were able to find someone else so quickly! It's a shame about Laura not working out—we all liked her when she came in for interviews."

Gray might not be great with people, but he didn't miss the slight censure in the HR manager's tone. She hadn't been happy about having to do rush paperwork for an employee she'd never even met. Apparently Martin Brayburn had been a fan of "group hiring" to make sure everyone had good rapport.

Gray wasn't even sure he knew what "good rapport" meant.

"I appreciate you helping establish Sophie into the system so quickly. I know it's not common procedure."

He tried for a grateful smile and was relieved when she softened slightly. "No problem. I'm sure she's wonderful if you hired her on the fly."

Wonderful?

Sophie was definitely not wonderful. She was more like…

Well, there really wasn't a word for Sophie Dalton.

When he'd seen her that night in Las Vegas, she'd just been so damn *inappropriate*. The hair, the sparkly eyelashes, the endless display of creamy skin. Those friggin' thigh-high boots that practically begged to be wrapped around a man's waist…

And the not-so-minor fact that she'd been the spitting image of the woman who'd broken his heart.

You stomped all over a stranger's dignity because of a woman you haven't seen in over a year. Well done, sir.

So Vegas had been a disaster.

And the train wreck that was the Dalton family dinner hadn't been much better. Gray had already been annoyed at himself for letting himself get talked into joining Brynn at her parents' house. He'd been having a brief wave of loneliness and she'd caught him at a bad time.

But he would have endured a lifetime of solitary evenings not to have to seen the horror on Sophie's face when she'd walked into the room and seen him.

Hell, *he* should have been feeling horror as well. Instead he'd felt dismay.

Dismay that the Las Vegas showgirl he'd been fantasizing about for the past two weeks was really an all-American girl next door. And sister to the woman he was seeing.

Not that he and Brynn were serious. Not even close. Hell, when she'd called to invite him to dinner, he'd barely been able to picture her face.

But that didn't mean he was okay with being attracted to her little sister. And he was definitely attracted.

There would be no more of that.

He'd learned the hard way that charming, manipulative women like Sophie were not for him.

Grayson Wyatt did not repeat mistakes.

"How'd you find her?" Ms. Jennings asked curiously. "Did she come recommended?"

Gray nearly snorted. The only person likely to recommend Sophie Dalton would be a gigolo or one of her patrons at that bar where she'd worked. Surely nobody in the *professional* world would want a piece of aimless fluff wandering around the office.

Then why did you offer her the job? his mind nagged.

He clenched his coffee mug in irritation at his own misstep. She wasn't supposed to accept. In fact, he'd been certain that she wouldn't. She'd made it perfectly clear that she couldn't stand the sight of him.

And yet, he'd misread her. No surprise there, but it didn't make the situation any less... dire. They'd barely been able to make it through dinner without suffocating each other with hostile tension. At least, he thought it was hostility. It was possible the tension was slightly more... sexual.

Either way, working in close proximity was a singularly bad idea.

Where is the wretched minx?

He glanced down at his watch with a scowl. "She's supposed to start today."

It had been nearly a week since the disastrous dinner at the Dalton household, but it had taken a few days for all the paperwork to go through. A few days in which he'd been certain she'd reconsider. A few days in which to order himself to grow some balls and back out of the arrangement.

But he hadn't. Backing out before she'd even had a chance to start felt petty.

Didn't mean he had to be happy about it.

Gray's office phone rang and he jumped at the chance to escape the awkward conversation.

"Ms. Jennings, would you excuse me?"

"Sure thing," she said with a wave. "I'll point Ms. Dalton to your office when she arrives."

Just wonderful.

"Wyatt," he barked into the phone.

"Ah, there's my favorite ray of sunshine."

Gray relaxed at the familiar voice. Ian Porter was his best friend from college and one of the few people besides his brother whom Gray knew in Seattle.

"How'd you get this number?" Gray asked.

"Sweet-talked the receptionist. She sounds cute."

Gray grunted noncommittally. He didn't know if Brayburn Luxuries' main receptionist was cute or not. He hadn't thought to look when he'd walked through the main reception lobby this morning. Hadn't thought to notice *any* of the employees, for that matter. Perhaps he should go make nice on his lunch break.

"So, what's up?" Gray asked curiously. Ian might be one of Gray's few friends, but they rarely talked on the phone to chitchat.

"I'm on marital damage control. I was supposed to invite you over to dinner this past Sunday, but I completely forgot, and Ashley's out for my blood. Come over this weekend and get her off my back?"

"I'd love to." Gray was glad his friend couldn't see his regretful wince at the belated invitation. If only Ian knew the hassle he could have saved Gray if he'd remembered to pass on his wife's request the previous weekend. Gray *could* have spent Sunday evening with his best friend and godson. Instead he'd been struggling to survive in enemy camp with a pseudo-girlfriend he didn't even want and her marriage-minded parents.

And Sophie. Ian could have saved Gray from Sophie.

Speaking of which…

Female laughter was disturbing the former quiet of the executive floor.

Familiar female laugher.

She was here.

"Hey, Ian, I gotta go. But I'll be there on Sunday. Can I bring anything?"

"A girlfriend? That would earn me extra brownie points with the wife."

"Absolutely no way in hell," Gray replied, his eyes scanning the glass wall for the source of the laughter.

Ian sighed. "Fine. Just bring some wine?"

"Done. See you then." Gray hung up the phone and froze when he finally spotted her.

Apparently the manipulative monster had already made a new friend. One of the sales associates whose name Gray couldn't remember.

Sophie caught his glare through the glass and her smile slipped as the sales guy…Brent? Brendan?…pointed her toward Gray's office.

Gray rose slowly from his office chair as she came trotting toward his open office door.

Do not lose your cool, he ordered himself.

He'd already done that in a jammed elevator. And again in the Daltons' bathroom. So far he was two for two in losing his mind around Sophie. Something he planned to put a stop to. Now.

Gray did a double take as he caught a good look at the woman standing in his doorway. There was no sign of the Sophie he'd seen in the elevator *or* the Sophie he'd met on Sunday. There were no hooker boots, obvious makeup, or scrappy little top that hoisted her breasts clear up to her chin. Not that he'd noticed.

But also gone were the ancient jeans that had fit just a tad too snugly around her tight backside. Gone was the defiant, ditzy persona she'd maintained around her parents.

This Sophie looked... well, exactly as a new CEO's assistant *should* look. Her light green skirt fell respectably to her knees, and her white blouse was conservative. He couldn't even criticize her high heels, even if they did seem too sexy. Because, to be fair, he'd seen a dozen women wearing similar styles on his walk to work.

The only indications that this was the same woman were the blonde *Playboy* hair and bright blue eyes.

Simply put, she was perfectly respectable.

Sophie hadn't made a single misstep in this conversion from hooker to tomboy to office assistant. He should have been pleased. Instead he felt... off-balance.

Off-balance from her conservative attire, off-balance from her placid smile. And *definitely* off-balance from the fact that his fingers were itching to unbutton those respectable buttons and see the *real* Sophie.

He was in serious trouble.

* * *

You can do this, Sophie reminded herself for the hundredth time that morning.

But looking into Grayson Wyatt's glowering gaze, she wasn't so sure. For starters, his gray suit was like a punch in the gut. It was identical to the one she'd admired in Las Vegas. Back when she'd wanted to jump his bones.

Back before she'd learned he was a jerk.

She was smarter now. Now she knew exactly what he was. An uptight, judgmental, socially impaired prick.

Whose eyes still made her...tingly. *Crap.*

She tried to think of something cutting and witty to say, but her brain seemed to be malfunctioning. Although she wasn't sure if it was nerves from the unfamiliar setting or nerves from *him*.

In happier news, he didn't seem to be handling her presence any better than she was handling his. He looked slightly constipated.

"Hi," she said, wincing at the weak opening. "Witty" apparently was not in her cards this morning.

He gave a curt nod but made no effort to welcome her into the office.

"What's with the glare?" she asked.

"What did you expect, welcome balloons?"

Sophie's patience frayed. She stomped closer to his desk. "Did you ever think to call? I assumed you were going to back out on our deal until that woman from human resources called and asked me to send over a formal application."

"I never back out on a deal, Ms. Dalton."

"But you wanted to," she accused.

"Of course I wanted to."

Sophie felt a little stab of regret at the certainty in his tone. His irritation at their situation didn't come as a surprise. And it wasn't like she wanted to work for this man. She'd only agreed to it with the intention of making his life miserable. And obviously what made him miserable was *her*.

But somewhere beneath her Old Testament–style revenge fantasies, a little part of Sophie wanted to make Gray change his mind about her. Impress him. She wanted to prove that she could do a good job and make him eat his horrible words in the elevator and in her parents' powder room.

"You may as well go set your bag down," he said with a resigned sigh. "I don't need you at the moment."

Sophie's jaw dropped slightly at the curt command and sheer irritability coming off of him in waves. "Are you kidding me? It's both of our first day on the job, and we're not even going to... you know, talk?"

He glanced up at her for a brief moment. "If we were new to each other, I would, of course, invite you in to sit down and fake interest in your life and what your hobbies were. But since we're past all that—"

"Really?" she interrupted. "Are we? The only thing I know about you is that you're trying to get into my sister's pants. And the only thing you seem to know about me is that I turn tricks on Saturday nights."

Gray finally gave her his full attention, but not until he'd made a show of rubbing his eyes like she was an exhausting toddler. "You're right, Ms. Dalton. I'm behaving badly. Please sit down."

"I think I'll set my purse down at my desk first," she said, turning on her brand-new patent-leather blue pump and flouncing out of his office.

But her initial surge of satisfaction about defying him faded almost immediately.

He *really* didn't like her.

The full magnitude of her situation settled around her like a storm cloud. It had seemed like such a harmless game on Sunday night, but now that she was actually here, she was realizing that she'd have to earn her paycheck.

And that meant pleasing Mr. High and Mighty.

"But not in the sexual way," she muttered to herself

snidely, remembering Las Vegas all too vividly. "Because he's not the type to 'pay for sexual attention.'"

Sophie identified her desk by the WELCOME, SOPHIE card next to one of those fancy corporate gift baskets. She'd bet her new shoes that it wasn't Gray himself who'd initiated the gesture. Flicking open the card, her suspicions were confirmed. It was signed "the team at Brayburn Luxuries" in a distinctly feminine scrawl. He probably wasn't even aware of its existence.

Setting her imitation designer purse down, she surveyed her workplace. Sophie let out a little squeal as she took in the view from the floor-to-ceiling windows behind her desk.

All of the Seattle landmarks sparkled up at her from the high-rise windows. Well, okay, not so much "sparkled," considering the fog, but still. There was the Space Needle, endless water, big-ass mountains. She could have been looking at a poster for *Sleepless in Seattle.* Minus the adorable image of lovelorn Tom Hanks and perky Meg Ryan before she'd gone all edgy and weird.

Her desk phone rang and Sophie plopped into her chair to answer it. "Hello?"

"Is that how you're going to answer the office phone line?"

Sophie swiveled around in her chair to stare through the glass walls to Gray's office. He was staring back. She really hated that he was wearing another of those dark charcoal suits. Men in modern, sexy suits were a major weakness of hers.

"Are you seriously calling me?" she asked. "From ten feet away?"

"Very astute, Ms. Dalton. Perhaps by the time we leave today, you will have managed to remember that you're not answering the phone at your sorority house, and you will have aspired to actually follow the directions of your *employer*."

"Do you have *any* friends, Mr. Wyatt?"

"Friends?"

"It's a tricky concept for someone like you, I'm sure. They're essentially people who place themselves in your company voluntarily."

Silence.

She watched through the glass as he broke eye contact and stared at a stack of papers on his desk. His expression was mostly unreadable, but for a brief moment, Sophie had the sensation that he was almost human.

"See if you can manage to be in my office within the next two minutes, Ms. Dalton. Surely even you can handle that."

Nope, definitely not human.

Sophie hung up and tapped her home-manicured nails against her fancy new desk.

The morning was not going as planned. He was supposed to be cool and indifferent, and she was to be polite and professional until she'd figured out a plan of attack.

Instead he looked ready to explode, and she hadn't even been trying to annoy him.

And already she was itching to see what was beneath that icy surface. That was so not part of the plan.

Sophie assessed her two options:

Stick it out and figure out how to work with Mr. Holier Than Thou, or…

Quit.

Quitting was the obvious choice.

The whole point of this respectable-job thing was to be, well…respected. That was pretty much out the window considering the one person who was now supposed to *save* her ego was the very same person who'd crushed it in the first place.

Even the luxury of working in a place where nobody spilled beer on you or "accidentally" brushed your boobs wasn't worth working for a man who'd seen you wearing little more than a bandanna tied around your waist.

Especially one whom you also had to face at family functions.

And the drive-him-out-of-his-mind revenge plan still held appeal, but she wasn't sure how to do that *and* be a competent employee at the same time. Her two goals were working against each other.

Something you should have thought about before getting into this mess, she chided herself.

So quitting it was.

Or...

Sophie contemplated a third option.

Leave the ball in *his* court.

It wasn't her usual course of action. She liked to be in control. But this way, Sophie couldn't be accused of being a quitter. More than likely he was already thinking of ways to get rid of her. And then *he* could be the jerk, and she could be the poor fired victim.

Mind made up, Sophie took her sweet time reapplying her lipstick. Not because she wanted to look her best, of course. At least, not *just* that. Mostly it was because the thought of making Grayson Wyatt wait on her was rapidly improving her mood. She added a dab of shiny gloss to her lower lip to make it look fuller. Then she checked her mascara and blush.

Primping complete, Sophie strolled over to his office,

taking care to let her hips sway just a bit. If this was going to be her last day on the new job, she at least wanted to get the most out of her brand-new outfit. Gray definitely seemed like the type who would prefer everyone to knock and await permission. So she barged in.

And blanched.

The office was *horrible*.

She didn't know how she'd missed it the first time she'd come in. Probably because she'd been too busy trying to avoid her new boss's death ray gaze. But she was getting a good look at it now. It was creepy. Even for Gray.

"Whooooo-eee!" she turned in a full circle. "I *love* what you've done with the place. Did you decapitate all these animals yourself? I'd ask if they were dead first, but I know better. Destroying creatures you deem beneath you is a hobby of yours, am I right?"

He looked up from his files, and the eyes that met hers betrayed nothing. Not even annoyance.

"They're not mine," he replied curtly. "The former CEO left the, um, decorations when he retired," he said finally. "I'd prefer something less cluttered."

"Wow, *you* liking no clutter? That's a shocker."

She was oddly relieved that the hunting paraphernalia wasn't his. Sophie was a bit of an animal lover and certainly didn't need one more reason to dislike him.

She settled uninvited into the chair across from him. "So, what's up, *boss*?"

Silence. Sophie waited impatiently while he finished whatever it was that he was reading. She accidentally-on-purpose let the toe of her supercute new shoe bump against his desk.

Thump. Thump. ThumpThumpThump. *THUMP.*

Finally he finished his reading and set it aside. She was pretty sure he'd just been staring at a blank piece of paper in order to make her wait on him, but considering she'd taken five minutes to put on lipstick for that same purpose, she didn't judge.

"First things first, Ms. Dalton—"

"Stop with that. Call me Sophie."

Gray paused. Blinked at her. Considered. "No, I don't think so."

She couldn't resist an eye roll.

"As I was saying, Ms. Dalton, there are a couple things I want to address before we discuss your long-term, routine responsibilities as executive assistant to the president."

"Oh, is *that* your title? I didn't see it plastered all over your fifty different nameplates."

His poker face didn't budge. "I understand that this job is a new…career direction for you. Care to explain why?"

Sophie's carefree attitude evaporated. He was poking in areas that nobody had access to. "I don't really see how my motivations are relevant."

Just fire me so we can get this over with.

He pressed on. "So you're telling me that quitting your waitressing job the very day after you got back from Las Vegas—"

"How did you know that?"

As if she needed to ask. Obviously Brynn had given him the details. Reason number eight hundred and fifty-four why it was a bad idea to work for someone who dated your only sibling.

Gray proceeded as though she hadn't interrupted. "You quit a waitressing job just days after I assumed that you were a prostitute. Are the two incidents related?"

"Maybe I just got tired of the lousy tips."

"So then you'd find a more upscale restaurant, you wouldn't just wiggle your way into the corporate world!"

Sophie sneered. "Says the man born in a white collar."

Gray leaned forward slightly. "I've met your parents, Sophie. I've seen the house you grew up in. Still want to talk to me about *white-collar*?"

She flushed. *Whoops.*

"Point taken," she grated out. "And since you're the one who brought up my family, aren't we going to talk about the fact that it's weird that you're dating my sister?"

"I thought we established the awkwardness of that connection in your parents' powder room."

Sophie shifted uncomfortably, remembering exactly how charged that particular confrontation had been. "Well, then you shouldn't have given me a job," she muttered.

"You weren't supposed to accept!"

Sophie sucked in a breath at his outburst. She couldn't help it—his reaction stung. She'd known all along that he'd been merely trapped by her sister's interference and that he didn't actually *want* to hire her. But a small, pathetic part of her thought that maybe he'd offered because he wanted to keep her around.

Fool, she thought harshly. Men like Gray did not relish connections with women who wore miniskirts and ratty jeans and whose résumés boasted how many shots they could carry on a tray. Somehow she didn't think he'd appreciate the nuances of a Buttery Nipple.

Oh God, do not put "Grayson Wyatt" and "nipple" in the same thought, she instructed her sex-starved brain.

"Ms. Dalton, what I was trying to get at with my questions...I need to know whether your decision to hastily quit your waitressing job had anything to do with my less-than-gentlemanly assessment of you in that elevator."

Sophie threw up her hands in exasperation. Clearly the man was not going to give up. "Okay fine. Yes. YES. The whole mistaken-for-a-hooker thing wasn't exactly a balm on my ego. And so, yes, I decided it might be time to change some things in my life. Happy now?"

His lips pressed into a firm line before he nodded once. "Okay."

"'Okay'? That's it?"

Sophie saw temper flash across his gaze and he very purposefully set one palm on his desk as he leaned forward. "What exactly am I supposed to say? My corporate life has just become a nightmare, and I have to accept that I have nobody but myself to blame. All because I hurt a party girl's feelings and inspired her to play dress-up."

Anger snaked down Sophie's spine and she stood up, slapping her own palms on his desk so she could get in his face. "*That's* why you regret insulting me? Because it led to this?"

As she said "this," she waved her hand between their two bodies, and Gray's eyes followed the motion of her hand before he halfway stood and put his face within inches of hers.

"Quit," he commanded.

Sophie could feel his breath on her face. "Fire me."

"And have a lawsuit on my hands? I don't think so. You'd sue me halfway to China."

"Well, I'm not going to add 'quitter' to my lengthy list of flaws, so if you want me gone, you'll have to haul me out by the hair," she shot back.

Sophie saw his fingers flex briefly and suspected there was nothing he'd like more than to follow through with her suggestion. But the hot, angry Gray was slowly fading.

Sophie watched with an odd pang of disappointment as the Ice Man returned, and he slowly lowered to his chair. For a moment he'd seemed so... alive.

"How about a compromise?"

She squinted warily. "What sort of compromise?"

"It's more of a trial period, actually. One week to see if we can put the past behind us."

Sophie considered. One week. She could do that. Probably.

People separated the personal and professional all the time, and half of her friends hated *their* bosses. Maybe her situation wasn't so different after all.

And the sad truth was, she *needed* this job. It was either this or ask her parents for a loan. Her stomach turned at the thought.

"Okay," she snapped, before she could change her mind. "It's a deal."

She expected him to respond with smugness. After all, she had just agreed to *his* terms. With no arguing. Everything she knew about him so far said he should be gloating.

Instead he looked... panicked.

But about what?

Once again, the flicker of humanity she thought she saw disappeared from his face in an instant.

"Fine," he said with a dismissive wave. "We'll reassess the situation next Friday."

She nodded in agreement. "And in the meantime? Anything you want me to do besides answer the phone and follow your bidding?"

His silver eyes seemed to burn hot before he shifted his gaze to the wall behind her. "How do you feel about decorating?"

Sophie shrugged. "Amenable." *I hope you like pink.*

"Amenable," he repeated. "That must be a first for you."

He waved his hand in the general direction of the dead animal gallery. "Get rid of all this. Donate it, sell it, keep it, ship it back to Martin Brayburn. I don't care what you do with it so long as you get it out. Once that's complete, we'll discuss what I want to replace it with. If anything."

"Should I be writing this down?" she asked sweetly.

"If you think you need to."

Sophie rolled her eyes. "Anything else? Boss?"

"Mr. Wyatt," he corrected.

"Whatever." She was already heading to the door.

"Sophie," he called, just as she was about to walk out.

She felt a weird jolt at hearing him say her first name. She ignored said jolt. "Yeah?"

"Do you think we'll be able to survive a week of... this?"

She didn't have to ask what he meant by "this." But of course neither one of them would put a name to it and say it out loud.

Not with their history. Not with their work relationship. Not with her sister.

"I don't know, Mr. Wyatt," she responded. "But it will be fun to find out."

CHAPTER FIVE

"I don't think Bambi would appreciate how much trouble you're giving me," Sophie muttered at the deer head that was staying stubbornly mounted to Gray's office wall. "Oh God. *You're* not Bambi, are you?"

The thought made her shiver, which in turn made her teeter on the ladder.

"Pull it together, Sophie," she commanded once she'd regained her balance.

She pushed Bambi out of her mind and tried to force herself to think of the hunting trophy as a *thing*.

Davie the Deer was the last to go, and was proving far more stubborn than Elvis the Elk, Morrie the Moose, and Benny the Bear.

Not that she'd gotten attached to the poor guys while she'd been taking them down or anything.

"Come on, Davie," she said, easing her hands around to where the plaque met the wall. "Work with me here. This looked so easy when Jeff did it."

Jeff Andrews was Brayburn's vice president of sales and had become one of her first friends at the company ever since he'd rescued her Red Vines from the vending machine on her first day. He'd offered to help her out, and she'd happily taken him up on it.

But after handily pulling down most of the heads, Jeff had deserted her. Something about couples' therapy with the wife. He'd seemed more excited about the dead animals.

"Focus, Sophie." She had to get the damn wall cleared before *he* returned from his dentist's appointment.

Today was it. The end of their one-week trial. Sophie couldn't afford to fail at the one task Gray had asked of her. As in, she *literally* could not afford it. Not after the whopping credit card bill she'd opened this morning. Unemployment was not an option. Even if the alternative was being employed by the devil.

Sophie took a deep breath and tugged again at the deer. Nothing. Kicking off her shoes, she let them drop to the floor and tried once more. She felt two nails break, and the obstinate deer head stayed exactly where it was.

She pulled back to glare at Davie for several moments. "I hate you," she whispered. "You're going to get me fired."

Feeling frazzled and desperate, Sophie grabbed at Davie's nose and pulled as hard as she could.

Davie stayed.

Sophie did not.

She let out a high-pitched squeal as she reeled backward on the ladder. Her last thought was that it was all Davie's fault as she started a graceless tumble.

Straight into Grayson Wyatt's arms.

She heard his grunt as she fell into him, her back slamming into his chest. The impact was hard enough to jar her teeth, but it was a heck of a lot better than breaking her neck on the office floor.

His arms shouldn't have felt familiar. Shit, *why* did they feel familiar?

Probably just reliving that initial moment of terror in Las Vegas, Sophie told herself, remembering the way she'd thrown herself at him then. Still, the sheer rightness of his embrace felt out of place, considering the wrongness of the moment. But she didn't move.

Neither did he.

Sophie felt his heart hammering again against her back. Her own stupid heart was beating a bit too fast, although she wasn't sure if it was from the near-death experience or her proximity to a very nice-smelling male.

One strong arm was wrapped around her waist, and the other banded protectively over her chest. Her toes weren't even touching the ground, but from some deep, abandoned part of her soul, she realized she hadn't felt this *safe* in as long as she could remember.

Her soul was apparently a fool. There was nothing *safe* about this man.

The fingers near her waist moved upward ever so slightly, and Sophie's eyes fluttered shut for a moment before she realized that he was merely adjusting his grip.

"You okay?" His breath was hot against her ear, and she couldn't seem to force any words out. She nodded and shifted slightly under his grasp, trying not to be too aware of the firm male body pressed against hers.

His fingers tightened again at her movements, and this time it was Gray who hissed out a breath. He set her down roughly and yanked his arms back as though she'd burned him.

She felt a flash of regret that the moment was over, but she steeled herself and turned around to face him, ready to deal with the lecture she instinctively knew was coming.

He didn't yell. Of course he didn't. But his eyes were screaming murder.

"What the hell were you doing?" His voice was as hard as she'd ever heard it, and she couldn't resist taking the smallest step backward. The ladder blocked her escape.

"I, um...just doing as you asked. Getting rid of the animal heads." She gestured toward the corner of his office where Jeff had set the remaining trophies.

His eyes never left her face.

"I see that. My question was why you were doing it by yourself. Do you have any idea how much those things weigh? Did you even *think*?"

Her embarrassment was starting to give way to indignation. "Don't talk to me like I'm a child. I was merely following your instructions!"

Gray blanched. "*My* instructions? When I asked you to clear out my office safari I didn't mean you had to do it yourself!"

"I didn't," she evaded. "Jeff helped me."

His eyes narrowed at that. "Jeff who?"

He stared at her blankly.

"Jeff Andrews?" she prompted. "Your vice president of—"

"I know who Jeff Andrews is, Sophie. What I don't understand is why one of my top-ranking executives is helping my secretary play with stuffed animals while I try to get my fucking teeth cleaned."

"Hmm, that's quite the potty mouth, Mr. Professional." Sophie huffed. Although part of her was happy to hear the f-bomb. It made the man somewhat more human. "Look, I can see that you're upset, and I can't really blame you. I'd feel guilty too if I were in your shoes."

"Guilty." He folded his arms over his chest. "You think I feel guilty?"

She nodded and patted his arm condescendingly. "Of course you do. The only reason I was wrestling that big deer down by myself is because I was paranoid that I'd be fired if I didn't! So really it's your fault I almost broke my neck."

"That's absurd."

"Is it? You gave me a one-week trial period of employment and then asked me to get rid of these stupid animals. It was either pull Davie down or get fired."

As far as explanations went it was a bit dodgy, but Sophie opted to stand her ground and see where it went. She was finding it sort of enjoyable to see him all worked up.

"You named the dead—okay. Okay." Gray closed his eyes as though praying for strength. "Ms. Dalton..."

"Sophie."

"Ms. Dalton, first of all, the one-week trial was in no way contingent upon your ability to redecorate my office. And second of all, if you *did* assume the two were related, why in God's name would you wait until the last possible moment on Friday afternoon to complete the task?"

Sophie waggled a finger at him. "Now, *that* I actually can explain. See, I *intended* to do it sooner, but it's taken me this long to find Davie and crew a good home. I couldn't just put them in the Dumpster, and none of the local donation centers accept...you know...dead animals. And Martin didn't get back to me until this morning because he's been in Europe, but good news! He'll take his babies back!"

"I'm so relieved."

"You don't look relieved. You look annoyed."

His jaw clenched. "Of course I'm annoyed! I came into my office expecting to catch up on filing and instead I find my assistant teetering idiotically on a ladder!"

"That would be upsetting to your delicate constitution," she murmured.

"For someone who is so paranoid about getting fired, you're certainly not taking care to get on my good side."

Sophie bit her lip. He made a valid point.

Poking the beast with sarcasm wasn't exactly the way to ensure long-term employment.

"Sorry," she said halfheartedly. "I'll try to be more biddable."

"I doubt you know the meaning of the word," he muttered as he turned and headed toward his desk.

She followed after him, deer mission abandoned. "Just out of curiosity, if the one-week employment trial wasn't based on the décor update, what *was* it based on?"

His head snapped up, and something hot seemed to run over his features. "You know full well what I was trying to determine. Whether or not we could avoid *that*." He nodded toward the ladder.

Sophie flushed slightly. Somehow she didn't think he meant her falling so much as his *catching* her fall.

She hated that he made her feel disoriented. Her eyes narrowed. What was he after? He'd made it clear that even if he was attracted to her, he didn't like her. Which meant only one thing…

The jerk was probably toying with her.

So she hit back.

"How's Brynn?" she asked, keeping her voice casual and plopping into the chair across from his.

His hands stilled from rummaging in his drawers, and she could tell the question had caught him off guard.

"I don't see how that's relevant."

Sophie took the high road and didn't rub it in his face that it was *very* relevant, given that he'd held her for a good sixty seconds longer than necessary when he was supposed to be interested in her sister.

Still, his response was reassuring and confirmed what she'd gathered from her latest conversation with Brynn. Their chemistry level was currently dwindling into the negative numbers.

Whenever Sophie asked one about the other, it was as if she'd just reminded them about a forgotten to-do list item. If Brynn's bored tone and Gray's indifferent expression were any indication, that "relationship" was dead before it even left the ground.

Not that Sophie cared one way or the other.

"Are you and your sister not on speaking terms?"

Sophie blinked in confusion at his question. "What?"

"You asked how she was. Since she's *your* sister, I must assume you two are estranged if you're asking a near stranger about her well-being."

His gaze was cool, and Sophie realized he'd seen right through her not-so-innocent question.

She made a big show of glancing at her watch. "Sooo, boss. It's nearly five o'clock on a Friday and I'm sort of trying not to freak out about whether or not I have a job to come to on Monday morning. Did I pass your little test?"

Sophie tried to keep the desperation out of her voice. Before the deer-and-ladder incident, and before she'd lost her mind and gone out of her way to rile him, she thought the week had actually gone pretty well.

Other than apparently thinking she was "too chatty" with the clients, he hadn't criticized her once.

He hadn't exactly complimented her either. But then, even if he had an employee whom he *didn't* loathe, he didn't seem the type to throw out bits of encouragement like *Good job stapling!*

Even though she *was* a pretty good stapler. Very precise.

Gray ignored her and pulled out a sheet of paper from a folder in his desk drawer. He alternated between reading the contents and looking over the top of the paper at her.

She struggled not to fidget. "What?" she finally snapped.

"You went to Stanford," he said thoughtfully.

Sophie frowned. "I never told you that."

"You double majored in biology and political science, with a minor in communications."

"Are you reading my résumé?" she asked in disbelief. She leaned across the desk to make a grab for it, but he pulled it out of her reach.

"The communications focus, I can see. The opportunity to talk nonstop probably appealed to you. But tell me about the other two. Biology and political science?"

"I see no need for us to go through this little interview exercise..." Sophie crossed her arms over her chest, feeling ill at ease. She didn't want to discuss anything personal with this man.

"Humor me," he said in a bland voice.

Sophie reluctantly settled back in her chair, but remained tense. Nothing set her on edge as much as someone analyzing her résumé. One could dig through her panty drawer, her purse, her Internet browser history...

But not the résumé. It revealed too much.

The only good news about this little scenario was that

she had plenty of practice with this routine. God knew she'd gone through it often enough with her parents, friends, Brynn, prospective employers... She could practically recite his next lines for him.

You have so much potential.

Is this job just a transition phase?

You're squandering your talent and top-notch education.

"What do you want to know?" she asked, mentally preparing her usual pat answers.

"Biology and political science don't exactly overlap in course loads. Did you have any career path in mind that would utilize both degrees?"

For a brief moment she considered setting aside her usual speech and telling him the truth. That the biology major had been for her dad, who'd assumed she'd go to med school. And the political science focus was for her mother, who'd long insisted on Sophie's destiny to be a lawyer.

Her mother had been wrong, as evidenced by the one very big omission on her résumé: her one-and-a-half-year stint at Harvard Law.

But there was a reason that Sophie didn't put her little law school dabbling on her résumé. People took a chance on those who'd just taken a little longer than average to make use of their college education. But *nobody* looked fondly on a quitter.

He was staring at her with unreadable cool eyes, and she changed her mind about telling him the truth. Grayson Wyatt didn't exactly invite her to spill her guts. Instead, Sophie launched into her usual rambling evasions. Better to sound like a ditz than a failure.

"Well," she said, winding a curl around her finger and fluttering her eyelashes. "It really came down to the cute guys. Biology had all those sexy, smart nerds. And poli-sci had all the confident alpha men. I mean, what girl could resist?"

He watched her for a moment, and then nodded once with something that looked like disappointment.

"That's it?" she asked snidely. "You're not going to grill me on why with a perfect college GPA, top-notch alma mater, and a couple impressive degrees to my name, I'm here fetching you coffee and figuring out how to rid your walls of animal heads?"

Gray shrugged. "If I thought you'd tell me the truth, I might ask. But if you're going to continue with your evasive bullshitting, I'm not going to waste my time."

Sophie scowled and tensed as she waited for him to move down the résumé. No doubt his interrogation over her education was just a lead-in to give her a hard time about her lack of office experience.

But he said nothing.

"I didn't bullshit you," she said finally.

He gave her a look.

"Well not *all* of it was lies," she amended. "I really do like cute boys."

His lips twitched in something that may have been a smile. "I'm sure you do," he said.

"You're not thinking about me as a call girl again, are you?"

"Ms. Dalton, I'm fairly certain that human resources would be in here pretty quickly if I started thinking about my assistant in such an intimate manner. Perhaps we could avoid such references going forward?"

"If I don't mention The Incident again, can I keep my job?" she asked.

His silence wasn't a good sign.

"Explain to me why you want this job," he said.

"Well, gosh, unemployment *does* have a certain appeal, but I find I'm rather fond of having money for frivolous things like food, rent, condoms."

"If you're trying to endear yourself as an employee, you're doing a miserable job."

She bit her lip. Why did she keep baiting this man? This was so not the time for her snark to come out in full force, and yet she couldn't seem to muster the polite, professional assistant routine around him the way she could everyone else in the office.

And even when she tried, he seemed to see right through it.

Gray leaned back in his chair and ran a hand over his mouth. "I'm not going to ask you to leave, Ms. Dalton. Despite our unconventional meeting and the fact that you don't seem to respect me in the least, you're competent. More important, people seem to like you. To be honest, I could use some of that popularity to help people get accustomed to my...style."

Ah, so Mr. Perfect was aware of his shortcomings. Interesting. "So you're keeping me around because I'm popular?"

"Something like that," he said.

Sophie considered. He had a point. She *was* good at that sort of thing. And it could be kind of fun to give a personality makeover to someone so socially stunted. Her brain was already bubbling with ideas.

"A project," she said thoughtfully. "How fun! I promise it won't be as painful as you think. I just need a month, and soon all of your weekends will be filled with golf rounds, cocktail parties, poker games..."

He winced. "Let's not get ahead of ourselves. I just meant that I could use your presence to buffer my . . . impatience."

"Oh, is that what they're calling it these days?"

He looked as though he wanted to smile but managed to resist the urge. Sophie was oddly disappointed. What would he look like without the pinched tension in his face?

"You have entirely too much of a smart mouth to be anyone's assistant, Ms. Dalton."

"For the last time, call me Sophie. This isn't 1793. First names in the office are normal."

"We're not *friends*, Ms. Dalton, we're colleagues. And casual workplace or not, I like to keep some semblance of mutual respect."

"Fine, if you want to act like an eighteenth-century dandy, who am I to intervene?" She steeled herself for the big question. "But . . . I can stay?"

"You can stay," he said quietly. "For as long as it suits you. Which, judging from your personality, I'd assume would be another few weeks before you move on to bigger and better things?"

Sophie tapped a fingernail against her lips. "Bigger things . . . such as dancing at bachelor parties and installing a pole in my living room to practice my moves?"

He gave one of his lopsided almost-smiles, and Sophie felt something warm and tingling in the vicinity of her lady parts. Annoying how the begrudging twitch of those unsmiling lips was somehow more rewarding than another man's full grin.

"So we're good?" Sophie asked tentatively.

"We're . . . okay. Just no more thigh-high boots, no more rambling stories about your childhood, and no more climbing up ladders."

"I make no promises," she said cheekily, before wiggling her fingers at him and heading toward the door. "Now if there's nothing else, I'll go find someone a bit more…suitable to pull down Davie, eh?"

"Fine," he mumbled. "Oh, and I did have one question."

She turned and waited.

"The coffee you brought me this morning. There was cream in there."

Sophie rolled her eyes. "Yes. There was."

"You've always brought me my coffee black before."

"Mm-hmm." She studied her chipped fingernails. "And you really thought I wouldn't notice that you dumped in two creamers as soon as I turned my back?"

She could have sworn she saw him blush. It was…cute? No, that wasn't quite right. But it was something.

"I think it's sweet that you didn't want to hurt Beth's feelings," she teased. "She informed me with great pride that she'd guessed that you like your coffee black."

"I think we're done here," he said, a distinct red creeping over his cheeks. "And don't tell Ms. Jennings about the cream-in-the-coffee thing."

Sophie raised an eyebrow. "Okay?"

He shrugged awkwardly and didn't meet her eyes. "There's really nothing to be accomplished by telling her that I don't like it black."

She cocked her head. "But you *don't* it like black."

"Just don't mention it, okay?" he snapped. "Honestly, is occasionally keeping your mouth shut *that* difficult?"

"Fine. Can I go?"

"Please do. And Sophie," he said, stopping her for the third time.

She sighed and spun around. "Yeesssss?"

"That, um... moment by the ladder?"

"Yeah?" Her voice had gone unintentionally husky.

"It meant nothing. It never happened. Got it? You and I... We're not... I'd never be—"

She felt the hot rush of humiliated anger. She might no longer be an actual prostitute, but apparently she was still a worthless tramp.

"I get it," she spat out. "You'd never be interested in someone like me. Loud and clear."

"Good, then," he said with a nod. "We're agreed, then—it was all a big mis—"

Sophie let the door slam before he could finish the sentence.

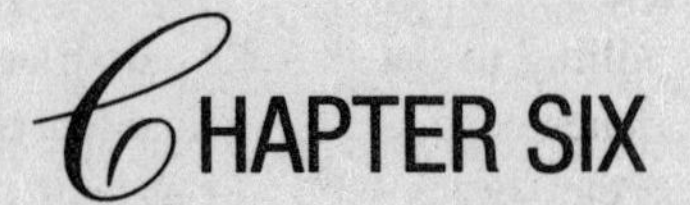

Gray mentally added yet another item to his list of Rules to Live By:

Never agree to another man's business meetings.

Martin Brayburn hadn't asked Gray for much upon his departure. The older man had bowed out graciously, leaving Gray to run the company as he saw fit.

Except for one solitary request: a meeting with Peter Blackwell and his son.

It should have been harmless. It could have even been *lucrative*. The Blackwells owned a chain of small boutique hotels on Maui. Nothing fancy, but the real estate was prime. And even better, they were looking to sell.

But that wasn't why Martin had requested Gray take the meeting. Peter Blackwell was Martin Brayburn's oldest friend, and his son, Alistair, was Martin's godson.

Martin's request had been personal, and Gray had agreed without a second thought. Something he was now regretting.

The meeting was a complete nightmare, starting with its

participants. The younger man across the desk was probably close to Gray's own age of midthirties, but the bloated frat-boy appearance and ill-fitting navy suit made him look like a pimpled intern.

Gray was willing to bet that Alistair Blackwell had no business experience beyond a childhood lemonade stand.

His father, Peter Blackwell, was at least respectable on paper, but instead of being the expected polished businessman ready to talk numbers, Peter had turned out to be an aging, sentimental entrepreneur with an elevated estimate of his company's worth. Gray was dismayed to hear a constant chorus of loyalty, family, and nostalgia, and not one solid reference to *profit*.

If the Blackwells thought Gray was going to buy their outdated line of Maui resorts based on some touchy-feely bullshit, they clearly hadn't done their homework. Maybe Martin Brayburn would have fostered such crap out of sentimentality, but Gray had no tolerance for it.

"...as I'm sure big Pops here will tell you," Alistair was saying in a faintly out-of-breath voice, "you can't be expecting us to roll over and play dead like a couple of happy pups, you know? Just because we're from the *islands* doesn't mean we don't know a thing or two about big business!"

Gray resisted the urge to stand up and walk out. After all, this was *his* office and he needed this deal.

"Mr. Blackwell," Gray said, putting an end to Alistair's rambling, "I'm sure you can understand the position that Brayburn Luxuries is in. We're very interested in the location of your properties, but all of our research has shown that the hotels themselves are quaint at best. Your asking price isn't realistic for a franchise that barely warrants a three-star rating."

Peter's mouth tightened into a thin line, and Alistair began another babble session. "Just because our bathrooms aren't marble, doesn't mean we're not located on the best little stretch of Hawaiian paradise—"

Peter held up a wrinkled, tanned hand. "Alistair, I'm sure Mr. Wyatt knows all about the waves and the state of our guest rooms. I think what he's telling us is that, regardless, Brayburn Luxuries isn't going to pay us what we want for our property."

Gray resisted the urge to plow his fingers through his hair. This wasn't going well. What he'd fully expected to be a slam-dunk negotiation was turning into a bloody war. Peter Blackwell was *supposed* to be a competent businessman who, after Gray's logical explanation, would understand that the hotel chain he'd launched decades ago was not worth his asking price.

And Alistair shouldn't even be here. Gray wished he could hand the younger man a twenty-dollar bill and tell him to go check out the Space Needle while the adults did the thinking. But judging from the way Peter gazed at his son in blind, fatherly affection whenever Alistair spouted his verbal diarrhea, Gray knew he had to tread carefully.

Problem was...he wasn't entirely sure how to do that.

Gray wasn't about to pay double the properties' worth just to appease an older man's ego. But neither was he willing to give up the deal. He needed a way to read these people quickly and determine their weak point. Trouble was, he didn't have the faintest clue how.

He tried once again to reach them with logic. "Mr. Blackwell, I'd like to reiterate that Brayburn is, of course, still interested, but we have to be realistic—"

"Who is that?" Alistair interrupted.

Gray stifled his annoyance and followed Alistair's gaze through the glass wall of his office.

Ah. Sophie.

Leave it to his little pain-in-the-ass assistant to distract his most pivotal, prospective clients at the most inopportune time. Not that she meant to, of course. But then, that seemed to be Sophie's MO. Making a mess of his life just by breathing.

Alistair was gaping, and even Peter seemed a little dazzled. Gray narrowed his eyes and tried to view Sophie objectively. As if she hadn't made it her life's purpose to get under his skin.

He scowled. Her long blonde hair fell in loose waves down her back, reminding him uncomfortably of the sex-kitten look she'd been sporting in Las Vegas. The memory of how her hair had smelled when he'd practically groped her during the ladder debacle made him even more uncomfortable.

He shifted in his seat.

Jesus.

Whether it was in an elevator, or her parents' bathroom or his own damn office, he couldn't seem to keep his damn hands off her.

Sophie Dalton is not for you, he reminded himself for the hundredth time.

Sure, she sent him a couple hot gazes and let her voice go all breathy when he got too close. But that's what women like Sophie did. They teased. They played.

And then they left.

He gritted his teeth and turned his attention to the Blackwells, but they were still captivated by the little blonde in the other room.

"That would be my assistant," Gray said, in delayed response to Alistair's question.

Peter reluctantly drew his eyes back to Gray, but Alistair continued to stare at Sophie's backside, all but salivating. Gray's annoyance with the man skyrocketed. "I'm assuming we can get back to *business*, unless there was something you needed, Mr. Blackwell?"

Alistair jumped, and Gray suspected that his father had just delivered a quick kick to his shin.

Gray tried to pick up where they left off. "So, as I was saying, while I can appreciate the value of the land, the value of the resorts themselves is unfortunately not up to Brayburn standards—"

Once again, he'd lost the attention of the two men he was trying so hard to impress.

"Excuse me, Mr. Wyatt?"

Shit. Sophie stood in the doorway and the effect of tumbling golden hair, ocean-blue eyes, and matching little outfit was even more distracting close-up than it had been from through the glass wall.

The Blackwells were enchanted.

Gray gave in to a sigh. "Yes, Ms. Dalton?"

"I just wanted to see if I could get you gentlemen a coffee-and-pastry tray, sir, if you haven't already eaten."

Gray had already had coffee and his usual breakfast of spinach and egg-white omelet at home, but he supposed there was no way he'd regain the men's attention until they'd had a close-up view. God, he missed his old assistant. Mary had been short, stout, and irritable. Gray wouldn't have had to deal with *her* distracting his most important clients.

"Thank you, Ms. Dalton, some coffee would be great."

"Coming right up. I'm sorry I didn't offer sooner. I didn't realize you had a meeting this morning."

Of course she didn't. Probably because he intentionally hadn't put it on the calendar she had access to. He'd hoped to spare the Blackwells the experience of Early Morning Sophie. The woman was pure menace before ten a.m. And *after* ten, for that matter.

So pretty much she was a nightmare around the clock. Always singing, smiling, dancing.

Yesterday she'd actually tried to sign him up for a book club.

Book club.

Today, however, her special brand of Sophie charm was working in his favor. The Blackwells couldn't get enough. Hell, neither could he.

Three pairs of male eyes watched as she trotted out of his office to fetch coffee, tight butt practically begging for male attention.

Twenty minutes later, Gray was no closer to making headway on the acquisition on this increasingly unappealing resort chain when Sophie returned with a carefully prepared tray. She must have sensed the importance of the meeting, because the tray looked like it belonged in Versailles, circa 1683.

"I thought I said 'coffee,'" he muttered. The tray was overflowing with croissants, mini quiches, doughnuts, bagels, and a large pile of fruit.

She balanced the tray on the corner of Gray's desk and ignored him completely, saving all her smiles for the Blackwells. "How would you like your coffee, gentlemen?" she asked. "Mr. Wyatt here takes his *black*, but I've brought cream and sugar, as well as a variety of flavored sweeteners."

Sophie shoved a mug in Gray's direction without looking at him, and he nearly smiled. She'd added cream.

"Just a pinch of sugar and a splash of regular old cream for me, dear," Peter was saying, suddenly taking on the persona of a kindly grandfather. This gentle old man sounded absolutely nothing like the stubborn hard-ass Gray had been dealing with five minutes prior.

"How do *you* like *your* coffee?" Alistair asked Sophie while unsubtly fingering his greasy comb-over.

She likes it with sugar. Lots of it, Gray thought.

"Mr. Blackwell, surely a confident man like you doesn't need someone like me to determine your coffee preparation."

Gray thought he heard traces of disdainful sarcasm in Sophie's tone, but Alistair ate up the compliment. "I'll try that hazelnut-flavored creamer there; I like things sweet."

Smiling serenely, Sophie prepared the coffee and handed it over to Alistair, their fingers brushing. Sophie flushed, and Alistair all but licked his lips.

"Sophie, how's your boyfriend?" Gray snapped abruptly. Cue the awkward moment of silence. A Grayson Wyatt specialty.

What the hell am I doing? Gray thought. He never blurted, he didn't call his assistants by their first name, and he certainly didn't ask about their personal lives.

She looked startled, but recovered quickly. "Oh, you mean Will? He's just a childhood friend who still hangs around. We're not together."

He stared hard at her. That was certainly not the impression she'd given him that night at her parents' house. She'd called Will her *date*. He should have figured she wouldn't stick with anyone long term. Will was probably just another of her playthings.

In an effort to break the awkward tension, Sophie glanced at the Blackwells and rolled her eyes. "In case you can't tell, Mr. Wyatt's a little overprotective of his employees. It's one of the reasons we all love working for him so much."

Gray cleared his throat in warning, but the other men seemed oblivious to her sarcasm.

"I could tell that straightaway about your boss here," said Peter. "His dedication to his people and his company is one of the main reasons I'm considering Brayburn Luxuries to acquire my company."

"How interesting, what kind of company?" Sophie asked, settling herself on the corner of Gray's desk like they were discussing favorite movies. Her hip was inches from Gray's hand, which he snatched back so quickly he nearly knocked over his coffee cup.

Get a grip, Grayson.

"Oh, just a little set of Hawaiian resorts I started a few years back," Peter was saying. "I'm getting too old to deal with all the maintenance and taxes. I'd hoped Alistair here would be taking over, but he's focused on his own career goals."

Like what, selling hemp bracelets on the beach? Gray wondered.

"I love Hawaii," Sophie gushed. "What island?"

"Just the prettiest little strip of Maui you've ever seen."

"It must be so hard to part with it," Sophie said to Peter, laying a hand on his arm.

The move *should* have seemed calculating and phony, but Gray had to give her credit: She was good. She made it seem genuine.

Peter blushed. "Oh, it's just business, I guess. The important thing in life is family," he said with an adoring look at his insipid son.

"Well, you couldn't choose better hands to leave your business in," Sophie said as she began assembling plates of food. "I haven't had the pleasure of working with Mr. Wyatt for very long, but he has the best reputation and is so smart with money."

Gray stifled the hollow stab of disappointment. He had a fleeting wish that she'd compliment his *person*. Not his accomplishments or his brains or his résumé. Just him. Just Gray. When was the last time anyone had looked beyond the suit?

And why did he even care?

Lost in thought, Gray barely noticed that Sophie was neatly concluding his meeting for him. In the span of fifteen minutes, she had sweetly trapped Peter into a second meeting next month to further discuss the offer.

She'd been equally adept at evading a dinner date with Alistair, which Gray was grateful for. The last thing he needed was his assistant dating his star client. Even if this particular client had as much use as a third nipple.

Gray shook the hands of both men, amazed at the difference in their mood after Sophie had worked her magic. They were all smiles and agreeability. Sophie showed them to the elevator with promises that she *absolutely* would check out their resort website, and *of course* she would read Alistair's blog.

He knew he should thank her for her interference, but he couldn't quite find the words. He felt an irritating combination of resentment and appreciation for the ease with which she managed people. And to give credit where it was due, Gray couldn't deny that she'd very likely saved an important business deal using nothing but perky breasts and fake smiles.

Was he annoyed or grateful? Or aroused? *Shit.*

She'd also surprised him by being savvy. And he hated surprises.

He sat down in the ugly orange chair she'd ordered for him and tried to get back to work. Only to realize that he couldn't focus on work. Instead he was thinking about life. His life. And how it suddenly seemed like nothing but a long series of workdays and lonely dinners.

It was a routine that hadn't bothered him before.

But now something felt *off.*

Gray knew exactly who to blame for his discontent, and she was currently tapping away on her computer, no doubt humming a Disney song or making a billion new friends on Facebook.

His eyes kept returning to her desk. Damn this glass wall. What had Martin Brayburn been thinking building an office with glass walls? There was no privacy. No peace of mind.

On his fifth glance, he did a double take.

She was no longer on her computer. She was smiling prettily up at a visitor. Of the male variety.

Gray's eyes narrowed when he saw that the visitor was Jeff Andrews. The observation shouldn't have upset him. Jeff was one of his best employees, and Gray himself had requested that Sophie work directly with Jeff on the Landers deal. It made sense that they'd be familiar with each other.

But the way Jeff's eyes kept dropping to Sophie's chest was a bit *too* familiar. He knew Jeff was married, but he seemed to remember Sophie mentioning something about Jeff and his wife going to counseling.

Gray scowled and forced his eyes to his computer screen,

but they kept drifting back to Sophie and Jeff. As far as his employees went, Jeff was actually one of Gray's favorites. Friendly, easygoing, smart…

But he wasn't feeling so friendly toward his colleague now. Why was Jeff looking at Sophie like that?

And why was Sophie leaning toward him?

Surely she wasn't actually attracted to the man. Gray tried to observe Jeff from a woman's perspective. The other man wasn't tall. Definitely shy of six foot. Didn't women like tall men? Then again, he supposed there were probably women that valued humor over height, and Jeff was one of those obnoxious joke-a-minute kind of guys. Sophie must go for the clown routine, because she was looking at Jeff in a way she never looked at *him*.

Gray waited impatiently for Jeff to come into his office and talk about whatever it was he'd come up to this floor to discuss. But when he looked up five minutes later and saw no sign of Jeff, his suspicions were confirmed. His vice president of sales hadn't come up to discuss business with the CEO.

He'd come up to flirt with the CEO's secretary.

Gray's mood officially moved from irritable to downright ornery, and he had the irrational urge to bring Sophie's mood down with him. This was a workplace, not a carnival. She should at least try to show some signs of being professional.

In a rare moment of pique, Gray wanted to get under *her* skin. To show her that life wasn't all about bunnies and rainbows and that she couldn't manipulate everything to go her way.

"Ms. Dalton, can you come in here for a moment?" he called.

She appeared at his doorway. "Sure, what's up?"

He noticed she didn't correct him and tell him to call her Sophie. Perhaps she didn't care anymore.

"When you've finished pulling last week's numbers, I was hoping you could do a quick personal favor for me. I'd do it myself but I'm slammed with phone calls over the next couple hours."

"Definitely, what do you need?" she asked. Her words were all acquiescence, but her expression had turned guarded.

"I need you to send some flowers."

"Flowers?"

"Yes, flowers," he said, feeling suddenly invigorated. "The biggest arrangement you can find."

"And to whom am I sending this blatantly cliché arrangement?"

"Whom do you think?" He smiled thinly. "Your sister."

It was a lousy thing to do. He'd had no inclination of pursuing things with Brynn, and now she'd probably get the wrong idea about his interest level.

And the stricken look on Sophie's face was supposed to make him feel satisfied. Instead he felt...petty.

What am I doing?

Gray had spent the past few weeks making a concentrated effort to separate his personal life from his professional life and now he here he was deliberately entangling the two.

He just hoped he could untangle them before he got in over his head.

Gray watched Sophie walk slowly back to her desk, noting the slight hunch in her shoulders. Something in his chest seemed to tighten at the sight.

Shit.

He was *already* in over his head.

* * *

Brynn was putting on her well-rehearsed big-sister-knows-best routine, but Sophie wasn't buying it.

"There's absolutely no way, Brynn. Why would I want to go on a double date with you and Gray? Hell, why would *anybody*?"

Brynn carefully folded her hands and placed them in her lap. "You're always saying how you and Grayson don't get along. I think spending some time together out of the office would do you both good. Allow you to see each other's non-work side."

I've seen his nonwork side. And that charming side of him assumed I was a hooker.

Sophie buried her face in her gin and tonic. "But a double date? What are we going to do, hang out with the high school kids at the ice-cream parlor?"

Will returned from the bar with refills on their drinks and took the seat beside Sophie. "What are we talking about?"

Sophie nodded toward Brynn. "She's still at it."

Will snorted and took a sip of Brynn's drink. "Get off it, Dalton. Only desperate couples go on double dates. If you're still begging, things with the iceberg must be a mess."

"My relationship is not a mess," Brynn said, grabbing her champagne glass out of Will's hand. "Well, actually, it's not quite a relationship. But we're... working at it."

Will gave her a derisive look. "I thought that nonrelationship was over. What's the point in giving it a second shot if you're already describing it as *work*?"

Brynn fiddled with the small napkin beneath her glass.

"Yeah, I kind of thought we'd agreed that it wasn't going anywhere too," she said in a small voice. "But then he sent these really beautiful flowers..."

"*I* sent the flowers," Sophie said grumpily.

"Because Grayson told you to," Brynn said pointedly.

Sophie took another sip of her drink, trying to wash away the sting of the memory. She didn't even know why Gray's request bothered her. It wasn't like she thought Gray would actually be interested in *her*. They might have enough sexual tension to burn down their entire office building, but he didn't even pretend to like her as a person. She'd forever be the slut in the elevator.

So of course she'd known that he wouldn't choose her.

But did he have to choose *Brynn*? They had about as much chemistry as two ice cubes. She thought that dull non-relationship was over.

On the plus side, whatever dopey affection Gray apparently felt toward Brynn didn't seem to be mutual. Sophie had been watching her sister carefully all night.

It was tricky to spot the differences between Happy Brynn and Worried Brynn. They both wore the same smile, never frowned, and never rose their voices. But unbeknownst to Brynn, she had a tell. She chewed her right ring fingernail when she was worried about something.

And right now, said fingernail was a mangled mess.

Trouble in boring land, Sophie thought with a little thrill of glee.

Still, denying Brynn such a simple favor felt...wrong. Spending an evening with Gray and Brynn together would be painful, but it wouldn't kill her.

Heck, it might even help dissolve whatever weird pull the man had on her.

And she and Will had pretended to be a couple plenty of times in the past for family parties and work events.

She could do this.

"So if we do this," Sophie said slowly, "what and where are we talking about? Just like dinner or drinks, right?"

Will groaned. "Don't cave, Soph. This entire conversation feels like something out of a teen movie."

Brynn gestured toward a group of leggy brunettes in the corner. "Speaking of teens, that little group of chlamydia carriers over there is making come-hither glances at you."

Will turned to look at the girls in question before giving a slow smile. "Very nice," he said with an appreciative second glance.

"Don't let us keep you," Brynn said with a wave. "In fact, since you've been such a good friend to Sophie all these years, I'll even give you a five-minute start before calling the cops and letting them know that there's a child predator buying appletinis for high school sophomores."

"To be fair, I think they must at least be juniors," Sophie mused. "Look at the one on the end; she has boobs."

"Damn fine ones too," Will said with a wink as he stood. "Much as I'm enjoying this riveting talk about that piece of granite you two call 'lover' and 'boss,' I'm sensing far more beneficial company over in that corner."

"That's disgusting," Brynn muttered as Will grabbed his beer and wandered away.

"Oh, come on," Sophie chided. "They're not really teenagers. They can't be much younger than us."

Sophie frowned when Brynn didn't respond. "Everything okay?" Sophie asked, noticing that her sister's eyes had gone from murderous to sad.

"I guess," Brynn said, not taking her eyes off her glass. "Just a little headache."

Sophie eyed Brynn's champagne. Alcohol surely wasn't going to help a headache, but she didn't say anything. Bossy, judgmental comments were Brynn's territory, not Sophie's.

"Are you sure you really want to date Gray?" Sophie asked, trying to keep her voice gentle.

Brynn nodded enthusiastically, but her eyes looked a little...numb.

Good lord, it's like she's a Stepford girlfriend, Sophie realized in horror.

"I think things could be great!" Brynn said woodenly. "Did he tell you I bought him a tie? He said he wore it today."

Sophie's heart twisted, but she pasted a smile on her face. Maybe things were more serious than she'd realized. Then again, Gray hadn't mentioned it, and Sophie certainly hadn't noticed anything special about today's tie.

She seemed to vaguely recall monochromatic stripes that looked like every other tie he owned.

This is your sister, she reminded herself firmly. *Be supportive.*

"Totally. It was just Gray's style," she said, patting Brynn's hand reassuringly.

"What was just my style?"

Sophie's head snapped up as she stared at her boss in confusion. "What are you doing here?"

Both he and Sophie glanced at Brynn, who was suddenly extremely preoccupied with her phone.

"You didn't tell them?" Gray asked, looking unbearably awkward.

Oh, Brynny, what did you do?

"No, no, of course we were expecting you!" Sophie lied, taking pity on him and patting the chair between herself and Brynn.

Gray sat, looking stiff as usual. Despite the fact that they were in a grubby little pub, he hadn't bothered to change out of his suit and looked painfully out of place.

"Look, if the double-date thing is uncomfortable, we can call it off," Gray said, glancing at Sophie.

"No, no. Not at all. It'll be nice to get to know each other better," she said lamely.

He looked vaguely queasy at the notion. "I'll need a drink," Gray said, glancing desperately at the bar.

He walked away and Sophie dug her nails into her sister's arm. "You seem to have neglected to mention that the double date was *tonight*."

Brynn's pale blue eyes pleaded with her. "A tiny omission, and only because I knew you'd say no. Please? I just thought that maybe he might loosen up a bit more around you and Will. When it's just the two of us, he's always so... guarded."

Sophie didn't have the heart to tell Brynn that "guarded" was simply who Gray was. Barbara Walters could take a shot at him and he wouldn't crack.

"Where's Will?" Gray asked, returning to the table with a beer.

"Oh, you know... he's over there," Sophie said, waving her hand over her shoulder.

She winced as Gray's eyes found her "date." She didn't have to turn around to know that her best friend probably had his hand on some twenty-year-old's thigh.

"I probably should have told you that Sophie and Will aren't exactly together," Brynn said hurriedly.

"I know. Sophie already told me."

Brynn's head snapped back slightly and her forehead showed the briefest ripple before resuming its usual smooth perfection.

Sophie felt a wince of sympathy for her sister. Gray was a workaholic, which meant that no matter how many flowers Brynn received, Sophie was still the one who would be spending more time with him. Not a fact that control-freak Brynn would take kindly to.

Still, Sophie's sympathy had limits. After all, this entire mess was Brynn's own fault. If she hadn't gone meddling in Sophie's unemployment status, then they wouldn't be in this awkward situation.

Sophie noticed that Brynn had barely touched her second glass of champagne, and was pressing her fingers into her temple. Apparently her little headache wasn't so little.

"Are you all right?" Gray asked, putting a hand gently on Brynn's shoulder.

Brynn gave a pathetic excuse for a smile and shook her head. "Just a sinus headache or something. I'm thinking maybe you all were right. This wasn't my best idea."

"You think?" Sophie said under her breath.

"I'm sorry about this," Brynn said weakly. "Maybe we should call it a night?"

Sophie glanced at her almost-full gin and tonic. "You guys go ahead. I'll stay and finish my drink. Plus I'll need to be Will's second if one of those girls' daddies comes after him with a shotgun."

"Let's get you into a cab," Gray said to Brynn, helping her to her feet. "You shouldn't be driving if your headache's that bad."

"You don't have your car?" she asked.

Gray shook his head. "I walked. I only live two blocks away."

"Oh, I didn't realize," Brynn murmured before shooting a nervous glance at Sophie.

Sophie pretended fascination with the football game on TV, trying not to react to what Brynn had just given away.

Brynn doesn't know where he lives. She's never been to his house. Never been in his bed...

Still, it didn't necessarily mean what Sophie hoped it meant. Could be that they'd only done the nasty at Brynn's town house.

Brynn's eyes fell on Gray's untouched drink. "You know, why don't you stay?" she said in her bossiest voice. "You haven't even had a chance to drink your beer."

"At least let me get you into the cab," he said stiffly.

Will materialized out of nowhere. "I'll drive her home."

Brynn sneered. "If you think I'm going to climb into your little identity crisis of a car, you're insane. I'll probably get an STD just from touching the seat belt."

"Yeah, because a cab is such a better option to avoid nasty diseases," Will said as he plucked Brynn's coat from the back of her chair. "C'mon, it'll give you a chance to critique my driving, and I know how turned on you get by nagging."

Brynn bit her lip, looking unsure of herself. She glanced at Gray, but as usual, his expression was a blank mask.

"Take Will up on it," Sophie urged. "It's pouring out, so you'll have a hard time finding a cab anyway."

"Fine," Brynn conceded. "But I get to pick the radio station, and we are *not* talking."

"Which sucks because I was so hoping to hear all about your Valentine's Day plans," Will snapped. "Let's go, I wanna get out of here before the Barbies over there realize I'm not going over to their place to play strip darts."

Sophie looked away as Gray and Brynn said good-bye. She thought she saw a tepid cheek-kiss out of the corner of her eye, but couldn't be sure. She waved after Brynn and Will, and watched as Gray resumed his seat and grabbed his beer.

"We can do separate tables if you want," Sophie said. "I didn't mean to trap you into spending more time with me than you have to."

He lifted a shoulder, but didn't seem to be anxiously glancing around for an escape route. She waited for her own compulsion to put distance between them to kick in, but the urge never came. Sophie almost smiled. Who would have thought that merely tolerating sitting at the same table with another person could be described as "progress"?

"So," she said, taking a sip of her drink, "things between you and Brynn, they seem… you know… well, how are they?"

He gave her a look. "Don't push it. No chatter."

Sophie mimed zipping her lips. "Got it. Brynn talk is strictly off-limits… So your sister called the office today. Jenna? She seems nice. You never mentioned what she—"

"Sophie," Gray interrupted.

"Yeah?"

"When we were trapped in that elevator, I asked you if we could be quiet and not talk. You said no."

She nodded. "Right. Because I am not a mime."

"Well, the thing is…" He looked at her, then looked away. "I'm asking you again. Can we sit here and not talk? Maybe catch this football game? People-watch?"

Sophie set her glass down with a sharp clink. "If you want me to leave, you can just say so."

This time he met her eyes. "That's the thing. I don't want you to leave. I want...company. But, you know, quiet company. Can you do that?"

Caught off guard, she looked at him more closely, taking in the strained creases around his eyes and the atypical wrinkles in his suit jacket. But it was the soft expression in his eyes that got to her. She felt something kind of warm and melty rush through her belly. Must be the gin.

But what if it wasn't the gin?

Oh dear.

Feeling off-balance, she found herself nodding. "Okay. Quiet company it is."

Gray didn't bother to hide the relief that flickered across his tense features. He shrugged off his suit jacket, and Sophie did her best to stare at the TV screen instead of his exposed forearms as he rolled his shirt up to his elbows. The more-casual Gray unnerved her.

Her mouth felt dry and she swallowed nervously. She couldn't help it. She didn't even know what she was going to say, she had to fill the silence. "So, have you ever wondered—"

Gray learned forward slightly, setting a finger gently across her lips to stop her words. He looked surprised by his own action, and then gave the smallest shake of his head.

"Okay," she whispered, unable to look away from his stare. The corner of his mouth turned up slightly. Sophie began to sweat. When had it become so freaking hot in the pub?

Then he turned slightly, and the moment was over. Gray put all of his attention on the TV screen, and Sophie let out a breath and tried to do the same.

She didn't know how long they sat there in companionable silence, but it got easier the longer they did. He wordlessly fetched them another round of drinks, and instead of feeling bored and panicked, she felt…content.

This is weird, she thought. *I'm playing the silent game with my boss.*

But then she found herself smiling.

Because it was also kind of nice.

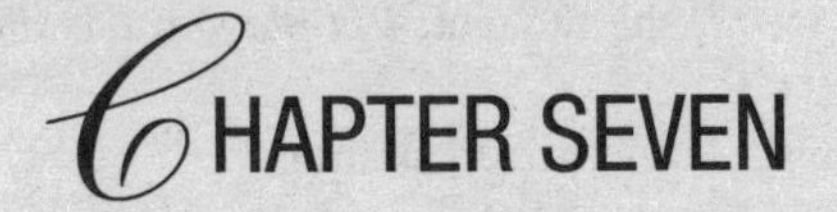

CHAPTER SEVEN

"Does this little toy car of yours have heated seats?" Brynn asked as she peered at the fancy buttons of his sports car.

Wordlessly Will punched a button and turned his attention back to the road. Brynn studied him out of the corner of her eye. They might not get along, but she'd known him long enough to know that silence and Will were never a good combination. Her body went on high alert.

"You shouldn't have offered me a ride if you were going to sulk the entire time," she said.

"Had I known you were going to chatter the whole way, I probably wouldn't have offered."

Brynn straightened her shoulders and gazed out of the passenger window and tried not to let his words sting. He'd never made a secret that he didn't like her, but she couldn't quite understand why her company was so repellant to him. And she *really* couldn't understand why someone as open, loving, and sweet as her younger sister had befriended such a selfish oaf. His entire existence revolved around casual sex and business ventures. He had zero substance.

"I don't understand why Sophie loves that bar so much," Brynn mused as she stared out at the line of red brake lights on either side of them. "It's so out of the way."

Will made a sharp turn to take a side-street detour, and Brynn braced her hand against the dash, surprised by sudden movement. She was about to nag him for driving like a freaking NASCAR driver when his outburst obliterated the sullen silence.

"Don't you ever get tired of being selfish?" he exploded.

She snapped her head around to look at his clenched profile. "Excuse me?"

"I'd just think you'd get sick of yourself after a while. I know I do." His knuckles tightened on the steering wheel.

"What—"

But he wasn't done. His voice took on a whining, high-pitched, mimicking tone. "*Sophieeee*, you need to sit through a hellish double date to make *my* life more convenient. Why doesn't everyone pick a bar that's closer to *me*? Mommy, Daddy, it's been ten minutes since you've praised all of my superpredictable accomplishments. Gray, why aren't you adoring me the way I deserve to be adored? Gosh, Will, you're so *mean* to me."

The unprovoked attack sent a river of emotions rolling through her, the anger hitting her hardest. How dare *he* of all people accuse her of being selfish?

The sharpness of her anger was followed quickly by an automatic denial. Will didn't even *know* her, not really. She was a good person. Sure, maybe she'd asked Sophie for an unfair favor, but Sophie was resilient. Nothing bothered her.

But as hard as Brynn tried to hang on to her anger, doubt

crept up her spine. Was he right? *Was* she selfish? Brynn didn't mean to be. She loved her sister and would never want to sabotage her happiness. But did Brynn even know what Sophie's version of happy looked like? Had she really stopped to assess what was going on with her sister, or had she just assumed that her own priorities were more important?

God, she *was* selfish.

The last emotion was perhaps the worst of all.

Hurt.

Hurt that it had to be Will of all people who'd held up the mirror and forced her to see her own narcissism.

Oh no. Not tears. Not now. She could not let Will Thatcher see her cry.

"Are you crying?"

"No," she said, the word soggy.

"Shit," he said softly.

Exactly.

He pulled over to the side of the road, and Brynn was surprised to see through the haze of her tears that they were outside of her condo building. Grabbing her purse, she fumbled at the door, desperate to escape Will and the flood of emotions he'd thrown at her.

"Thanks for the ride," she muttered tersely.

Again with the damn manners! She should have told him to go screw himself, but even at her most vulnerable, she couldn't get the words out.

"Brynn," he said softly, putting a hand on her arm.

"Don't you dare," she hissed, turning to face him, suddenly not caring that he was seeing her with puffy eyes and black rivers of eye makeup running down her cheeks. "Don't you dare insult me, outline every single flaw I have, and then turn around and try to make it better. You wanted to hurt me and you succeeded. At least have the balls to own your victory."

"I never meant to hurt you," he said, not breaking eye contact. "I just couldn't stand the way you were trying to push Sophie down so you could pull yourself up."

"Of course, we wouldn't want your poor precious Sophie to suffer," she said scathingly, hating the words she heard coming out of her mouth.

"This isn't about Sophie!" he said more sharply. "This has never been about Sophie!"

"Oh really?" She scoffed. "So it's just coincidence that you're taking her side on everything. You just don't want to see *me* happy, so you're doing your best to ensure my relationship with Gray never has a chance."

"You don't even like the guy!" Will yelled. "This isn't about Gray or Sophie, it's about you trying to control absolutely every little detail in your life because you don't know what you really want."

"I do know what I want! I want Gray. He's perfect for me. Smart, successful, genteel…"

"The man's a Goddamn mannequin, which is exactly what you *think* you want because you can ensure he fits into your plastic life."

"Why are you acting like this?" she whispered, staring into his blazing blue eyes. "I know we're always bickering, but you've never been cruel before."

"God, Brynn." He turned away and stared out the front of the car, running his fingers through his blond hair and muttering a string of curses.

"I don't expect an apology," she said quietly. "I know better. I just want to know why."

"Why? Why?!" His voice had taken on an agitated tone, and he sounded completely unlike the controlled and manipulative Will she knew so well.

"*This* is why, Brynn."

A rough hand slid behind the nape of her neck and jerked her over to the driver's-side seat. Firm lips slammed down on hers as he held her head still and took control of her mouth.

She parted her lips on a surprised gasp and his tongue flicked teasingly across her bottom lip. Brynn moaned. She didn't know if this was supposed to be her punishment, her embarrassment, or simply more ammunition that he could use against her, and she didn't care.

She didn't care that they hated each other, didn't care that she was lying awkwardly across the middle console of his car like one of his groupies.

She didn't care that he probably had some sort of agenda or that she was most certainly going to regret this in the morning.

Because at this moment, all she cared about was kissing Will.

His tongue slid against hers in a silky stroke and she moaned again. Winding her arms around his neck, Brynn pressed closer, letting her tongue tangle with his in a kiss that wasn't civilized or rehearsed or practiced. Kissing Will was a lot like dirty dancing. It was heady, instinctual, and it gave her the urge to move her hips.

They kissed like they argued. Savagely, taking as much as they gave. His hands tilted her head to the side so he could press deeper, and this time it was Will who let out a low groan. His mouth broke away from hers, and his lips softly pressed against the side of her mouth, skimming along her jaw before gently brushing her cheeks, her eyelids.

Reality crashed down as Brynn realized what he was doing. He was kissing away her tears. He cupped her face gently, as though using his lips to try to erase the pain he'd caused.

And suddenly it just felt too…tender. Animal passion had been safe. She could blame that on the champagne and their anger.

But kindness and tenderness from Will…she couldn't…she wouldn't…

She pulled away sharply.

"Brynn," he said quietly, reaching out to her again.

"Don't," she said. "Just don't."

Clutching her purse, she scratched at the door again, shoving it open in clumsy haste. She set one foot out into the stormy night before hesitantly looking back at him.

"You won't…you won't tell anyone about this, right? We'll just chalk it up to a moment of absurd insanity?"

Any softness that might have been in his eyes vanished. "Don't worry," he snapped. "Your secret is safe with me. You think I want anyone knowing that I failed to get a hot reaction from Ice Princess Brynn? You're just as cold as everyone thinks you are."

She didn't let his words sting. She was already numb.

"Good night, Will," she said stonily as she climbed out of the car. "If you've given me some sort of disease, you'll be hearing from me."

She'd barely slammed the door before he peeled away from the curb with a squeal of tires. *Typical*, she thought. Slowly her snarl faded as she stood hunched in the rain, staring after his long gone taillights.

That was a mistake. The realization came as a shock.

Because Brynn Dalton did not make mistakes.

CHAPTER EIGHT

"I didn't even know Seattle had a baseball team," Gray said under his breath, as he studied the elaborate retractable roof of Safeco Field.

"Easy, there," Ian said as he handed Gray another beer. "I'll have you know that the Mariners are well ahead of your White Sox this year."

"They used to be your White Sox too," Gray said, taking a sip of beer.

"Sure, but then I moved here. And now I'm a Mariners fan," his best friend said succinctly.

"That's just as well—you'll never have to worry about the hassle of getting World Series tickets."

"You just wait," Ian said, his eyes tracking a line double into center field. "This team will become your favorite."

Gray shook his head. It seemed like yesterday that he and Ian had been buying nosebleed tickets to White Sox games when they needed a break from studying for their Northwestern finals. Like Gray, Ian was a Midwestern transplant in the middle of Seattle's greenery. He'd moved to the Pacific Northwest several years prior.

As two of Gray's closest—okay, *only*—friends, Ian and his wife, Ashley, had been a major factor in Gray accepting a job in Seattle.

Them, and an intense desire to get away from a toxic ex-fiancée.

Ian's son squirmed impatiently in his seat. "Dad, can I have some pizza?"

"Now? You just finished your pretzel."

"I know, but I'm hungry again. And the pepperoni looks *really* good," said the perpetually hungry-for-junk-food Ryan.

"He has a point," Gray said, not taking his eyes off the field. "The pizza looked awesome."

"Ashley's going to kill me," Ian said with a shake of his head. "She hates when he eats crap."

"It's a ball game," Gray replied. "What are you supposed to feed him, kale?"

"What's kale?" Ryan asked, thumping his baseball glove with his tiny fist.

"My point exactly," Gray said. "Get the man some pizza, Dad!"

Ian sighed. "I'll be back. Ryan, make sure your godfather doesn't drink my beer."

"Beer's gross."

"Totally," Gray replied, taking another sip of his "gross" beer.

As Ian went to fetch the offending junk food, Gray watched his godson out of the corner of his eye. He didn't know Ryan well. They saw each other every couple years or so, but that was practically an eternity to a kid. Ryan was a new person every time Gray saw him.

When Ian had invited Gray to tag along on the father-son outing, Gray had waited for the usual rush of apprehension. Small talk was hard enough without figuring out what to say to a first grader. But instead of making a polite work excuse, Gray had found himself accepting. Wasn't this why he had moved to Seattle? To make connections with people?

"How's school?" Gray asked, realizing he'd been brooding.

"Good," Ryan said with a small shrug. "My teacher's pretty cool. And I got second in the science fair."

"That's cool. Got a girlfriend?"

Ryan's small body convulsed in dramatic dry heaves. "Girls are gross."

"Cooties?" Gray asked knowingly.

"I dunno. They're just stupid. I like baseball way better."

Gray smiled into his beer. Sometimes he thought he liked baseball better too. There was none of the drama, and the rules of the game were straightforward. With baseball, there was no worrying about why sometimes a woman looked at you like she wanted to curl up in your arms and stay there, and other times she looked at you like you were an inconvenience she had to somehow explain to her family.

Baseball had no distractingly wide blue eyes or slim curves or smile a man could drown in.

The beer turned slightly sour in Gray's stomach as he realized he hadn't been thinking about Brynn.

"One pepperoni pizza, coming right up!" Ian announced, scooting past the row of knees as he made his way back to them. He plopped a small box into Ryan's lap as he passed, and then, settling into the middle seat, handed another box to Gray.

"Am I off the hook from healthy eating too?" Gray asked, as he opened the personal-sized pizza box.

"We're splitting it," Ian said as he handed out napkins like the most experienced of dads. Gray nearly smiled at the gesture. Hard to imagine this was the same wiry frat boy who once refused to let anyone be admitted to his house party unless they could eat nachos with no hands.

The three of them settled into companionable male silence and watched the Mariners battle a close game. They weren't exactly bringing in the runs, but neither were the opposing Yankees, so all in all it was a relatively well-paced game.

"How's the job going?" Ian asked as he finished off Ryan's barely touched pizza. "All settled in?"

"Fine," Gray said. "A challenge. Brayburn Luxuries has genius behind it, but I'm not sure Martin was as adept at the operational aspects as he fooled everyone into thinking. I find that most of my time is spent trying to find records of previous deals and the contact information for existing clients. It's pretty fuc—" He glanced at Ryan. "Pretty messed up."

"You were going to say 'fuck,'" Ryan announced disinterestedly as he blew bubbles into his Coke.

"Ryan!" Ian exclaimed. "Where'd you learn that word? Are you trying to get me in trouble with your mother?"

Ryan shrugged. "Mom's the one who said it. The other day in the car when some other car cut in front of her. She told me never to tell you."

A slow smile broke out over Ian's face at the spousal ammunition his son had just unknowingly handed over. "Did she, now? Son, did I ever tell you how much I love you?" He pulled Ryan close to his shoulder for a moment, and at six, Ryan was still young enough not to be embarrassed by such displays.

Gray looked away, disturbed that the casual gesture gave him a vague sense of discontent that hadn't been there a few months ago. With their identical blond hair and brown eyes, they were the classic father-son baseball duo. Gray felt like an outsider. It was a feeling he'd long become accustomed to, but it had never bothered him quite so much before.

"Okay, so work's not great, but it'll get there," Ian said, returning his attention to Gray. "You'll turn it around in no time. It's why Brayburn selected you as his replacement."

"I guess," Gray said noncommittally.

"Well, *that's* the enthusiastic businessman I know so well," Ian said with a raised eyebrow. "What's the deal, you homesick or something? Got your period?"

Gray didn't bother to respond to that, and took a sullen bite of pizza.

Ian pressed on. "It's your bratty siblings, isn't it? Jenna is still giving you crap for not taking her ice-skating when she was nine, and Jack's still treating you like an impersonal stranger."

Gray tensed at that, but it was nothing he hadn't heard before. Hell, it was nothing he hadn't *thought* before. "The twins are fine," he said. "Jenna's actually coming to visit in a couple weeks. I doubt we'll be spending any white Christmases together anytime soon, but they seem to have forgiven me for whatever it was I did or didn't do when they were kids."

Ian nodded thoughtfully, having met Jack and Jenna often enough to know that those relationships were nothing they were going to solve before the end of the ninth inning.

"Woman problems, then," Ian said.

Gray's chewing slowed for a moment, and his jaw tensed, but he said nothing.

Ian chuckled. "I fucking knew it."

"Dad, you said—"

"Look, the moose!" Ian said quickly, pointing at the Mariners' mascot dancing on top of the dugout. "Why don't you go see if you can shake his hand?"

Needing no further encouragement, Ryan scampered down the stairs, holding his too-large cap with one hand, glove held protectively in front of him just in case a fly ball happened to find its way into his waiting mitt.

"You're still with the gym rat, right? Your assistant's sister?"

Gray growled at the mention of Sophie. "I don't want to talk about her."

"Who? The girlfriend or your assistant?"

"The assistant. I specifically look forward to weekends because it's the one area of my life that Sophie hasn't bulldozed with her good moods and chatter. And don't call Brynn my girlfriend. She's just…a woman I'm seeing. Sort of."

Barely.

He'd only spoken to her briefly since her ridiculous plan of a double date had exploded. He should definitely call her. Maybe arrange dinner for tomorrow.

Gray frowned. The idea didn't hold as much appeal as it should.

And the hell of it was, Gray should be feeling guilty about the way the failed double date had gone. Not just because he'd sent Brynn home with another man, but because Gray hadn't cared.

Weighing even more heavily on his conscience was the fact that sitting in companionable silence with Sophie had been a good deal more enjoyable than several of his strained silences with Brynn.

Which was ridiculous. Brynn was perfect for him. She had a respectable career, cared about her image, read the news, and paid attention to politics. She wasn't wedding- or baby-crazy.

Didn't have distracting curves or wear inappropriate clothes or act like she was chronically on the verge of throwing glitter at random passersby.

He realized that once again, Sophie had wedged into his thoughts.

He tried to push her back.

Maybe it was time to take things with Brynn to the next level. He'd already waited longer than average to pursue any sort of physical relationship with her. Gray kept telling himself it was because he didn't want to rush Brynn.

He refused to consider that there were other motivations for his reluctance to sleep with Brynn.

He waited for the idea of Brynn in bed to appeal. Nothing. Not the slightest stir. He felt…bored.

"I don't think we're working out," Gray muttered. Hell, it hadn't been working out from date one, but neither one had a good reason to firmly break it off. Perhaps because they were both too damn polite.

And polite wasn't good enough.

Ian dug a hand into a bag of peanuts. "Ashley will be disappointed. She's been trying to marry you off forever."

"She has?" Gray asked with genuine surprise. He'd always figured that women didn't see him as the husband type. He either got labeled as a consummate bachelor or a love-'em-and-leave-'em prick. It wasn't a reputation he fostered, per se, but he'd become resigned to it. He obviously lacked something that women were looking for when it came to long-term commitment.

At least that's what Jessica had told him.

Ian's voice jerked him back to the present. "Sure, Ash always has about a half-dozen single women in her book club alone who are dying to meet you. She's described you as being the strong, silent type. Women love that shit."

Gray grunted.

"So what happened? I thought you liked Brynn."

"I do," Gray said truthfully. "That's the trouble. I like her. That's it."

Ian paused in munching his peanuts. "Sounds simple. Maybe simple's what you need after Jessica..."

Gray remained silent as he watched the Mariners' third baseman hit into a double play. "It's kind of boring," he said finally.

"No offense, but 'boring' is kind of your thing these days. I thought you liked things predictable."

"I do," Gray said, his mood turning increasingly surly. He didn't like all of Ian's questions. They were hitting disturbingly close to a nerve he hadn't felt in a long time.

He felt his friend watching him out of the corner of his eye and tried not to squirm. "What?"

"It's the other one," Ian said with a slightly awed tone.

"What?"

"Your girlfriend's sister. Your employee."

"What about her?"

"You like *her*," Ian accused. "*That's* why things aren't working out with the perfect sister. You like the imperfect one. The one that looks just like your ex-fiancé. Because that's healthy. Not."

"I never should have told you about her resemblance to Jess," Gray said shortly, taking a sip of his beer. "What gave you that idea?"

Ian continued to watch him. "The way you talk about her. You should have heard yourself that first night you found out she'd be working for you. It was the most I've heard you talk in years."

Gray grunted. "Sophie is...Everything about her is wrong."

"Mm-hmm. Bet she's hot," Ian said, turning his attention back to the game.

"She's a mess."

"She's gotta be hot," Ian muttered again, under his breath.

Gray noticed that for all his talk about "hot" women, Ian's eyes had never left his son. Ryan was now wearing a big foam finger and, at the mascot's beckoning, stood atop the dugout and helped to lead "the wave." Ryan's face glowed with pure youthful ecstasy.

Had Gray ever been that happy? He couldn't remember.

Flagging down the beer vendor, Gray handed over some money and pushed Ian's twenty-dollar bill away. "My turn," he grumbled.

"So if it's not the younger sister who's under your skin, why are you planning to ignore a beautiful woman who hasn't done anything wrong?"

Gray gave Ian an annoyed look. "Are we still talking about this? What are we, sorority sisters now? Shall I order us some ice cream and Chardonnay?"

Ian continued to look at him.

Gray sighed and relented. Maybe talking about Sophie would clear his head.

"Okay, so Sophie might *kind of* be getting to me. But not in the good way, just...She's just always there."

Ian whistled. "I was right. You *are* hitting on the help."

"Don't call her that," Gray snapped more sharply than he'd intended.

Ian glanced at him in surprise, and Gray leaned forward, putting his elbows on his knees, the game temporarily forgotten.

"Shit," Gray breathed. "I don't know what to do. This girl drives me crazy. And she's my *assistant*, for Christ's sake. She's gorgeous but snotty. She has these massive self-esteem issues and yet is incredibly determined in what she wants. Most of the time I think she hates my guts, and yet sometimes there are these looks..."

"Hold on, let me get us some tampons," Ian said.

Gray glowered, even as he deserved it. Babbling wasn't his style, but he'd never been in a relationship that gave him so many headaches. Hell, this wasn't even a relationship. It was just...an inability to escape from the other person.

Sophie was too bubbly and unpredictable. Too much passion, not enough substance. Maybe that made her sort of magnetic, but should he be investing his valuable time thinking about her? Definitely not. He had a business to run, siblings to look out for, a godson to take to baseball games, and a girlfriend to make love to.

Plus, he wasn't her type. She went after the flighty, artistic types. The party boys. There's no way she would think of him as anything other than an experimental fling. Not that he wanted her to.

He just wanted...

"Maybe I should take Brynn to dinner tomorrow. Somewhere fancy that requires her to wear a black dress. Women always wear sexy underwear under a black dress, right?"

Ian frowned. "Wait, I thought we were talking about Sophie?"

"We were. And we agreed that she's completely inappropriate. So now we're talking about Brynn. Who's very appropriate."

Ian didn't respond, and Gray's head dropped forward slightly in resignation. "I'm in trouble, aren't I?"

His friend lifted a shoulder. "Could be worse."

Gray pictured the colorful, obnoxious chaos that was Sophie. Brynn's sister. *And* his assistant.

Whom he couldn't get out of his head.

"Actually, Ian…I'm pretty sure that this is as bad as it gets."

CHAPTER NINE

For the tenth time in five minutes, Sophie silently cursed Brynn for ditching her at yoga class. She'd thought there was nothing worse than having to fold herself into yoga positions next to perfect Brynn. But she'd been wrong.

Having to fold herself into yoga positions *without* perfect Brynn to mimic was much, much worse.

Sophie glanced at the woman next to her and tried to copy her constipated-cow position. The anorexic-looking instructor roamed around the room, reminding them to "just breathe." As though *breathing* would somehow fix life's problems.

Sophie felt a firm hand pressing into the small of her back. "Bottom up to the sky," the instructor whispered. Sophie hitched her ass into the air, feeling very much like a dog ready for mating.

So much for Brynn's claims that yoga would foster "constructive sibling time." Tonight, Sophie was the lone klutz in a room full of aging Cirque du Soleil understudies.

"Sister bonding, my ass," Sophie grumbled under her breath as they moved into yet another awkward pose. Her swearing earned her a glare from the elderly woman. Sophie gave an apologetic smile, but the woman had already folded herself into a bow and wasn't paying attention.

Brynn had proposed yoga as something fun they could do together. Brynn had been a yoga master practically since emerging from the womb, but she'd signed them up for an intro class so that they could have "sister bonding."

Sophie could think of about a million different ways they could bond. Wine. Gossip. Reality TV. Nachos.

Instead, she was writhing around on a little purple mat. Alone.

Sophie swallowed her bitterness and tried to remind herself that her sister had a good reason for skipping the yoga torture tonight. A *really* good reason.

Sophie knew from experience that breakups were the worst.

And as of this afternoon, Brynn and Gray were no longer a couple.

Which had shocked...absolutely nobody.

Even Brynn hadn't mustered the energy to act surprised. Her sister had been a half bottle deep in Chardonnay when she'd called Sophie, and had been rambling on about how they'd been dating three weeks and hadn't had sex.

Sophie only hoped Brynn hadn't heard her sigh of relief at that crucial revelation. Not that anything would come of it, but Sophie's mind was at ease knowing she hadn't been having sex dreams about the guy her sister was actually having sex with.

Yes, sex dreams about Grayson Wyatt.

Talk about a nightmare.

A really hot nightmare.

The instructor motioned to Sophie to tilt her pelvis up and Sophie nearly moaned as images of last night's dream flashed through her mind.

Gray's head lowering to her neck.

Her hands tugging at his belt.

His lips on her—

"Sophie, loosen your hips," the instructor scolded. "Watch Margaret. You see how her lower body is open? You look closed-off."

Eighty-year-old Margaret looked seconds away from a yoga-induced orgasm.

Sophie nearly whimpered.

She surreptitiously checked the clock in the corner of the room. Only five more minutes and she could get her Friday night started. As usual, she had a truly exciting night awaiting her. Wine, a new romance novel featuring a surly duke, a nice salad. If she was feeling productive, maybe a little self-pedicure.

Finally the torture ended.

She smiled at the older lady next to her as they rolled up their mats. "You have great form," Sophie said. "I haven't seen you in here before, have I?"

"This my first class, but I've been doing yoga DVDs for years. And I practice daily. I'm heading over to the Pilates class after this, if you want to join."

"Well, that sounds..." *Awful.* "...lovely, but I do believe I hear a nice Merlot calling my name."

The Merlot was actually in her gym bag. Along with a bottle of Chianti. Which pretty much meant she should be signing up for AA about now, but it's not like she was actually *drinking* the bottles at the gym. She just hadn't had anywhere else to put them after Will dropped them off at her office. He got a killer discount from an ex-girlfriend and was always hooking Sophie up with new vintages.

"Oh, I don't drink the alcohol," the fitness freak was saying. "I prefer a nice cup of green tea."

Of course you do, Sophie thought.

As if anyone needed any further proof that she wasn't cut out for this yoga business, Sophie hadn't rolled up her mat tightly enough and couldn't snap the buckles around it. The flexible, antibooze grandma had to help her.

Finally she was on her way out of the hellhole, her body begging for a hot bath and her baggiest clothes, when she realized she couldn't find her keys in her purse. Sophie groaned as she remembered she'd last used them to open the printer toner box this afternoon.

Which meant the keys were likely sitting on her office desk.

So much for the imminent bubble bath.

Sophie trudged back toward the office, praying that the security guard would be around to let her in.

How had her Friday devolved from perfect to crappy?

When she'd left her house that morning, she'd felt great. And looked great. The guy behind her at Starbucks had bought her latte, *and* she'd had a blind date set up for that evening. Then she'd gotten to the office and received an actual *compliment* from Gray on the report she'd put together on the potential Blackwell deal.

But within the span of a couple hours, she'd spilled coffee on her dress, her date had canceled on her, and Gray hadn't spoken to her the rest of the day.

So now she had crotch sweat from yoga, her only date was a fictional duke, and she had to go back to the miserable office, where her boss had likely put another pile of work on her desk. At least she had the wine on hand.

She might suck at everything else, but she was pretty sure she'd make a kick-ass alcoholic if she put her mind to it.

The security guard was none too happy to be pulled away from his paperback, but Ralph was willing enough to let Sophie into the office once she promised home-baked chocolate chip cookies on Monday morning.

If only all men could be managed so easily.

Sophie found her keys buried beneath the expected pile of new work. She was contemplating "accidentally" knocking the files into the recycling bin when she heard the rustle of papers. She glanced toward Gray's office, startled to see a lamp on, despite it being well after business hours.

And there was Gray.

Apparently she wasn't the only one whose Friday night had a faint whiff of loser. Except that her boss wasn't here because he'd forgotten something. In fact, he looked like he'd never left, and was hunched in the same position as when she'd left a few hours ago.

He looked... lonely.

Sophie's stomach clenched. At least she knew Brynn was cozy at home, drowning her sorrows in ice cream with her girlfriends.

Gray had no one.

She glanced at her watch. It was nearly seven. If she hurried, she could probably make it home in time to see whatever trashy reality show was geared toward single women with no plans on a Friday night.

Gray still hadn't seen her, so it wasn't like he'd know that she'd abandoned him to a Friday night even more pathetic than hers. Sophie might be alone, but at least *she* wasn't working. She tugged her wine-stuffed yoga bag farther up her shoulder and quietly picked up her keys. Should she say hello? What if he just wanted some peace and quiet?

Or worse, what if he didn't *want* to be alone?

Maybe she'd just pop her head in and say hi. He'd probably be horrified to realize she existed outside the hours between nine and five, but she couldn't just sneak away.

He turned his head slightly to grab another file and her heart lurched as she saw his profile. He didn't just look lonely. He looked sad.

And if there was anything Sophie couldn't turn her back on, it was a sad creature. She clenched her fingers around the keys, inexplicably nervous.

"Gray?" she called out, as though she'd just now realized there was someone else in the building. His head snapped around as he spotted her through the glass wall, and she was relieved to see that while he didn't quite smile at her (that would be a first), neither did he look annoyed at the interruption.

"What are you still doing here?" she asked, moving toward his office and leaning against his doorway. "It's seven o'clock."

"Working," he replied, gesturing to the stack of files and his laptop.

"Have you eaten?" She didn't know why she asked. She'd only meant to say hello and make sure he wasn't, you know...like suicidal or something.

But close-up, he looked even more lonely and pathetic than she'd expected.

"Eaten?" he repeated.

"Yes, Gray, food. Normal people consume it to give them

energy, joy, maybe a little extra padding around the middle?"

He stared at her, and she had the unsettling feeling that it had been a really long time since someone had cared about whether or not he'd had anything to eat.

She sighed. "I'll order pizza. You're not a freaking vegetarian or something, are you?"

"You saw me eat chicken at your parents' house."

"Well, sure, but I also watched you drink black coffee, which I know you hate. I hardly think getting verbal confirmation of your eating habits is unwarranted."

"I don't need any pizza. I can eat when I get home."

"Which would be, what? Frozen dinner? Scrambled eggs? Please. It's Friday night. Come on, humor me. I can't indulge in a meat lover's combo alone."

"You're eating pizza? Here? With me?"

"Why not?" she said with a shrug.

At least this pizza would totally be guilt-free. Calories didn't count when you were just feeding your lonely boss.

Once again, the thought of Gray being lonely caused a funny fluttering in her stomach, which she chalked up to hunger pangs. Thirty minutes later she was down in the lobby, tipping the pizza boy and eagerly inhaling the scent of Romio's house special.

Trying not to drool, she stopped by the office kitchen to grab some paper plates and napkins. As an afterthought, she also grabbed a fork and knife because Gray seemed the fastidious type.

Sophie paused and remembered her gym bag.

Oh, why the hell not? She grabbed a corkscrew that some of the sales guys kept around for spontaneous in-office happy hours. Pizza went better with wine, as did awkwardly intimate dinners with one's stilted boss. Armed with a bottle of red and a box of greasy heaven, Sophie walked back into Gray's office without knocking.

His eyes flicked to the pizza box. Then to the wine. He raised an eyebrow.

"Don't go all prudish on me," she said as she set the box on the corner of his desk. "It's a Friday night, and I fully intend to enjoy this bottle of wine even if it's not on my couch like I'd planned."

"Nobody asked you to stay, and I certainly didn't ask you to bring your booze."

She must have become immune to him, because she didn't even get riled at his lack of gratitude.

"Oh, so you don't want me to share?" she asked innocently as she wrestled with the ancient corkscrew.

His answer was to stand and pull the bottle and opener out of her hands. His big hands proceeded to open it like a pro before pouring liberally into two plastic cups. Her lady parts purred. Now *this* was a Gray she could start to like.

Sophie handed him a plate with two pieces of pizza before selecting a slice for herself. *Just one*, she thought as she mentally counted the calories. Her metabolism was pretty good, and supposedly the hellish yoga helped to keep her backside from wobbling. But even the best of genes would struggle to overcome these puddles of grease.

"So what are you working on?" she asked once they'd settled into chairs.

"You're going to make me converse, aren't you?" he said.

"Absolutely. It'll help build your character. Oh, and here, I brought you a fork. I figured a tidy man like yourself wouldn't approve of eating with his hands."

His eyes flicked to hers, and she thought she read something like dismay. The stony gray depths were somehow warmer than usual, and they seemed to ask, *So this is what you think of me?*

She looked away, unsettled.

He picked up the pizza purposefully with both hands. "I'm trying to make sense of Martin's shorthand," he said, gesturing at the multiple piles. "There are about eight hundred different-colored file folders, pen ink, and highlighters. But I don't seem to be any closer in deciphering the method behind the color coding."

"I think maybe he just thought black ink and standard manila folders were boring," she said around a huge glob of cheese.

He picked up his cup of wine and stared at her over the rim. "Boring? You're telling me I've wasted hours trying to figure out what blue highlighter was supposed to signify and he just was trying to add some color to his life?"

Sophie shrugged. "Yeah, his secretary left a couple of notebooks behind with commentary on Martin's quirks. I just found them this afternoon."

That was a lie she didn't feel particularly guilty about. The notebooks had been there all along, but the thought of helping Gray before now just hadn't appealed.

Not when he looked like he wanted to call an exterminator every time he looked at her.

"What else did these notebooks have to say? Anything else that can save me time? Despite what you probably think, spending Friday night in the office isn't *exactly* my idea of the good life."

"Oh? Did you have big plans?"

Sophie instantly regretted her question. She'd forgotten that he and Brynn were originally planning to see a play tonight. Probably something scholarly. She hadn't meant to rub the breakup in his face.

"Did you speak with your sister?" he asked after a pregnant pause.

Sophie nodded as she picked at a piece of pepperoni. "I didn't really get the details, just that, you know...you guys decided it wasn't working out."

He didn't say anything more, and Sophie was unsettled by his lack of reaction.

Was he more torn up about the breakup than she'd expected? He hardly looked like a man glad to be done with a going-nowhere relationship.

"Do you, um...want to talk about it?" she asked. *Please say no.*

"Talk about what?"

She sucked in a breath for patience.

"The fact that you just ended a relationship? That usually registers a blip on the human emotional scale."

"Oh. No, I don't want to talk about it."

"No problem," she said, happy to dodge that particular conversation. "Shall I go get Martin's assistant's notes? We can go over them while we eat and see if there's anything that would help you."

"Your sister's great," he blurted out.

Oh, here we go. She sat back in her seat and grabbed for her wine. Sophie wasn't exactly in the mood to hear yet another person begin a tirade about Brynn's excellence, but she couldn't cut off a guy who'd just been dumped. Or at least she was *assuming* Brynn had done the dumping. Her sister's message hadn't exactly been clear, and she doubted she'd get all the gritty details from Gray.

"Yes, Brynn's wonderful," she replied warily.

"We just didn't suit."

"'Suit'?" she repeated. "You do realize that phrase went out of style back around the time of Prohibition?"

"You know what I mean," he said as he stared into his wine. "Everything worked on paper, but in person, nothing clicked."

That's because you two are the same uptight, overachieving, perfectionist freak. Suddenly her good intentions began to evaporate. The thought of Brynn and Gray in all of their sophisticated and successful glory made her stomach churn.

"Are we having a bonding moment here, boss?" she asked snidely. "Shall I grab some tissues and ice cream to go with the pizza and wine?"

"Never mind," he said gruffly.

"I'm sorry," she said, feeling like crap. There was no need to take out her personal issues on the poor man. He shrugged and reached for the pizza box. He slid another piece onto her plate before getting one for himself.

So much for just having one, she thought as she dug in.

"So what's real the story with you and Will? Is it like one of those on-again, off-again things?" he said, breaking the companionable silence.

"What's with all the talking?" she teased gently.

Gray shrugged again, suddenly looking less like the powerful, disinterested boss and more like a shy new kid in town. "I don't usually enjoy your variety of constant rambling—"

"Nice, Gray, just when I was starting to kind of like you."

His eyes met hers and he continued. "But I don't know anyone in Seattle, and you seem to be the only person I can talk to."

Oh. *Oh.* And just like that, her irritation evaporated and was replaced by something downright melty. She pushed the uncomfortable sentiment aside. The last thing she needed was to start letting her guard down around her boss.

"I'll grab those notebooks," she said, almost knocking over her wine in her haste to stand.

"Sophie."

"Yeah?"

"You never answered my question about you and Will." His eyes burned into hers and she suddenly wished she'd had a couple fewer sips of wine. Or maybe a few more. Everything was fuzzy.

What was it he'd been asking?

Oh, right. Will. Best friend.

"Oh, Will and I are just friends. We've always been just friends," she said with a wave of her hand.

"Then why did you tell me he was your date at your parents' house?"

Sophie snorted. "Well, let's see, I'd recently endured the humiliation of being stuck in an elevator with a man who assumed I was a whore, while wearing little more than a thong. And *then* the same man shows up at my parents' house as my perfect sister's perfect new boyfriend. So after that, did I want you to think I was single and lonely as well as pathetic and slutty? No, not really. So, I let you think I had a fake boyfriend. Sue me."

Her voice pitched up at the end and she felt her cheeks flushing as she stared him down. Her attempt at cute and snarky had derailed into melodramatic and lame. She stood abruptly and walked quickly from his office, annoyed to feel the prick of tears as she gathered the notebooks from her desk.

Sophie took a deep breath. She needed to get out of there. She'd just hand over the notebooks and let him continue with his loser evening. Alone. She marched back into his office and nearly collided with his solid form. He put his hands on her shoulders to steady her, and she jumped back from the heat of the contact.

"Sorry," Gray said quietly, flexing his fingers and putting them back to his sides, as though even the briefest of contact with her made him itch. He cleared his throat but didn't move out of the way. "Look, I'm sorry for prying about Will. I was just curious what a woman like you would be doing with a guy like him."

"You mean what would a rich entrepreneur want with a lowly secretary?"

"Stop it," he said sharply, sounding very unlike his usual calm self. "Quit talking about yourself as if you're toilet paper."

"Perhaps if you quit treating me like an irritant I wouldn't be so defensive!"

"This has nothing to do with me," Gray said. "I made one single misassumption about you in a dark elevator. It was a mistake. I hadn't slept, I hadn't eaten all day, I hate confined spaces, and frankly, I *really* wasn't at my best that night in Vegas, okay? But ever since learning that you *weren't* a prostitute I have treated you with nothing but respect. And yet you continue to goad me and verbally sabotage yourself every chance you get. Why is that, Ms. Dalton?"

He took the tiniest step forward and she swallowed hard, resisting the urge to move away from him.

Her brain was struggling to think of a retort, so she blurted out the first thing that came to mind. "Don't call me Ms. Dalton."

"Why, is it too *respectable* for a screwup like yourself?"

Sophie flinched, knowing his sarcasm was only playing

off her own words, but it still stung. "It has nothing to do with respectability," she snapped. "I just want you to think of me as a person. I want to hear you say 'Sophie.'"

Oops. That had *not* come out right. Now he was going to think she was partial to hearing her name from his lips. At the thought of his lips, her gaze fell to his mouth. What was wrong with her? The wine was messing with her head.

But he still hadn't moved away. And he didn't exactly look repulsed.

"Okay," he said slowly. "Sophie, then."

As if the moment needed to be any more charged, the lights in the office turned off as they were programed to do every few minutes in the evening unless their sensors detected movement.

It would only take the slightest step to trigger the lights back on, but they stood still for a moment longer in the darkened office. The air felt thick with conflicted electricity, but Sophie wasn't sure what was at the root of the weirdness.

Just minutes ago they'd been talking about Brynn, and now…

Now she wanted to kiss her boss. Badly.

She could just imagine his horror if she leaned into him. Here he was trying to intimidate her, and she wanted to jump his bones.

Except…Gray seemed to be doing a little leaning of his own. And was it her imagination, or were his lips a lot closer than before? All she had to do was move a couple of inches and…

No.

Sophie sidestepped quickly to move around him just as she saw his arm reach for her. They stared at each other as the fluorescent lights flickered back on.

"Yikes, that would have been awkward to explain to HR, right?" she asked brightly. "Us standing alone in the dark, you about ready to strangle me for being a silly little twit."

"I'd never hurt a woman."

"Jeez. Calm down, I was *kidding*. Where should I put these notebooks?"

"Just leave them on the desk. I think we're probably done for the evening."

"Meaning?" she asked.

"Meaning I appreciate your willingness to help, but I can't take up any more of your weekend time. It was already inappropriate to let you order pizza. Which, of course, you can expense, by the way. The wine too."

"Another HR strike against us," she said, trying to lighten the mood. "Company money going toward booze for two."

He ignored her.

She moved past him and set the books on his desk. "Fine, I'll leave these for Monday, but only if you promise to do the same."

"I still have a couple things to wrap up," he said, not moving from the doorway.

"Oh, come on," she said. "Go home. Go watch baseball or drink beer or whatever it is you do for fun. Throw darts at children. Boil bunnies..."

She glanced over at Gray as she began piling up their plates and froze. His mouth looked different. Lopsided just slightly. Almost as if...

Grayson Wyatt was smiling. Sophie's world tilted just slightly.

I must really need to get laid, she thought. All it took was some dark lights and a pathetic excuse for a smile and she was ready to hump the one man on earth who could barely stand her company. Definitely time to get out of there.

"Well, okay, then, I'll take off, if you're sure you're okay with me ditching you," she said flippantly. "You know me, any chance to put off work sounds great."

His smile faded, and the gray eyes turned back to dull slate. "I'll see you on Monday, then," he said.

"Monday," she agreed with a forced smile.

Sophie quietly gathered up her gym bag and took one glance back at Gray, who was staring out the window. She ached to go to him.

Instead, she walked away.

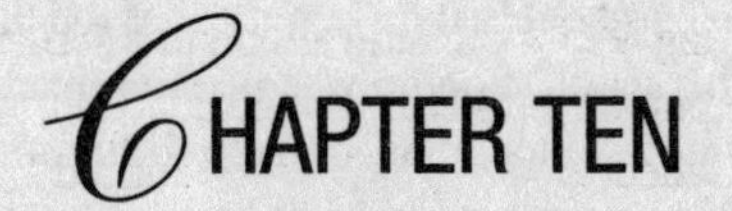

CHAPTER TEN

To say that Gray's life had been disorderly for the past couple of months was an understatement. His once-calm routine had been turned upside down, and no matter how carefully he planned his days, fate continued to throw him one curveball after another.

And he knew exactly when the turn from comfortable to chaos had occurred.

Right about the time he'd encountered a certain blonde firework in an elevator. He no longer thought it was coincidence. Fate had apparently delivered Sophie as some sort of trial, and the woman was turning out to be absolute hell on his nerves.

She'd become both invaluable and intolerable as an assistant. She anticipated his every need before he asked. Her cheerful social skills on the phone easily smoothed over any feathers he inadvertently ruffled by his lack of inane social niceties. And she'd apparently read Martin's secretary's notes cover to cover, because in addition to her intuition about every single business deal, she now knew staff birthdays and the names of potential clients' children and had memorized the menus of every business caterer in Seattle.

But as much as he relied on her, most of the time her presence soured his mood. Sophie was just too much. Too much energy, too many smiles, too Goddamn infuriating.

As if all that weren't enough, he had yet *another* frustrating woman to reckon with.

Jenna was due at the Seattle airport in an hour, and Gray hadn't a clue how he was going to pick up his little sister *and* manage his meeting with the Blackwells. Hell, he didn't even know how he'd double booked himself in the first place, other than that he'd avoided giving Sophie access to his calendar after she'd begun booking thirty-minute "mental breaks" into his work schedule.

"Sophie!" he barked.

She threw him an arch look through the glass and took her precious time strutting into his office. She was wearing some sort of dress that looked like cotton candy and her shoes had bows on them. *Bows.*

"Why are you yelling?" she asked.

"I don't yell."

"Your voice was raised."

"I had to raise my voice to get your attention," he ground out.

"You've never raised your voice before to get my attention when I'm at my desk. I can hear you just fine with your normal voice-of-doom volume."

"Sophie."

"Gray."

"You are possibly the most annoying assistant ever. I should fire you."

Her blue eyes narrowed as if daring him to try. "Did you call me in here just because you're cranky?" she asked.

Her impertinence should have rankled him, but instead he felt the odd urge to smile. But smiling would only encourage her, so he scowled instead.

"I need a town car."

"Has Seattle driving become too much for you?" She studied her fingernails.

"It's not for me. I need it sent to the airport to pick up my sister."

She stared at him. "You've got to be kidding me. Your sister is coming to visit, and you're having her picked up in a town car instead of meeting her yourself?"

He flinched. "I'm busy."

"With what, world domination? Practicing your glare? Take an hour off, for God's sake. I'll clear your calendar."

"I would, but it's the Blackwells. Remember them? You had them eating out of your palm and now they're coming back to discuss a potential deal. Today, of all days."

"Don't get pissy with me. If you'd let me manage your calendar like assistants are paid to do, you wouldn't be in this pickle," she said primly.

"I'm not in a pickle. Just get the damn town car, would you?"

"Is this sister your *only* sister?"

"Yes," he said wearily.

"Your baby sister, right?"

"Yes, she and Jack are twins. I can sketch you a family tree later, but for now I just need you to get me the car."

"Doesn't Jack live around here? Why can't he pick her up?"

"Because he has an exam today. She's twenty-four, not in

junior high. She can manage to get home from the airport without a big brother escorting her."

Even as he said it, his gut gave a sharp twist of guilt. Of course Jenna would be fine in a town car, but he wished he *could* pick her up personally. Their relationship was cordial, but he'd never had the closeness with the twins that they had with each other. Something he'd been meaning to rectify for years, but could never quite find the time. Or the method. He just didn't have the ability to easily converse in the way that came so naturally to Jack and Jenna.

Sophie got that assessing look that Gray now knew meant trouble. He wished for the hundredth time that the assistant assigned to him was someone uncomplicated and professional. Someone like Brynn.

Although if Brynn had been his assistant, he wouldn't have been able to date her. Because CEOs did *not* date their assistants unless they wanted a lawsuit on their hands. Something he'd nearly forgotten the previous Friday night. It was amazing what months of celibacy could do to a man. He'd almost pulled a page from the *How to Be a Sleaze* handbook and made a play for his secretary.

Thinking about how close he'd come to kissing Sophie made him uneasy.

Neither of them had mentioned it, but if the sexual tension had been simmering before, it was nearing a boil.

He didn't like it.

She opened her mouth again, and his strained temper exploded. "Whatever you're thinking, just drop it," he snapped. "All I need is for you to make a simple phone call and have them pick up Jenna Wyatt. Her cell phone number is in my contact database. Nothing weird. No limo, no flowers, no welcome committee."

"You got it," she said with suspicious calm. "I'll order some sandwiches and have them delivered to the conference room. You should meet them in there instead of your office. They won't be as intimidated if it doesn't feel so much like your turf. You'll get further with men like them if they don't feel threatened. "

Gray just shook his head. Most of Sophie's ideas on social manipulations were beyond him, but as long as she continued to help the business, he'd humor her. Plus, it would get him out of this atrocious orange chair. He hated the thing almost as much as he'd hated the uncomfortable rocking chair that Martin had left behind, but he wasn't about to give Sophie the satisfaction of complaining. The woman was at her best when she goaded him into talking, snapping, or yelling.

It seemed to be in his best interest to keep the upper hand. And if keeping the upper hand meant sitting every day in a chair that looked like it was covered in Halloween spray paint, so be it.

A quick glance at her desk verified that she had in fact picked up her phone to call the town car. Relaxing slightly, Gray pulled up the Blackwell file on his computer. He'd spent all of the previous evening researching the proprieties, but no matter which way he looked at it, the buildings themselves just didn't warrant the Blackwells' asking price. In order to bring the buildings up to Brayburn standards, he'd either have to implement major renovations or tear the damn things down and start from scratch.

It wasn't going to be a pleasant discussion. Gray could only hope that the son wouldn't tag along this time. It was bad enough that he had to go toe to toe with the stubborn Peter Blackwell. Watching Alistair sniff after his assistant's tight little ass like a randy dog would be more than he could handle.

His cell vibrated and he saw his brother's name. "Jack. Aren't you supposed to be taking a test right now?"

"Easy, big brother. It doesn't start for another twenty minutes. Are you on your way to pick up the monster?"

"No, I had a conflict. I sent a car."

He was met with silence on the other end.

"I had to, Jack; this deal is huge," Gray said, hating that his tone sounded defensive. "I'm already struggling to keep this company above water as it is."

"I get it," Jack replied shortly.

Sure you do. "Let's meet up for dinner later. What time are you free?"

They settled on a time for what would likely be an uncomfortable family dinner. They'd fall into the usual Wyatt routine of Jack and Jenna chattering eagerly like the Bobbsey twins while Gray would awkwardly try to insert himself into the conversation.

The twins had enough manners to make polite inquiries about Gray's life, but he winced at the lameness of his own inevitable answers.

No girlfriend. I tried, but she turned out to be too perfect and I got bored.

No social life. I don't know how to make friends.

What's that? My secretary? Yeah, I mistakenly implied that she humped for money and she now spends every hour of the day pushing my buttons.

Dinner with the family would be only slightly worse than eating alone. Or eating pizza with Sophie.

That had not been his wisest decision. He'd just felt so damn alone. Even Sophie's constant rambling seemed preferable to the endless solitude. But then she'd started berating herself and he'd lost his temper. He still wasn't sure exactly what it was that had had him advancing on her like a lion stalking a helpless mouse. For all her damn spunk and spice, there was a big hole where her self-worth should have been.

Despite the fact that Sophie was smart, attractive, and competent, she seemed to think that she was slumming it because she wasn't a neurosurgeon or quantum physicist. And he'd just been sick of hearing about it. He'd wanted her to feel special. Wanted.

Well, not wanted in the sexual way. Okay, *maybe* in the sexual way.

But damn, he hadn't been prepared for her to show up in her tight little yoga pants and all that hair pulled back into a perky ponytail. And the way she'd worried about making sure he'd eaten...

He knew better than to be reeled in. Jessica had pulled a similar stunt by bringing him homemade chicken soup when he was sick, and look how that had turned out. He'd gotten soup, and his partner had gotten into his fiancé's pants. Oddly, what bugged him most in hindsight was that the blasted soup had tasted like it had come from a can. *Homemade, my ass.*

Maybe he should call Brynn again. Perhaps he'd been too hasty in ending their relationship before giving it a chance. She was everything he was looking for. Successful, lovely, calm...

No. He was bored just thinking about it. Plus it would mean enduring more Dalton family dinners, and no woman was worth that.

Still...he needed a girlfriend. Someone to talk to. Ian

was great, but weekly sessions at the gym with another dude weren't the same as lingering dinners with a woman.

But finding the right woman had proven a hell of a lot more difficult than any business venture he'd undertaken. He'd given up on dating in Chicago after Jessica, and the Seattle dating pool hadn't been much better. He wasn't even sure what he was looking for anymore.

Gray did, however, know what he *wasn't* looking for. He didn't want someone too cheerful and talkative. And maybe it was time to try a brunette this time—someone serious and focused. Someone who wouldn't wear a miniskirt to a business function just to piss him off.

His eyes unwillingly fell on his assistant. Someone not like Sophie.

* * *

"Where's that cute little Sally?" Alistair Blackwell asked around a mouthful of his third salami panini.

Gray clenched his teeth. The thought of this creep lusting over his assistant was not improving his mood. It was becoming rapidly apparent than Alistair's only purpose in joining them for the day was free food and getting into Sophie's pants.

"I believe Ms. Dalton is on her lunch break," Gray replied coolly.

Actually, Gray had no idea where Sophie was. He hadn't seen her since he'd requested she call a town car, but he assumed she was off eating a fancy overpriced salad at one of the nearby restaurants with the other office women. He hated to admit it, but he almost wished she were here to work her nauseating female magic on the Blackwells.

As if Sophie had read his thoughts, he heard the sound of familiar female laughter. Finally she was back from her froufrou girly lunch. Really, she couldn't have waited to do an extended lunch on a day when his personal and professional life weren't in mayday status?

Slowly his mind registered that he was hearing the laughter of two women. Both sounded familiar.

His spine stiffened in realization. *Oh God.*

Alistair, completely oblivious to the turmoil running through Gray's mind, seemed delighted to see not one, but two females approaching through the glass partition.

"Well, well, your pretty Sally has a pretty friend," he said, all but licking his lips.

"My assistant's name is Sophie," Gray ground out. "And that pretty friend you're ogling is my little sister."

He didn't have to turn around to know it was Jenna. The low, cynical chuckle and the raspy jazz-diva voice were all too familiar. Gray had spent the past decade trying to keep the twins away from his professional life, and Sophie had managed to undo years of careful maneuvering in one afternoon.

"Sophie!" Alistair was booming, heading toward the door of the conference room. "I was wondering when we'd get to see your pretty face."

"Mr. Blackwell," Sophie cooed. "It's so lovely to see you again. Allow me to introduce Mr. Wyatt's sister. This is Jenna, visiting us all the way from New York. I just picked her up at the airport."

Sophie shot Gray a triumphant look, and as much as he wanted to drag his assistant into his office by her hair, it was hardly the time to address her misunderstanding of the words "town car."

Gray settled for sending her a glare. *We'll talk later.*

She smiled back at him. *You're welcome.*

"Gray, aren't you going to say hello to your sister?"

He jolted guiltily. He'd been so busy glaring at Sophie that he'd forgotten all about greeting Jenna. His sister looked beautifully dangerous, as always. Dressed in tight black pants and some sort of knit top, she looked every bit the New Yorker she'd been for all of the past three months.

Before that, she'd been a Southern belle. Before that, a cowgirl.

Dark hair fell in thick waves around Jenna's shoulders, and one perfectly groomed brow arched above a gray eye not unlike his own.

"Hello, brother dearest. It was so thoughtful of you to send your assistant since you couldn't make it in person. I'd have thought you'd have just sent a town car, but this was a nice personal touch."

Gray smiled thinly.

"You're quite the assistant, Ms. Dalton," Peter was saying to Sophie as Gray awkwardly hugged his sister. "You fetch lunch, answer phones, and pick up your boss's sister from the airport..."

"What other services do you offer, Soph?" Alistair said with a grin, his eyes fixated on Sophie's breasts.

And that was quite enough of that. Gray stepped forward between Sophie and the Blackwells.

"Jenna, it's great to see you, but as you can see, we're just wrapping up a business meeting here. Let's meet up for dinner later?"

"By all means," his sister purred, her expression betraying nothing.

Alistair finally managed to tear his eyes away from Sophie's chest and did a double take as he took in the full impact that was Jenna. His sister was stunning, which had been hell on an older brother while she was in her teens. Now that she'd blossomed into a confident and edgy woman, she'd become downright dangerous. Her eyes were the trademark Wyatt gray, except hers tilted upward slightly, giving her the look of a predatory cat. A slim body and long silky chestnut hair had attracted the attention of many a modeling scout. Which Jenna had, of course, pursued, if only to irk both of her brothers.

The combination of Sophie's sunny glow and Jenna's sultry smirk was too much for the Blackwell men to handle, and Gray sensed their already-iffy focus starting to wane.

"We'll get out of your way," Sophie said smoothly, apparently sensing the tension in the room. "I'm sure both Mr. Blackwells here are eager to get back to work."

"I was just about to suggest we men get back down to business. You took the words right out of my mouth," Alistair said, puffing up slightly. "Ladies, I'd love to entertain you, but I've always been a man of focus, I'm afraid. Occupational hazard."

"I completely understand," Sophie replied with a straight face. "I couldn't bear it if little women like me and Jenna here distracted you."

Jenna snickered, and Gray sent Sophie a warning glance. Now was not the time for her to show the Blackwells her sugar-coated fangs.

"Perhaps we could all grab dinner after," Alistair suggested with a lingering glance at Sophie's shapely calves.

"Son, I'm sure they have a nice family dinner planned," Peter said chidingly. "We don't want to intrude."

Jenna laughed softly. "You don't know the Wyatts that

well, then," she said. "For us, family and business go hand in hand. Dinner just wouldn't be the same unless work crept into it, right, Gray?"

The accusation stung more than Gray wanted to admit, but he gave a tense smile. "I'm sure Mr. Blackwell was just being polite with his offer. I can't imagine what all of us would have to say to each other over a meal."

Sophie shot him a look. *Watch it. Coddle them.*

"But," Gray amended hastily, "if you're in town tomorrow night, dinner would be great. It'd give us a chance to talk about your property in a more informal setting. Maybe get to know each other better."

Sophie smothered a laugh, and Jenna tilted her head to the side and eyed him suspiciously.

"Actually, we need to fly out tomorrow morning," Peter said. "It's my wife's birthday tomorrow, so we need to head back to the islands. But no need to schmooze us over dinner. I think we've come about as far as we can in this discussion, don't you think?"

Shit, Gray thought, his mind reeling for ways to save the deal. "I have just a few more points to wrap up if you have the time," Gray said hastily. "Jen, I should be done here within a couple hours, if you want to grab drinks."

"Sounds great," she said with surprising agreeability.

"Unless..." Sophie began.

Oh no. No. No. No. But, of course, she kept going.

"Well, I'm just thinking, neither Jenna nor the Blackwells here have really seen Seattle. No harm in killing two birds with one stone. We could all see something of the city, and finish the evening with a dinner? Gray's buying."

Great. Now she was a fucking Girl Scout troop leader using company money?

"I'm game," Jenna said.

"I could probably find the time." Alistair looked ridiculously pleased with himself.

"Well," mused Peter, "I suppose we all need to eat, and I wouldn't mind hearing a local's opinion on Seattle. Especially a beautiful local."

Sophie laughed prettily, and Peter blushed slightly, smiling at her like a fond father.

The realization settled over Gray like a storm cloud. He had to do this if he wanted to save the deal. Sophie was the key to this whole damn thing. The Blackwells weren't interested in the bottom line. They were vain, old-school fools who wanted to be flattered, pampered, and appreciated. They wanted someone to tell them that their property was special and important, regardless of its price tag.

He needed Sophie. And this dinner.

"Fine," he said, dreading the impending painful evening. "If nobody minds, I'd like to include my brother, Jack. He's expecting to see Jenna."

"The more the merrier," Sophie cooed.

Barf.

"I'll call Jack," Jenna said.

Gray closed his eyes briefly and counted to ten. He could do this. It would be hell, but somehow he was going to have to find a way to spend the evening with his estranged siblings and his two most difficult clients.

At least Sophie would be there.

Although for the life of him, he didn't know if that would make the evening better or worse.

* * *

An hour later, Gray was drinking a lukewarm beer and watching his client hit on his sister, and his brother hit on his assistant.

He wasn't sure what bothered him more: the way Alistair was staring at Jenna's chest as she ran verbal circles around him, or the way Jack's and Sophie's heads were tilted together as they laughed over their beers.

"I had no idea that Seattle was a bowling town," Peter said as he sipped his whiskey.

"I don't know that it is," Gray admitted. "But tourist options are limited on rainy days, and Sophie insists that this is a Seattle classic."

Sophie's head snapped around and she gave him a defensive glare. "What was I supposed to do, drag them through a soggy Pike Place Market? Maybe show them how much they *can't* see in the fog from the top of the Space Needle?"

"Calm down," Gray muttered. "Nobody's attacking your bowling idea."

"Are you having fun?" she asked him in a warning tone.

Fun? He *should* have been having fun. Everyone else was. But instead of joining in with the laughter and the flirtation, Gray had somehow ended up pairing off with the elderly Peter instead of chatting with his brother and sister. Instead of flirting with Sophie.

He felt like a decrepit old man watching the kids run around and have a good time.

"Yes, Ms. Dalton," he replied. "I'm having *fun.* In fact, it was just this morning that I was thinking I haven't been bowling in so long. Thanks for the opportunity."

She narrowed her eyes, but Peter seemed to take Gray's comment at face value, because he nodded agreeably.

"You're up, champ," Jack said, grabbing Sophie's knee to get her attention.

Fantastic, they had nicknames now. Jack must have felt Gray's gaze burning a hole in the back of his hand, because he removed it quickly from Sophie's leg with a questioning eyebrow as if to say *Yours?*

Gray avoided his brother's silent inquiry by staring at the scoreboard, where he was placing...fifth. Out of six. Even Alistair was beating him. Peter at least was a good deal behind him, but the man had arthritis, for God's sake. Nobody expected Peter to do anything other than gently push the ball down the lane with two hands.

Surely Gray could do better than this. It wasn't like he'd never bowled before. He could remember a couple of birthday parties as a kid. So it had only been, oh, about twenty years since his last game.

Meanwhile, the blonde demon in his life had just thrown yet another strike, which had her tied in first place with Jack. The two of them were now doing some sort of victory dance that involved lots of touching.

This was just great. At this rate, Gray's *next* bowling experience would probably be at the birthday party of his nieces and nephews as they squealed about how this was the place where their parents first met.

The thought of mini-Sophies and -Jacks put him in an even worse mood, so instead he studied the other flirtatious couple. Alistair had abandoned Sophie almost immediately after discovering that she was the better bowler. Pudgy losers like Alistair didn't like to be beat in anything, even something as ridiculous as bowling. Jenna was barely better than Gray, which made her fair game for the younger Blackwell's attention.

As Gray watched Jenna lay a hand on Alistair's arm, he wondered why she wasn't ripping her lame suitor to shreds. His sister wasn't exactly approachable, even to eligible men. There was no way she'd waste her time with this overweight lecher boy currently trying to correct her bowling form. And yet her usual venom wasn't seeping from her pores. Interesting.

He took another swallow of beer and made a concentrated effort not to scowl at the whole lot of them. Peter excused himself to the restroom, and Sophie fluttered into the vacated seat, filling his senses with...cinnamon?

She smelled like a freaking bakery. He'd noticed the sweet and oddly alluring smell the other night when he'd cornered her in his dark office like a creepy predator.

"You're scowling, boss."

"You think?"

She sighed as though dealing with a difficult child. "Really, this is the best thing. Peter is smiling, and Alistair...well...Jenna knows what she's doing, right? I mean her humoring him will work in your favor, but she can't possibly be attracted, can she?"

"*Jenna* knows how to handle herself." He hoped.

"I'm guessing that's your Mr. Darcy way of implying that *I* can't handle myself?"

"Who's Mr. Darcy?" he asked, his frown deepening. "And why does he get to go by his last name, while you've been calling me Gray since the moment you met me?"

She sighed again, wearily. Clearly he'd disappointed her somehow. Again. "Never mind about Mr. Darcy. I take it you haven't told your siblings about our little elevator misunderstanding?"

"Tell them what, exactly, that I thought my assistant

turned tricks? No, I didn't mention it. In case you haven't noticed, we're not exactly prone to chatting."

"I noticed. But the tension is only because you're sitting here in the corner like the freaking Grinch. They *want* to talk to you, but your body language is telling everyone to fuck off."

"I am not having this conversation with you."

"Why not? You owe me; I picked your sister up from the airport."

"Which expressly disobeyed my orders! Town car! I said to get Jenna into a town car!" he exploded.

Several pairs of eyes landed on him. Even in the noisy bowling alley, his voice had carried. Jack gave him a reassuring smile, but Jenna just rolled her eyes in disgust. She abruptly pushed past a startled Alistair and stalked off to the bar.

Sophie looked at him with a censorious expression. "You really should go talk to your sister. Now she thinks that you just wanted to put her into an impersonal Lincoln."

"That's exactly what I intended. Then we wouldn't be in this dreadful bowling alley," he mumbled.

She poked him in the side. "Go. This is your *sister*."

He glanced over his shoulder and saw Jenna flirting with the tattooed bartender. Knowing her, she'd go home with the man just to irk him, end up with hepatitis C, and blame Gray for the whole thing.

Avoiding Sophie's eyes, he got to his feet to go talk with Jenna.

"Wait, you can't go *now*." She tugged at his pant leg. "It's your turn!"

He smoothed away the wrinkle she'd made in his trousers and glanced up at the scoreboard. Sure enough, there was his name blinking next to the string of small, single digits. "You play for me," he told Sophie.

She snorted. "And ruin your stellar average? I don't think so."

"Just toss it into those divots that run down the side of the path."

"Those would be the gutters, bro," Jack said. "And by 'path,' I'm guessing you meant lane?"

"Whatever," Gray said. "Would someone just play for me?"

"I'll take care of this," Alistair said smugly.

"That's wonderful," Gray said. "Just great."

He hesitated for a moment, the smell of fresh cinnamon buns wafting up to him and filling him with an odd sense of longing. Or was it nostalgia? Unable to resist, and propelled by a rare sense of impulsiveness, he bent down until his lips nearly touched Sophie's ear.

"Why do you smell like Christmas morning?"

He felt the hitch in her breath, and felt a little unhinged himself by the closeness. Jerking back, he avoided her eyes and headed toward the bar.

"What were you expecting, harlot perfume?" she called after him.

Hiding a smile, Gray slid onto the bar stool next to Jenna. She didn't acknowledge his presence. He debated his options. Jenna and Gray tended to communicate mostly in sarcasm. Jack was the only Wyatt to ever learn the art of friendly conversation. But he could feel Sophie's eyes boring into his back and knew she wouldn't be a fan of anything less than he and Jenna singing "Kumbaya" by the end of the conversation.

"I'm sorry I didn't pick you up at the airport," he said quietly, gesturing to the bartender for another beer.

Her body stiffened slightly, and he knew she was debating whether to accept the olive branch or rake him over the coals. He was betting the coals. It was easier than dabbling in emotion.

But she surprised him.

"It's okay," she said finally. "I know you're busy trying to save the world one precious hotel at a time."

Gray bit his tongue to keep from snapping that it had been his *precious* hotels that had put her and Jack through law school and enabled the purchase of the designer purses he bought her every year on her birthday.

"Yeah, well, this is one hotel that I won't be able to add to my collection," he said bitterly, nodding back toward the Blackwells.

"Oh, I don't know about that." Jenna snuck a cherry from the garnish tray and winked at the bartender. "I suspect that perv and his old man might be warming up to the idea of selling to you," she said.

He set the bottle to his lips and shook his head. "I don't think so. I've tried every angle, and they just won't bite."

"Not *every* angle."

He raised an eyebrow.

She gestured toward her chest. "You lack these. The only numbers men like the Blackwells deal in is cup size."

Gray choked on his beer. "Aside from the fact that I absolutely do not want to be hearing about my little sister's breasts, is *that* why you've been letting that buffoon dry hump you out there? To help my company?"

She shrugged, looking unsure of herself. "It seemed the least I could do. Sophie mentioned that you were in the middle of a tough deal, and when she orchestrated this entire charade, I thought maybe I could lend a hand. Or a boob."

Gray's head spun, both with the idea that the deal could be saved and that his sister had actually gone out on a limb for him. The only thing that *didn't* surprise him about this conversation was Sophie's interference.

"So you're doing this because my pesky little assistant ambushed you in the airport? How did she even find you?"

Jenna smiled and snagged another cherry. "She was standing there at baggage claim holding a sign with my name on it. You know, kind of like a town car driver would have done?" She shot him a side look.

"At least a town car driver could have delivered you to my condo or wherever you wanted to go. Sophie's meddling got you trapped into *bowling*."

"Well, actually," she said, spinning around on her bar stool to look at their group, "it's been oddly fun. Sophie's great."

Gray grunted.

"Are you two...you know...?" Jenna wiggled her eyebrows.

He sputtered on his beer. "She's my assistant, Jen. That would be...No. She's an employee."

"So? Does your company have a policy about coworkers dating?"

"What? I don't know." He did know. They didn't have a policy.

She kept pressing. "How about subordinates dating bosses? Is that off-limits?"

"Who cares? Why are you bringing this up?"

She smiled her cat smile at him, and got to her feet. "Call it feminine intuition."

"Or I could call it...delusion. And have you not noticed how much she resembles a certain almost-sister-in-law of yours?"

Jenna gave him a disgusted look. "I told you from day one to stay away from that one. And sure, they look a little alike, but it took me all of five minutes to see that Sophie is nothing like Jessica. Not in the way that matters."

Gray's stomach knotted as he considered Jenna's words. If business had taught him anything, it was that tingling sense you got in your hands when you knew you'd made a mistake.

He flexed his fingers. *Yup. Definitely tingling.*

"How are things in New York?" he asked, annoyed to realize that his voice sounded gruff.

Jenna's smirk showed she was on to him, but she'd apparently finally done some maturing because she let it go instead of pushing his buttons like she would have a year ago.

"You know, New York is pretty great. It feels like this one might stick."

Gray had his doubts. Jenna thought every city would stick, but she rarely lasted more than a year. Still, if she could let things go, so could he, so he just nodded.

"Boyfriend?" he asked casually.

His sister gave him a look. "If I tell, are you gonna arrange for a background check?"

Gray winced. She knew about that?

"No," he lied.

Jenna stood and dragged him to his feet. "No big-brother prying tonight. *My* life isn't the one in deep crap right now. Come on, let's go land you a hotel deal. And maybe improve your bowling skills. You're embarrassing the Wyatt name."

He followed her back to the group and tried to avoid looking at Sophie. She'd either give him a smug *I told you so* look, or she'd be grinning at him like a proud mother. But as usual, he lost the battle, and couldn't seem to help glancing at her. What he saw was neither gloating nor pride. She looked almost... affectionate.

Which *might* have lifted his mood if Jack's arm hadn't been around the back of her chair.

Maybe it didn't even matter if he'd been wrong about Sophie. Even if she lacked Jessica's more manipulative qualities, they had one very important detail in common.

Neither one wanted him.

"Gray, my man," Peter said in a whiskey-soaked boom. "Let's get over here and discuss what you did in that fancy Chicago-based company of yours. Sophie and Jack tell me that a couple years ago you were responsible for turning around that set of fancy resorts on Barbados? Hell, those are five-star celebrity destinations now! I had no idea you had that kind of experience."

Gray shot a glance at his brother and Sophie, who sent matching winks his way.

He couldn't hide his victorious smile. Finally he was back in his element. He might suck at apologies, gratitude, and chitchat, but this? *This* he could do.

By the time the group was sitting at a long bench table at a nearby pizza parlor, Gray was feeling the best he'd felt in weeks. The Blackwells had just left to return to their hotel, but they were going to sign. He knew it. His business instincts were buzzing with victory, and they were never wrong.

He wondered if he should thank Sophie. It never would have happened without her interference. If it was up to him, the meeting would never have left the conference room and would have ended hours ago. Probably with the deal dead in the water.

"So, Sophie," Jenna was saying as she wound a piece of mozzarella around her finger. "You seeing anyone?"

All eyes fell on Sophie, and Gray was annoyed to realize that he wasn't the only one who seemed extremely interested in her response. Jack had gone completely still and was watching her carefully.

"Um, no. Not really," Sophie said.

Gray squinted. Was she blushing? The Sophie he knew didn't blush, but there was a distinct pink tint to her cheeks. He wondered what caused it. Or who. Not Alistair, certainly. Jack? The two of them had been inseparable most of the evening.

A fact that depressed him more than he wanted to admit.

"I can't believe that," Jenna was saying. "You're so sweet and pretty."

Gray's eyes narrowed in on his sister. He knew that tone. It was the same one she'd used when she'd brought three puppies home without warning. The same one she'd used when she'd wanted to borrow his car without her driver's license. That tone meant trouble.

"What about my brother?" Jenna asked, her gray eyes all innocent curiosity.

Gray and Jack exchanged a wary glance. Both knew they should shut up their sister. But both wanted Sophie's answer first.

"Oh, um, you mean Jack?" Sophie asked, her voice coming out on a squeak.

Gray felt a funny twist somewhere in the middle of his chest. He should have been prepared for it. Of course she'd assume that Jenna had meant Jack. Who would think of dowdy, grumpy Gray when they could have the funny, charming version?

"Ugh, not Jackie," Jenna said with a face. "He's still reeling from Avery."

"Don't," Jack said, his voice uncharacteristically curt.

"Uh-huh—so you never see each other?" Jenna pressed.

"We're... friends," Jack said with narrowed eyes.

Sophie nibbled at a breadstick and watched them curiously.

"Anyway," Jenna said, waving away her brothers' glares. "Jack's no good for you, Soph. I was talking about Gray."

He froze with his beer halfway to his lips and wondered if it would be inappropriate to drag Jenna out to the parking lot by her hair and put her in a cab. He wanted to look at Sophie, but didn't think he could bear to see what kind of amused disdain would be written all over her face.

"Gray's my boss," she said quietly.

A good, safe answer. A disappointing answer.

"Oh, sure, but if he weren't, you'd go for it, right? He's cute," Jenna said. She leaned over to pinch his cheek, and Gray batted her hand away with a warning look. Which she ignored.

"I'm pretty sure I'm the last woman on earth your brother would be interested in."

Gray's eyes flew to Sophie. An interesting choice of words. Was she saying that she would be interested if she thought he was? He silently begged her to meet his eyes so he could read her expression, but she didn't look away from Jenna.

"Huh," Jenna said, apparently realizing that she'd pushed the conversation as far as it could go.

Gray's shoulders had just started to relax when his sister piped up again. "Hey, Soph, you should join us for dinner on Friday."

He pinched the bridge of his nose. This was too much. He could barely handle Sophie nine-to-five during the week-days. If he had to start seeing her on weekend evenings, he'd lose his mind.

"Oh, I couldn't interrupt family time," Sophie said.

"Please, you've seen this 'family.' We're hardly the Brady Bunch. An outsider helps smooth the waters. Plus I need another girl to keep me company while the two of them argue about baseball."

"She's right, it'll be fun. And Gray's a fantastic cook," Jack said, giving Sophie a soft elbow in the side.

Gray choked. "Who said I was cooking?"

Jack shrugged. "You're good at it. And we all know Jenna isn't civilized enough for any decent restaurant."

"Hilarious, Jack," Jenna purred. "Sophie, did you know we had a comedian in the family? But Jack's right. Dinner at Gray's sounds great."

"Of course it does," Gray muttered. "All *you* have to do is show up and drink my wine."

"Exactly. So, Sophie, you in?"

Gray spared his assistant the briefest of glances. "I'm sure she has other plans on a Friday night."

Sophie's blue eyes locked on his. "Actually I don't. And dinner sounds great. I'd love to come."

Shit.

CHAPTER ELEVEN

Sophie stood outside the condo building of one grumpy Grayson Gregory Wyatt and wondered at what point she'd completely lost her mind.

She also wondered what kind of uptight fool advertises a full name like Grayson Gregory on their building call box.

I'm going to kill Jenna.

Gray's sister had only been in town for a week, but Jenna had firmly inserted herself into Sophie's life as though they'd been lifelong friends. Shopping trips, happy hour at the local wine bar, spa day . . .

And now this.

She'd known exactly what Jenna was up to when she'd suggested dinner. Sophie was a little sister herself. She knew all about the set-up-the-big-sibling routine. Sophie had gone through a brief phase of matchmaker, trying to set Brynn up with the wrong men.

She knew firsthand that these things never went well.

But Gray's eyes had been begging her to decline.

So *of course* she'd had to accept.

Plus, the three of them clearly didn't have the whole "family" thing figured out. Not that the Daltons were perfect, but at least they didn't avoid conversation with one another. If Gray was left to his own devices, he'd end up treating the twins like either children or clients.

If anyone needed to build solid familial relationships it was Gray Wyatt.

But what had sounded like a harmless idea on Tuesday was a lot more daunting when she was actually standing in front of her boss's condo building on a Friday evening.

Sophie thought uncomfortably of the last Friday night she'd spent with him in the office. She certainly didn't need a repeat of those uncomfortable emotions.

At least tonight the twins would be there as a buffer. No chance of her getting the hots for her sulky employer with his siblings looking on. She glanced up at the high-rise condo building. It looked like a museum. No doubt, the interior of his condo would be more of the same. Monochromatic, cool, and tidy. Boring.

Still, a promise was a promise, and so here she was. Sophie slowly reached out and punched the button next to his pretentious-as-shit name. Dinner in a restaurant would have been awkward enough, but actually going to her boss's home officially crossed the fragile boundary between professional and personal. She had no idea why Gray had agreed to it, but it could have something to do with the fact that Jenna had the personality of a Rottweiler and biceps like Jillian Michaels. One did *not* mess with her master plan.

A flash of sanity demanded that Sophie turn and run, but then she heard Gray's rough voice on the tinny intercom.

"Yeah?"

"It's me," she said.

"Sophie?"

"Um, no, this is Mimi, the hooker from Vegas? You called for a genital massage?" She smiled at the elderly couple approaching the building, hoping they were hard of hearing.

"I'm so amused," Gray's voice crackled through the intercom. "I hope you like Top Ramen, because that's all you're—"

Sophie punched the call button again to end the cheery discussion and scooted in the front door behind the couple. They turned to size her up, and she gave them her sweetest smile. "You don't mind if I slide in behind you, do you? My boyfriend's a little grumpy because I forgot it was our one-month anniversary. Honestly, how is a busy woman supposed to remember these little things?"

The blue-haired woman's expression softened, and she patted Sophie's shoulder. "Oh, don't you stress about a thing, dear. Men pretend they don't care about that stuff, but they're so sensitive! Walter here pouted for a nearly two hours when he thought I'd forgotten our forty-eighth wedding anniversary."

Walter harrumphed, sending his white mustache twitching. "That's bollocks. I was just upset that the tennis tournament got canceled for those blasted cheerleading competitions!"

"I didn't exactly see you reaching for the remote to turn the station away from those scandalous little skirts."

Walter flushed slightly. "My arthritis was acting up, Joyce. You know I can't just go gallivanting around the living room trying to find the remote."

The little woman rolled her eyes at Sophie. "You see what

I mean? They're sensitive. Now you go right on up there and make amends with your man. Cook him a nice meal and maybe give him a little nookie!"

Sophie smothered a smile at the throwback to a different era. She didn't have the heart to tell Joyce that "her man" would actually be cooking *her* dinner, and that nookie was so not an option.

Saying good-bye to the now-bickering couple, Sophie found her way to Gray's apartment, giving a perky knock. She tugged nervously at the hem of her tight white sweater. She knew this wasn't a date, of course. But maybe she'd taken a *few* extra minutes getting ready.

And the results were worth it. She was wearing her cutest (and tightest) jeans, and the sweater she'd just picked up from Nordstrom. The cashmere kept it classy while the tight fit made it sexy. Not that she wanted to be sexy. He finally answered the door, and all thoughts of her own appearance vanished.

Because Gray looked...gorgeous.

She realized this was the first time since dinner at her parents that she'd seen him outside of a suit, and while he admittedly filled out a suit very nicely, casual was a surprisingly good look on him. He wore dark jeans that were either designer or personally made for him, because he looked like a freaking male model. The gray sweater was layered over a crisp white shirt and made his eyes look, well...actually they looked downright stormy and pissed.

But it was a sexy picture nonetheless.

"How'd you get into the building?"

"It's called charm—I'll write a report on it on Monday so you can begin to understand the how the concept works. Short version: you smile at people and they like you more."

His scowl deepened and he braced an arm on the doorway, blocking her entrance.

"Okay." She sighed. "I can see I'm moving you along too fast on the path toward not being a dick. Lesson number one: invite me in."

"Jenna's not coming."

Sophie blinked at that. "Why not? Is everything okay?"

"Oh, everything is fine. Just some apparent stomach bug," he replied.

She chewed her lip. This was not ideal. Although Sophie was *technically* here to provide a buffer among the Wyatt siblings, what she really needed was a buffer between her and Gray. This would be all the more awkward with just herself, the two brothers, and no fellow female influence.

"I hope she's okay," Sophie said. "You and Jack must be bummed to not see her on her last night in town."

"Oh, I'm not so sure Jack *won't* be seeing her," Gray muttered, still not inviting her in.

Sophie had gotten pretty good at interpreting this man's moods and mumbles, but she was now officially confused.

"What's going on?" she asked pointedly, folding her arms self-consciously across her chest.

"We've been set up," he said, not meeting her eyes. "Jack thought dinner tonight was canceled, and I don't think Jenna ever had any intention of showing up."

Suddenly everything became clear in Sophie's mind, and she couldn't help but laugh at how well Jenna had played her cards. The setup was even more blatant than Sophie had expected.

"Why are you giggling?" He glanced at her sharply, as though surprised to see her still there.

"Just admiring your sister's tactics. Well, the least you

can do is let me in. I'm guessing you cooked for four, right? You may as well feed me."

"I'm not so sure this is a good idea," he said.

"Oh, it's a horrible idea. This will be a complete disaster," she agreed, slipping under his arm and scooting into his apartment. "But it'll build your character."

"Fine, but don't expect me to entertain you. You eat, then you leave. I have things to do."

She laid a hand on his arm. As expected, he stiffened, but she kept her hand there anyway. She couldn't help it. She was by nature a warm, affectionate person, and she was tired of always trying to hide that around him. Besides, if anyone needed a little dose of harmless human contact, it was this man of stone.

"I'll leave if you want," she said, meaning it. "But I'll be stuck going home to a dinner of cereal, and whatever you have cooking in here smells amazing."

He stared at the spot above her head before nodding shortly. "Sorry about this. I never meant for you to get caught up in the disaster that is my family dynamics."

"Relax, Gray. I'm glad to be here. Besides, it might be good for you. I know too well that one-on-one interactions are not your forte. Practice can't hurt."

Sophie froze, realizing how that had sounded. She had practically proposed a *date*. With her boss. Who didn't like her.

She ordered her impulsive brain to back the heck out of this impending disaster. But then Gray frowned. And for some reason, his reluctance solidified her resolve. She had promised to help him with his innate lack of social skills. Who said that had to be exclusive to the office?

And besides, she was starving.

"You're my assistant," he said. "This just seems... wrong."

"Don't be such a stiff. It's just one night, and nobody has to know. On Monday you can go back to grumbling orders to Ms. Dalton. And if you're on good behavior tonight, I may even start calling you Mr. Wyatt in the office as a little reward."

"Indefinitely?"

"Let's say for one day. For Monday, I promise to be perfectly respectful and boring. If you can go the entire night maintaining the facade that you're interested in me for more than my filing skills, then I'll even call you sir. Deal?"

His eyes lit at the idea of a challenge. "You're meaning to tell me that you'll actually be docile and unobtrusive for an entire day if I pretend you're my girlfriend?"

Sophie's heart seemed to skip for a split second at the word "girlfriend." That hadn't been what she'd meant by this little experiment.

And yet she still wasn't turning and running. She pasted a smile on her face as though she played these kinds of charades every day.

"Eh, let's say *almost*-girlfriend," Sophie said with a nervous smile. "Let's pretend it's the third date, and that we're moving in the direction of a committed relationship."

There. That seemed harmless enough.

He ran a hand over his short dark hair. "This is insane. I don't know why the hell I agreed to this dinner in the first place, and now I'm stuck with *you*."

"That's lovely. I have to say, you're a pretty awful boyfriend so far."

"Sorry," he said gruffly. "That was rude. I'm never at my best around you."

His eyes seemed to warm a moment, and be still her little stupid heart, but she almost wished that he was interested in her for real. Then again, he hadn't even *once* glanced down at her strategic sweater. Clearly he wasn't interested in her as a woman.

So much for my investment in a push-up bra that weighs more than a Thanksgiving turkey, she thought.

"Lesson number two," Sophie said, setting her purse down and shrugging off her coat. "Always offer the lady a drink."

She started to set her coat on top of her purse, but he snatched it from her and hung it in the hall closet. "Very good," she said. "That was a test."

"It's not like I've never had a guest over before. I'm not completely without manners."

The way he stalked toward the kitchen sort of undermined his claim on manners, but she let it go. Baby steps.

Peering around curiously, she took her first look at Gray's condo. She almost grinned when she saw it was exactly what she'd expected. The floor seemed to be made of honest-to-God concrete. There were a couple of cool-toned area rugs to break it up, but still. Concrete was concrete.

The walls were a shocking white, softened only by a handful of depressing-looking metal structures. Either he'd completely overpaid his decorator or he'd gone shopping himself at Home Depot. The living room off to her right was clearly unused, and she wandered into his personal office, running her hand over the built-in bookshelves.

This room at least had a bit of warmth. She wondered if it was the only one he spent any time in. The walls were still white, but a large colorful painting of an old-fashioned bar took up one wall, and the other held a few photographs, most of them pictures of Jenna and Jack.

She could easily picture him here, relaxed in the large leather easy chair with some brainy book in his lap and a glass of whiskey on the side table. What the man really needed was a dog. Maybe a Labrador or a spaniel. Something friendly to sit by his feet and banish that chronic look of loneliness the man wore around him like a cape.

Sensing eyes on her back, she turned around and saw Gray standing in the doorway, two wineglasses in hand.

"Don't you ever read fiction?" Sophie asked, accepting the wineglass he handed her. "There are dozens of biographies, and not a single one seems to be fewer than a thousand pages."

Gray gestured to the bookcase on the far end of the room. "Take a look at the top shelf."

Sophie wandered that way, taking a sip of excellent Chardonnay. She immediately saw what he wanted her to see and a laugh bubbled out. "Harry Potter? Really?"

He shrugged. "Biographies are my preferred reading material, but I enjoy well-written fiction once in a while. Plus I wanted to see what all of the hype was about."

"You reading about a boy wizard." She shook her head, completely unable to picture it.

"Quit snooping through my stuff. Come into the kitchen."

She followed him out of the office, pleased to see that he seemed more relaxed than when he'd first opened the door. Maybe it was just the lack of pinstripes, but he didn't have his usual wary expression. Jeans suited the man, Sophie thought. She found herself studying a surprisingly yummy-looking backside.

"Quit checking out my ass."

She choked on her wine. *Caught.*

"I'm just mentally cataloging potential areas of improvement on behalf of your future wife. Do men do squats, or is that more of a Hollywood actress exercise? And—*wow*. Look at this kitchen!"

Her exclamation earned her what might have been a half smile. "I like to cook."

"So do I, but I don't have like five ovens," she said, looking around in awe. The kitchen was a restaurant-sized industrial masterpiece. This was no standard-issue luxury kitchen. It was clearly custom-built for someone who knew their way around food.

"I'm a little embarrassed to have assumed the extent of your cooking skills was toast," she said with chagrin. "Did I really force delivery pizza on you with the mistaken assumption that it was the best meal you'd have all week?"

"I didn't mind," Gray said, not unkindly.

Sophie snorted. "Says the man who has about a dozen French cookbooks whose names I can't pronounce."

She plucked one of the fancy cookbooks from the shelf and was surprised to see that it wasn't just for show. It was splattered and creased and littered with his neat handwriting.

"What I'm making tonight is actually from that book," he said, nodding toward the cookbook in her hand. "There'll be more than enough food since I was assuming a party of four, but I think we can make a pretty good dent."

"I'll pretend you didn't just imply your fake girlfriend was fat."

He gave her a look. "You know you're not fat, Sophie."

She raised an eyebrow. He was flirting now? Nah. Then his gaze *finally* drifted down briefly to her chest.

Okay, *maybe* flirting.

Perhaps the bra and new sweater had been worth it after

all. Brynn had been right. There were ways other than obvious cleavage to call attention to the girls.

Thinking about her sister made her feel guilty. Would Brynn mind that Sophie was cozying up to her ex-boyfriend in his home, about to eat a home-cooked French meal? Hell, had Brynn *been* here before? She hadn't that night of the awkward double date, but she could have come over at some point after that.

The thought bothered Sophie more than it should, considering this wasn't even a real date.

Gray snapped his fingers in front of her face. "Where'd you go?"

Pushing Brynn out of her mind, she settled onto one of his bar stools, taking another sip of wine. "Oh, I'm just wondering exactly how experimental you're thinking of getting tonight."

He raised an eyebrow at her, and she felt unexpectedly tingly.

"*Food*, Gray, I was talking about food."

The corner of his mouth hitched up in what she was beginning to realize was his version of a smile. "Ah. Well, in that case, let's get you started on the first course before you do that hungry sulky thing."

"Okay, you have to know that discussing a woman's appetite and generally implying she's a glutton isn't exactly going to get you laid, right?"

"I thought we were just talking about food," he said archly.

"We are," she sputtered, blushing. "I just mean, you know... for future reference with other women. Real women."

"Are you saying a part of you is fake?" he asked, his eyes dropping again to her chest. She was appalled to find her nipples tightening. Luckily he couldn't notice through the eight layers of push-up padding. God bless Victoria and her secret.

"Wow, accused of selling sex *and* of being plastic by the same man. How is it that we haven't killed each other yet?"

He gave her a real smile this time, and she warmed a little at this slightly more friendly Gray.

"Would you like to help cook?" he asked.

"Not really, I'd much rather watch the master and drink all of your delicious wine."

He nodded and pulled a tray of grilled asparagus out of the fridge. "Don't touch that yet," he snapped as she reached out to grab one. "I'm not done."

She watched, fascinated as he proceeded to poach a couple of eggs and add them to the platter. Strips of salty prosciutto were added to the sides of the plate, and he finished the whole thing off with a drizzle of some fancy-looking olive oil and balsamic vinegar and croutons.

By the time he took a seat at the bar next to her, her mouth was watering.

"First course is served," he said, handing her a fork. She was just about to spear a perfectly grilled vegetable when he grabbed her hand.

Startled by the contact, her eyes met his, and her mouth went from watering to dry. The man was more adept at seduction than she'd given him credit for. With nothing but a sultry look and the touch of a hand, she was practically panting.

"Don't tell me I don't get to eat this," she joked, trying to break the unexpected tension.

Gray picked up his wineglass. "I'm a big fan of celebrating the food I cook before eating it."

She blinked in confusion. "You want to pray?" Not that there was anything wrong it, but she hadn't pegged him for the type.

"No, I just meant that I thought we should do a toast," he said quietly.

And then she melted just a little more, because his expression had gone from looking seductive to slightly embarrassed. Feeling a rush of warmth for this complex, emotionally challenged man, she set down her fork, and dramatically cleared her throat as she picked up her wineglass.

"Ahem. I'd like to toast my dreamboat of a fake almost-boyfriend, who is, in addition to being a cuddly laugh-a-minute hottie, also a damned good chef. Not that I'd know because he won't let me actually *eat* the food, probably because he thinks I'm annoying, gluttonous, and slutty, but—"

Gray clinked his glass to hers and let out a half laugh. She couldn't help smiling back. She felt oddly proud of coaxing humor from someone who so seldom smiled. As she dug into the decadent dish, her sister crept back into her mind. Was Sophie sitting in the same spot Brynn had sat in when they were dating?

Was Sophie once again merely playing a part, whereas Brynn had been the real deal?

They ate in companionable silence, and common sense told her to keep quiet, but the wine flowing through her system had other ideas.

"What does Brynn think of your cooking?" she blurted out.

"We never quite made it to that stage." He pushed a crouton around on his plate. "I don't think I'd know what to talk about."

"You seem to be doing fine with me," she said, trying to keep the gloat out of her voice.

"Only because you forced your way into my life like a battering ram. My options are to talk to you or go deaf from your incessant chatter."

"Be still, my heart."

"How hungry are you? I was thinking I could put together a quick salad."

"I doubt anything you cook from that book is quick, but sure. A salad sounds great. Where'd you learn to cook like this, anyway? Mom? Grandma?"

Gray stood and pulled greens from the refrigerator. "No, my mom died when I was a kid, and the only grandmother in the picture was my father's mom. Not exactly the warm, fuzzy, culinary type."

The fact that Gray had grown up without any maternal influence didn't surprise Sophie in the least, but it made her sad all the same. It also explained quite a bit about Jenna's rough edges and Jack's excess of superficial charm.

She'd also learned from Jenna that their father hadn't exactly been the warm type either. Lack of a softer influence had resulted in one very jaded big brother. Over martinis, Jenna had let it slip that Gray had absorbed the majority of their father's attention, but not in the way a son would hope for. The senior Grayson Wyatt had continually berated his eldest son for being quiet and wimpy. Gray had been sent away to boarding school with instructions to become more *likable*.

Sophie winced as she realized that her own comments about making him more approachable might add to open wounds. How must it feel to always be told that you're not appealing enough? To be shy, but told that in order for someone to like you, you had to be more talkative?

Had anyone ever told Gray that he was sufficient just as he was? That he was successful and kind, even if he had no idea how to show it?

She doubted it.

Not that he was faultless, of course. That chronic scowl had to go, she didn't care how introverted he was. But at the same time, she no longer was sure she wanted him to smile just because it was *expected.* Sophie was beginning to like the fact that Gray's smiles had to be earned. They felt more like a reward worth reaching for instead of a superficial grin freely given.

Perhaps most startling of all was the fact that the two of them weren't quite as different as she'd assumed. They were both struggling to reconcile being true to themselves while managing the expectations of others. He with being more approachable, and she with being more conventional. On the one hand, they wanted to be open to self-improvement. On the other, they didn't want to compromise their own values.

"Please tell me you're not having some sort of melodramatic womanly moment over there," Gray said as he drizzled some oil over a bunch of exotic-looking greens.

"I totally was. You want to hear about it?" she asked.

"Absolutely not."

She told him anyway. "I was just thinking how we have more in common that I would have guessed."

He sighed and put a salad in front of her. "Is listening to this optional?"

"Quit being so emotionally closed-off," she said without heat.

"And this is why I don't read *Cosmo.*"

Sophie dug into her salad, pleasantly surprised that something so simple could taste gourmet. "Hey, this is really good. You should open a restaurant. And you still haven't told me how you learned to cook like this."

He shrugged awkwardly. "I kind of stumbled into it, really. At some point after college I realized that I wanted to be able to make something other than grilled cheese. So I went to cooking school. Le Cordon Bleu, actually."

"Isn't that where professional chefs go?"

"They take anyone with enough money."

"Ah, so you bribed them. Fair enough. You pay for cooking school, you pay for sex. It all makes sense."

He let out a low growl. "When do we get to drop the prostitute thing? I'm making dinner for you, and I think in return you should quit making cracks about that night."

She bit into a perfectly crisp green bean and considered. "I will under one condition."

He muttered a string of obscenities which she pretended not to hear.

"I promise never to bring it up again if you tell me what *exactly* about me made you think I was a hooker. I mean, I know I wasn't exactly classy, but it was *Vegas*. I was hardly the only one in skimpy attire."

He looked almost hopeful. "If I address the elevator incident, we can move on?"

"Promise. I will never ever imply that you once wanted to pay me for sex."

"I never wanted—" He broke off, realizing that she was baiting him.

He was really getting better at this whole reading-of-the-people routine. She felt so proud.

Gray's jaw tightened, and his voice sounded gruff. "It was just those damn boots. They were awful. I figured no self-respecting woman would wear them."

Sophie let out a half laugh. "You made a snap judgment based on my shoe choice?"

He lifted a shoulder and continued eating his salad.

She shook her head. "Talk about judgmental crap."

"Talk about slutty shoes."

That made her smile ruefully. "And to think I spent a good hour getting ready that night. All my hard work defeated by the wrong shoe selection. I was *this* close to picking a very respectable sandal."

"Now can I ask *you* something?"

She raised an eyebrow. "Very good, Gray. Showing interest in your date is progress."

He ignored her attempt at evasion. "Two questions, actually. First, why did you quit law school?"

Sophie blinked at the unexpected change in topic. She thought carefully about how to respond. Did she even know anymore? Her twenty-three-year-old self seemed like a distant stranger. "I don't really know," she said slowly. "It's like one day I was contentedly going through the motions of the path I'd always been on, and the next day...everything just felt wrong."

"So...you wanted to go into the restaurant business?"

Sophie laughed softly. "Very delicately put. And no, not really. I suppose you could say it was a very delayed form of rebellion. I'd done everything I was supposed to up until that point. Good grades, the "right" extracurricular, the right school, wholesome boyfriend...When I fell off that path, my parents flipped. There was a whole lot of talk about being respectable, and not a whole lot of dialogue about happiness. I guess in turn I tried to get as far away from their path as possible."

"By becoming a cocktail waitress," he finished for her.

"Well…it was that or a hooker," she said with a sly smile.

He took a sip of wine. "Which leads me to my next question…Why are you still so preoccupied with what happened that night? It was a simple mistake, and we've already established that neither of us was at our best. Add to that a freak elevator malfunction. But you can't let it go. Why is that?"

She let out a long breath and pushed her salad aside. "I'm going to need more wine for this discussion."

He complied, refilling both their glasses without comment. Then he turned and studied her, his dark eyes latching on to hers with uncomfortable intensity.

She looked away and idly ran her finger along the stem of her crystal glass before speaking.

"So, the thing is," she began slowly, "my career path hasn't been exactly typical for a Stanford graduate. The alumni house is hardly pounding on my door begging for interviews."

She took a swallow of wine, feeling his intent gaze still fixed on her profile.

"And I guess I've always known that I'm better at being *liked* than being admired," she continued. "And I'm okay with that. Mostly. But being mistaken for a prostitute somehow felt like rock bottom, you know? Like I'd been able to handle the *You can do better* pep talks up to a point, but…"

She broke off, not knowing how to explain herself and worried she'd revealed too much.

He didn't let her off the hook. "But when I thought you were at the bottom of the employment food chain, you doubted yourself and began to wonder if your family was right about you?" he guessed.

"Yup, that pretty much sums it up," she said glumly.

"Hey," he said softly, nudging his knee against hers.

She raised her eyes to his, ignoring the flip of her belly.

"You're not inferior to anyone. You have skills that nobody else in your family has. Hell, the way you handled the Blackwells? I've never seen anyone wrap someone around their finger so efficiently. That kind of skill is worth something. *You're* worth something."

The last sentence came out in a mumble, and he tensed his jaw, probably from the uncomfortable sensation of saying something nice. Sophie wanted to give him a hard time about the uncharacteristic softness, but she felt too warm and melty to ruin the moment. This kind of affirmation coming from anyone would have given her a flutter.

But coming from Gray? She felt like grinning.

What would it be like to lean into him for just a moment? To beg for more reassurances. To hear that he liked her. That he respected her, just as she *was*, not for what she could be.

Before she knew it she was leaning, and from the way he was staring at her mouth, she wasn't the only one who felt the pull of whatever was going on there. He moved imperceptibly closer and Sophie held her breath, not daring to let herself think. Not about work, not about Brynn, not about Vegas.

Kiss me, she thought.

Gray drew back so quickly he nearly knocked his plate off the counter.

"Anyway, I just wanted you to know," he said gruffly, grabbing their plates and standing.

Sophie shook her head and tried to shake off whatever had just flashed between them. She took a deep breath and ordered herself not to be disappointed.

You are not to make out with your boss, you are not to make out with your boss…

She repeated the mantra in her head as he dumped their barely touched salads down the garbage disposal with a fierce scowl. She had the insane urge to press her lips against the crease between his eyebrows.

How had the night turned so quickly from dreaded family dinner to downright sexy?

The taciturn, irritable version of Gray never made her feel off-balance. But this flirty, sweet version made her wary. *This* Gray could too easily slip past her guard, and the last thing she needed was to fall for someone who would never approve of her. Throwing a few morale boosters her way was one thing, but someone like Gray would never be in a serious relationship with someone as unfocused as her. Hell, Brian had been a freaking nomad, and even *he* thought she was floating aimlessly through life.

The thought depressed her more than it should. Most of the time she couldn't stand Gray, and now she was thinking about a relationship?

They needed to abort this cozy chatter before she did something crazy. Like grab the lapels of his crisp white shirt and kiss him senseless. And every instinct in her body told her that getting personal with Grayson Wyatt could only lead to heartbreak.

"Can I help with the main course?" she asked too loudly.

He glanced up, looking relieved that she wasn't going to continue their bonding moment. He'd probably reached his quota of emotional availability for the year.

"You can chop the parsley," he replied. "You can't possibly mess that up."

"Gee, thanks," she said, sliding off the bar stool. "Do you have an extra cutting board?"

He slid the garlic he was mincing to the right side

of his cutting board and gestured to the space he'd just cleared. "Grab a knife. Parsley's in the produce drawer of the fridge."

Unsurprisingly, his fridge was both well stocked and well organized. She took her time browsing through the assortment of fancy cheeses and meats and wide array of produce. It had more variety than her local grocery store, she marveled as she checked out some expensive-looking ham.

"Quit fondling my meat, and just get the damn parsley."

"Cliché sexual references, boss? I didn't think that was your style," she said as she grabbed the parsley and a knife and settled beside him at the cutting board.

Despite her intention to keep things completely professional between them, she couldn't help but notice the domestic coziness of them sharing a cutting board. He seemed to think the same, because his eyes slid to hers and he gave her a shy smile.

She followed the motion of his hands as he adeptly minced several garlic cloves. He looked so at home with his cooking utensils. It was strange to think that the same hands deftly handling the chef knife were the ones she'd seen typing, holding a phone, or shooing her out of his office.

Awkwardly, Sophie began chopping the parsley. She'd never thought much about her chopping technique before. She'd watched plenty of Food Network and could whip up the occasional spaghetti or stir-fry without embarrassing herself. But after watching him go all Julia Child on her, she felt strangely inept.

Her eyes slid again to his hands, trying to mimic what he was doing. Noticing that he used shorter, more efficient chopping movements, she tried the same—

"Ouch!" she exclaimed. "Son of a..."

She'd never exactly been keen on blood, and the sight of red fluid covering her hand had her swaying.

"What the hell?" Gray said, grabbing her by the wrist. "You've cut yourself!"

"Wow, nothing slips by you." she said dazedly, staring down at her bloody hand. It was hard to see around the *Braveheart*-worthy puddle of blood, but it looked like a major gash was running along her index and middle fingers right below the knuckle.

"You're going to need stitches," Gray muttered.

"Just get me a Band-Aid," she said, humiliation beginning to sink in around the queasiness. "It's only a little nick."

But Gray had grasped her wrist and wrapped a towel around her fingers. "Into the car, now. We're going to the ER."

"Are you freaking kidding me? Just get me another glass of wine and another towel or something. Maybe some tape." Her hand began to throb. "Actually, make that wine a whiskey. But I'm not going to the hospital because I cut myself chopping *parsley*."

"I can see your bone, Sophie," he said as he ushered her out of the apartment, down a stairwell, and into the garage. Throbbing finger or no, she wasn't so out of it that she didn't notice the careful way he tucked all of her limbs into his black BMW or the way he quickly ran his hand over her hair.

Then again, that could have been the woozy at work.

"Just great. I'm even a failure at cutting herbs," she muttered, throwing her head back against the headrest and clutching the towel more closely around her fingers. The blood had soaked through the folded dish towel and she was beginning to realize the sheer stupidity of what she'd done. She couldn't even blame the wine. Sure, she'd had a glass, but most of her intoxication had been from watching the man next to her.

Distraction by lust. It happened to the best of women, right?

Through the haze of pain and humiliation, she realized that Gray drove just like he did everything else. Quickly, quietly, and with no unnecessary movements.

"How are you feeling?" he asked, glancing over at her.

"I'm feeling really great, Gray. For the first time ever I was getting the impression that maybe you didn't hate me, and then I go and ruin the night by nearly slicing off the fingers of my dominant hand. So yeah, I'm great. Maybe later we can go shoot puppies at close range."

"I never hated you," he said quietly.

And then he reached over and briefly set his hand on her knee before he jerked it back to the steering wheel.

Despite the fact that her hand was wrapped in a blood-soaked towel, and that she was about to spend her Friday night in a hospital waiting room, she couldn't hide a giddy little smile.

CHAPTER TWELVE

Somehow Gray had never imagined that his personal version of hell would include an emergency room waiting area, the frantic parents of his secretary, and her scarily stressed-out sister, who *also* happened to be an ex-girlfriend. Will Thatcher had shown up as well, although he at least seemed calm.

Resisting the urge to press his fingers against his temples, he turned to Will, the only one of the group not either wringing their hands or scowling at him. "Would you please explain to me how it is that you all ended up here for a very minor finger injury?"

Will shrugged good-naturedly as he dug into his second bag of peanut M&M's. "Soph's dad used to run this emergency room. There's no way you could have snuck beloved Dr. Dalton's youngest daughter through here without the whole fam finding out. M&M?"

"No. Thanks."

"Tell us again how this happened?" Sophie's mom asked, shredding her thumbnail to pieces with her teeth.

"Calm down, Marnie. Dr. Hoyne said it was nothing a few stitches wouldn't fix," Sophie's dad said while rubbing his wife's back.

Marnie hissed. "Oh, and what does Richard Hoyne know!"

"True, med school teaches those docs *nothing* these days," Will said.

"I heard that, William," Marnie said.

"Dr. Hoyne is a fine ER doctor. I trained him myself," Chris said soothingly.

"So she's not going to lose her fingers?"

Oh Jesus. Gray pinched the bridge of his nose. Of all women, the one who had to go and slice her finger was an employee. And of all the *employees*, he had to end up with the one whose dad was a retired doctor and had apparently handpicked the entire emergency room staff.

"I just don't understand how this happened," Marnie asked.

"I didn't realize I owed you a report," Gray snapped, losing his temper.

"Don't get snippy with Mama Dalton," Will said. "You're the one cavorting around with your secretary on a Friday night, chopping off her fingers."

"Yeah, how is it that you ended up spending Friday night with my sister?" Brynn asked, stopping her pacing for the first time since arriving.

"Oh, here we go," Will said, noisily crunching his M&M's.

Gray avoided Brynn's accusing look. He hadn't expected to see his ex-girlfriend again, and definitely lacked the quick thinking to smooth over the situation.

What the hell am I doing here? Just when Gray was about to make a cowardly exit, the doctor finally came out.

Frankly, Gray couldn't understand why they'd all been banished to the waiting room in the first place. It wasn't like privacy was needed to sew up a couple of fingers.

"Hi, everyone, thanks for waiting," the doctor said somberly, as though he'd just finished rebuilding Sophie's spleen from scratch.

Dr. Hoyne shook Sophie's dad's hand. "I have some good news. Sophie's going to be just fine."

"Oh good, we were *so* worried," Will said, earning a punch from Brynn.

"Will she have any permanent nerve damage?" Marnie asked, her hand pressed against her lips.

Seeing the genuine maternal concern, Gray felt some of his irritation fade. Yes, in the grand scheme of medical emergencies, this was barely a blip on the radar. But to the Daltons, one of their own was wounded.

Hell, Gray felt like one of *his* own was wounded. Not that Sophie was his, even if it had felt that way for a few strange moments in his condo.

However, surrounded by her family and friends, who *really* knew her, he suddenly felt out of place. At the end of the day, he was just her boss. And no matter how blatantly the attention-starved little minx had flirted with him, he wouldn't be the one she wanted to see right now.

"Which one of you is Mr. Wyatt?" the doctor asked Will and Gray.

Will pointed to Gray and grinned as if he were a sixth grader passing the blame for some pulling a girl's hair.

"Great, come with me," the doctor said. "Sophie's asking to see you."

Silence settled over the group.

And just like that, Gray no longer felt out of place. He

felt like grinning. Sophie wanted to see *him*. Even after he'd flirted with her, made her help him cook, and then barely spoken to her while they waited for her name to be called, she was asking for him.

Of course, she probably hadn't realized yet that she had an entire get-well committee on hand. Swallowing awkwardly, he followed the doctor down the sterile hallway.

All boyish hopes that Sophie might anxiously be waiting on the hospital bed for Gray to check on her faded when he heard her laugh all the way down the hall. Instead of finding a wounded bird holding a broken wing, he found a preening peacock, sitting hip to hip with an elderly man, giggling over what appeared to be an ancient photo album.

"Oh, Gray!" she said, her face glowing and smiling, instead of somber and in pain. "Meet my new friend, Mr. Bronson. He was just showing me pictures of when he and his wife went to the circus in Paris and the baby elephant escaped."

Gray couldn't figure out if he wanted to smile or just walk away in exasperation. He'd spent the past twenty minutes enduring glares from her overbearing family, and she was in here discussing baby circus animals with a man who looked like Santa Claus.

Her gaze fell on the doorway behind him and her smile faltered slightly.

"Mom? Dad? What... Wow, everyone's here. What's going on?"

"We came to see if you were all right, of course!" Marnie said, dashing to her daughter's side and grabbing for her wrist. "Oh gosh, what a huge bandage."

"Mom, seriously, it's just a few stitches on each finger. I'll be completely back to normal before my next dump."

Everybody except Mr. Bronson winced. The old man patted her knee. "It's good to be regular, dear."

Sophie's welcoming smile was long gone, and she fixed Gray with a glare. "Really? You called my entire family because of a little cut finger?"

"Oh no, that was me, dear," said the plump redheaded nurse who had just entered the room. "I just sent your parents a text message to say how pretty you'd gotten over the years! I wasn't thinking that they'd probably freak out that an emergency room nurse was seeing their daughter. Sorry, everyone. I just didn't think..."

"Obviously," Gray muttered.

"Don't worry about it, Anna," Sophie said with a reassuring smile. "I'm sure my family and friends feel silly for rushing down here."

"On the contrary, Soph. I, for one, was *terrified.* I actually stopped at the hospital chapel on the way up here," Will said as he dug through a basket of lollipops intended for six-year-olds.

"Knock it off, Will. Don't mock the chapel. And don't belittle Sophie's injury," Brynn snapped.

"Says the big sister who was more focused on ogling her ex than worrying about Sophie," Will muttered under his breath.

Gray stiffened awkwardly. This was a conversation he didn't want to have...ever. Sure, he owed Brynn an explanation, but not *here*.

Sophie apparently agreed, because she scowled fiercely at her family.

"Dad, you can't go abusing your hospital connections just to spy on your kids. I'm sure Anna or Dr. Hoyne could have told you over the phone that it was just a finger scratch and not head trauma."

Both parents looked away guiltily.

"And Brynn," Sophie said pleadingly, "*please* quit looking at me like I just shot your cat. Nothing happened between Gray and me; we were just together for work reasons."

Brynn sputtered, obviously not enjoying being called out. "I wasn't worried about that, I was just surprised..."

"And bitchy," Will said around a neon green lollipop. Did the man never stop eating?

"And *you*," Sophie said, turning on Will. "Thank you for coming down, but come on. You didn't know better? You couldn't have run interference?" She glanced meaningfully at Brynn.

Will shrugged, unperturbed as ever. "Brynn called me saying that there'd been an accident and that she was worried about you."

"*Brynn* called you?" Marnie asked.

"And you actually came?" asked Dr. Dalton.

For the first time since Gray had met him, Will seemed to falter. "I came for Sophie, obviously. I was worried."

Awkward silence settled over the group.

Gray wondered what his next move should be. Did he try to explain to the family why their daughter was at his home on a Friday night? Out of habit, he looked to Sophie for guidance. She was forever giving him hints on appropriate social behavior.

But not this time. She was too busy staring at the bandages on her fingers like she could heal them with her eyes.

Gray cleared his throat nervously. "Ms. Dalton, if you're feeling better, I think I'll let you spend time with your family. I'll see you on Monday. Unless, of course, you need a ride home," he finished politely.

Sophie's head snapped up, her wide eyes blinking up at him.

"*Ms. Dalton?*" Will said. "What a stiff."

Gray wanted to snap that he wasn't deaf, but confrontation wasn't really his style. Neither was playing nursemaid, and he silently begged Sophie to excuse him from this awkward mess.

"Sure, I can get a ride home from my parents," Sophie finally replied, sounding uncharacteristically formal. "Thanks for taking the time out of your schedule to drive me over here. I apologize for the"—she shook her injured hand in a little wave—"inconvenience. Hopefully it won't adversely affect my typing skills on Monday."

That made his head snap around and he met her gaze. "For God's sake, you know it's not your work I care about—"

Will cleared his throat.

"I should go," Gray said finally.

Hating himself for his curtness, but feeling completely out of his element, he walked quietly out the door and nodded an awkward farewell before escaping into the blissful anonymity of the hospital hallway.

Traces of conversation followed him as he headed for the parking lot.

"Good Lord, did the man just bow to us?" Will asked.

"Interestingly, William, some men understand the basic concepts of being a gentleman," Brynn said.

"How, by screwing his secretary?" Will asked.

"Now, I'm sure it wasn't like that. He doesn't seem the type to be interested in our Sophie," Marnie said. "They said they were working."

"On what, French cooking lessons? Or French something else?"

"Can we please go now? Please?" The faint request came from Sophie, and the pleading quality of her voice almost had him turning around. She sounded nothing like herself.

But he kept walking. He didn't know the first thing about playing hero.

"Gray, wait up a sec." His heart sped up for a brief second when he thought it might be Sophie coming after him.

He watched her approach, waiting for some sort of sting of regret that he'd let this beautiful woman walk away from him. At the very least, he expected some sort of physical regret that he hadn't even tried to get her into bed.

But as he watched Brynn come toward him, he felt nothing. A removed appreciation, maybe. She was still lovely, and he could see them being friends. But any lingering hope that they might get back together faded for good. There was nothing here but friendship potential.

"Can I get a ride home?" she asked. "I know it's out of the way, but I don't want my parents to have to drive me and Sophie, and Will...that's just not happening."

He was a little surprised by the request, but didn't really mind. "Sure. My car's parked just out front."

She smiled in thanks and tucked her arm companionably in his. Gray waited for the alarm bells to go off in his paranoid mind, but nothing happened.

Brynn seemed more thoughtful than flirtatious, and he relaxed slightly.

While they waited for the elevator, Gray had the uncomfortable sensation of being watched, and he warily glanced back toward Sophie's room.

Two very wounded eyes were blinking back at him, and he felt a stab of panic that he was seeing her here with Brynn. But before he could explain that this wasn't what it looked like, her parents swooped around her, leading her in the opposite direction.

She didn't look back.

* * *

Sophie gave the printer a soft kick. So much for her "minor" finger injuries not interfering with her work. The stitches from her parsley incident had been minimal, but the splint holding the two injured fingers immobile made even the simplest actions awkward.

Everything took her twice as long, from curling her hair, to typing up expense reports, to going to the damn bathroom.

Sophie's patience had been fraying all week, and today she'd reached the breaking point. Hence the printer-kicking. She'd hoped to get out of work early today to stop by a friend's birthday dinner, but instead it was seven o'clock and she was still stuck in the office. There was a pile of sales reports that needed to be printed before tomorrow's board meeting, and, naturally, the printer with the built-in hole punch was out of ink.

Her choices were to try and figure out how to change the toner herself or use a different printer and do the hole-punching by hand.

Neither option would get her out of the office in the next hour with her crippled fingers.

On top of it all, she was spoiling for a fight and she knew exactly who she wanted to pick it with. Except the object of her frustration wasn't exactly the type to lower himself to a good old-fashioned yelling fest.

He was more the ice-out-the-enemy type of fighter.

Something he'd been doing very well all week.

It had been six days since The Episode, and other than giving her curt work-related requests, Gray hadn't spoken to her. He'd barely looked at her.

Either he was being a complete chickenshit, or whatever fuzzy feelings Sophie had felt that night at his house had been completely one-sided.

She glared down at the red, blinking error light. Stupid printer. Stupid job. Stupid Gray.

Stupid Sophie. That was the real crux of her anger. She was mad at herself for letting herself think that she might matter. Mad that she'd been ready to go back to his home after the emergency room and have a nice homemade crepe, and instead he'd left her there to go home with her dad while he walked away with his ex-girlfriend.

She felt the now familiar heat of embarrassment that always made her fingers tingle, and she shook her hand. Normally she liked Brayburn's copy room. It smelled like paper and productivity. And since she was the only one that used the one on the executive floor, it usually felt like her private haven when the rest of the office felt too chaotic.

But tonight her precious copy room felt like a prison holding her back from the bubble bath that awaited her at home.

Resigning herself to the battle ahead, she found a stool and carefully teetered up its wobbly steps toward the toner boxes on the top shelves, giving a little grunt of triumph when she managed to grab the box and crawl back down the stool without falling and shattering her tibia. She so did not need another ER visit.

But getting the box down was only the start of the battle. This wasn't a simple open-the-door-and-drop-it-in type of deal. Sophie stared down at the indecipherable images masquerading as instructions. Why didn't they just *tell* you how to change the cartridge?

What was this first picture supposed to be? It looked like a UFO sitting on top of a tractor.

"Need some help?"

Sophie closed her eyes. Of course he would be here. She didn't even muster the energy to feel surprised. Even if she hadn't known the rough voice by now, Gray was the only one who stayed in the office this late. He probably considered it a sacrilege to leave the office before the nightly janitorial crew had left.

"Go away," she breathed, not turning to look at him.

Not exactly the cool professionalism she was hoping for, but she'd been trying for cool professional all week. It was Thursday, and her feet hurt, her hand was throbbing, and she just wanted to go home.

Instead of granting her request, he came up beside her and pulled the toner box toward him.

"Give that back," she snapped.

"You need two hands to do this," he said, apparently immediately understanding the hieroglyphics on the box.

"I have two hands."

"Yes, but only eight fingers." He still hadn't lifted his eyes from the box.

She tried to pull the box back toward her. "CEOs do not change printer toner. Their assistants do."

"What are you doing here so late?" he asked, finally turning his head toward her.

Her stomach gave a jolt at the eye contact, and in a second she went from irritated to hot and bothered. This whole desire-to-hump-the-boss thing was starting to get really inconvenient. Particularly since it wasn't mutual.

"Oh, you know, just wanted to spend more time in your dazzling company," she said with her biggest smile.

"I'm sure whatever work you still have can wait until tomorrow."

"Not unless you want to hand-draw your sales report for the board tomorrow."

His mouth clamped shut and she gave him a knowing look. "Exactly."

"How can I help?" he asked, still not moving.

"By going away. Maybe falling out the window." Losing the battle with her aching feet, Sophie finally relented and eased out of her shoes, surprised they weren't filled with blood. She certainly wouldn't have pulled out the new camel peep toes this morning if she'd known she'd be working a twelve-hour work day.

She let out a sigh of relief and wiggled her toes.

"I liked them on," Gray said roughly.

For a moment she thought she misheard him, but the hot look he was giving her said otherwise, and was like a match on her already-frayed temper.

"Don't do that," she hissed, waving the spike of her heel at him. "Don't you dare *flirt* after a week of acting like a robot."

He batted the shoe out of his face and glared down at her. "What the hell are you talking about?"

"Did we not share a meal on Friday night, Mr. Wyatt?"

His expression grew wary. "We did. And on Monday I had lunch with Beth Jennings, and on Tuesday I had dinner with Jeff Andrews. What of it?"

"Really? Did you cook for them? Did you nearly kiss them? Did you tell them that they were *worth something*?"

Her voice broke and she brought up her shoe again as protection.

"Sophie," he said softly.

"Don't. No pity. Not from you."

"Put your damn shoe down."

"No." She waved it at him. "I have to put this toner in and then I'm going home and eating nothing but carbs and butter."

Sophie told herself she was glad when he turned away. This was *her* copy room, and it wasn't big enough for the both of them.

But instead of leaving, he pulled the toner box away and tore it open before she could respond.

"I'll do it," she said, trying to grab for it.

He batted her away as though she were a fly and, turning to the massive machine, opened a couple of hidden doors, slid a couple of panels, and in the span of a couple of minutes had replaced the toner and was putting the old one in the bag to be recycled.

"You didn't have to do that," she said, not quite willing to say thank you, but grateful all the same. She was pretty sure she'd be still trying to open the box.

The red light on the printer flicked to green, and the machine began methodically spitting out neat piles of hole-punched paper. They stood side by side in silence as they watched it work. Their hands were less than an inch apart. All she had to do was extend her pinky finger, and...

The machine slowed to a stop, and Sophie made a grab for the papers and her shoes.

"Thanks again for the help," she said, backing out of the room.

"You're done now, right? You can go home?"

"Almost. I just need to put them in the report binders and get them into the conference room."

"I'll help," he said, following her to her desk.

"Would you stop? I can do this!"

"I know, but it's my project you're working on. I've given you too much to do. I'm sorry. It won't happen again."

"It's not too much," she muttered as she awkwardly tried to open the binder with her maimed hand. "It's just this damn splint. It slows me down."

"All the more reason for me to apologize. You wouldn't have the splint if I hadn't forced you to help cook," Gray said quietly. He gently pulled the binder from her hands. "I'll do this part. You just hand me the paper."

She wanted to tell him to go to hell, but he was being so damn decent, and telling him off felt needlessly petty. She *hated* when he was nice. Which, she had to admit, was more often than she gave him credit for.

Once again, the task went twice as fast with his assistance, and by the time she laid the last binder at the head of the conference room table, it was only seven thirty, not midnight, like she'd feared.

She moved toward the door only to find Gray standing there watching her. She quickly turned to the window rather than face him, her pulse humming with... something.

It wasn't anger. Her temper from earlier had mellowed, and she was no longer itching to start a fight.

She was wanting something much more dangerous than a fight.

"I've never seen the view from up here at night," she said. There. That was a safe topic. Very platonic.

Except Sophie hadn't bothered to turn on the conference room's light, preferring to work by the city lights outside. She regretted that decision now. The darkness was decidedly romantic.

He shoved his hands into his suit pocket and came to stand beside her as they stared out at the Seattle skyline. It was a clear night, and the city felt both peaceful and alive. "This is one of my favorite times in the office," he said. "I do my best thinking up here after everyone's gone."

Sophie gave a rueful smile. "And here I've gone disturbing your peace. As usual."

"As usual," he agreed.

Sophie couldn't help the wince. At what point would his rejection stop stinging?

She turned to go, leaving him to his dark solitude, but he grabbed her hand. "Don't."

He stared down at their joined hands for several moments before very slowly lacing his fingers with hers. It was one of the sweeter and strangely most erotic sensations of her life. Holding hands wasn't supposed to be sexy.

But holding hands with Gray was.

She didn't know how long they stood there, two mismatched souls holding hands in the moonlight, but she didn't want it to end.

"Gray," she whispered, still not looking at him. "I—"

"Don't, Sophie," he said, giving her fingers a squeeze.

It was hardly the first time that Gray had silenced her, but she was getting damn tired of it. For once she hadn't been about to pry or pester or annoy him. She'd just wanted to talk. Hear his voice. And he denied her even that.

She peeled her fingers away from his and walked out of the conference room, back to her desk. Her eyes were watering as she picked up her purse and began stuffing her belongings into it.

So the man wanted quiet? She'd give him that. He wanted solitude? He could have that too.

In fact, he could pretty much have those things the rest of his life, because no woman in her right mind would—

A firm hand jerked her around so roughly that her purse fell to the ground. Sophie's eyes went wide as she stared up into his angry face. This was a Gray she hadn't seen before. There was none of the earlier gentleness, and the soft look in his eyes had been replaced by something hot and fierce.

His mouth was on hers before she could move.

She stiffened for the briefest of seconds before relaxing into him. Sophie heard herself gasp at the unexpected rightness of it. She'd thought about this moment. Dreamt about it. She'd expected it to feel wrong.

But there was nothing wrong about the mouth moving slowly over hers, his lips taking hers in quiet demand. She tentatively kissed him back, and when his hands slid up her arms to cup her face, she slid hers around his waist, pulling him even closer. Their bodies fit together like the last pieces of an impossible puzzle.

Gray groaned, using his lips to coax open her mouth and slide his tongue against hers in silky rhythm. There was nothing slow and gentle about the kiss now, and she clawed at his back and kissed him like he was the last man alive.

Her hands moved to the buttons of her shirt, but she only had half of them undone before she realized that he was one step ahead of her. Her blouse was fully unbuttoned, and he was roughly tugging it down her shoulder. His mouth moved to the crook of her neck as his hand found her breast over her lace bra and they both moaned.

"God, Sophie," he said against her neck. She wanted to tease him that there was supposed to be no talking, but she didn't feel like teasing. At least not that kind.

Her uncoordinated hands had finally undone the last of

his shirt buttons when they heard the unmistakable sound of keys jingling in the hallway.

Please keep going, she silently begged the owner of the keys.

But the jangling stopped right outside the office doors.

"The janitor," Gray whispered, pulling back abruptly. Sophie was unprepared at the sudden loss of his support, and stumbled off-balance, catching herself on the side of her desk.

Her desk. Horrible reality flooded over her. She had nearly just had sex with her boss in the office.

Who does that? she screamed at herself.

She heard a key turn in the lock, and she'd barely pushed her arms through the shirt Gray tossed at her when the door opened.

The fluorescent light spilled in from the hallway, and Sophie squinted against its harshness.

A very startled-looking janitor blinked at them as Sophie held her purse in front of her half-buttoned shirt and tried to look natural.

"Mr. Wyatt?" he said, clearly confused.

"Hello, Walter," Gray said in his usual calm voice. "Come on it. We were just finishing up a couple of sales reports."

If Walter suspected anything, he was too kind to show it, because he merely nodded and gave her a shy smile before wheeling in his cleaning cart.

"I'll drive you home," Gray said quietly in her ear. But she knew that tone. This wasn't the Gray who had cooked dinner for her, and it certainly wasn't the Gray who had kissed her senseless.

This was the cold Gray. The one from the elevator.

She should have known that any kind of intimacy would only blow up in their faces. This was the type of man that pushed away anyone who got beneath his defenses. Gray was already fully dressed, looking for all the world like he'd just come from a nice business lunch instead of fondling his secretary on her desk.

"I'll be fine," she said, her voice crackling as she finished buttoning her shirt.

"Sophie—"

"This was the worst kind of mistake. Don't even try to deny it."

And he didn't. Just stared at her with cool gray eyes. "Yes, it was a mistake. It won't happen again."

Sophie gave a curt nod and grabbed her shoes to keep from having to make eye contact. "I'll see you tomorrow," she said brightly, before heading toward the door without looking back.

He said nothing.

By the time she exited the elevator, she was a sobbing mess.

This job at Brayburn was supposed to be her path toward respectability, and she was messing everything up.

Nobody would respect the girl who fell in love with the boss.

CHAPTER THIRTEEN

"Sophie Claire, are you listening to me?"

Sophie switched her cell phone to her other ear as she threw yet another rejected shirt on the bed. Her entire wardrobe was office-ready, but not even remotely first-date-ready. When had *that* happened?

"Sorry, Mom, what?"

Phone conversations with her mother were trying on the best of days, and painful when her mother was attempting to coax Sophie into yet another "self-improvement plan."

Marnie let out the smallest of dignified sighs. "I was saying that Blair has an opening this weekend and is willing to take you on as a client. Don't you think a little change to your look would be nice? I'm thinking darkening the blonde to something more natural. Maybe getting rid of the length? You're not sixteen anymore, you know..."

"Brynn's hair is the same length as mine," Sophie said as she held up a green dress in the mirror. She made a face and tossed that in the reject pile. Mint green only looked good when she had a bit of a tan. Not something she could claim at the moment.

"Hmm, is it?" her mother was musing. "I suppose so, but Brynn wears hers straight, so it's more age-appropriate."

"Well, Brynn is older than me," Sophie said with sham cheerfulness, "so when I'm her age, then we can have this chat, okay?"

"So what should I tell Blair?"

Tell him to take a flying leap. Or her. Sophie had no idea what gender her mother's beloved hairstylist was, and she really didn't care.

"Mom, I've got to go. I have another call coming in."

"You do not. Who is it?"

"Good-bye, Mother. I'll see you Sunday," Sophie said, hanging up before her mother could attempt to launch her next campaign for Sophie's betterment.

She tapped her phone against her chin as she surveyed her bedroom. There were now more clothes discarded on her bed than there were clothes in the closet, and she still didn't know what to wear. For that matter, she didn't even know what this date entailed.

Michael seemed like a decent enough guy. He was one of Will's friends from college who'd just moved to the area, and Will wouldn't set her up with a creep.

And yet, she hadn't heard from him once since he'd first called to ask her out, despite his promise that he'd call with more details. He'd probably forgotten, since, being a guy, he had about three wardrobe options to choose from instead of a thousand.

She glanced at the clock on her nightstand. She had two hours until he was supposed to pick her up. Would it scream "high-maintenance" if she called and asked where they were going? A restaurant was a restaurant, but what if he was one of those creative types who had planned a picnic? She certainly wouldn't be able to think about getting romantic if she had the Seattle spring breeze blowing up her cute skirt.

Screw it. Finding his number in her phone's address book, she took the plunge.

The creaky voice that picked up was so unlike the masculine voice she remembered that she had to double-check that she'd called the right number.

"Michael?" she asked.

"Yeah?"

"Hey, it's Sophie Dalton."

A pause.

"Oh shit."

Sophie closed her eyes. "You're sick, huh?"

"More like half-dead. I haven't moved in two days. I completely forgot about our date."

Sophie began hanging up dozens of shirts. The only thing she'd be wearing tonight was her sweats. "No worries," she said. "You can't help being sick."

"Still, I should have called," he said with a nasty cough.

"Please. You sound like a tuberculosis patient. I'm sure you had other things on your mind."

Like dying.

"I'll call you later this week for a reschedule?"

"Absolutely," she said with as much enthusiasm as she could muster. "I hope you feel better."

Sophie tossed her phone into the pile of clothes and sat on the edge of her bed. She waited for the expected rush of disappointment.

It didn't come.

If anything, she was bummed that it was the first sunny

Saturday of the year and she had no plans. But she was oddly indifferent to being dateless. Michael was probably a nice enough guy, but if she was honest with herself, she'd only agreed to go out with him for one reason.

To forget The Kiss.

It had been almost two weeks since she'd nearly jumped Gray's bones in the office, and the two of them had been circling each other like wary cats. He'd retreated behind a mask of ice, and Sophie had responded like a petulant four-year-old, needling him in every way that she could.

But neither one had mentioned what happened that night. Just like they hadn't mentioned the dinner at his house, or the emergency room visit that had followed. It was like two eighth graders who couldn't have a straight conversation and needed a mutual friend to pass notes.

Except there was no mutual friend in this case. And they weren't immature eighth graders. They were scarred, wounded, emotionally crippled adults.

Who could not be more wrong for each other.

Sophie's phone began to vibrate, and she groaned as she dug it out of the pile of halter tops and miniskirts. Probably her mother calling to remind her not to swear on the first date. Or any date.

Finally finding her phone, Sophie stared down at the name and number.

Definitely not her mother.

"Hello?" she asked. This had to be a pocket-dial.

"Sophie."

Not a question. He'd called her intentionally.

"Gray," she replied, relieved that her voice sounded calm. "I am not coming into the office on a Saturday, I don't care how far behind you are on your plan of taking over the world."

"That's not why I'm calling."

"Oh," she said, flopping back on the bed. "Finally got up the courage to use my call-girl service, then, huh? I'll have you know, I'm not cheap—"

"Would you like to come to a dinner party tonight?"

All of Sophie's snark flew out the window and she sat up in confusion. "You mean like a date?"

He cleared his throat nervously. "Well, I mean, there'd be other people there. My friend Ian and his wife. Maybe their son, although I think he might be off at a birthday party or something."

Sophie stared at the generic flower print hanging above her dresser in disbelief. "You want me to come with you to your friend's house? For dinner?"

"That's what a dinner party usually means."

She pulled the phone away from her ear and frowned at it briefly. "This is sort of out of nowhere for someone who had his tongue down my throat and then didn't talk to me for two weeks."

"You didn't talk to me either, Sophie. And don't think I don't know you swapped my coffee for decaf and pulled all the cheese off my sandwich before giving it to me. Very mature."

Yeah...not her best moves. She'd been desperate to provoke him.

"All right, I'll go," she said simply.

"You will? You don't have plans?"

"No," she said on a sigh. "I was supposed to have a date tonight, but he got sick."

"You were going on a date?"

There was something low and menacing in his voice, and Sophie couldn't hide a smile. Maybe the man wasn't so indifferent after all. "Yes, Grayson. A date. But he has consumption, so I'm free now."

"What?"

"Never mind. What time?"

"Is an hour too soon for me to pick you up?"

"Gee, I'm glad I wasn't a last resort or anything."

He was silent for several seconds. "It took me this long to work up the courage."

"Oh." The admission melted her annoyance slightly. Okay, it melted it *completely*. She was practically mush. "I can be ready in an hour."

"Great," he said, not bothering to hide the relief in his voice. "Bring a sweater or something. Ashley is insisting we sit outside even though it's barely sixty degrees out."

"Honey, in Seattle, this is practically beach weather," Sophie said, pulling out a pair of blue capris, a white tank, and a yellow cardigan she'd stolen from Brynn. "Now go away. I need some time to don my hooker gear."

"Don't forget the boots," he said before hanging up in her ear.

Sophie did a ridiculous little happy dance when she hung up the phone, before taking a deep breath and telling herself to pull it together. It was just a dinner party. With chaperones. Not a marriage proposal.

But it was the first time that Gray had been the one to initiate spending time together. And for a man whose emotions needed a wheelchair, that *had* to mean something.

* * *

"Holy crap," Sophie said as she took in the treelined drive of Ian's house. "Is it a requirement that all of your friends be fellow CEOs or pirates?"

Gray gave her a sidelong glance before parking next to an enormous fountain. Yes, an honest-to-God *fountain*. At someone's house. Sophie was suddenly relieved that she'd had the foresight to be waiting on her front porch when Gray had picked her up. No way was he going to see the inside of her studio apartment now. His best friend probably had showers bigger than her entire home.

"Ian's an attorney," Gray said as they climbed out of his car. "He owns his own practice."

"Jeez, no wonder my parents didn't want me to drop out of law school. Do these people have their own stable? A carriage house?"

Sophie didn't know much about real estate, but Ian's address alone screamed "money." Medina was one of Seattle's richest suburbs, with many of its homes located near the water. It was minutes from downtown, and yet far enough away to have a view of downtown.

In other words, rich-people heaven.

Not her scene.

"Quit being a snob," Gray said, as he led her along the walkway toward the front porch.

"I'm not," Sophie said, trying not to squirm when he briefly set his hand on the small of her back. She wished she better understood what this was. A dinner party at his college friend's could hardly be considered a date. But he'd invited *her*. Not Brynn, not some perfect potential girlfriend.

That had to mean something. Damned if she knew what. He'd barely spoken to her on the ride over. An open book he was not.

"I'm not a snob," she said again, resisting the urge to see if the perfect hedges were fake. "It's just intimidating, you know?"

"You weren't intimidated at my place."

"Well, sure, but your place, while nice, is hardly on par with this," she said, gesturing to the enormous grounds and slice of waterfront view poking around the right side of the enormous white house. "No offense."

"I don't have need for all this space," Gray said distractedly. "Not for one person."

Sophie paused and stared at the back of his gray polo shirt. "Are you telling me you *could* afford this? If you wanted to?"

Gray glanced back and gave her an exasperated look. "What is with you? I've seen your parents' house. It's nearly as big as this. I'm guessing you hardly grew up on food stamps."

"That's my parents' money," she said defensively. "I'm not sure if you're aware, but cocktail waitresses can't exactly afford Bentleys. And it's not like Brayburn's paying me all that much. Perhaps we should discuss a raise."

Gray grabbed her hand and pulled her none too gently up the brick steps to their front door. "Just behave. Please." He gave the door an impatient knock.

Sophie ran a finger over the door frame. "White. How is this possible? How can they have a perfectly white front door without a single scuff or speck of dirt?"

The pristine white door in question swung open, and Sophie's first thought was that Gray was right. She had been a prejudging, stereotyping snob.

Ashley Porter was wearing cuffed jean capris, a plain white T-shirt, and those boat shoes that Sophie thought only people in the Hamptons wore. But the shoes were well worn, and the T-shirt had some sort of red stain near the hem. Hardly the immaculately groomed housewife that Sophie had been fearing.

The woman herself was beautiful in a completely unintimidating sort of way, her dark brown hair worn in a short pixie cut that only woman with perfect features could pull off. She had clever, friendly brown eyes and a wide mouth completely devoid of lipstick.

"Took you guys long enough," she said as she ushered them in. "We were wondering how long you were going to stand in our driveway arguing."

Sophie blushed, but the other woman's voice held no accusation.

Ian wandered into the foyer with a beer in hand and gave Sophie a friendly hug as though they were old friends instead of total strangers. "Good to see you, Sophie. I see you've met Ash, my nagging shrew of a wife."

Ashley shook Sophie's hand before giving Gray an enormous hug, looking a bit like a friendly fairy cuddling up to a grumpy bear. Then Sophie glanced at Gray's face and almost stumbled. Not only was he *enduring* the hug, he was actually smiling. And the relaxed affection was unlike anything she'd seen on his face before. She felt a sudden liking for these people she barely knew for being people he could relax around.

"You have a beautiful home," Sophie said as she followed them into the kitchen. The inside was even more stunning than the outside. Ashley's decorating taste ran toward soothing neutrals, which perfectly accentuated the floor-to-ceiling windows and the stunning view of Lake Washington.

"Thanks," Ashley said with genuine pride. "I wish I could say it's always this clean, but the truth is I took advantage of Ryan's slumber party today to get everything back in order. Gray mentioned we have a six-year-old son?"

Sophie nodded.

"We lucked out and got a calm one, but that doesn't mean my life doesn't revolve around tripping on soccer balls and pulling action figures out of the sofa cushions."

Her voice lacked any real irritation, and Sophie felt a spurt of jealousy. Ashley seemed to have it all. Handsome, successful husband, great kid, beautiful home. And even in her casual clothes, she had an air of confidence that Sophie had spent years trying to fake.

"Ian, did you fix the grill yet?" Ashley asked distractedly as she wrestled with a corkscrew.

Ian caught Sophie's eye and shook his head before turning back to his wife. "I certainly did. Gray, come admire my skills. I just need a quick detour to the garage to grab my tools."

"Ian!" Ashley said. "You said you'd have it fixed by the time they got here."

"Ash, I'm thinking maybe the grill isn't meant to work until Memorial Day. It's a sign that we should be eating indoors."

"*We're eating outside*," Ashley said as she poured two liberal glasses of white wine for herself and Sophie. "That's why we have the heaters. Which *are* working, right?"

But Ian had already disappeared into the garage. Gray shot Sophie a glance. "You okay if I go help Ian?"

"Don't worry, I promised Ian I wouldn't interrogate her," Ashley said, handing Sophie a glass.

"Just like he promised to fix the grill?" Gray said with a rare grin.

Ashley pointed to the French doors leading out to an enormous patio. "Go. I need girl time."

"Don't scare Sophie off," Gray said with a small smile.

Sophie blinked in surprise. He was talking about her as

though they were together. Which they weren't. But he was out the door before she could figure out what he'd meant.

"He likes you," Ashley said as she patted a bar stool at the center island. "It took him forever to admit it, even to Ian. But he wouldn't have brought you here otherwise."

"He hasn't brought over women before?" Sophie was trying for casual curiosity, but it came out as insecure prying.

Ashley shrugged. "Not since Jessica. He's mentioned he was engaged once?"

"Yeah. Wasn't exactly liberal with the details, though."

"Shocker."

Sophie smiled. "You know him well."

The other woman tilted her head. "So do you, apparently."

"We work together. It's my job to read him."

"On weekends too?"

Sophie took a long sip of her wine and shifted in her seat. "I don't really know what this is. I thought he was just bringing me along to make the situation more comfortable, but I've never seen him as comfortable as he is with you guys, so obviously that's not it…"

Ashley shook her head. "He comes over every couple weeks or so. No buffer needed."

Sophie was more confused than ever.

"It's like I said," Ashley said gently. "He *likes* you."

A sharp rapping at the glass had them both looking up to see Ian staring in the kitchen window, miming shoving something in his mouth and pointing at the fridge.

"Oh crap, I forgot all about the bruschetta," Ashley said. "I kind of wanted nothing to do with it after a tomato exploded all over my shirt. Sorry, I meant to change first, but I'm comfy."

Sophie smiled. "Believe me, I like it better this way. I was picturing someone like my mother. Frosty hair, ever-present pearls, and designer slacks."

Ashley snorted. "Not my thing. Grab that wine while I get the appetizers. Let's go feed the menfolk."

By the time the four of them were sitting around the outdoor table to a delicious dinner of barbecue chicken, grilled corn, and all-American potato salad, Sophie was feeling like part of their little dinner-party family.

The way Gray had his arm around the back of her chair and kept toying with the ends of her hair didn't hurt either. She was starting to get the warm, glowing feeling that Ashley might be right.

Perhaps he *did* like her.

She grabbed her wineglass and leaned toward him just slightly, relishing the warmth from the wine, the toasty outdoor heaters, and the horribly attractive man by her side.

"So, Sophie," Ian said, taking a long pull of his beer, "how's your sister dealing with you stealing her boyfriend?"

Sophie choked on her wine and gave Gray a panicked look. He merely stared back with a raised eyebrow.

"Oh, Gray and I aren't... We're not... I didn't steal anybody," Sophie said, feeling suddenly sweaty. These damn heaters. Damn wine. Damn man.

Ashley and Ian exchanged a conspiratorial look, but Ashley apparently took pity on her and changed the subject. "So, Gray, do you talk to Mary often?" Ashley asked.

Ian gave them a bland look. "No."

"Who's Mary?" Sophie asked.

"His old assistant," Ashley explained. "He tried to bring her out to Seattle with him, but she didn't want to move. But I'm betting he never spent time with *her* outside of the office."

"Ash," Gray said mildly. "You're going to make Sophie uncomfortable."

Sophie's mind was reeling. What was going on here? Since when was Gray the one to make a situation more comfortable? That was supposed to be her job. And why was he not refuting them?

"Gray, you're going to give them the wrong idea," she murmured softly, even as she kicked him not so softly under the table.

"What idea is that?" he replied just as softly, giving her a private smile.

"That we're...you know...a *thing*."

He shrugged. "I can't control what they think."

"It's true," Ian said unapologetically. "We'll make our own assumptions regardless of your excuses."

Sophie hated that she was blushing, and Ashley gave her a sympathetic look before she stood and began gathering dishes. "Soph, would you mind grabbing that platter? We need more room on the table for dessert."

"Absolutely!" Sophie said, shooting to her feet. She'd grabbed the plate and was in the kitchen before Ashley had stacked more than two plates.

"Sorry about that," Ashley said, as she came into the kitchen. "The three of us have always been open with one another. It's unfair to expect you to spill your guts when you've just met us."

"It's not that," Sophie said, fiddling with a piece of paper towel. "I actually have chronic verbal diarrhea. Spilling my guts is kind of my thing. It's just...I don't know what Gray is after. And I can't afford to be wrong, you know?"

"Yeah. I get it," Ashley said, giving her a sympathetic glance.

Needing some space, Sophie threw the paper towel aside. "Is the bathroom down the hall?" she asked.

"Second door on the left."

The hallway was covered in mismatched picture frames, most of them containing photos of a child whom she assumed to be Ryan. There had to be at least two dozen pictures of a darling blond boy from babyhood to Little League.

At the far end of the hall was Ian and Ashley's wedding picture, and she couldn't help but grin at their elated young faces. Her eyes fell on the best man and she did a double take.

Gray. The short dark haircut hadn't changed a bit over the years, and he had the same fit, lean build. But the gray eyes were less guarded than the ones she saw on a daily basis. And younger Gray was actually smiling.

"Cute, weren't we?" Ashley said coming up beside her.

"You still are," Sophie said truthfully. "I had no idea Gray had so many teeth."

Something sad flashed across Ashley's pixie-like features. "Yeah, well. He's always been quiet and reserved, but back then he wasn't quite so…"

"Emotionally handicapped?" Sophie supplied with a smile.

She expected Ashley to smile back, but she gave a small shake of her head. "I was going to say 'wounded.'"

Sophie's smile faded, and she stared again at the picture of Gray. She was so used to seeing his lack of social charms as a character flaw. What if it was an emotional scab that she kept picking at?

"What happened? The fiancée?" she asked Ashley.

The other woman gave a short nod. "It was a rough one."

For some reason, Sophie had a hard time picturing Gray being hurt by a woman. He seemed the type to let the messy emotional stuff roll right off of him.

Ashley seemed to be studying Sophie for a minute before directing Sophie's attention to another picture. "That's Jessica."

The picture seemed to be at a celebration of some sort. Gray had his arm around a blonde woman, and Sophie leaned in for a closer look.

And felt like she'd been kicked in the stomach.

"She looks *just like me*."

Ashley nodded. "This picture doesn't even do your similarities justice. The facial features are uncanny. Ian mentioned that Gray thought there was a resemblance, but seeing you on the front porch took my breath away. It was like déjà vu."

"Wow, no wonder he's had such a hard time liking me," Sophie muttered. "What happened exactly?"

Ashley looked away guiltily. "It's not really my story to tell. I shouldn't even have shown you this picture. I just thought you should know. She's the reason he insists he'll never get married."

There was another kick in the stomach. Much harder this time.

It doesn't matter.

Why should it matter? One kiss and an arm around the back of her chair did not a soul mate make.

"Really?" Sophie asked, grateful that her voice didn't croak. "I didn't know. I mean...we've obviously never had that kind of discussion."

Ashley gave her a knowing look. "I'm not trying to rush you to the altar, of course. But if you are looking for an eventual husband and father of your children, well...it's always better to know sooner, isn't it?"

"Thank you for telling me," Sophie said, not really sure if she meant it. Navigating this weird thing happening with her boss was hard enough without knowing she was basically a ghost from his past.

As for the whole *Gray will never get married* thing, well...that just wasn't her problem, now, was it?

After using the restroom, Sophie helped Ashley finish doing all the dishes, but her previously light, giddy mood had evaporated. Her eyes kept straying to Gray's profile as he and Ian still sat at the outdoor table.

At Ashley's request, Sophie took dessert out on the patio and began dishing up strawberry shortcake with more force than necessary.

"Here," she snapped at Gray. She shoved the plate in his direction and sucked in a sharp breath when she felt his fingers brush deliberately against hers. And linger.

He stared up at her with hooded eyes, and Sophie jerked her hand back so quickly that she bobbled the plate, leaving Gray to make a quick grab for it with two hands.

"Sorry," she muttered as a strawberry fell into his lap. The pink stain on his perfectly pressed khakis was immensely satisfying.

He gave her a questioning glance, which she ignored. She couldn't help it—she was mad. Mad that he hadn't trusted her enough to mention a rather significant detail about his past.

Really, he might have *mentioned* that she just happened to be the spitting image of a woman who'd spit on his heart.

And it wasn't just anger rippling through her.

It was fear.

What if his apparent growing attraction had nothing to do with Sophie herself and everything to do with the fact that she resembled someone that he wasn't over?

Was she just a stand-in for the real deal? First Brynn and now Jessica. Hell, she was apparently even second choice to Mary, his old office assistant.

It seemed that she couldn't escape her role of backup plan in Gray's life.

When everyone had been served dessert, Sophie reclaimed her seat next to Gray, but there was none of the casual intimacy of before. He must have sensed her mood, because there was no arm around the back of her chair, and no playful brushing of his knee against hers.

Sophie felt strangely like crying and she wasn't even sure why.

Ian and Ashley kept the conversation easy and light, but the contentedness she'd felt during dinner had evaporated. By the time their hosts were showing them to the door, Gray and Sophie were like two strangers.

Ashley gave her a questioning look as she hugged her good-bye, and Sophie just shrugged. She didn't know how to explain why she and Gray had gone from easy to enemy in the span of ten seconds. She only knew that it was something they seemed to be damn good at.

If dessert had been awkward, the ride home was downright painful.

Gray didn't say a word, which was pretty much par for the course in their relationship. But for the first time since she'd met him...hell, the first time since she could *remember*, Sophie didn't have the urge to fill the silence with happy, useless chatter.

The silence was uncomfortable, but stewing in it was oddly gratifying.

Gray pulled up in front of Sophie's apartment building just as it started to rain. That too was satisfying.

Still, being sulky didn't mean she had to be rude, and she couldn't very well just climb out of the car and slam the door.

Especially when the man hadn't actually done anything wrong.

Not directly.

"Thanks for the evening," she said finally, as he put the car in park and turned toward her. "Ian and Ashley are really great."

Gray gave a curt nod, and Sophie gave him several seconds to come up with a bland, polite response, but he remained silent.

Fine. Go ahead and be an emotionally closed-off hermit.

"Well, good night," she said, giving up on him and reaching for the door handle.

He stopped her with the briefest of tentative touches on her arm. "What happened?"

"What do you mean?" Sophie hoped playing dumb never went out of style, because it was damn handy.

"Something happened. You were there with me at dinner...and then dessert came out and you were...gone."

She thought about not responding. Leaving him in the dark about what made her tick just like he did to her. But then she saw his eyes and the vulnerability there, and she couldn't just leave it alone.

"Why didn't you tell me that your ex-fiancée and I could have been twins?" she asked, keeping her tone as neutral as she could. She didn't want a fight. Just answers.

Gray's eyes closed. "Goddamn it, Ashley."

"It wasn't her fault," Sophie said, fudging slightly in defense of her new friend. "I saw a picture of you two on their wall. It was like looking in a mirror. I didn't think it was possible for two unrelated people to look so alike except in the movies."

"Me neither," he said roughly. "Learning otherwise was not a pleasant surprise."

"You should have mentioned it."

"Why? I haven't seen Jessica in over a year, and she has no part in my future. And I don't owe you any explanations about past relationships."

True, but…

"So you're over her?"

"Completely. I was relieved when it was over."

The shuttered pain in his eyes said otherwise. "Then why are you letting her determine your future?" Sophie asked, keeping her tone gentle.

"What are you talking about? I just told you that I don't even want to see the woman again."

Sophie turned to face him more fully. "Yeah, but you went from putting a ring on someone's finger to never wanting to get married? That screams 'emotional scarring.'"

She expected him to get defensive, or at the very least, angry at Ashley again about spilling the beans about his marriage phobia. Instead he looked confused. "What does the fact that I'll never get married have to do with any of this?"

Sophie stared at him aghast. The man genuinely had no concept of why his refusal to ever marry would impact Sophie.

It was clear he'd never even come close to putting the two thoughts together.

And that made Sophie's heart sink more than if he'd responded with anger. "So you really don't want to get married? Ever?"

He shook his head. "No. I have nothing against marriage, it's just not for me."

"Why, because one woman stomped all over your icy little heart? Get over yourself."

He flinched. "Jesus, Sophie."

Her face flooded with the heat of remorse. She hadn't meant to say that. She didn't even mean it. "I'm sorry. This really isn't my business, is it?"

"No, it's really not."

And that told her all she needed to know. But she had to check...

"So the kiss at the office, and everything that happened tonight...the touching, and letting the Porters think we were *something*...that was just...what?"

Gray leaned his head back on the headrest and stared through the windshield, which was now completely blurry with raindrops. "Look, Sophie...about tonight...I shouldn't...I didn't mean...I'm not good at this."

"You're joking."

Her sarcasm earned the tiniest of smiles, although it was gone almost immediately.

"Look, Gray...you haven't really spared my feelings in the past. Why start now? Just let me have whatever you're stuttering over."

He swallowed and turned to look at her. "I know the impression I gave you tonight. And that night in the office. And, hell, however many other times. But I don't think I'm ready for a relationship."

"With me, or with anyone? Because you seemed to be doing fine with Brynn."

"How do you figure? We broke up after a month, and the relationship went nowhere."

Hmm. A good point.

She moved on.

"If you don't want a relationship, why invite me along tonight? Why play with my hair? Is this a game?" Her voice broke slightly, but she was beyond caring.

He had the decency to look guilty, but Sophie was hardly mollified. She'd been a gooey, contented mess, and he'd been playing with her?

"I'm sorry. I shouldn't have... You make me forget sometimes."

She blinked in confusion. "Forget what?"

"That women like you are all wrong for me."

"Women like me? Or women like Jessica?"

"Same thing," he muttered.

Sophie resisted the urge to slam her head on the dashboard. "I knew it! You're shoving me off because I remind you of your bitch of an ex. That's junior high territory, Gray. *Really* ridiculous."

His expression turned fierce and he turned on her with blazing eyes. "You want the whole story? Here it is... Your crack a minute ago about someone stomping all over my icy little heart was dead-on. *Except it wasn't icy then.* And it hurt. So you'll forgive me if I'm not anxious for a repeat."

I wouldn't break your heart, she wanted to beg. But she knew that look. And there was no room for negotiation. She wanted to fight. To insist that he give her a chance. But she couldn't risk it.

Because he could break *her* heart too.

"So what now?" she asked, trying to sound calm and mature.

There would be an Oreo-involved breakdown once she got upstairs, but for now she had to hold it together. She didn't want her messy emotions to get all over his pristine car.

"What do you mean?" he asked warily.

"Well, I mean...I work for you. It's not like I can just conveniently disappear like any other failed first date. Do I look for another job? Or do we try to pretend this whole thing never happened?"

To her surprise, he gently reached out and took her hand. A jolt of electricity seemed to rip up her arm and, more inconveniently, to all of her lady parts. Sophie bit her lip to keep from throwing herself into his arms and begging him to at least let her be a one-night stand.

Casual sex is not part of your self-respect project, she reminded herself. *You deserve to be more than a booty call.*

"I'd like it if we could be friends," Gray said, jolting Sophie out of her horny pep-talk.

Wait, what?

"What?" she asked.

The corner of his mouth turned up slightly. "I know, it's the oldest line in the book. And not one that I've uttered. Ever."

Sophie let out a horrified laugh. "It's a really horrible line. And it never works out."

"It did for you and Will."

"That was different..."

"How?"

I never wanted to keep Will chained up in my bedroom as a plaything. I never wanted to devote my life to making him smile the way I do with you.

"We were kids when we dated. And it was barely dating," she said.

"Please, Sophie. You know this isn't easy for me."

"Define 'friends,'" she said warily.

He looked completely confused, and she melted. He probably didn't know *how* to define it. Other than Ian, she wasn't sure he really had any friends.

"I don't really know," he said looking embarrassed. "I just was hoping... You make me smile. I don't want to lose that."

It was like an arrow to her heart. If she made him smile, why wouldn't he give her the chance to be more than a friend? And yet she couldn't refuse him. Not when he was staring at her with confused gray eyes.

He doesn't even know what he wants, she thought. *This is what I get for falling for someone who's an emotional vault.*

"Okay. Friends it is," she said reluctantly.

His relieved smile reassured her that she'd made the right decision. Somewhere along the line she'd learned to *care* for this complex man.

She couldn't just walk away. Even though staying would break her heart.

CHAPTER FOURTEEN

Brynn Dalton maintained a very a strict list of Do Nots.

Perms. Trans fats. Cubic zirconia. Tequila. Glitter nail polish. Airplane bathrooms. Casual sex. William Thatcher.

The last two items of her list were completely unrelated, of course. At least, they were supposed to be.

But then that kiss in the car had happened, and Brynn couldn't seem to separate "Will" from "sex." And after an uncharacteristic three glasses of Pinot Grigio, it was getting a lot harder to remember why exactly "William Thatcher" and "casual sex" were on her Do Not list at all.

Combining the two wouldn't be so horrible, would it?

Yes. Yes, it would be very horrible, said her brain.

But fun. Really hot, sexy fun, said her loins.

Clearly it was her loins that had done the majority of absorbing the three glasses of wine she'd just consumed at her monthly sorority reunion.

She wasn't drunk. Just tipsy. And tipsy was not something Brynn did often because it left her feeling reckless.

Brynn Dalton did not *do* reckless. Come to think of it, she should probably add it to her Do Not list. Nothing good ever came from being impetuous. That was where STDs, unwanted pregnancies, and broken hearts came from.

And yet here she was, standing outside Will Thatcher's home and debating the unthinkable.

It bothered her that he lived in a homey town house. Hotshot bachelors like William Thatcher were supposed to live in monolithic high-rises. Brynn had been here before, of course. He'd hosted an anniversary for her parents two years earlier, and she'd also been by a couple of times to pick up an inebriated Sophie.

But she'd never really picked up the details before. Like a friendly blue welcome mat. Why would a man who could barely be civil have a welcome mat?

The dark green of his front door was also all wrong. Hunter-green accents were for *her* future home. They did not belong at the enemy's abode. And the dented brass knocker looked like it had been well used. Probably by a constant stream of female visitors.

The flower pots bothered her more than anything. They were empty now thanks to Seattle's chillier-than-usual winter, but she couldn't help but wonder what he planted in the summer months. Flowers? Herbs? Or maybe something more stark and manly, like palms. Not that she could see him out here watering the damn things. Or maybe she just didn't *want* to picture it.

Brynn squeezed her eyes shut and told herself to walk away. Contemplating a one-night stand with public enemy number one was dangerous enough. Humanizing the bastard would be a disaster.

Damn Carrie for pushing that last glass of wine. Although

it wasn't really fair to blame her friend. It wasn't like Brynn didn't know her own limits. The monthly sorority reunions were notoriously boozy. Granted the sugary Jell-O shots of college had given way to overpriced wine bars, but her group of girlfriends still knew their way around their drinks. Brynn usually limited herself to one or two glasses, but she had the day off tomorrow, and she'd really hoped that third glass would help rid her of the itchy feeling.

Instead it had led her here. Enemy territory.

"This is insane," she muttered. "I'm not *that* drunk."

There were plenty of less dangerous men with whom she could scratch her itch. That accountant she'd gone on a date with last week would probably be willing. Or an ex? She thought briefly of Gray but quickly discarded the thought. They hadn't slept together when they were dating, why would they sleep together after they'd broken up?

Besides, something clearly was happening between him and her sister. Not that Brynn could actually see something developing there. They wouldn't make it past the first date when Sophie insisted on rowdy karaoke and Gray wanted to go to the opera. Something she'd told him straight-out when he'd driven her home after the emergency room the other night. Sophie would kill Brynn if she knew she'd interfered, but Brynn hadn't been able to resist the opportunity to talk with Gray.

The soft looks that Sophie had been shooting Gray were not harmless employee-to-employer glances. Brynn hadn't seen her sister look at anyone that way in years. Sophie choosing to care about something was a rare gift, one that Brynn had made damn sure Gray knew to either accept or return with care.

Gray had assured her that he had no intention of hurting

Sophie, and Brynn believed him. But that was sort of the thing with men, wasn't it? Sometimes they hurt you whether or not they intended to.

The reminder that men and pain went together was enough to jar Brynn back into sanity.

Time to get away from there.

She was pulling out her cell phone to call a cab when it started vibrating. Her stomach dropped when she saw the incoming number.

"Will?"

"Brynn." His voice was low and gravelly. She felt the smart part of her slipping away, and her reckless feeling increased tenfold.

"Hi, um... why are you calling me?" she asked in a too-casual high-pitched voice.

He was silent for several moments. "What are you doing on my front porch?"

Oh God. She squeezed her eyes shut. "You know?"

"I saw the cab and watched you teeter up my walkway in death heels. Pretty sexy shoes for an orthodontist."

Brynn scowled at that. She hated how he always undermined her career, as though being an orthodontist meant you had to be frumpy and wear clogs.

"Yeah, well, I was just leaving," she grumbled.

The door opened so suddenly that she nearly fell forward. Their eyes locked for several heated moments, and, moving on unspoken agreement, they silently hung up their cell phones without saying another word.

Will braced his arm on the doorjamb as though barring her entrance.

Not exactly a welcoming start, Brynn thought with a pang.

Then his hand slid up several inches as he lifted his eyebrows in invitation, leaving just enough room for her to slide under his arm if she wanted to.

She wanted to.

Swallowing dryly, she ducked under his arm so she was standing in his foyer. He closed the door with a quiet click, and they still said nothing.

She studied Will closely, waiting for smugness or mockery, but his face was carefully blank.

"I um...I just thought I'd stop by. You know, to say hi, and stuff," she said, her voice husky.

His eyebrow quirked at the mention of "stuff," but instead of giving her a hard time, he just nodded and gestured toward the kitchen. "Let me get you a glass of wine."

"Oh gosh, no. I've had plenty," she said, following him into the kitchen.

He paused in opening the fridge. "You're drunk?" Something like disappointment flashed across his face.

"No, just a little buzzy. And getting less so by the minute."

"Coming from a not-so-great date?" he asked, pouring her a glass of ice water.

"No, just a girls' night." She lowered herself onto the leather bar stool and fixed her eyes on her glass as he poured himself some sort of amber-looking liquid.

"And you came by to say hi," he said, taking a long swallow of his drink.

"Mm-hmm," she said, tracing a drip of condensation down the side of her glass.

The wine buzz was fading, but the recklessness wasn't.

Her mind kept returning to The Kiss from the car. It had been running over and over through her brain like a track on repeat. And the more she thought about it, the more she wanted to do it again. Take it further.

But not like this. He was supposed to be his usual crude self. She wanted hot, meaningless anger sex. Something she could walk away from without so much as a bruise on her emotions.

This quiet, contemplative Will set her on edge. She didn't know how to speak with him in any language other than "feud."

Why didn't he call her bony or snobby or vapid and set her temper off so that she could storm out? Storming out was immature, but smart. Practical. Necessary. Storming out was very Brynn.

And that was the problem. She was sick of herself. She wanted a break from being the organized, uptight, no-sex-before-the-eighth-date goody-goody.

Who better to give her a night's vacation from *perfect* than a man who spent more on condoms in a year than he did on food?

Brynn shook her head to try and clear it. She was making herself dizzy with all of this waffling. Either she wanted to jump his crass bones, or she didn't. *Make up your mind.*

And then the most disturbing thought of all hit her. What if he didn't want her?

She'd taken for granted that he was a womanizer, but for all her complaining about him going through women faster than a toddler went through Cheerios, he'd never made a move on her. Not in high school, when they'd run in the same social circles. Not in college, when he'd practically lived at her house over Christmas break. And certainly not in their adult life, when their once-harmless bickering had turned into very real dislike.

Not until that rainy night in his car, and she still wasn't sure that the kiss hadn't been more about punishing her than passion.

The thought of being rejected by Will was almost enough to bring back the practical, self-preserving Brynn. And yet still she didn't move.

Just do it. You have the rest of your life to be boring.

Brynn set aside her untouched water glass and stood.

Keeping her eyes locked on his moody blue gaze, she slowly made her way around his kitchen island. She continued her slow approach until there were only inches between them. Still he didn't move or speak.

Brynn let her eyes move over him the way she'd seen him check out women a thousand times before. He was wearing a tight black T-shirt, jeans, and a scowl. He looked like every woman's bad-boy fantasy. *Perfect.*

Licking her lips nervously, she pulled the glass from his hand and set it on the counter. She felt a little thrill of gratification when something dark and dangerous flashed through his normally bored eyes.

She hesitantly ran her manicured fingernails lightly over his rib cage, closing her eyes in ecstatic panic when she heard him suck in a sharp breath.

Rough fingers clamped around her wrist. "Brynn, wait—"

No! Desperate to stop him from thinking this through, she rose to her toes and kissed him. It was a soft kiss, just the merest brush of her lips against his. But still, she shuddered. He tasted warm and smoky and strangely addicting.

She kissed him again, lingering this time. His lips moved just slightly beneath hers. Not quite returning the kiss, but not pulling back either.

He's letting me decide, she realized. Whatever she was

feeling was nothing like the manic passion of the car, and that alarmed her. This kiss was softer. Nicer.

And every instinct was screaming that "soft" with William Thatcher was dangerous. "Soft" wasn't what she was here for. She wanted hot, animalistic sex on the floor of his bachelor pad, not soft, heady kisses in his homey kitchen.

Determined to banish all traces of tenderness, Brynn wound her arms around his neck and pulled his head down to her. Her lips were firmer this time, and she nipped at his bottom lip. He stiffened, and for a fraction of a second she had the horrible sensation that he was going to pull back. Push her away.

He doesn't want me, she realized in horror.

Then Will moved so quickly that she nearly lost her balance. Sliding one arm around her back, he hoisted her onto the kitchen counter, even as his other hand slid around the back of her head.

She closed her eyes and waited for the crush of his lips, but his fingers clenched in her hair and held her still. His eyes had gone so dark they were almost black, and he stared into hers with an unreadable expression.

"You'll hate me if we do this," he said gruffly.

"I already hate you."

"Then why are you here?"

She almost laughed at that. She had her legs around his waist and he had to ask? "Isn't that kind of obvious?"

"Just sex?"

"Yes. And just this one time. And, Will...if you tell anyone about this, I *will* kill you."

His head tilted back slightly, and something unidentifiable flashed across his face before he resumed his usual bored expression.

"Well, if it's one-time sex you want, you've come to the right place," he said with an evil little grin.

Then his mouth closed over hers, and she resigned herself to the inevitable.

She was going to become one of William Thatcher's women.

CHAPTER FIFTEEN

Of all the ways Gray expected to be spending his first truly sunny Saturday in Seattle, it wasn't at a company picnic.

A picnic that he was supposedly hosting.

With the help of his assistant.

Who was supposedly just his *friend*.

And yet here he was on a gorgeous late-May afternoon, surrounded by balloon bouquets, blow-up obstacle courses, beanbag tosses, and the spouses and children of his employees.

It should have been a disaster.

But as usual, Sophie had been right. Everyone seemed to be loving it. He'd lost count of the number of times that someone had clapped him on the back with the affirmation that Brayburn Luxuries was an even better place to work now that it was under Gray's considerate care.

Wives had simpered at him, grateful that in a world of corporate schmucks with no soul and no family, that they were lucky enough to belong to a "work family" that respected and supported the homelife.

Gray hadn't bothered to explain that he'd had nothing to do with it. That every last detail, from DJ down to the corn on the cob, had been masterminded by the world's biggest people-loving tornado.

Sophie.

He looked around for his erstwhile assistant, hoping she'd see that he was smiling and shaking hands just like she'd instructed. While lending half an ear to some hyper little man from finance, he finally spotted Sophie over by the games tent.

Yes, she'd set up a *games tent* for a three-hour event. And yes, it was ridiculous.

But damn if people weren't loving it.

His plastered-on smile faltered as he saw who she was talking to.

As if it wasn't enough that Jeff Andrews had become a permanent fixture at Sophie's desk over the past couple of weeks, it would seem that he needed to drool over Gray's assistant at work events as well.

Since they were *friends*, Sophie had felt the need to explain that Jeff had just finalized a messy divorce and was in need of a friend. Sophie, being Sophie, had taken Jeff under her wing in an effort to "distract him from his pain."

Gray, being a man, was reasonably sure that the main focus of Jeff's personal life at the moment had nothing to do with missing his ex and everything to do with coaxing a sympathetic Sophie into bed. He narrowed his eyes as Jeff playfully tugged at Sophie's ponytail.

Flirting with coworkers, especially subordinates, was unprofessional and lowbrow.

He promptly ignored the voice in his head that whispered, *Hypocrite*.

"...and that's how my wife and I learned that athlete's foot was contagious!" the bumbling employee from finance was saying, with a proud grin at having captivated the CEO's attention for all this time.

"That's, um...that's..." *Why the hell were they talking about this? And what was this man's name again?*

"Oh, there's my wife now!" the athlete's foot expert said proudly. "Keri! Keri! Over here, babe! I want you to meet Gray!" He blanched for a moment. "It's cool if I call you Gray, right?"

No, it's absolutely not cool. "Sure," he said weakly. "Call me Gray."

"My wife will think it's so cool that I'm on a first-name basis with the company's CEO," he said with a delighted grin.

Sure enough, the wife *was* impressed by her husband's lofty connections, and it took Gray another ten minutes of listening to conversation about sausage-making before he could politely remove himself. Gray began making his way through the throng of people, hoping his expression said "pleasant, but busy." He couldn't handle much more of this chatter. Overall, the afternoon hadn't been horrible, but if he had to make one more inane comment about the great weather or the merits of the Seattle school districts, he'd probably need a sedative.

Pretending an interest in the food, he kept one eye on Sophie as she continued to giggle with Jeff. Didn't she have better things to do than flirt? Caterers to coordinate? Wallflowers to soothe?

"Great party, Mr. Wyatt," said a low feminine voice to his left.

Glancing down, he saw Beth Jennings, his HR manager.

"Thanks," he said, grateful to find someone he could relax around. Beth knew him well enough by now not to expect inane rambling. His eyes slid again to Sophie, whose hand was settled on Jeff's forearm, and his fist clenched around his plastic utensils.

It's your own fault, he told himself. The "friends" routine had been his idea.

He just hadn't expected her to embrace it quite so damn readily. She'd moved easily into the role of platonic, helpful friend and bidding assistant. It was annoying, really.

The only hint that there had ever been any tension between them happened in the office elevator on Monday. The elevator became more full than usual, and Sophie, in making room for more passengers, had become pressed against him. His body had tensed immediately at the brief contact, and from the hitch in her breath, he had a feeling she wasn't exactly immune either.

But the moment was over before he had a chance to smell her nearness, and in the moments that followed she'd chatted happily about a date she had planned for later that night. He'd told himself the knot in his stomach had everything to do with annoyance at her rambling, and nothing to do with jealousy.

His life was back to the way he wanted it.

No more stressing about saying the wrong thing, and no more constant worrying about what she thought of him.

"Earth to Mr. Wyatt," Beth was saying. "You got a little preoccupied with the beans there."

She nodded toward the pot of baked beans that he'd been stirring with angry stabbing motions. "Sorry," he said, dropping the spoon.

"Oh, it's no problem. I know you have a lot on your mind

trying to make a good impression on all of these employees after the legacy left by Mr. Brayburn. But I have to tell you, as much as we loved the man, he never put on anything like this. Major brownie points."

"It was all Sophie," he said truthfully. He'd agreed to the event and shown up, but he couldn't rightfully claim any part of its success.

"She's great, isn't she?" Beth said fondly, glancing over to where Jeff was now feeding Sophie a piece of pie. "You know, I never thought her and Jeff… well, I mean… I hadn't realized that they were so close until recently."

Gray grunted, willing Beth to talk about something else. Some*one* else.

"You know, I always thought… well… I guess you never can tell."

"You always thought what?" he asked sharply.

Her smile slipped slightly and she began to look nervous.

Great, Gray. Very smooth. He tried again. "What did you think?" he asked with a strained smile.

"Well," she said nervously, licking her lips and fiddling with her hamburger bun. "After the weird dynamic I saw between you and Sophie that first day, and the way you were always getting under each other's skin, well, I guess I maybe thought…"

"Yes?"

She let out a nervous laugh. "Oh, it's just a little gossip. But for those first few days, I thought that maybe you and Sophie had a… well, a *thing*. Crazy how misperceptions start, isn't it?"

"Yes. Crazy," he said quietly. "Ms. Jennings, if you'll excuse me, I really should be making my rounds."

"Of course," she said with a wave of her hand.

His plate full of food he didn't want, Gray searched around for somewhere to sit. The handful of picnic tables were half-full with chattering families and coworkers who knew each other. Despite his title, or perhaps *because* of it, he knew nobody beyond their name, face, and job description. He didn't know their hobbies, their children, or their favorite sports teams.

But he knew Sophie.

Although, he wasn't even sure he knew her anymore. In the past two weeks, she'd been her usual chatty self with him. Perhaps more so. But it felt superficial. He was now seeing the same Sophie that she presented to everyone else. She was still sarcastic, but nothing like the gutsy spitfire he'd met in the Las Vegas elevator and who'd gone toe to toe with a brand-new boss who'd openly disdained her.

He didn't like it.

He wanted the old Sophie back. The one who breathed fire but also lit *him* on fire. But he knew he couldn't have that.

Abandoning the idea of eating, much less finding somewhere to sit, he surreptitiously dumped his paper plate in the garbage. After he shook hands with a few more people he barely knew, he began making his way toward the activity tent.

Not because that was where Sophie and Jeff continued to laugh like an old married couple, he told himself. He merely wanted to determine if there were employees over there whom he hadn't greeted yet.

"Hey, guys," he said casually.

They broke off their conversation as he approached, and he pushed away the uncomfortable sensation that he was obviously an outsider in their party for two.

"Hey, boss," Jeff said with his usual easy nature. "Great party you've got here."

"It wasn't really my idea," he said honestly, his eyes settling briefly on Sophie, who was watching the festivities with a little smile on her face.

"Yeah, this has Sophie all over it," Jeff said with a laugh. "She totally saved my butt last week when I was trying to plan a wine-tasting party for my staff. Couldn't have done it without her."

Gray didn't miss the casual possessive note in Jeff's voice and stifled a surge of resentment and the urge to snarl that Sophie was *taken*.

Especially since Sophie wasn't *looking* at him. Gray couldn't even accuse her of giving him the cold shoulder, she just seemed...disinterested.

Which was exactly what he'd wanted.

"Gray!" called an out-of-breath voice. He tore his eyes away from Sophie's profile and looked to the source of the panting. Here was the stout Stan—now he remembered the man's name—of the athlete's foot, rushing toward him, Keri in tow. Gray stifled a groan.

"We just completed The Castle," Stan said, panting slightly from his speed-walk across the park. "You've gotta try this thing!"

"The Castle?" Gray asked blankly.

Keri gestured toward the huge blow-up jungle-gym monstrosity on the far edge of the park. "Over there. It's been the hit of the party. At first it was just the kids that were competing, but now the adults are going through. It's a race to see who can get through it first."

That sounded like...hell. Gray glanced toward Sophie with a raised eyebrow.

"The event coordinator highly recommended it," Sophie said with a shrug. "Apparently it's becoming quite the rage at corporate events, assuming employees don't mind a little physical activity."

What had happened to the days of cocktail parties? What was wrong with standing stationary and drinking a nice Scotch?

"That's great," Gray said awkwardly.

"Who won?" Jeff asked Stan and his wife.

Dammit. He should have asked that.

"I did," Keri said proudly as Stan pouted.

"It was my socks," Stan said defensively. "They're new, and therefore very slippery. I'd recommend taking your socks off before going through, Gray."

Gray didn't know which disturbed him more: the athlete's foot expert discussing going barefoot, or the fact that they apparently expected him to fumble his way through a blow-up tower in front of his entire company.

"Oh, I'm not really dressed for that," he said noncommittally.

Sophie snickered. "Yeah, I'm sure your jeans and polo shirt are really going to hold you back. It's not like you're wearing a suit."

He met her eyes. They both knew the only reason he wasn't wearing a suit was because she'd called him that morning with a stern lecture on looking approachable and "not looking like a stiff."

"Come on, Gray, the people will love it," Jeff said, taking a sip of his beer. "The oh-so-proper CEO scooting through a plastic tube on his belly? It'll be great for your reputation."

Gray narrowed his eyes looking for an underlying insult, but Jeff's face remained pleasant, and the sausage-making couple bobbed their heads in agreement. "I shouldn't," he said with sham regret. "I still have a ton of people to meet. But *you* should," he said to Jeff. "You're a vice president; it should have the same effect."

"He can't," Sophie said. "Jeff's got a bad ankle after his last tennis match."

"Oh, and whose fault is that?" Jeff asked teasingly.

She shrugged innocently. "It's not my fault you didn't listen to my warning about my killer backhand."

What the hell? They're playing tennis now? Together? She'd never asked *him* to play tennis. Friends did that kind of thing, right?

"I'll go if you go," he blurted out.

Four pairs of startled eyes glanced at him.

"Who are you talking to?" Jeff asked.

"Sophie," Gray said, daring her to meet his eyes. "Come on, the president against his assistant? It'll be great for company morale."

He'd chosen his words deliberately. She was all about company morale. She narrowed his eyes at him, and he could see her mind reeling with possible excuses.

Finally she nodded. "All right. You're on. But you should prepare yourself for a crushing loss. I'm extremely agile and flexible. It'll be no contest."

"I'm bigger. And taller."

"I'm scrappy."

"I lift weights."

"I play tennis," she snapped back.

"Okay, then!" Jeff said with a laugh. "Let's see this battle go down, shall we?"

And suddenly Gray felt the lightest he had in weeks. Sophie had let her fake cheerful mask down for the first time since The Talk, and it felt good to have her back, if only for a moment.

Just this one stupid activity, he told himself. Just this one last moment to draw out the real Sophie. Then it was back to professionalism and talks about the weather.

* * *

Kicking off her sandals, Sophie stared up at the beast called "The Castle." When she'd signed the contract to have the damn thing set up, she certainly hadn't pictured herself going through it. It was supposed to be for kids.

She watched as the two teens in front of her began climbing up the tubes that marked the entrance to the death trap. A crowd of spectators cheered and someone wearing a striped ref outfit held a stop watch.

Why had she agreed to this?

She studied The Castle more closely, trying to gauge what it was like inside. There were a couple parts of the maze with see-through nets, and from what she could tell, The Castle was basically a combination of slides, ropes, ramps, and awkward-looking ladders. Most of the obstacle course was hidden from view, but every now and then she could see the two agile teenagers laughingly struggling to keep their feet as they pushed each other aside in a race to get to the next tube.

"Are you sure this is meant for adults?" Sophie asked a Castle employee.

"Oh, definitely," said the pudgy worker, who looked like she couldn't fit through the small spaces of The Castle if someone paid her. "Usually it's the adults who end up hogging the whole thing after the kids have had their fun."

"Yeah, *fun*," Sophie muttered as she tucked her shirt into her shorts. Her cute yellow sweater set really wasn't meant to be tucked into anything, but she'd take the fashion faux pas in order to keep this party family-friendly. Last thing she needed was to give all of Brayburn Luxuries a glimpse at her less-than-toned belly.

Where the hell is Gray? she wondered as she looked around. *This was his damn idea and now he's nowhere to be found. Maybe he chickened out.*

Nope. There he was, laughing with Jeff as though the two were old long-lost friends. For a while there she'd thought that he might actually be jealous of Jeff, but obviously that had been her imagination. Or wishful thinking.

Because why would he be jealous if they were *just friends*?

It was better this way, she told herself for about the millionth time in the past month.

To be honest, he'd surprised her. She'd figured that his suggestion of being friends had merely been his polite way of saying *Get lost*, but to his credit, he did seem to be making an effort to actually be friendly. He'd invited her on a couple of morning coffee runs, rambled to her about sports (as though she would ever care), and even asked her advice on what to get Jack and Jenna for their birthday.

There was nothing romantic about it in the least. Nothing but buddy-buddy platonic chitchat. And that's what irked her the most. It would have been cleaner if he'd merely decided to blow her off completely. That way she could just give him the finger, quit, and move on with her life.

But the man was actually *trying*. He was stretching his stilted, introverted ways and trying to reach out. Granted, it wasn't in the way that she wished. And certainly not the way that her lady parts wished. But it was something.

The part of her that was a sucker for wounded creatures wouldn't let her turn her back on him while he was clearly trying for self-improvement. However, the man didn't look quite so wounded and needy at the moment as he laughed with Jeff and flirted with Rachel, the new receptionist.

She found herself scowling at him. How dare he volunteer them to bounce around like idiots inside of an inflatable death trap, and then look completely unfazed.

Catching his eye, she jerked her head at him, gesturing for him to get over here so they could get this over with. He raised an eyebrow at her, but began making his way toward her. The yells on the other side of The Castle indicated that the kids in front of them were making their way through the final obstacle.

"You ready for this, Dalton?" he asked.

"I can't believe I agreed to this," Sophie muttered.

"Scared of losing?" The man looked downright giddy.

She scoffed. "We both know this is ridiculous. We're going to look like fools, but I suppose it will be good for your people to see you when you're down."

Gray's eyes followed her movements as she reached behind herself and pulled her foot back toward her butt, unconsciously moving into a pre-run routine.

"Are you *stretching*?"

Blushing, she dropped her foot. "No. Maybe. Gotta stay agile, you know?"

He rolled his eyes as The Castle employee headed toward them.

"You guys ready?" she asked.

"No," Sophie grumbled.

But Gray gave a nod and kicked off his shoes, practically grinning as they stepped up to the starting line. Who would have thought that an inflatable toy and a bit of competition were all it took to coax a full smile from the man?

Word had apparently gotten out that the CEO and his assistant had lost their minds, because the crowd of people had doubled, and the whoops of encouragement and laughter grew deafening.

"You'd think they were watching gladiators," he said.

"I'd be the gladiator," Sophie replied. "*You'd* be whatever weakling they throw in there, who gets mutilated."

"That's not very *friendly*, now is it?"

"On the contrary," she said. "It's quite friendly. See, if we were *more* than friends, I might let you win for your delicate pride and all, and because I wouldn't want to deal with you sulking over dinner. But since we're *just friends*... well, then I don't have to see you over dinner, now, do I? Therefore... I'll happily beat you."

She didn't even know what she was talking about. Where had this case of verbal diarrhea come from? Gray looked at her with a thoughtful expression on his face, but didn't respond.

"Okay, guys, are you ready to RUMBLE?" hollered the way-too-enthusiastic Castle referee.

"On your mark..."

Shit.

"...Get set..."

Dammit.

"GO!"

A whoop of laugher escaped Sophie as she and Gray rushed forward, pushing each other out of the way in order to be the first one up the tube.

"Hey!" Gray said, as she jabbed her elbow into his side. "You fight dirty."

"Pussy!" she mumbled back, all thoughts of keeping this affair family-friendly forgotten.

Thanks to her pointy elbows and sharp fingernails, she managed to get to the tube first, giggling as she squeezed her way through the tight opening. It was more yielding than it looked, but it still required an awful lot of wiggling.

"Nice view," she heard Gray mutter from close behind her as he followed her through the narrow opening.

"Enjoy the angle while you can," she said back. "It's the last time you'll get this close."

She yelped as a palm smacked her behind, just as she made her way into the next chamber.

"You spanked me," she sputtered as she found herself in a pit of plastic balls that went up past her waist.

"No, no," he said, looking around for the passageway out of the chamber. "I was just helping your hips fit through that narrow opening."

She let out a little growl as she struggled to push through the sea of plastic balls, wading toward some sort of shaky-looking ramp. "Hey, no fair!" she exclaimed. "You're taller, so you can reach higher."

"Just like it was way easier for you to wiggle through that last tube because you're smaller. Well, except for your hips."

"My hips are fine," she said, self-consciously touching the offending body part.

"Yes, they are," he said matter-of-factly as he hoisted himself up the ramp using the strategically placed handles. He'd already shimmied up the squishy slope by the time she'd pulled herself to the base of the ramp.

"See you at the end," he hollered as he moved out of sight.

Snarling obscenities at him, she struggled to reach the lowest handle, wondering how children had managed this thing. Then again, kids were like monkeys. Twenty-eight-year-old women? Not so much.

Grateful that this particular part of the challenge was out of sight of spectators, she tried unsuccessfully to levy herself up to the next platform before she slid down again and again into the plastic balls.

She finally managed to get a decent grasp on two of the handles, and was debating where to make her next grab when she saw a hand extend in front of her face. Glancing up, she saw Gray's laughing eyes stare down at her.

"Need some help?" he asked casually.

"No," she said primly, conscious that her face was red and sweaty and that her arms were beginning to shake from the effort of supporting all of her weight.

"Come on, Soph," he said, wiggling his fingers at her. "I won't tell anyone."

Sophie knew she had plenty of faults, but pride had never been one of them. When faced with the choice of dealing with a gloating man or languishing among plastic balls, she'd tolerate the testosterone overload. Grasping his arm, she allowed him to pull her up. When she lay gasping at the top of the platform, she paused a moment to catch her breath. "Do you think that's that hard for everyone?" she asked him.

"No," he said simply. "Guess you shoulda stretched your arms in addition to your quads, huh?"

She punched his shoulder. "You're not supposed to help me, you know."

"Yeah, well, it was either that or listen to you bitch in the office on Monday, so I was really doing the company a favor."

"This is ridiculous," she said as they began crawling on their hands and knees through a tunnel toward the next horrible challenge. Suddenly the roar of the crowd got louder and she realized that they were in the part of a tunnel that was visible to those watching. Fixing a smile on her face, she grinned and pretended to flex her muscles, while horribly self-conscious of how foolish she must look.

"Somebody get the tissues ready," Gray called to his laughing employees. "Sophie's going to need someone to comfort her when she loses!"

"Oh, so you're making jokes now," she muttered, as they cleared the tunnel and found themselves in a chamber surrounded by nets.

"I just wanted to give Jeff a man-to-man heads-up that he'll have a chance to cheer you up when you emerge a sulky loser."

"I'm not sulky. And I'm not going to lose. And why would Jeff care?"

"Oh, come on," he said. "You're going to tell me you two aren't dating?"

"I don't have to answer that," she said stiffly. "But…no, I'm not dating Jeff."

"Well, he's interested," Gray muttered as he began testing the nets for support.

Sophie had suspected as much herself, but wasn't about to admit it to her boss. "I'm not so sure I like this chatty Gray. I think I liked you better in Vegas when you were all hostile. You weren't so annoying."

"I think you like me annoying," he said with a wink before he began to climb up the side of the wall. "It ensures we have more in common."

Rolling her eyes, Sophie followed him, finding this particular hurdle much easier than the previous. In fact, her lighter weight made it easier for her than it was for Gray, since there wasn't as much pull on the net. Neither of them spoke as they concentrated on getting to the top.

"How long is this thing?" Gray muttered as he joined her at the top of the platform. "I thought it was like a minute-long adventure."

"Are you kidding? It took the kids before us almost ten minutes, and they're a hell of a lot more limber than we are."

"Speak for yourself."

"Oh, come on. You're hardly Tarzan."

"Me, Tarzan. You, Jane."

"This new side of you is giving me a headache," she said, even as she found herself smiling.

Oh hell, she thought as she looked down at the winding slide in front of her. "They want us to go down that? Onto what?"

"I'm guessing they're not going to have us land on cement," Gray said.

"Still, what if I land funnily on my hand? The stitches are out and it's healed," she said as she hesitantly settled into a sitting position, "but what if—HEY!"

Gray planted a palm against her back and gave her a shove. With a squeal she went sliding into darkness before landing indelicately on what seemed to be a very bouncy mattress-like trampoline.

"Look out," Gray called from the top of the slide, and she rolled to the side so she didn't get crushed.

"Shit," he muttered as he landed with a grunt. "I think you

might have been right. This was not my best idea," he said as they lay on their backs, trying to catch their breath.

Sophie couldn't help it. She started giggling. After all that they'd been through, who'd have thought it would come to this? Both of them panting, slightly sweaty, and completely defeated by a pile of plastic, nylon, and nets. Turning his head to look at her, he smiled back, and then he too was laughing.

"Nobody can see us here, right?" he asked.

"Nah, I think they designed this as a reprieve. It lets the oldies like us catch our breath without prying eyes."

"Good," he said firmly.

And then he rolled toward her, and before she knew what was happening, Sophie found herself pinned between the padded floor and a hard male body. His mouth took hers with such fierce possession she gasped from the shock of it.

Unlike the kiss in the office, which had been a slow and deliberate exploration, this kiss felt like a brand. The insistent pressure of his lips against hers and the slick rhythm of his tongue left her brain no room to wonder or consider or analyze. There was nothing to do but feel.

He used his arms to brace himself above her, but wanting to feel more of him, she slid her hands around his shoulders and tugged, urging him to put all of his weight on her.

Gray complied and they both groaned at the contact. She didn't know how long they stayed there, her arms locked around his neck, and his hands framing her face as they learned each other's taste, their heads tilting this way and that without their lips ever breaking contact.

She felt his him grow hard against her thigh, and she rubbed herself against him. He swore and nipped her neck with his teeth. Dimly, Sophie became aware of the laughter outside dying out, and worried questions from the outside began to pierce her passion-drugged consciousness.

"What happened to them in there?"

"Are they stuck?"

"Should we send someone in after them?"

Turning her head to the side slightly, she pushed her hands against Gray's shoulders. "Gray," she said, her voice sounding husky.

"Mmm," he said as his lips roamed over her face.

"We have to get moving. They're going to send someone in after us. They think we're stuck."

Slowly he pulled back from her, and for the briefest moment she saw some new expression in his eyes that she hadn't seen before. Something that went beyond desire or amusement. But it was gone before she could identify it, and she saw the moment reality slammed back into him and his eyes retained their usual cool, overcast expression.

With a fluid movement, he pushed to his feet, pulling her with him. "This way," he said roughly, pulling her toward the next, and hopefully final, tunnel.

"Okay, so I guess we're not going to talk about that," she said in an attempt at lightness.

He didn't respond, and merely shoved her up onto the next platform before pulling himself up beside her.

"Last stretch, Dalton. You ready to lose?"

"Oh, you're on, Mr. Wyatt."

And with that, they both broke into a run, pushing their way through a net room filled with foam tubes hanging from the ceiling. He had the advantage of strength, but her smaller size allowed her to more easily navigate the small spaces. They pushed and pulled at each other in an attempt to get ahead as the laughing crowds cheered them on.

"All right, Sophie!" she heard Jeff call. "That's my girl!"

Gray paused momentarily, giving Sophie just the last bit of advantage she needed to dive toward the exit tube ahead of him.

She felt his hand grasp around her ankle and let out a girlish squeal as she tried to kick free. He held firm, and despite her squirming, he managed to get even with her as they each tried to push the other aside long enough to squeeze through the one last tube.

"You should let me win," she gasped. "People will like you more."

"When have I ever cared if people like me?" he muttered back, his own breath sounding a bit short.

She bit his forearm.

"What the hell!"

"Whoops. Instinct took over," she said.

"Exactly what instinct is that, bobcat?"

He nudged her to the side, and she lost her advantage as the tubes fell back into place, blocking the exit.

"Argh, just let me through!" she exclaimed laughingly.

"Earn it."

She went to nip him again, but he grabbed her disheveled ponytail and held her teeth away from his body.

"Christ, Sophie," he said with a laugh. "I think you might be my..."

He broke off, and then shook his head as if to clear his brain.

"I might be your what," she goaded. "Nemesis? Thorn in your side? Your demon?"

His lips quirked slightly and he laid his mouth against her ear in the pretense of pushing past her. "I think you might be *mine*," he whispered.

And just like that, her world faded away. She forgot about the fact that she looked like she'd lived through a hurricane, forgot that there were a hundred people waiting for her to squeeze through an inflatable tube, and forgot that this man had once been everything she'd hated in the world.

Her shock paralyzed her, and his gray eyes glowed down at her before he gave her suddenly limp body a gentle shove, and with some kind of ridiculous war cry, he went diving through the tunnel ahead of her.

The crowd erupted in applause, and pulling herself together, she followed him through, careful not to let her now-damp sweater set ride up. She emerged to a crowd of people patting Gray on the back, and Jeff was there to pull her to her feet.

"Good show, Sophie," Jeff said with a warm smile. "I thought you guys had died in there."

"It was touch and go, believe me," she said, as she was surrounded by her rowdy coworkers.

Stan Michaelson had fashioned a makeshift gold medal and was trying to place it around Gray's neck, and her boss grinned almost boyishly as everyone clapped him on the back and demanded to hear about his technique.

Sophie smiled and laughed, and joined in with the chatter, but inside she was shaking at what had just happened. She willed Gray to look at her, just once so she could confirm that she hadn't misheard him. That the kiss hadn't been a dream.

But he was uncharacteristically hamming up his victory for his audience, and seemed to have forgotten that she existed.

Jeff slung an arm around her shoulders as he led her away from the crowd. "What time do you think this party's wrapping up?"

Sophie glanced at her watch. “Oh! Crap! Any minute. I have to go talk with the coordinators. We only have this picnic area reserved until six o’clock.”

She started to dash off, but Jeff grabbed her arm.

“Have dinner with me?” he asked.

“Oh, um...” Sophie glanced up into Jeff’s classically handsome face. She’d always liked him, and the old Sophie might have even had something of a crush. But now he seemed so...bland.

“Come on, Soph, it’s not a marriage proposal. Just food,” he teased.

“Sorry, Jeff. She already has plans.”

Jeff and Sophie both spun around to see Gray standing a few feet away. She raised a challenging eyebrow at him, but didn’t break eye contact. What game was he playing now?

“Oh. Sure, sorry, boss,” Jeff said in obvious puzzlement.

“It was, um, part of our bet,” she said nervously to Jeff, hoping to avoid any awkward explanations. “I said I’d buy Mr. Wyatt dinner if he won.”

“That’s not why we’re having dinner,” Gray said, walking toward them.

“Okay, okay,” Jeff said raising his hands in bemused surrender. “I’ll let you guys work out whatever you need to. See you Monday.”

“Jeff...I...” Sophie said awkwardly, as he began to walk away. Jeff waved a hand at her as though dismissing the entire episode.

“Don’t worry about it, babe.” He winked and then spotted the cute receptionist. “Yo, Rachel! Wait up!”

“Hmm, he moves fast,” Gray said blandly.

“What was that about?” she hissed at the gloating man beside her.

"Let's go, I'm starving."

Her jaw dropped. "Just like that? And what do you mean, you're starving? I had Seattle's best caterers here. Didn't you eat?"

"I don't want that stuff, I want my cooking," he said as he began storming toward the parking lot.

"Snob," she said. But she found herself trailing after him, trying to figure out whether this was a continuation of their manufactured "friendship," or a follow-up to the kiss.

Hell, maybe it was just a caveman routine. He didn't want her, but didn't want Jeff to have her either. His whispered words echoed through her mind again, and she nearly stumbled at the memory.

I think you're mine.

She skidded to a halt as reality sunk in. "I need to go make sure clean up is under control."

He turned around. "So make a phone call."

She narrowed her eyes.

He narrowed his right back. A challenge.

"Okay, I'll go with you, but I'm not helping you cook," she said.

"As if I'd let you anywhere near a knife."

"Is this like a...friends' dinner?"

He signed and moved toward her. Leaning down, he stamped an impatient kiss on her lips. Pulled back. Did it again, lingering this time. Well, that answered that question.

Friends didn't kiss like that.

"Okay?" he asked impatiently.

"Okay," she said quietly.

"Excellent. Now let's get going. I want to stop and get a first-aid kit on the way."

CHAPTER SIXTEEN

"I can't believe you made me eat so much," Sophie groaned as she curled up on Gray's couch, pulling her bare feet beneath her.

"*I* can't believe you made me start a fire," he replied.

Sophie snorted. "By 'start a fire,' I suppose you mean flipping a switch and letting the gas flames roar to life?"

"Still, it's May. You're wearing shorts and sandals. A fire feels incongruous."

"It's *cozy*," she corrected as she accepted the glass of dessert wine he handed her, loving the casual way he let his fingers brush hers as though they'd done this a thousand times before. As though they hadn't spent the past months either ignoring each other or clawing at each other's throats or tearing out each other's hearts.

He settled on the couch next to her, not quite touching, but close enough for her to feel his body warmth. Sophie longed to lean against him, but as much progress as they'd made today, she wasn't sure he was ready for companionable contact.

She'd never seen Gray like this. He was easy, comfortable. Perhaps not quite chatty, but he'd lost that wary, nervous look he'd always worn like a suit of armor.

Was this a date?

As with their first disastrous dinner, the food had been fabulous. He claimed that he would just "whip something up," which, in the Wyatt home, apparently equated to veal carpaccio, beet and arugula salad, and some sort of delicate fish in a delicious vanilla-saffron sauce.

Sophie had been the one to keep the conversation light and easy, as was her expertise, but he'd more than held his own, even opening up about his hopes of improving his relationships with Jack and Jenna. They both stared quietly into the fire for a moment, and for the first time in longer than she could remember, Sophie felt content.

There was nobody she had to impress or comfort or appease. She could just *be*.

She realized it had always been that way with Gray. At first, she hadn't bothered trying to impress him because the effort would be futile. He'd seemed determined to dislike her.

But then she'd quit trying to impress him for a different reason. Somewhere between typing up his reports and bowling with his family, Sophie realized that Gray didn't *want* her to put on a show. In fact, the times when he seemed to withdraw the most were when she was at her most cute. The more she sparkled and charmed, the more sullen he'd gotten.

Gray had always seemed to want to see the *real* her. And somewhere along the line, she'd begun to let him.

She rotated her body slightly, and, resting her cheek

against the back of the couch, she stared up at him. He glanced at her briefly, but turned away just as quickly.

"What now?" he asked. But his tone was without rancor or annoyance, and she smiled. When had his abrupt irritability started to make her grin like a fool?

"Tell me about Jessica," she said, the words coming out in a rush. It was a risk, and she mentally crossed her fingers that he wouldn't shut down.

He didn't respond for several moments, and she panicked, realizing she'd pushed him too far and too fast. But Gray was full of surprises tonight, and although he wouldn't look at her, he finally spoke.

"You mean Ashley and Jenna haven't spilled the whole sad story?"

"No. They alluded to it being a *Titanic*-type situation, but both insisted that it wasn't their story to tell."

"It's not really something I talk about."

"Okay," she said, not wanting to scare him off. "I didn't mean to pry, it's just so strange to think of you..."

He gave a sad smile. "Of course you mean to pry. And what, is it hard for you to imagine me on one knee pouring my heart out?"

A mental image flashed through Sophie's mind, and she felt sucker punched. She *could* imagine it. Suddenly she longed for it. But it wasn't Jessica that she pictured. It was herself. Smiling down at Gray. *He* wouldn't be smiling, of course, but his eyes would be...loving.

She shook her head slightly to block out the painfully impossible image. *Too fast, Sophie. The man is just now beginning to speak in full sentences. Let's not rush him to the altar.*

Taking a steadying breath, she smiled easily at him. "I

just can't picture a loner like yourself as the marrying kind," she said teasingly.

Liar, her heart said.

"Yeah, neither could Jessica," he said without expression.

"Tell me about her."

"No."

"Gray."

"Sophie."

"Did we not fight our way through a pile of plastic balls today? Did we not shimmy up a net like a couple of chimps?" *Did you not kiss my brains out and tell me I was yours?* she added silently.

His lips twitched. "That was different."

"True, it was. Different in that there were about a billion people that could have seen and overheard. Here it's just the two of us. Nobody but me, wanting to know about you."

Take a chance on me.

He glanced at her briefly, then looked away. Glanced back again. "It's not a good story, Sophie."

"Breakups rarely are. C'mon, spill. I'll tell you about all of my ex-boyfriends."

"I don't want to hear about ex-boyfriends."

"Jealous?" she teased.

He didn't respond, but she saw a little tic in his jaw.

Sophie sighed. "Okay, fine. We won't talk about your precious Jessica. I'll just ask your brother. Jack's much more forthcoming. And friendly. And—"

"She left me," he said sharply, staring down at his wineglass. "She'd been sleeping with a partner of mine for months. Someone I considered a friend. He got drunk at our engagement party and announced to two hundred people that he'd been fucking the bride-to-be."

"My God," Sophie said. She'd sort of suspected cheating, but not a public spectacle of it. "Did she try to deny it?"

Gray snorted. "Nope. Didn't even blink in guilt. Just told me that I should have seen it coming. That someone like her couldn't be expected to be satisfied by a mannequin. I think there was something in there about me not having a heart worth caring about."

Sophie gasped, both at the cruel words and the carefully removed tone with which he said them. She felt waves of guilt. Hadn't she been guilty of thinking the same thing about him since day one? She wondered how many of her careless observations about his lack of emotion must have reminded him of Jessica's words.

"Gray," she said, laying a hand on his arm.

He surprised her by turning his hand up to grasp hers, his thumb rubbing her knuckles as he looked down at their clasped hands.

"Don't try to put a Band-Aid on this one, Sophie. Let it be."

She swallowed, her heart hurting at his ragged expression and what it meant.

"You loved her," she said with surprise.

She'd assumed that whatever he'd had with Jessica must have been a sterile, businesslike arrangement. A mutually beneficial convenience.

But the raw expression on his face said otherwise.

"I thought I did," he said in answer to her question. "It felt something like that. She was friendly and pretty, and everyone liked her. She could make me laugh."

"Like me," she said, as he confirmed what she'd suspected. His initial dislike of her hadn't just been because of her hooker boots. Everything about her had been like salt on his most painful wound.

"Are you calling yourself pretty?" he teased.

She smiled back. "Aren't I?"

His eyes roamed over her face, warming every spot they touched. "You're beautiful."

She clucked her tongue. "Well played, Mr. Wyatt. Bet you've been practicing that delivery in the mirror—"

And then he kissed her. *Really* kissed her.

Not a kiss out of anger or frustration or an attempt to prove something. He was kissing her because he wanted to. And she was kissing him right back.

He set both of their wineglasses on the table, but before he could reach for her again, she'd launched herself at him, straddling his lap.

"I should have known it would only be a matter of time before you tried to take control," he said.

"*Tried* to take control?" she asked. She ground her hips slightly against the bulge in his jeans. "Feels to me like I *am* in control."

"Oh yeah?" He leaned forward and nipped at the tip of her breast. Even though it was through the layers of her shirt and bra, she gasped.

"Are you sure we should do this?" she asked breathlessly.

"No. I'm never sure of anything with you."

They stared at each other, both aware that they were on a ledge from which there was no turning back. She willed him to make the first move. Without breaking eye contact, he slid his hand behind her neck, then his fingers tangled roughly in her hair. He pulled her close but didn't kiss her again. He seemed to be waiting for her permission.

Lost in the storm of his eyes, she felt herself leaning forward slightly, her lips parting.

He needed no further invitation. His arm slid around her lower back, pulling her toward him as his other hand tugged her face roughly down to his. If the kiss in the park today had been *unexpectedly* steamy, she went into this kiss fully expecting the rush. And it delivered.

Gray may have initiated the kiss, but Sophie took it over, rubbing her body against his in blatant want, even as she kept her mouth light and teasing. She wouldn't let him take the kiss as deep as he wanted, and she loved the growing tension in his body. Finally he simply clamped his hands on her hips and held her against him, allowing her full reign over him. She tasted everything she could reach.

The kiss was every bit as hot as the one earlier in The Castle, but this one had an extra layer of emotion. Somewhere under the burning haze of sexual desire she felt the pull of something else.

This kiss wasn't just about this moment. It held the promise of something more. Much more.

Pushing the thought out of her mind, she bit his bottom lip. Gray growled, and had apparently reached his limit in allowing control to someone else because he pulled back and took over. Suddenly, she was her back on his leather couch, staring up into eyes that had gone nearly black. His hands slid to her waist and held her still.

They were both breathing heavily, and she tried to resist the urge to say something witty. It wasn't exactly a moment for talking, but she saw the same confused emotion in his eyes that she was feeling, and she longed to say something to lighten the mood.

They weren't ready for this kind of intensity. She opened her mouth to make a joke, but Gray set two fingers over it, brushing her lips softly. He tore his gaze away from her face, and his eyes roamed over her body, leaving a trail of fire everywhere he looked.

Touch me, she thought.

As if hearing her plea, his hand slowly began stroking along her side, his fingertips just barely brushing the undersides of her breasts before they swept idly back down to her waist. She let her hands do some exploring of their own, learning the shape of his shoulders and the slope of his chest. He'd changed into a casual white button-down when they'd gotten back to his house, and her fingers toyed with the buttons, searching his eyes for any indication that he was going to back out.

Then his hands slid back up over her breasts and squeezed softly. Nope, he definitely didn't want to stop. She closed her eyes and arched her back as his thumbs began brushing against the tight peaks of her breasts. Sophie wanted his mouth *there*, but he continued toying with her, alternating with playful tweaks and slow caresses.

Her fingers resumed their mission of unbuttoning his shirt, loving each inch of skin she revealed. She raked her nails slightly down his chest and he sucked in a breath before pulling her into a sitting position. All pretense of patience gone, she tore at his shirt as he tugged awkwardly at her cardigan.

When he roughly pulled her shirt over her head, he groaned at the sight of her in a bra and jeans. She wasn't exactly wearing her sexiest lingerie, but luckily she'd skipped the ugly nude-colored bargain bra this morning and had settled on a very respectable baby-blue demi-cup.

He looked at her nearly exposed breasts as though he wanted to devour her. She *wanted* him to devour her. Instead he merely ran one finger along the top slope of her right breast.

"Pretty," he whispered.

Sophie wasn't sure what caused her to melt more, the feel of his lips pressing soft kisses all over her exposed chest or the whispered compliments. When he reached behind her to unhook her bra she could do little more than sigh his name.

His mouth wrapped around her nipple as his hand slid down her stomach to the button of her jeans. For a man so restrained in other areas of his life, he was surprisingly aggressive in this one. He knew just went to suck, when to lightly lick, when to tease, and when to gently rake his teeth over the sensitive tip. Sophie barely registered her jeans being removed, but she suddenly became very aware of the warm hand sliding into her panties.

Sophie responded with a hoarse gasp, and she felt his victorious smile against her breast, but she couldn't begin to think of something smart to say to put him in his place. Right now she was all his. She had no idea whether a few seconds or an eternity had passed, but when she felt herself reaching the brink, she frantically clutched at his shoulders.

"Gray, no. Not like this. I'm going to—"

But it was too late. Her body was too far gone, and she went over the edge of ecstasy, her body rocking in silent shudders. When it was over, he gently peeled her panties down her legs and tossed them aside before smiling gently down into her flushed face.

She struggled not to blush. Hell, she struggled not to pass out. She would have bet money that she couldn't take any more of his touch, but then his hand slid over the inside of her thigh and she reconsidered.

This gritty sex maniac was nothing like the restrained businessman she knew so well. Gray pulled her to her feet and swept her into her arms like some sort of damn romantic hero.

"This is nuts," she muttered against his neck. "Definitely don't want to know what the employee handbook says about this."

"We are *not* going to think about that now," he said with a groan, shouldering open his bedroom door.

She was thrown rather unceremoniously onto his bed, and before she could catch her breath, he was on top of her, struggling out of his own jeans.

"Sophie," he muttered, kissing her neck with hot open-mouthed kisses.

"Mmm?"

"This is going to be fast. I'm not...it's just...it's been a long time."

It shouldn't be the type of thing a woman wanted to hear in bed, but she couldn't help a small smile at the admission.

Good, she thought. She didn't want to be the most recent in a long line of bed partners. And then she stopped thinking altogether as he roughly pushed her thighs apart and pushed inside her with one firm stroke. She gasped at the wonderful invasion, instinctively lifting her hips, struggling to accept him completely. He began to move in steady, methodical strokes as she met his fierce rhythm.

His hands held her hips in a possessive grasp, and she remembered his words at the park. Mine.

Mine.

She sensed he was close, and urged him to go faster, wanting him to experience the same ecstasy she had minutes before. Sophie was so focused on enhancing his pleasure that she was caught by surprise when she felt his fingers at her center again, circling in the perfect rhythm to his strokes.

She arched her back even higher and cried his name. He buried his face in her neck and she felt him gasp against her as they reached the peak together, shuddering and clinging to each other in confused wonder.

When they'd finally caught their breath, he rolled to his side and brushed her hair out of her face. She turned her head to look at him, feeling strangely shy.

"What now?" she asked.

"Are you asking me what happens Monday?" he asked warily.

"Well, it's a valid question. I mean, I did just shag my boss."

"Correction. Your boss shagged *you*."

Sophie narrowed her eyes at him. "I should have known it would be this way with you."

"What way?" he asked innocently.

"Argumentative."

"Honey, arguing is the last thing I want to do with you right now," he said as his hand slid over her side.

Honey. The word made her feel squishy inside.

"All right, then," she said with a catlike smile. "No arguing."

But there were other ways to get on top. She rolled over him until she straddled his hips and had his hands pinned above his head. Gray eyes sparkled up at her, and for a moment her playful mood faltered at the warmth she saw there.

Look how far we've come, she thought.

He apparently misread her, because he started to tense and pull back.

"God, Sophie, you're right, we really shouldn't be doing this."

Shaking her head, she put her hand over his mouth. They'd have to deal with it eventually, but not yet.

"Just one night," she said quietly.

Gray nodded slowly, before pulling her face down to his. "One night," he agreed.

And they made it one hell of a good night. She lost count of the number of ways they loved each other.

It wasn't until Sophie slowly drifted off to sleep in the early morning that she realized the noise in the back of her mind wasn't *just* a postsex hum.

It was a warning bell.

Chapter Seventeen

Sophie rolled over the next morning in a foreign bed and was dismayed to see the sun streaming in the window. She groaned. So much for leaving in the early morning hours. Sneaking out of a man's bedroom at five in the morning had never been a particular forte of Sophie's. She hated early mornings in general. It usually took a bullhorn and an electric prod to get her moving in time for work.

And that was assuming she was in her own house with her own coffeepot, her yellow fuzzy robe, and the *Mamma Mia!* soundtrack.

She squinted at the empty bedroom, not at all surprised that she didn't see Gray. No doubt he'd already ran a half marathon, baked a baguette, churned his own butter, and acquired six new companies before she'd even taken her first morning pee.

Sophie pulled herself out of bed, wishing for something to tie back the hair that she knew was in a tangle of curls. She'd found that while men *thought* they had a thing for bedhead, what actually turned them on was hair that had been styled to *look* like bedhead.

The real thing? Not so good.

The clothes situation was even trickier since she seemed to remember that hers were last seen scattered around his living room. And there was just no way in hell she was about to go prancing around his house naked.

Not for any man, and certainly not for her boss.

Oh God, I've slept with my boss. This sort of thing really was not supposed to happen outside of tawdry romance novels and old movies.

She should be ashamed. She'd just taken one huge step back for womankind.

But right now she wasn't thinking of herself as part of the general women's movement, or as some sort of trashy stereotype. She was thinking like a woman who'd just slept with the man she loved. Sophie plowed her fingers through her hair and tugged at the tangled curls.

I'm in love with Gray.

She wasn't sure why the realization was such a shock. She shouldn't have been surprised. It was merely the latest in a string of really, really bad choices. But it didn't have to be a disaster. She just couldn't let him find out.

Not that he'd be able to pick up on it. At least if she had to fall in love with the wrong guy, she'd picked one with absolutely zero people-reading skills.

Sophie stood abruptly and went to his closet, pulling on the first shirt she saw. It smelled vaguely like him, and she hated herself for sniffing it.

"That's an interesting look."

Sophie closed her eyes briefly at the sound of his voice, and finished buttoning his shirt. She'd never understood how in the movies, a man's shirt fell to midthigh of the heroine after a night of bumping uglies. All of those actresses must be midgets, because a standard men's shirt on Sophie barely covered her ass.

You can do this, she told herself with a deep breath.

She braced herself for a disapproving and closed-off grump. Instead, she saw that he looked relaxed and maybe even a little bit happy. If she'd fallen for grumpy Gray, she could *really* lose her heart over this sweeter version.

"Morning," she muttered, tugging at the hem of his shirt and tucking a crazy curl behind her ear. "I, um...left my clothes downstairs, so..."

He gestured to the dresser, where her clothes lay in a perfect pile. Of course.

Sophie blanched. "You folded my thong?"

"At least I didn't iron it," he said, handing her one of the coffee mugs in his hand, which she accepted gratefully.

"Thanks. I'll be out of your way just as soon as this caffeine kicks in. Mornings aren't really my thing."

"I know," he replied, mouth hitching up in his trademark half smile. "I've seen your morning self, remember?"

"Like I could forget. I *work* for you."

Gray winced, and she regretted the sharpness of her tone, if not the words. It had to be addressed, for both their sakes. He couldn't like the stigma of sleeping with his subordinate any more than she enjoyed the skeeviness of having sex with the person who determined her salary.

It was almost disturbingly ironic—she was far closer to prostitution now than she'd ever been in her slutty Vegas boots.

"Why do you do that?" he asked quietly.

"It can't just go left unsaid. What happens tomorrow? Do

we pretend this didn't happen? Do I ride you on your desk and dare anyone to question the CEO's personal choices in mistresses?"

"Stop it."

She took a sip of coffee and stayed quiet, but inside she was seething. It was easy for him to ignore the issue away. He had a six-figure salary and everyone's unwavering respect. He could bang a transsexual pole dancer, and people would just quietly murmur that he deserved his privacy.

But not someone like her—if news like this got out, she would be *that girl*. The one who was sleeping with her boss to get ahead. The cocktail-waitress-turned-secretary who'd seduced the CEO. The slut.

"Sorry," she said finally. "I think it's better if I just go."

He nodded slowly, and she stifled the wave of hurt that he'd agreed so readily. She handed him the coffee mug and grabbed her pile of clothes.

"May I use your bathroom?" The idea of putting on dirty underwear didn't exactly appeal, but she could hardly go skipping back to her apartment wearing nothing but a man's business shirt. She also wasn't sure how she was going to get her car, which she'd left at the park. But she wasn't about to ask him for a ride. She'd have to spend the upcoming week's Starbucks money on a cab.

More reason to be mad at Gray. He was depriving her of skinny vanilla lattes *and* her self-respect.

Ten minutes later, she'd done the best she could with the wrinkled clothes and raccoon eyes and ventured quietly into his kitchen. Her inner five-year-old wanted to make a dash for the front door, but that would only make Monday morning more awkward, so she opted for a quick and painless farewell.

She should be used to the sight of Gray behind the stove by now, but seeing him cook some sort of elaborate-looking egg dish had her shaking her head. Really, how was a rich and handsome chef not married by now?

Sophie cleared her throat in the doorway, feeling more awkward in front of him this morning than she had in that elevator months ago. "I left your shirt on the bed. I figured you'd probably want to dry-clean it or something."

He lifted an eyebrow. "Didn't you wear it for less than two minutes?

"Well, yeah, but...it probably smells like girl."

"There are worse things." His gray eyes crinkled slowly around the corners and it was almost enough to have her falling into his arms and begging him to love her just a little bit.

"Well, I'll be going, then," she said with a smile she didn't feel, jerking her thumb toward the front door, feeling like a fool. Like he didn't know where the exit was.

His face went flat again. "At least have some eggs. I've made enough for two."

Whatever he was making smelled amazing, but she couldn't handle sitting next to him, sharing a meal as though they were in a relationship of some kind. This had been a mistake, pure and simple. The sooner they ended it, the better they'd both feel.

"You don't have to do that, Gray. I appreciate the gentlemanly approach this morning. Most guys would have made up some excuse about having their mother stop by to get me out of the house, but we both know that last night was..."

Wonderful, intense, the best sex of my life.

"A mistake," she finished.

He ignored her and slid the omelets onto two plates before carrying them to his dining table. They'd always eaten at the island before. The kitchen table seemed far too intimate.

"Come sit," he said, already digging into his food. "It's getting cold."

Sophie chewed her lip and glanced toward the front door. Maybe just a few bites. Just so that she could explain to him that this could never happen again and that he couldn't tell a soul. She dropped into the chair across from him and watched him. He was eating his mushrooms and eggs very precisely, as though completely unaware that he had company.

"You eat your omelet with a knife?" she asked.

"It's called Continental style. Europeans do it."

"Which would totally make sense. If you were European." Sophie dug into the decadent-looking breakfast, ignoring the knife like a normal American.

"So what do you want to do today?" he asked casually.

Sophie's fork clattered to her plate. "Don't do that."

He finally set his silverware aside and looked at her. "I want you to stay."

"Why?" she asked, genuinely puzzled.

"I want to spend time with you."

"Since when?"

"Since—just, I don't know. Please?"

Somehow his sulky, frowning expression was infinitely more effective than puppy-dog-style begging or standard-issue flattery. She knew instinctively that he didn't *want* to want her to say. That he was just as annoyed by this connection between them as she was, but every bit as reluctant to let it end.

"If I stay, are we going to talk about us?" she said around a succulent mushroom.

"What do you think?"

"Right. You're not so much about the talking. But we can't just ignore it."

He sighed and resumed eating like some damn Regency duke. She decided to wait him out, and several minutes passed as they ate in silence.

"I don't know how to explain anything," he replied finally, sounding a little lost. "I don't really know what I want, or what's going to happen on Monday. I just want..." His eyes met hers, and she melted at the bewildered longing in them.

"Yes?" she prodded quietly.

"I'm tired of being alone every weekend," he said, eyes locked on a mushroom.

She swallowed against the sudden rush of emotion, and slowly the intention of running away faded. She knew that by not leaving immediately, she was signing herself up for the most intense heartbreak of her life, but she couldn't walk away. Not now.

"Okay," she said quietly. "I'll stay. But you're taking me to the mall to buy some underwear."

The relief on his face made her heart twist, and she turned her attention to the eggs before he could read her expression.

"I like lace," he said, plucking a mushroom off her plate. "Lacy panties. Tiny ones. Black is nice."

"Oh really, you prefer your women in tiny black lacy panties? That's completely new to me, since most men I've been with preferred faded white granny panties. This is so original of you!"

"If you're going to talk about past boyfriends, I won't cook for you. We'll be stuck getting horrible, soggy Chinese food."

Sophie secretly loved cheap, crappy Chinese. Preferably straight from the box. But she could give a little. "Fine. I can be bought by fine French cuisine. Ooh, what about crepes? What are we going to do today, anyway?"

He raised an eyebrow.

"Oh no, Mr. Wyatt. No more hanky-panky until I have my clean panties. And we need an activity."

"That *is* an activity."

"Such a man," she muttered. "How about a movie? Museum? Walk in the park?"

"I want to play Monopoly," he blurted out, looking completely surprised by his own admission.

Sophie couldn't help her laugh. "You own Monopoly?"

"Well...no. But we could buy it. They still sell it, right?"

"Yeah, pretty sure they still sell Monopoly," she said gently. And if possible, she fell just a little more in love. She was willing to bet that this man's opportunities for board games had been few and far between.

Picking up their plates, Sophie cleaned up, and turned back to find him watching her with an odd expression, which she ignored. They had to keep this light or the entire weekend would explode in their faces.

"Shall we?" she asked brightly. "A panty and Monopoly expedition?"

Ten minutes later, they were in Gray's car, engaged in a heated argument over the radio station, both wearing slightly goofy smiles. *Please don't let this weekend end*, Sophie thought.

"I get to be the banker," Gray was saying. "I'm good at it."

"You drive like a grandpa. I think that bicyclist just passed us."

"I'm safe," he replied.

"Yes, that's *very* shocking to everyone who knows you. I'm driving home."

"No. No way," he said, turning on his blinker a full five minutes before the turn toward the mall.

"Fine, then. I think Victoria's Secret has a sale on white, full-coverage cotton diapers."

Gray groaned. "You kill me. What the hell am I supposed to do with you?"

But Sophie couldn't bring herself to respond. The answer in her heart hurt too much.

CHAPTER EIGHTEEN

"Can I take you out again?"

Brynn looked up at the handsome man standing on her front porch and wondered why she didn't feel more than an indifferent hum.

Evan McCain was perfect for her. Handsome, successful, conventional. A lawyer. Stable. But the first date, which was perfect on paper, had been merely pleasant. All of her usual criteria were fulfilled, but she couldn't seem to muster any excitement about a future date.

She studied his classically attractive face, and assessed. Her parents would love him—he was the ultimate son-in-law material. Her friends would approve. He'd fit in perfectly at Trish's elaborate dinner parties.

Sophie would be the only one less than impressed. She'd write him off as "too perfect," which had never made sense to Brynn. What was better than perfect? Brynn had never understood why Sophie craved unpredictability, passion, and change. It was so messy.

But for the first time in her adult life, Brynn was beginning to wonder if her sister might be onto something. Perhaps Brynn was missing out on some crucial factor by only dating men who fulfilled her carefully configured checklist of required qualities.

She thought briefly of Will, but immediately pushed him away. Talk about a man who had none of her required qualities. Well, except for the looks, of course. Will was definitely handsome, if you liked the obvious, male-model thing.

Brynn hadn't seen him since the depraved scene on his kitchen floor a month before. He'd called a couple of times, but she hadn't picked up. He was probably calling to gloat that he'd found her underwear, which they'd been unable to locate during the awkward morning after. Brynn wasn't adept at spontaneous sexual encounters, and she certainly had no idea how to handle the aftermath of that particular mistake.

She'd was ashamed to admit that she'd even lied to her family about having to work on Sunday nights in order to avoid seeing Will at dinner.

"Brynn? Have I lost you?" Evan asked with a gentle smile. "How about next weekend?"

Oh, what the hell. The guy may be as exciting as Wonder Bread, but she was sick of being single.

"Sure!" she agreed with more enthusiasm than she felt. "How about Friday?"

Evan gave a quick victorious grin, perfectly masculine without being chauvinistic. It should have been appealing. Hell, even a month ago, it *would* have been appealing. Right up until the moment she found herself pinned against the wall of Will Thatcher's bachelor pad.

"Kiss me?" she said suddenly to Evan. He looked slightly surprised at her forwardness, but plenty willing.

She regretted her impulsive request as soon as Evan's head dipped toward hers. But maybe the kiss of another man would banish the demon of *that* man. She tried to lose herself in Evan's kiss, she really did. But the harder she tried, the more she realized it wasn't right.

When they finally broke away, he too seemed aware of the lack of chemistry.

"You're sure about Friday?" he asked.

Brynn forced a smile. "Of course! I look forward to it."

He gave her a small smile, looking a lot less interested than he had before their lackluster kiss. He made some noncommittal comment about double-checking his schedule and calling her.

Brynn had given enough polite brush-offs in her dating career to recognize when she was receiving one, but she couldn't bring herself to care that this was probably the last she'd see of Evan the lawyer. She couldn't blame the guy—from the way she'd kissed, he probably thought she was frigid.

She sighed and let herself inside, anticipating a hot bath, a good book, and a cup of tea.

The sight of the man sitting on her couch had her screaming like a banshee and dropping her purse. "What the hell are you doing here?"

Will held up her latest issue of *Cosmopolitan* without glancing up from the magazine. "Did you know," he said, "that the average American woman has seven sexual partners in her life? Isn't that interesting?"

Brynn took a deep breath to steady her pounding heart.

"Which notch is Evan on your bedpost?" Will asked thoughtfully. "Five? Fourteen? Thirty?"

"You were spying on me?"

He shrugged. "Open window, perfect hearing. Very awkward."

Brynn let out a snarl. "Get out of my house. How did you even get in here?"

He sighed as though she was being an unreasonable child, and reluctantly set the magazine aside after dog-earing a page. "If you must know, your mother gave me a key. I stopped by to fix their computer and she asked if I could drop off the pie dish you left at their house."

"My house isn't even *remotely* on your way home. You mean to tell me that my mother expected you to drive all the way out here for a six-dollar pie dish?"

He merely watched her, somehow managing to look both amused and disinterested. "No. I volunteered," he said simply.

"Why would you do that?"

"To spy on you and Romeo, of course. Who was he? Accountant? Chiropractor? Does he supply the retainers for all your snaggletoothed teens?"

Brynn gave a small, secretive smile as though the thought of Evan got her juices flowing. "He was a lawyer. Very rich. *Very* handsome."

Will snorted, and followed her into the kitchen. "He sounds absolutely riveting. How was the kiss?"

"That's some pretty thorough spying," she said in response.

Brynn pulled down two wineglasses even as she told herself that he would absolutely not be staying. "Why are you here? And no more crap about my pie dish. I'm not really in the mood for company. I'm tired, cranky, and sort of..."

"Horny?"

"I was going to say *pissed* that you're in my home, unexpected, without asking. If you've come to apologize about our...episode, let's get it over with and then you can leave."

He frowned and stepped closer. "Why the hell would I be apologizing? I don't apologize for fucking, Brynn. Not when the woman is as willing as you were."

A blush crept over her face. She *had* been willing. More than willing.

"You're not seeing him again," Will said.

"What? Who?"

"That idiot that was stupid enough to leave after one kiss."

"The Neanderthal routine doesn't suit you, William. What can you possibly care about who I date?"

The expression that flashed over his face might have been hurt, but it was gone before she could identify it. "Did that night mean so little to you, Brynn? You're already looking for your next conquest?"

She looked at him more closely. "Aren't you? Wasn't what happened between us just the latest move in the power game we play?"

And then she saw it again. It wasn't just hurt. It was vulnerability. Had that night mattered to him? Did *she* matter to him?

"Never mind," he said roughly. "I'll be going. I didn't mean to intrude upon your postdate euphoria."

The moment had passed and damn if she didn't want it back. "No, Will, wait." She reached out a hand, but stopped before she touched him. "Can't we just...can't you..."

"What?" he asked, watching her intently. "What do you want?"

"I... I just wanted to make sure that you hadn't told anyone about us."

His eyes went colder than she'd seen them. "No. Not a soul. You weren't worth the bragging rights."

That stung, but she didn't let herself swipe back. "You should go. And I'm sick of skipping my own family's dinners so that we can avoid each other. Maybe you could miss one once in a while?"

Will gave her a disgusted look. "Exactly how old are you, Brynn?"

She blushed, but stood her ground. "Look, I know it's immature, I just... I can't see you after knowing that we..."

She shuddered a little at the intensity of the memory, and saw immediately that he misinterpreted the reaction as disgust.

"All right. If that's what you want."

His voice was so dead that she almost panicked. Almost begged him to take her again. But instead she gave a businesslike nod. "Good, then we're agreed. It doesn't have to be forever. I just need a little space."

"Baby, I'm about to give you all the space you need," he said with a blank expression.

"What's that supposed to mean?" she yelled at his retreating back.

But her only answer was the resounding slam of her front door.

CHAPTER NINETEEN

Sophie hurriedly closed the e-commerce website she had up on her work computer when Gray walked by. He was growling into his cell phone as he passed, but he gave her a small wink.

Her toes curled. She couldn't help it.

Watching as he headed toward the kitchen, she pulled up the website browser window again. She couldn't believe she was shopping for *ties*.

She felt oddly giddy about it, even if she was mostly doing it out of guilt. She'd thrown out one of his ties last night. The one Brynn had gotten him.

For starters, it was the clothing equivalent of a coma. And second... well, it was just *weird* to see something in his closet that her sister had picked out.

And even though Gray hadn't seemed the least bit fazed by her demand, she was feeling just the tiniest bit guilty. Just because the man was practically made of money didn't mean he wanted to be throwing his clothes out on a whim.

So she was buying Gray Wyatt him a new tie. One that left *her* mark on him.

Now if she could only decide between the purple penguins or the salmon-colored polka dots…

Sophie's eyes bugged out when they caught on the clock. It was practically noon and she'd barely started her work. The tie would have to wait. She bookmarked the site and reluctantly pulled up the Blackwell deal. Negotiations were nearly final, but the details seemed to change every second Sophie thought she'd finally get the chance to hit print.

She tried to force herself to focus.

Coming into the office after sleeping with Gray hadn't been nearly as awkward as she'd feared. He treated her more or less like normal. And if he sometimes asked her to stay late and, ahem, "visit the copy room," well, that was just fine by her.

Granted, nobody else in the office knew that they were bed buddies. Just the way she wanted it. And the way Gray wanted it. Which, okay, maybe bugged her, just a little. Not that she wanted their mattress acrobatics going out in the company newsletter or anything, but she couldn't hide the suspicion that he was ashamed of her.

Knock it off, Sophie. Disparaging self-talk was so last year.

Digging through the papers on her desk, she looked for the notes Gray had left her after his call with Peter Blackwell this morning.

"Where the hell is it?" she muttered, rummaging through the stacks. Some people would call the mountain of crap "disorganization." These people didn't understand the appeal of structured chaos.

Finally she found the paper she was looking for. Under

her coffee mug. And her water glass. She winced as she saw that the classy notepaper with Gray's initials at the top now resembled a well-used coaster.

She bit her lip as she realized she'd have to ask him to rewrite the notes. He wouldn't mind. She knew the information was locked up all neat and tidy in his database of a brain. But she hated having to ask. She didn't want him to think she was getting careless just because she could.

Standing and adjusting her new yellow skirt that she'd blown most of her bonus on, she headed toward the kitchen to find Gray. Perhaps she could dump a little Baileys in his coffee to soften the blow. Or perhaps show a little cleavage...

Don't be a floozy. She mentally saluted her inner voice. "Got it. Today's to-do list: do not be a floozy."

Sophie paused around the corner to the kitchen when she heard Gray talking to someone. It was Jeff Andrews. She felt a moment of panic. She hadn't seen Jeff since the picnic, but if anyone suspected that something might be happening between her and Gray, it would be Jeff.

"You going to keep working on the Blackwell deal personally?" Jeff was saying.

Sophie relaxed. Nothing but a little harmless work discussion.

"Yeah, I promised Peter I'd stay on board until the end. He's old-fashioned like that," Gray responded.

"Makes sense. So what do you need from me?"

"I'm heading out to Maui at the end of the month. I'd like you to come along. Get your initial assessments of renovation and marketing costs."

Jeff whistled. "You're a tough boss. A work-related trip to Maui?"

"It won't be all fun. I need someone to help run interference when Peter's twit of a son tries to insert his obnoxious self in the middle of things."

"Sure, no problem. But why not just have Sophie keep at that? Rumor has it she's been running circles around the younger Blackwell."

Sophie had been about to enter the kitchen once she'd established it wasn't a confidential conversation, but she paused when she heard her name.

There was a pregnant pause, and Gray spoke again. "Sophie's not coming."

She frowned. Not at the words necessarily, although she'd have loved an expenses-paid trip to Hawaii. There was something odd about Gray's tone. Like he was surprised and baffled that Jeff had even suggested that she go.

"Oh, sorry," Jeff said, sounding sheepish. "I didn't mean to imply anything inappropriate... I just meant that I thought Sophie would be going along for note-taking or dinner reservations or whatever. It's the biggest deal of the year. Nobody would think twice if you brought your assistant."

Sophie made a mental note to buy Jeff a coffee on their next Starbucks run.

Gray made a derisive noise that had Sophie's spine doing a weird tingling thing. "I hardly think Sophie's contributions would be worth the price tag of a round-trip plane ticket to Hawaii. I'm sure the Blackwells have some girl at the resort who can staple and push the buttons on the fax machine just as well."

Something bright orange exploded in front of Sophie's eyes and she realized it was anger. Or perhaps humiliation. She took a deep breath and tried to get ahold of her temper, but it was no use. She'd already rounded the corner and revealed her presence to both men.

"Hey, Soph," Jeff said nervously. At least he had the decency to look guilty. Gray, on the other hand, looked completely unperturbed. Worse, his eyes looked almost *affectionate*. How dare he belittle her very existence in the company and then give her a come-hither glance in the next instant? *I'm just his plaything*, she realized in horror.

"Sorry to interrupt," she said. Gray's eyes went instantly wary at the silky danger of her tone. "Mr. Wyatt, I was just coming to ask for some more information from your Blackwell meeting this morning. But I won't worry about it, because I'm sure Mr. Blackwell has *some other girl who can do it just as well*."

Gray's eyes widened slightly, while Jeff made a choking noise and began backing out of the room.

"Sophie," Gray said in a low voice, "let's go into my office and talk."

"Why, so you can fuck me and then give me menial tasks that apparently any little woman could do? Tell me, Gray, is it just in the office that I'm replaceable, or am I replaceable in your bed too?"

Sophie knew she was way over the line of appropriate corporate behavior, but she was beyond caring who overheard. She wouldn't work here much longer anyway, and if it negatively impacted the employees' perception of Gray, the jackass more than deserved it.

His lips pinched together and he gently took her elbow and led her out of the kitchen. She jerked her arm free, but followed him to his office. It was fitting, really. They'd done some of their best fighting in that office. Might as well have their last one there as well.

He calmly closed the door behind her before reaching out a hand. "Sophie, please. It's not what you think."

She made a scoffing noise. "You weren't exactly vague, Mr. Wyatt. There really wasn't much there that could have been misinterpreted. You think my job is useless."

"No, of course not."

"But you think any old person can do it."

He hesitated for the briefest moment. "Well, no. Not anyone."

There it was again, that big red anger ball of fire blowing up in front of her eyes so she couldn't even see straight. "You made my job sound like a joke!"

He tried to move toward her again, but she took another step back.

"I didn't mean it like that," he said. "I didn't mean anything against you personally. I was just thinking in terms of the expenses and the necessities, and..."

"And you don't need little old me to do something a monkey could do?"

"Stop it," he said sharply. "Don't do that."

"Don't do what? Don't call attention to the fact that you're being completely demeaning?"

"No, I mean don't take all of your personal issues with your family and put them on me. I've never considered you inadequate."

"I *heard* you, Gray. You think this job is unimportant. You think *I'm* unimportant."

"I would have taken you with me to Maui in a personal capacity," he said quietly.

It was the wrong thing to say. "Oh, would you have?" she asked sweetly. "What would you have done, kept me stashed in your hotel room while the important people had important discussions?"

"Sophie, try to be rational. Do you really think this

Blackwell deal requires your presence on a professional level? If so, then I'll be glad to hear your case. But don't try to use your employment as your entire sense of validation. Don't do that to yourself. Do you even *like* this job? I hardly get the sense that filing is your life's passion."

He had her there. She didn't *dislike* her job. The pay was good and she liked being around the man she loved all day long even when it was painful. But the job itself didn't thrill her. It had long ceased being a challenge.

Still, she wanted her job to *matter*. This was supposed to be her path to respect. Instead she was no better off than she had been mopping up tequila. Why did everyone seem to think it was okay to treat her occupation as some sort of insignificant hobby? She'd never given Brynn crap for fitting metal to teeth all day. And she'd never told her mom that knowing twelve ways to explain the benefits of a walk-in closet hardly was going to change the world. Who were they to decide what was worthy and what wasn't?

"I thought you were different," she said finally, feeling some of the fight go out of her. "I thought you understood."

"Different how? Understand what? Help me out here," Gray said impatiently, spreading his hands to the sides in exasperation. "You want me to tell you that being a secretary's the most important job in the world? News flash, it's not. *None* of our jobs are. If you want to base your entire self-worth on your paycheck, go ahead, but don't expect me to walk on eggshells and blow smoke up your ass."

"I'll grant you that we're not exactly saving the world here, but how am I supposed to spend my life with a man who thinks I'm disposable?"

She closed her eyes in dismay as she heard what she'd just said. She'd implied lifetime togetherness with a man who didn't want marriage. Sophie prayed that he'd missed her slip. Or at least would ignore it.

He didn't.

"That's another thing, Sophie. I've never promised a *lifetime*. What we have is special. It's fun. But you've known that I don't want to get married, so I don't know where you get off acting like I've just threatened some grand happy ever after. You've known this wasn't forever. I've never lied about that."

Sophie reeled. She hadn't even realized how much she'd thought the night after the company picnic had changed things between them. But here he was telling her otherwise, in what was probably the longest speech of his life.

And it told her everything she needed to know.

"Gray?" she said sweetly.

"What?"

"I quit."

"What? Now? I didn't mean you had to quit effective immediately. We'll need time to find a replacement, and for you to train them..."

The fact that his first thought was business solidified her decision even as it broke her heart.

But she knew what she had to do. "That's not my problem, Gray. If you insist on me coming in for the next two weeks, I will because it's standard business protocol, but I should warn you that they'll likely be very awkward for both of us."

"Why's that?"

She smiled thinly. "Because I'm not just quitting Brayburn Luxuries."

His eyes went cold and flat, and she saw that he understood.

"I'm also quitting *you*," she said softly.

She hadn't been expecting a reaction, and she didn't get one. He stood there staring at her, his expression unreadable.

"You know the worst part of all this?" she said, making her way toward the door.

He said nothing, but steadily returned her gaze as she continued to speak. "I've been spending the past several months hating Jessica. Hating her for what she did to you. The cheating thing... well... that was still wrong of her. But her assessment of you as lacking was dead-on. There's nothing beneath that suit but ice."

Something stark and hopeless flashed across his features and almost had Sophie wanting to take back her words. Almost.

But she was done letting people spit all over her existence like she was some vapid butterfly who wouldn't care. Everything was becoming clear to her now. That moment in the Las Vegas elevator had felt like rock bottom only because she'd let other people make her feel that way.

No more.

She was done living for other people. They could take the stingy, withheld respect that she'd been so desperate to earn and shove it up their ass.

Without a backward glance, Sophie opened Gray's office door, and stopped only long enough to grab her purse. She didn't bother to look back and see if he was watching her. It didn't matter.

Sophie Dalton was taking her life back. Even if it meant walking away from the man she loved.

CHAPTER TWENTY

Sophie clung to her anger like a security blanket. It was the only way to stave off the soul-sucking pain that lurked beneath the rage.

And by Sunday night, that anger hadn't abated. In fact, it had expanded. And it was no longer just Gray who was in its crosshairs.

"Mom, Dad, I'm here!" Sophie called, wiping her feet on the mat to remove the mud.

Seattle residents loved to brag about how great their summers were, but the truth was there was still plenty of rain. Even in June. And tonight's storm was a doozy. Perfect for her mood.

"Sophie, dear, you're late," her mother said, coming into the foyer and putting a spatula-holding hand on her hip. "And you know I hate those jeans. I was so relieved when that 'worn' look went out of style, but you still insist on—"

"Mom," Sophie said. "My jeans are just fine for a *family dinner*. And I'm not even ten minutes late. Brynn and Dad show up late all the time and you don't so much as blink at them.

Marnie blinked rapidly, clearly surprised at having her lecture interrupted. "Well, honey, they do run late from time to time, but it's different. They have very..."

"What? They have something *important* going on? They have a *good reason*? Well, so do I."

Her mother's nostrils fluttered. "Sophie, please don't be petulant. It's unattractive."

Marnie turned on the heel of her designer pump and marched back into the kitchen.

Confusion temporarily dampened Sophie's anger as she absorbed the blunt truth that her own parents seemed to think she didn't matter.

Were they really still that mad at her for not finishing law school? Was that what all of this was about? Was having a daughter they could brag about at the country club really more important than said daughter's happiness?

Sophie knew that they loved her, of course. She could always count on them to come help her out if she got a flat tire, or needed help moving, or nearly chopped her fingers off while cutting parsley. But caring was no longer enough for Sophie.

She wandered into the kitchen and poured herself a generous glass of wine. Her family was deep in a riveting conversation about "the club's" upcoming tennis tournament. Sophie started to tune out, but their ignoring her was like Miracle-Gro on her little seed of anger.

The four of them had used to all play tennis together. And the real kicker was that Sophie was better than all of them. Something they'd conveniently forgotten since she didn't play at "*the club*."

"Do you guys need another person?" she blurted out.

Three pairs of startled eyes fell on her. Their confused expressions burned into her and gave her courage. "What? I'm pretty sure my backhand still beats all of yours."

"Sophie, hon, you have to be a member to play," her dad said gently.

"Oh." She'd forgotten that part. "Is that like really expensive or something?"

She already knew that a membership to their country club was out of the question. Especially since she was now unemployed. "Well, it'd be nice to be included as a guest once in a while," she said softly.

"Sure, you can come with me anytime," Brynn said smoothly. "I didn't realize you still played."

Probably because you've never bothered to ask.

"Where's Will?" Marnie asked, setting a platter of avocado crostini in front of them. "These are his favorite. He's usually here by now."

Sophie snagged a piece of bread and got ready to drop her bomb. "Will moved to Boston."

The reaction to this announcement would have been comical had she not been so annoyed with the lot of them. Marnie's salad tongs were frozen in midair. Her father's crostini seemed stuck halfway to his mouth. Brynn's crystal wineglass was now in a million pieces at her feet.

"What do you mean, he's moved to Boston?" Chris said as Marnie rushed to help Brynn clean up. "We just saw him last Sunday and he didn't say a word about it."

To me either, Sophie thought.

Will had come by last night to say good-bye, catching Sophie completely off guard. Her best friend was moving across the country and hadn't breathed a word about it. In the span of a week he'd put his town house on the market, sold his car, hired movers, and signed a lease on an apartment in downtown Boston that he'd never even seen.

But it had taken about five seconds to see that this wasn't a careless move.

Spontaneous, yes. Slightly insane, sure. But she knew Will better than anyone, and if he was making a move like this, it was for good reason. It had stung that he hadn't been able to share that reason, but Sophie hadn't pushed. She hadn't exactly been spilling her guts to him lately either. Even the best of friends were allowed their secrets.

"He's sorry he didn't say good-bye," Sophie said to her still-stunned family.

That Will hadn't been able to stick around to say good-bye to her family still confused her. The Daltons were the only family Will had. She'd begged him to postpone his flight by a day to say good-bye in person, but he'd insisted he had to get to Boston immediately.

"Well, that's just...just...I don't know what to say," her mother sputtered, speechless for once.

"He said he'll be back someday, Mom," Sophie said gently. "And I'm sure he'll come visit."

Marnie just shook her head and went back to dressing her salad with a shell-shocked expression. Chris returned to watching his baseball game with a forlorn look. Nobody else in the family could tolerate his reciting of sports stats like Will could.

Brynn was washing spilled wine off her hands. Or at least that's what she was supposed to be doing. It looked a lot like staring out the window looking ready to puke while letting the water run.

"You okay, Brynny?" Sophie asked.

"What? Oh, sure. Did Will say why?"

Sophie shook her head. "Nope. Maybe he just wanted a fresh start."

Her sister remained silent.

"Brynn, the water?" her mother said.

"Oh, right," she muttered, returning to the task of washing her hands.

Marnie and Sophie exchanged a puzzled look. What was that all about? If anything, Brynn should be happy to get Will out of her life. It's not like there was any love lost between those two. Sophie shrugged at her mom. She'd pester Brynn about it later. And from the wrinkles on Brynn's normally perfectly smooth forehead, whatever was eating at her was going to be juicy.

Without Will's easy, carefree presence to diffuse the usual Dalton stuffiness, the evening had a strained, stilted vibe. Marnie seemed to be still miffed with Sophie, although Sophie wasn't sure it was for being tardy, the hole in her jeans, or the fact that she'd defended herself instead of apologizing.

Brynn continued to do the strange moody thing that *really* didn't look good on her.

These were the types of evenings that the old Sophie would take charge of, sprinkling little bits of false cheer.

But not tonight. She didn't have it in her. No matter how many times she told herself not to think about Gray (at least fourteen times every minute), she kept seeing the blank look in his silver eyes when she'd walked away from him.

She also kept seeing herself as she'd spent the weekend, wearing her baggiest pink sweats, eating nothing but corn chips and waiting for the phone to ring. It hadn't.

The four of them shoveled food in robotic silence, until

uncharacteristically, it was Sophie's dad who finally tried to break the icy silence.

"Excellent roast, Marn," he said as he sawed furiously at the dry piece of meat. Sophie rolled her eyes. The roast wasn't even close to excellent. Sophie missed the days when her mother had worked full-time and they'd had a housekeeper who put perfectly passable casseroles in the oven. But since retirement had left Marnie feeling useless, she'd filled the void by buying a library's worth of cookbooks.

Money would have been better spent on cooking lessons on how to actually *use* said cookbooks.

Sophie poked at an underseasoned potato and wished Brynn would bring one of her perfect boyfriends over more often. At least then Marnie tried to cook something other than a massive chunk of meat left to dry out in the oven for hours.

But Brynn hadn't brought anyone over since that disastrous dinner with Gray.

Just look how *that* had turned out.

"Sophie, about your new job..." Chris said when Marnie failed to preen over his dinner praise. "I've been thinking, I bet a company like that would help pay to put you through business school. Then you could actually be one of the big guns instead of just working for them."

As her father's words penetrated her brain, Sophie let out a hysterical little laugh that had all three family members staring at her warily.

"I don't think so, Dad."

Chris looked disappointed, but not surprised. Marnie's lips pressed into a thin line. Sophie waited patiently for a follow-up question she knew wouldn't come.

So you like your job, then?

What about the other areas of your life?

How's Gray? What's going on there?

As expected, nobody spared her a second thought once they'd established she wasn't angling to be CEO, and conversation turned to Brynn's latest patient, who had an entire extra set of teeth.

Sophie quietly watched her family, feeling as though she was viewing them from a great distance.

There was her mother with her composed "interested" face as she listened to her successful older daughter discuss maxillary lateral incisors. And here was Sophie's dad, nodding knowledgeably, even though Sophie was pretty sure he'd never had to get near a maxillary whatever during his days of sewing up appendices and ruptured spleens.

Last, Sophie studied Brynn, whose placid smile didn't reach her eyes as she recited words Sophie didn't know. None of the words were fewer than fifteen letters.

This can't possibly be what Brynn wants out of her life, Sophie thought. *It's certainly not what I want.*

Sophie's fork clattered noisily to her plate, startling everyone into silence.

"Sophie, that's expensive china," her mother said with an exasperated look.

"And it's *fine*, Mother. Even if it weren't fine, this is the most predictable pattern in all of yuppie America and it's a *plate*. It's *replaceable*."

Marnie's mouth dropped open slightly, but Sophie was already moving on to her next target.

"And Brynn? Noooobody cares about the incline of Tiffany so-and-so's molars. I mean, do *you* even care?"

Finally, she turned to her father. "Dad, no daughter wants to disappoint her father, and I'm tired of doing it over and over, so let's just have it out once and for all. I'm never going to be a lawyer. Or a doctor, or some high-level executive. I appreciate that you gave me the opportunities and education to make those things possible, but it's just not the path for me."

"Soph, you say that now, but..."

"I'm almost twenty-eight, Dad. Still young, but hardly some dewy college student trying to figure out what to do with my life."

"And what *are* you doing with your life, Sophie?" her mother asked. "Serving cocktails? Now you're spending your days making copies and fetching coffee..."

Sophie held up one finger. "Actually, that last bit isn't quite true any longer. I quit."

The number of stunned silences at this lovely family dinner was starting to get comical, and Sophie almost smiled.

"But why?" her father asked. "It's only been a few months..."

Sophie shrugged. "Because I was shagging my boss and it got complicated."

Another of those silences. "You and Gray?" Marnie mused. "I never would have thought..."

"That he'd be interested in me?" Sophie finished for her mother. "Yeah, me neither. Turns out we were both right."

Sophie's righteous fury had been briefly exhilarating, but saying Gray's name out loud had taken the wind out of her sails and she felt her anger slip away to reveal what it had been hiding all along. Pain.

"That's not what I meant," Marnie said, her voice uncharacteristically gentle. "I didn't think you'd ever be interested in someone like him. He was so...formal."

"Not so much," Sophie whispered. "Not underneath."

Brynn came around to Sophie's side and knelt by her chair, wrapping a comforting arm around her waist. "I'm sorry, Soph. What happened?"

Sophie scanned her sister's face. "Aren't you upset? I mean, I slept with your ex. That's a sibling no-no."

Brynn rolled her eyes. "Please. The only reason I was even remotely upset when we broke up was because it was an inconvenience. And I think I knew on some level that you two had... well, something."

Sophie's eyes watered at the unexpected acceptance. "You're a better person than me."

"Never," Brynn said, squeezing her hand. "Now tell us what happened."

"About what you'd expect. He just saw me as a temporary toy."

"And you? How'd you feel about him?"

Sophie rolled her eyes up to look at the ceiling in an effort to keep the tears from falling. "Oh, you know. True love, and all that nonsense."

The dishes rattled as Chris pushed back roughly from the table. "Where does this guy live? Nobody makes my Sophie cry."

Sophie let out a watery laugh. "Thanks, Dad, but it wasn't his fault. Just one of those things that didn't work out."

She tried to take another bite, but let her fork drop again. "You know, I think I'm going to go home. Sorry to ruin dinner."

Her parents nodded, looking uncomfortably out of their depth. She didn't blame them, not really. The Dalton family didn't communicate in scenes and tears. But before she let them off the hook, she had one more thing to say.

"You know, getting rejected by a guy who doesn't think

I'm good enough is one thing. I can move on from that. Eventually. But you guys are my *family*. I shouldn't have to try so hard to be good enough. It should be enough for you guys that I'm happy, even if I'm not impressive."

"Sophie, you know we love you," her mom said, looking on the verge of tears.

"Yeah, I know, Mom. But I need that love to stop being so judgmental."

"I'm not—"

"Yeah, you are. If it's not my jeans, it's my hair, or my job, or my friends, or my hobbies. I'm never going to be Brynn. Stop trying to make me."

Brynn shifted awkwardly. "Don't bring me into this."

"I love you both equally," Marnie said, her voice wavering.

"I know," Sophie said, letting her voice soften. "Respect us equally too, okay? And if you don't, fine, I guess. But I'm done caring about it, so get used to these jeans."

Sophie gave her dad a hug, which he stiffly returned, and she planted a kiss on the top of her mom's blonde head.

The parental units weren't exactly vomiting out apologies, but they looked thoughtful. Maybe that was something.

Brynn followed Sophie out to the front door and watched in silence as Sophie put her shoes on. There were things to be said between them as well, but Brynn seemed to sense that Sophie had reached her emotional conversation quota for the evening.

"Call me later?" Brynn said after Sophie had grabbed her purse.

"Sure. Probably tomorrow."

They hugged, and Brynn tucked a wayward curl behind

Sophie's ear. "Soph, you know all that stuff you were saying about just wanting to be happy?"

Sophie nodded.

"Well... *are* you happy?"

Sophie looked out at the pouring rain and considered. "No. Not yet. But I'm learning how to be."

Chapter Twenty-One

Sophie was secure enough with herself to be able to admit her worst faults. The most prevalent flaw at the moment? Complete cowardice.

"Thanks again for meeting me," Sophie said to Beth Jennings as they stood outside the Brayburn Luxuries office building. "I know that coming down on a Saturday night isn't ideal, but I couldn't make it earlier in the week and I need to pick up my stuff before Monday."

She hated lying to Beth, but coming on a Saturday was the only way Sophie could retrieve the belongings she'd left in the office without risk of running into Gray.

"No problem," Beth said as she buzzed open the front door. Sophie still had her key to the Brayburn office suites, but she'd lost electronic access to the building on the day she'd quit.

"Do you mind if I leave you here?" Beth asked, holding the door open for Sophie. "My friends invited me for a last-minute drink at a bar just up the street, and I'd love to meet up with them before it gets too late."

"Oh! Of course," Sophie said, guiltily. "Are you sure it's okay if I just let myself up?"

"Sure," Beth said with a shrug. "A little against protocol, but it'll be our little secret. Just leave the keys in your desk drawer and I'll grab them on Monday. Rachel packed all of your personal stuff into a box, but you may want to take a quick look around and make sure she didn't forget anything."

"Will do. And thanks again for coming all the way down here. I owe you one."

"Don't worry about it. You'd do the same for me. Hug?"

Sophie smiled and embraced her friend. Waving one last good-bye to Beth with a promise to stay in touch, she headed toward the elevator. Hitting the button for the fourteenth floor for the last time, Sophie waited for the usual wave of bittersweet emotions to hit her. She was well practiced at leaving jobs, and the series of emotions was always the same.

Regret at leaving new friends.

Excitement about future opportunities.

Doubt that she was making the right choice.

This time, she experienced the expected first and second emotion, and she braced herself for the third. It was always the worst.

But the doubt never came. She was making the right decision in leaving. There was no "maybe" this time. She'd enjoyed her time at Brayburn, save for the painful last day, but she'd never belonged here. She'd never invested herself, never let it define her, never let herself excel.

Sophie had nothing but respect for assistants and corporate staff of all natures, because it was a hell of a lot harder than people knew. But it wasn't her passion. It was time to move on.

The past weeks since leaving Brayburn had been the most enlightened of Sophie's life. It had been painful to realize that her chronic job-hopping had never been about spontaneity and following her heart. It had merely been a method of avoiding herself.

She'd spent years surfing on a wave of ambiguity over what to do with her life, which she should have tackled after graduation. But instead, she'd just avoided it. By never investing in anything, she could never be accused of failing. Never be disappointed.

But no more. It hadn't taken much reflection to realize that she didn't *like* office buildings and paperwork and suits. Didn't like staplers or copy machines or multi-line phones. Hell, aesthetics aside, she didn't even really like high-heeled shoes.

The only aspect she'd liked about this environment had been the *people*. Sophie loved people. She loved watching them, talking with them, learning them. And she could admit now that she was damn *good* with them. The highlight of her time at Brayburn had been discovering what made people like the Blackwells tick. Seeing them as people instead of clients. As personalities instead of customers.

People were her passion, and she knew in her gut that this new insight was her path to true job satisfaction.

Granted, she still didn't know exactly what that meant career-wise. Therapist, milkman, teacher?

But she had a little money saved up. Enough to provide a financial buffer while she figured it out. She'd gotten so adept at *not* being what other people expected her to be, that she'd failed to figure out what she *wanted* to be.

Stepping off the elevator, Sophie took a deep breath. This was the part she'd been dreading. Seeing Gray's office again.

Seeing the place of his first smile, their first fight, their first kiss.

Their last words.

Refusing to look toward Gray's darkened office, Sophie marched to her desk with a mission.

Grab the box and get out. Fast.

She took a quick glance through the contents of the box. The potted orchid that Brynn had bought her, which Sophie had barely managed to keep alive. A condom from Will, "just in case." A picture of her family. Some sort of fancy pen from her father that Sophie had never used for fear of losing or breaking it.

Her hand hesitated as she picked up the last item. It was the small bowl of creamers she kept at her desk to ensure Gray's coffee was always perfect. She cringed, remembering how much she'd treasured his small half smiles when she'd gotten it just right.

She shook her head in shame. How could she have been so foolish? All that effort she'd put into pleasing the man, and the entire time he'd merely been seeing a competent secretary. A replaceable one, apparently.

Sophie had been stupidly trying to win a smile from *Gray*, when really all he'd expected was that she earn her paycheck from *Mr. Wyatt*.

Sophie stared down at the small packages of half-and-half. They seemed to represent everything that had been wrong about the pseudo-relationship. She pulled the garbage can out from under the desk and, with slow purpose, turned the delicate glass bowl upside down, listening as the small plastic containers crashed into the trash can.

"Ms. Dalton. Is that company property you're disposing of?"

The glass bowl slipped from her fingers, shattering on the floor as she spun around with a shriek.

She should have been prepared for this. *Of course*, Gray would be here. Their entire relationship had been based on a series of coincidental meetings. It made sense that their final meeting would be yet another disastrous accident.

"Working on a Saturday night is pathetic, even for you," she said with as much disdain as her thudding heart would allow.

Gray stood framed against his office door, arms crossed. She wished he were wearing a suit so she could distance herself from the CEO. But his dark jeans and casual gray shirt made her long for the man, not the employer.

"I'm not working tonight," he said.

"So you're just here hanging out?" she asked breezily. "I suppose that makes sense. At least in the office you have the occasional janitorial visit. At home you're merely *alone*."

She didn't know where the cold words came from. It was as if cruelty was the only way of keeping her heart from shattering. He said nothing, just looked at her with unreadable gray eyes.

"Did Beth tell you I was coming by?" she asked tentatively, confused by his intense gaze.

"She mentioned it, yes."

"And you didn't think it would be wise to be *anywhere else* when I got here?" she asked incredulously.

"That kind of would've defeated the purpose, wouldn't it? I specifically asked Ms. Jennings when you'd be collecting your belongings, and she seemed to have this crazy idea that Saturday evening was the only *possible* time you could squeeze this into your schedule."

His raised eyebrow said it all. He saw right through her.

"I've had a busy couple weeks," she said weakly.

He nodded once, but only continued looking at her with a steady gaze. Almost as though he were looking for something.

"Didn't Beth think it was weird when you asked about me?" she blurted out.

"Probably."

"That wasn't your best plan," she said stiffly. "Now she probably thinks something is going on between us."

"Yes, she definitely thinks that. Well, actually, everyone does after your yelling in the kitchen."

The part of Sophie that had played assistant for so long slipped out, because she rushed to reassure him. "Well, she may have her suspicions, but it'll blow over. And she's in human resources, so she's pretty much the dead end of the gossip train."

"Ms. Jennings isn't dealing in suspicions any longer, she's dealing in facts."

"You *told* her... that we... you know..."

"Not in those words, no. But I told her that I'd lost something, and I wanted it back. I think she put the pieces together."

Sophie tried to process, but her brain didn't seem to be keeping up with her racing heart.

"What did you lose?" she whispered.

"Come on, Sophie," he said as he stepped closer. "You're smarter than this."

At the reminder of his assessment of her intellect, she stiffened. "I'm not coming back here, Gray. I'm not going to be your disposable assistant, and I sure as hell am not going to tiptoe around, trying not to embarrass you while waiting for you to decide that our relationship has run its course."

He moved closer still, and she became captivated by the heat in his eyes. She hadn't seen this expression before from him, and she felt nervous. So much for her being a people person. She'd never felt so confused.

"You don't embarrass me," he said, reaching for her hand. "You couldn't. You're the best part of me."

Every self-preserving instinct in her body was screaming at her. *Pull back. Run. Kick him in the balls.*

She stayed. "What are you trying to say?"

"I want you back," he said simply.

"As your secretary or bed partner?"

His eyes flashed angrily. "Don't."

"What else am I supposed to think? You made it perfectly clear that my role in your life was to lie on my back, while you could find any old employee to take care of your stapling."

He opened his mouth, but shut it again, looking frustrated. She nearly softened. Like a foolish woman in love, she found it endearing that he was pushing himself so far out of his element for her.

But she couldn't relent. Whatever plan he had in store for them would involve rules and boundaries and heartache. It would never work.

"I have to go," she said softly.

He swallowed and nodded. He looked panicked, and she longed to help him with whatever he was struggling with, but he was no longer her personal project to be tweaked and prodded.

Blinking back tears, she grabbed her box and headed for the door. As far as closure went, it was a total bust, but sometimes cleaner was better.

"Sophie," he called hoarsely.

Keep walking.

"Don't, Gray," she whispered, slowing her steps.

"Do you love me?"

The question sounded like it was torn from his throat, from his heart, and she faltered.

Her tears fell freely now. "You have no right to ask me that. No right."

"Do you?" His voice was closer now.

"It doesn't matter," she said quietly.

"It matters," he said roughly, close enough now to grab her shoulder. "It matters."

He turned her toward him, but she sucked in a sob and refused to look at him.

"Don't do this," she begged. "I can't be what you want."

"You *are* what I want."

The desperation in his voice made her look up, clutching the flimsy cardboard box to her like a security blanket. What she saw nearly undid her.

His eyes were damp and pleading. *Please*, they said. *Please.*

But he remained silent, and she knew he wouldn't know how to say what was written on his face. He wouldn't ever be able to say it, and she deserved to hear it.

She tried to turn again, but he held her still, his throat working in obvious effort.

"Let me go," she said quietly. Firmly. She could do this.

"I can't." He shook his head. "I can't."

Sophie smiled sadly and pulled away. "I'm not the one for you, Gray. You're looking for a good-time girl, and I know you think that's me, but—"

"Dammit, would you stop talking like that!" he growled like an animal in agony.

"I want a family!" she said, her voice breaking. "I want a husband who's proud of the stuff he burns on the grill, and a baby who yanks out my earrings, and a big dog who will probably smell when it rains. You don't want any of those things!"

His fingers tightened on her upper arms, and he shook her so hard she dropped the box, the spilled contents lying ignored at their feet. "I'd want them with you."

Her heart gave a jolt, and she closed her eyes. He wouldn't be so cruel as to torture her.

"I love you, Sophie," he whispered hoarsely.

She thought her heart would explode in ecstasy and pain. He couldn't possibly know what he was doing.

"Gray, listen—"

"No, *you* listen. I think I fell for you somewhere between that damn Las Vegas elevator and you picking up my little sister from the airport. My feelings hit me over the head when we were in that Goddamn blow-up maze at the company picnic, but I didn't know what to do, what to say..."

Sophie's mind reeled. "But...my job...and you don't want to get married..."

"Forget all that," he said desperately. "You know I'm new at this. Bad at it. And I'll continue to mess everything up. But you have to give me a chance."

Don't weaken, Sophie. Turn away.

She didn't move.

"You have to," he said, his voice breaking. "You can leave Brayburn. Or stay. Come to Maui, or not. I don't care. But you can't leave me. Please don't leave me."

"No," she said, her voice breaking. "I won't. I can't."

His arms closed around her tightly, and she realized how much these past weeks had cost him. And her.

"What you said about Jessica—"

Sophie closed her eyes in pain and put a hand over his mouth. "Don't. I never should have said it."

"Then you think I'm someone worth liking?"

"Not exactly..." she said coyly.

"Loving?" he asked, voice hopeful.

"Perhaps."

"Tell me."

"Tell you what?" she teased.

"Sophie." He rested his forehead on hers.

"I love you," she said with a wobbly smile. She framed his face with her hands. "I love that you barely know how to smile, and that you care about your siblings more than you possibly know how to express. I love that you *totally* cheat at Monopoly, and that you hit on your secretaries like a common pervert."

The relief in his eyes had her crying all over again.

"Just one question, Ms. Dalton," he said, resting his forehead against hers.

"Yes, Mr. Wyatt?"

"How much is this going to cost me? I've come to learn that you're a *very* high-end call girl."

Sophie pinched him. "Doesn't matter. I'm worth it."

She felt him smile against her temple. "Yes, you are."

Epilogue

"I called the restaurant to let them know we'll be a little late," Sophie said, hanging up the hotel phone.

Gray wiggled his eyebrows. "We could be a little *later*. Make time for some afternoon delight?"

"You already got a little afternoon delight! Twice. And don't call it that."

He shrugged as he added a gray tie to his gray suit.

Sophie smiled and shook her head at the monochromatic ensemble. There were some things that couldn't be changed, even in the course of a seven-month relationship. Gray's wardrobe was proving to be one of them.

But the important things had changed.

Gray was still CEO of Brayburn Luxuries. His new assistant was a tiny, stern woman named Ida who refused to address him as anything other than Mr. Wyatt, no matter how many times he asked her to use his first name. Ida had also removed all of Sophie's bright decorating choices and replaced them with soothing taupe and ivory accents. Gray's office was now nothing but a bunch of boring neutrals. Exactly as he liked it.

Sophie was on her way to getting her teaching degree. She hadn't decided on a subject or a grade level yet, but as soon as Gray had suggested she'd make a great teacher, she'd known immediately that it was the right fit. It would be a long road getting there, but Sophie had finally found a career path that excited her and that she was proud of.

She still had a couple years of school ahead, but she already ached for the first day of teaching with a bunch of expectant faces looking up to her. Of course, they'd probably have to call her Ms. Dalton. Good thing she was used to that by now.

As for her parents...they were trying. They'd even thrown her a congratulatory party when she'd been accepted to Seattle University's teaching program. Of course, her father hadn't been able to resist the briefest of lectures on how small teachers' salaries were, and her mother had given Sophie's short skirt a panicked look. But overall they were learning to let her be her.

Brynn too had been supportive of the changes in Sophie's life, although if Sophie's life was finally getting on track, her older sister's seemed to be teetering on the edge of... well, Sophie wasn't sure what exactly. It wasn't like Brynn had joined a commune or bought a Harley or pierced her belly button, but in the past few months there had been something vaguely off about Brynn. A restless impatience that Sophie had never seen before. She'd tried talking to her sister about it, but Brynn had feigned ignorance. Sophie itched to dig deeper, but she knew firsthand how it felt to have someone meddle in your life, so she was trying to let her sister have her space.

"What's with the frown?" Gray asked, tugging at a blonde curl.

Sophie shook off her concern. "Nothing. Just musing."

"There will be no musing in Vegas," Gray said. "Here, I've got a surprise for you."

She raised an eyebrow as Gray began digging through his suitcase. She never thought she'd hear the word "surprise" come out of Grayson Wyatt's mouth.

He turned around with a boyish grin, and Sophie let out a horrified laugh as she saw what he held in his hands.

"My hooker boots!"

"It took me forever to find them," he said, smiling fondly at the cheap, fake leather. "What were you thinking, hiding gems like these under your bed?"

"Well, gosh, you're right. They do bring back *such* fond memories, I should have put them on the mantel."

"Is that sarcasm I sense?"

"From me?" Sophie asked, wrapping her arms around his waist and pressing her nose into his neck.

He nibbled her ear for a split second before gently pushing her aside. "None of that, you harlot. Here, put these on."

Sophie stared at him. "I am not wearing those to dinner."

"Why, you worried about some surly man hitting on you in the elevator?" he asked, giving her bare legs an appreciative glance.

"I'm pretty sure I'll be stuck with a surly man, regardless of shoe choice," Sophie said, reluctantly accepting the boots. "You *really* want me to wear these? When you said you wanted to go to Vegas to celebrate a year since we first met, I didn't realize you wanted to actually celebrate the *hooker* part of it."

"I thought I was being sweet," he said with mock affront. "Don't women like reliving a couple's first meeting?"

"Not when the first meeting involves a near-death experience and ultimate humiliation. And I told you I wanted to stay in one of the tacky hotels. You picked the same boring one as before," she grumbled as she reluctantly pulled off her black pumps and slipped into the boots. "God, I'd forgotten how uncomfortable these are."

"Oh, quit whining," he said, pulling her out the hotel room door and toward the elevator lobby.

Gray punched the elevator button and leaned in for a kiss, pulling back when they finally heard the elevator arrival chime.

"Hey, it's the same elevator as before!" Sophie said in happy realization. "What are the odds?"

"One in eight," he replied, guiding her into the elevator. "Or twelve-point-five percent. There are eight possible elevators, so the chances of us getting this one—"

"Oh jeez," she said, cutting him off. "Just when I think you're finally beginning to understand romance..."

Suddenly the lights went out, and the elevator jolted to a sudden stop. "You've got to be kidding me," Sophie said incredulously. "What are the odds of *this*? You'd think they'd have fixed—Gray, what the hell are you doing down there?"

Sophie squinted through the dark to find him.

"Hold on, I have a light," he grumbled.

"You carry a flashlight now?" she asked, still struggling to see his figure. "Although I guess it's not a bad idea at *this* hotel—"

She broke off again as a tiny stream of light flicked on. It served as a spotlight for one very large, very sparkly diamond ring.

Dimly she could see Gray's shadow outlined behind it.

He was on his knee.

"Oh my God," she whispered, a shaky hand covering her mouth.

"Marry me," Gray commanded gruffly.

"Is that a question?" she asked with a choked laugh.

"More like a plea," he said. "Please hurry up and decide. I can't imagine all the germs on this elevator floor."

"You planned this," Sophie realized in wonder. "You were actually crazy enough to ask them to stall this elevator?"

"You said you wanted romance."

"I can't believe I'm wearing a miniskirt!" She plucked the ring out of the box and inspected the flawless solitaire diamond.

"Sophie, if you don't answer my question, so help me—"

"Yes!" she burst out. "Of course, yes."

"Thank God," he said with relief. "Do you have any idea how many palms I had to grease to organize this whole debacle—"

Sophie threw herself at him, both of them falling awkwardly to the ground. "You did this for me," she said, gazing down at his face in the dark.

"I'd do anything for you," he said simply.

"I love you," she whispered.

"I know."

Sophie bit him.

"Fine. I love you too. If someone would have told me a year ago I'd be in love with a blonde prostitute—"

She broke off his words with a messy kiss. "How long did you arrange for us to be stuck in a black box together?"

"I, um, didn't exactly specify. I wasn't sure how long it would take to talk you into it."

"So we might have some time?" she asked playfully.

"Probably. I implied that you were a little high-strung, so they'll probably err on the side of caution and leave us in here awhile."

"Then I guess it's convenient that I'm wearing a tiny little outfit."

His hand slid up the back of her thigh. "I guess it is."

"Wanna make babies?"

"Will they be quiet and well behaved, and read nonfiction?"

"No chance in hell."

"Then yes. Definitely," he said as he began untying her halter top.

* * *

Eleven minutes later, the elevator began moving again, and they straightened their clothes as best as they could.

"Well, I guess I finally know your rate," Gray said as he helped her retie her top. "I should have left a diamond ring on the dresser a year ago, and we could have skipped all the past few months and gotten straight to the good stuff."

"But then we'd never have experienced the awkward family dinner, or The Castle, or the Blackwells..."

"Speaking of the Blackwells, what do you say to a honeymoon in Maui?" he asked.

"Will Alistair be there?"

"I can probably arrange it. Assuming he doesn't have a mosquito convention."

"Then absolutely. I'm in. Ugh, I don't suppose you have a handkerchief," she said, struggling to right her appearance.

He pulled one from his pocket, predictable as ever. "I

thought you were supposed to save the one I gave you last time as a memento," he said as she carefully removed her smeared lipstick.

"I believe what I said was that I *wasn't* keeping it."

"I thought you women were supposed to be attuned to romantic inklings."

She snorted. "Maybe. Doesn't mean I didn't set your handkerchief on fire."

Gray grabbed her left hand and ran a thumb over the new diamond. "You're sure about this, Sophie? You think I can be a good husband?"

"I'm sure about *you*," she said confidently, smiling into his worried face. "I can't wait to spend the rest of my life annoying the crap out of you."

Gray's lips closed over hers, and it took them several moments to realize that the elevator doors had opened, and that a crowd of people were staring at them. The same hotel manager from before came rushing over.

"Mr. Wyatt, I hope everything is—well, I mean—will your companion be joining you for dinner?" Mr. Clinksy finished awkwardly, clearly unsure how to handle the unusual situation.

Gray smiled down at his new fiancée. "Indeed she will." Sophie and Gray walked away from the elevator lobby for the second time in the same year.

But this time, they were going in the same direction.

Will Thatcher is exactly the type of sexy bad boy that good girls like Brynn have always avoided.

But Will is out to show Brynn that this imperfect man might be the best mistake of her life…

Please see the next page for a preview of

Made for You.

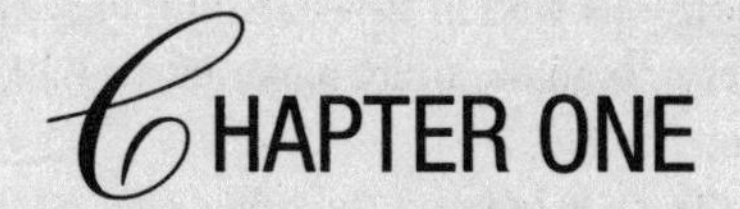

CHAPTER ONE

Accept the aging process with grace and decorum.

—Brynn Dalton's Rules for an Exemplary Life, #32

Distributing toilet paper was not on Brynn Dalton's life list.

Neither was crying in a public bathroom at her own birthday party.

But if there was one thing Brynn was starting to suspect, it was that life's plans went to hell after thirty.

"Excuse me, um…ma'am? Would you mind passing some toilet paper? This roll is empty."

The slightly embarrassed question from the neighboring bathroom stall caught Brynn on the verge of a sob, and she blinked rapidly to keep the tears at bay.

"Oh. Sure." She kept her voice composed. Her voice was *always* composed.

Brynn carefully tore off six squares of toilet paper and folded them neatly. She was about to pass them under the stall when she paused. The tidiness of the bundle annoyed her. So instead of handing it over, she set the folded squares on her knee and slapped at the toilet paper roll again until she had an enormous wad of tissue. Brynn very slowly, very intentionally crumbled the toilet paper into a ball.

Much better.

Plus, now the poor lady on the other side wouldn't be in the awkward position of having to ask for some more toilet paper. And Brynn Dalton was *very* good about not putting people in awkward situations.

Brynn leaned down slightly and thrust the wad of tissue under the stall wall.

"Thanks," came the relieved voice. "You'd think a classy place like this would have enough TP stocked, huh?"

"You'd think," Brynn agreed politely. Not that she gave a hoot about the toilet paper stocking policies at SkyCity's private event venue.

"You here for the party?" the voice asked.

"Mm hmm," Brynn said, becoming aware that she was on the verge of entering full-on conversation from a toilet seat. What kind of crassness was this? Weren't bathroom stalls supposed to be sacred places?

"Do you know the birthday girl?" the voice persisted.

Brynn gave a grim smile at that. "Oh yes."

"Never met her," the other voice said. "I'm just tagging along as the date of one of her friends."

"Oh, nice," Brynn said, struggling to keep her voice polite.

Brynn heard Chatty Cathy's toilet flush. *Finally*. "Well, see ya," the voice said. "Good luck."

Good luck? What exactly did the stranger think Brynn was doing in here that required "luck"?

Then again, she had been in here for the better part of twenty minutes. And come to think of it... what *was* Brynn doing in here?

She knew only that she couldn't be out *there*. She'd rather be watching her dignity melt away while passing out toilet paper to strangers than face what awaited her:

Her thirty-first birthday, and a room full of people just itching to spot that first gray hair.

Brynn breathed a sigh of relief as she heard the sink faucet turn off, as the swish of the swinging door indicated that the talkative woman had returned to the party. *Finally* Brynn could commence what she'd come in to do in the first place.

Wallow. In private.

"Brynn! Brynn Dalton, are you in here?"

The door to the women's restroom banged against the wall and the click of a fast-paced high-heeled walk echoed through the marble bathroom.

Crap. Caught.

In an uncharacteristic burst of cowardice, Brynn contemplated lifting her feet above the ground so that her sister wouldn't be able to spot her shoes beneath the stall walls. She knew full well that Sophie Wyatt wouldn't think twice about crawling around on hands and knees until she spotted her prey.

Then again, knowing Sophie, she also wouldn't hesitate to look *over* the bathroom walls.

Resistance was futile.

The *tap-tap* of Sophie's heels paused outside the stall where Brynn sat hiding.

"I know you're in there, Brynn, I can see your boring brown shoes."

Brynn glanced down at her designer pumps. "They're not brown. They're nude."

"Seriously? *Nude* doesn't even count as a color."

Brynn's brow furrowed. What did she mean, nude wasn't a color? The saleswoman at Nordstrom had told her that nude heels would make her legs look "impossibly long."

She tried to look at them through her more flamboyant sister's eyes. Okay, maybe the shoes were a *little* boring.

Just like you.

She pushed the disparaging thought out of her head. Self-pity wasn't Brynn's normal style, but it had been steadily fighting for room in her brain ever since she'd learned that the birthday she'd been hoping to sweep under the carpet was turning into a damn circus.

Brynn heard the neighboring stall door swing open and the clatter of Sophie's heels on the closed toilet seat. Warily, Brynn glanced up and saw her sister's accusing blue eyes staring down at her.

"I knew it!" Sophie said. "You're not even *going*. You're hiding in there."

"Well if I were *going*, I certainly wouldn't appreciate the audience," Brynn mumbled.

Sophie waved away this objection. Younger sisters didn't put much stock in the value of privacy. Sophie folded her arms on top of the stall wall and rested her chin on her hands. "You okay?" she asked, her voice softening.

Brynn shifted uncomfortably, increasingly aware that the toilet seat cover was not meant for long stays. Exactly how long had she been in here? She'd only meant to hide out for a minute or two to catch her breath, but if Sophie had sniffed her out, her absence must have been noted.

"I thought I specifically said no surprise parties," Brynn said, trying to keep her voice calm as she addressed her sister.

Sophie's brow furrowed. "When?"

Brynn's fingers went to her temples. "When? How about every birthday for the past decade?"

"I thought all that fussing was about your *thirtieth* birthday. I didn't know it applied to thirty-one as well."

The tick in her temple increased and Brynn fought to keep from screaming at her sister. But the thing was, she knew that the warped logic made sense in Sophie's bubbly, carefree head.

Just as she knew that Sophie would never have thrown this party if she'd suspected Brynn wouldn't like it. Despite her occasional bouts with obliviousness, Sophie was one of the kindest, sweetest people Brynn knew.

But it didn't change the fact that everyone in her acquaintance had seen the big fat 31 cake on the table, and now knew her precise age. And instead of looking at what she'd accomplished, they'd be looking at what she *hadn't* accomplished.

No husband. No fiancé. No baby on the way...

All of which would have been fine if those things hadn't been part of *The Plan.*

"I'm really sorry, Brynny," her sister was saying. "It's just that we haven't really done *anything* for your birthday since you turned twenty-one. I thought you'd be sick of quietly toasting with Mom and Dad like we do every year."

"*Quietly* is the operative word there, Soph."

"But this is classy! It's the Space Needle. It's not like I dragged you to Cowgirls Inc."

Brynn stifled a shudder at the very thought of straddling

a mechanical bull or doing body shots, or whatever they did at Cowgirls Inc.

"It is a lovely party," Brynn said, belatedly realizing that she might be hurting Sophie's feelings. A party of this magnitude must have taken months to plan, and here Brynn was acting like it was an execution.

Get it together.

Taking a deep breath, Brynn stood and opened the stall door and walked calmly to the bathroom mirror. She heard Sophie noisily clamber to the ground and follow her.

"You look pretty," Sophie said, looking at Brynn's reflection.

"Even with my brown shoes?"

"I guess they're not so bad," Sophie said kindly. "They're very *you.*"

"Gee, thanks." But Brynn didn't take offense. Not really. They *were* her. And normally she took pride in being consistently subdued.

But today...

"I'm thirty-one, Soph," she blurted out.

"You always were good with numbers," Sophie said. "You know what else we could go count? The huge number of presents, and even bigger number of people here to see you."

"See me what, turn old and wrinkly right in front of their eyes?"

"Okay, stop," Sophie said, planting her fist on her hip. "Do you have any idea how obnoxious you sound? Thirty-one isn't even close to old, and you know perfectly well that you don't look a day over twenty-five."

Her sister's criticism chafed at Brynn's raw nerves. "Give me a break, Soph. Like *you've* never had a sense of panic over an impending birthday?" Brynn snapped. "I distinctively remember you going on a rampage about how your eggs were going to turn into raisins when you turned twenty-nine and Gray refused to turn his office into a nursery *just in case*."

"Yeah, but that's *me*. You know perfectly well that I am the whiner of the family. *You* always rise above pity parties. I thought it went against your moral code, or whatever you call that notebook of yours."

"It's my life list, not a moral code." She hated how snobbish her tone sounded.

Sophie's eyes narrowed. "Wait a minute. *That's* what this is about. Your stupid list."

Brynn began rummaging in her purse for her lipstick. Her *nude* lipstick. The same color she'd been using for almost a decade. "That's not it," she said primly.

Sophie snickered. "Oh it *sooo* is. Isn't there a thirty-five before thirty-five clause or something in there? Or is that an entirely separate list, not unlike your *Thirty Things to Do Before Thirty*, and your *Fifty Before Fifty* list."

"If you're going to make fun of me, I'm not going to talk about this with you," Brynn said as she applied a careful swipe of the lipstick.

But Sophie had already latched onto the topic. "Your hyperorganized little mind is running through all of the things you were supposed to have done by now. That's why you want your birthdays to slink by unnoticed."

Something squeezed in Brynn's chest. "I just...I thought I'd be engaged by now."

There.

She'd said it.

And she knew how it sounded. She'd practically delivered a death blow to feminism. Modern women didn't need a husband. Brynn didn't need a husband.

Except... it was on her *plan*. And what was the point of having a plan if you didn't stick to it?

She didn't bother looking at Sophie to gauge her reaction. She already knew her sister would be incredulous, and possibly a little outraged.

But Sophie wouldn't get it. How could she? Her younger sister had married the man of her dreams before the age of thirty, and was happier than she'd ever been in her life.

"But Brynny, it's just not your time," Sophie said softly. "And I thought things with James were going great? He's looking for you, by the way."

James.

Right. She felt even more ridiculous for stressing about her marital status when she had a perfectly wonderful boyfriend. A boyfriend who was currently stuck making small talk with people he barely knew because she was lamenting the lack of a shiny ring on her fourth finger.

She was pathetic.

"Listen," Sophie said, helping herself to the sugar-free gum from Brynn's purse. "I know you probably have some grand plan of where you're supposed to be by this exact date. But it doesn't always work like that. Or you know, maybe marriage just isn't in the cards for you."

Again, that tightness in her chest. *Dammit.* "It is," Brynn said firmly. "I know it is."

"Okay," Sophie said with strained patience. "Then it will happen. Someday. But hiding out in the bathroom isn't going to get you there any faster. I hardly think James's going to get marriage-minded with a woman who spends inordinate time in the restroom."

True. So true.

Brynn gave her sister a spontaneous hug. "I love how you always say the right thing in the weirdest way."

Sophie hugged her back before tugging at the hem of her flouncy blue cocktail dress and dropping into a small curtsy. "I do my best."

"You know, you might have given me a *hint* about this party so I could have dressed accordingly." Brynn looked her sister up and down. "You're not supposed to outshine the birthday girl."

Sophie waved her hand. "Please. Outshine perfect Brynn Dalton? Impossible."

Brynn gave a forced smile. Because once upon a time it had been *very* possible to outshine Brynn Dalton. But now wasn't the time to take a trip down memory lane. Although, come to think of it, the whole hiding-in-the bathroom thing was an all too familiar blast from the past.

A past that involved crying in the bathroom through most of second grade. And third...and pretty much every horrible day up until she'd finally begged her parents for braces, contacts, acne medication, and a regimented weight-loss program.

At fifteen, she'd finally figured out how to do it right. It had been the start of her lists. Lists that kept her from ever, ever being the one that stood out from the crowd to be pointed and laughed at.

Her lists and plans had kept her from ever having to sit alone at lunch, or hook up with a guy who was out of her league.

Her lists were her life. And she wasn't about to fall off the wagon at age thirty-one.

Besides, coming in second place to Sophie was just fine with her. God knew she was used to it.

Her sister was especially sparkly tonight. Sophie's blue dress was the perfect color to offset her bright blue eyes. And unlike Brynn's own boring "brown" pumps, Sophie's were a shocking orange. The look should have been garish, but instead was completely charming.

Charm was something the younger Dalton sister had in large doses. If Brynn was the smooth and reliable one, Sophie was the fun, alluring sister. Even Sophie's *hair* was more fun. Despite the fact that their long blonde hair was almost identical in color and texture, Sophie's was always styled in a mess of wild yellow curls. Brynn's own long hair was kept perfectly straight. A style that suited Brynn perfectly even if it did feel a bit...boring.

"Not boring. Respectable," Brynn reminded herself under her breath. And she'd learned early on that there were a lot worse things to be called than boring.

"Yeah, yeah," Sophie said as she dragged Brynn toward the bathroom door. "You're respectable, *and* you're beautiful, rich, and successful. Everyone adores you. Blah blah. The only person who RSVPed *no* to your party was Aunt Philly, and that's just as well because now we don't have to hear about her hemorrhoids. But—"

"There's a but?" Brynn interrupted.

Sophie paused at the door and spun back around. "You have to promise me to loosen up. Forget that damn list for once. Drink too much champagne and have drunk sex with James back at his place."

Brynn carefully kept her face blank. She and James hadn't been having much of *any* sex lately, but there were some things even one's sister didn't need to know.

"Fine," Brynn said reluctantly, "but if Mom starts on one of her rampages about how I'm not getting any younger..."

"I'll handle Mom," Sophie said as she shoved Brynn through the door. "You just get yourself some bubbly booze, and embrace another fabulous year in the life of Seattle's most gorgeous orthodontist."

"Yeah, because the competition is pretty stiff in that category," Brynn said as she plucked a glass of champagne from a passing tray.

"There you are," said a familiar male voice from behind Sophie and Brynn. "Everyone's been wondering what happened to you two."

"Ladies room," Sophie said, sliding an arm around her new husband's waist.

Gray Wyatt raised an eyebrow. "The entire time?"

Sophie raised an eyebrow right back. "Do you really want details?"

Gray grunted, and fell silent. Silence was something Grayson Wyatt did a lot of. Brynn should know. She'd dated the man for about five seconds of tepid boredom before he and Sophie had spontaneously combusted. Not that anyone ever remembered Brynn and Gray's romantic history. Probably because it hadn't been the least bit romantic.

"Thanks for the party, Gray," Brynn said. "I know you're friends with the owner of the restaurant."

Gray gave a polite nod. "The planning was all Sophie. If it was up to me, I would have planned something more..."

"Dull? Bland? Introverted?" Sophie supplied.

Gray's amused gray eyes met Brynn's over Sophie's head. "I was going to say mellow."

Sophie sniffed. "Yawn. People like you and Brynn have plenty of mellow in your life."

"Has anyone seen James?" Brynn asked, scanning the room for her boyfriend. He could hold his own in social situations, but she felt bad leaving him alone this long. Especially since he'd probably helped coordinate this whole disaster with Sophie. She should at least say thank you.

"He was talking with your dad," Gray volunteered, taking a sip of his whiskey.

"The usual medical mumbo jumbo?"

"Yep. Didn't understand a word of it," Gray confirmed.

"Great," Brynn muttered. She was glad her father and boyfriend got along. She just wished they were able to connect on something other than ER policy and the latest heart-valve technology.

"Seriously, I don't know what you two talk about," Sophie said as she eyed a tray of passing spring rolls with a critical eye. "James is nice, but the man's like a machine. He's practically been a part of the family for the past year, but I still can't get more than small talk and lengthy lectures out of him."

"You thought Gray was a machine when you first met him," Brynn countered.

Sophie cuddled up to her husband's side with a coy grin, and Brynn stifled the sting of jealousy at the easy connect between her sister and her husband. "Well I may have made a mistake about that," Sophie said softly.

"A mistake? You?" Gray said blandly.

"Just the one. Unlike you and Brynn who have so much red tape running every which way that you couldn't *possibly* make a mistake. You're both overdue. Mistakes build character..."

But Brynn couldn't hear her sister over the rushing in her ears.

He. Was. Back.

Look away. Look away now from The Enemy.

But she couldn't tear her eyes away from the tall blond man currently ogling a redhead in a killer black dress. His dark jeans and white shirt should have been too casual for the occasion. But nobody would notice that he was underdressed. They'd be too busy basking in his wide smiles and hot gazes.

Why was he back?

"Brynn, are you listening to me?" Sophie asked. "I was just explaining how maybe if you would slip up every now and then you wouldn't have to hide in the bathroom on your birthday."

Sophie couldn't have been more wrong about Brynn not making mistakes.

Because once upon a time, she'd made the most elementary of all mistakes.

And he was staring right at her.

THE DISH

Where Authors Give You the Inside Scoop

From the desk of Kristen Ashley

Dear Reader,

When the idea for LADY LUCK came to me, it was after watching the Dwayne Johnson film *Faster.*

I thought that movie was marvelous, and not just simply because I was watching all the beauty that is Dwayne Johnson on the screen.

What I enjoyed about it was that he played against his normal *The Game Plan/Gridiron Gang* funny guy/good guy type and shocked me by being an antihero. What made it even better was that he had very little dialogue. Now I enjoy watching Mr. Johnson do just about anything, including speak. What was so amazing about this is that his character in *Faster* should have been difficult to like, to root for, especially since he gave us very few words as to *why* we should do that. But he made me like him, root for him. Completely.

It was his face. It was his eyes. It was the way he could express himself with those—*not* his actions—that made us want him to get the vengeance he sought.

Therefore, when I was formulating Ty Walker and Alexa "Lexie" Berry from LADY LUCK in my head, I was building Ty as an antihero focused on revenge—a man who would do absolutely anything to get it. As for

Lexie, I was shoehorning her into this cold, seen-it-all/done-it-all/had-nothing-left-to-give woman who was cold as ice.

I was quite excited about the prospect of what would happen with these two. A silent man with the fire of vengeance in place of his heart. A closed-off woman with a block of ice in place of hers.

Imagine my surprise as I wrote the first chapter of this book and the Ty and Lexie I was creating in my head were blown to smithereens so the real Ty and Lexie could come out, not one thing like I'd been making them in my head.

This happens, not often, but it happens. And it happens when I "make up" characters. Normally, my characters come to me as they are, who they are, the way they look, and all the rest. If I try to create them from nothing, force them into what I want them to be, they fight back.

By the time I got to writing Ty and Lexie, I learned not to engage in a battle I never win. I just let go of who I thought they should be and where I thought they were going and took their ride.

And what a ride.

I'm so pleased I didn't battle them and got to know them just as they are because their love story was a pleasure to watch unfold. There were times that were tough, very tough, and I would say perhaps the toughest I've ever written. But that just made their happy ending one that tasted unbelievably sweet.

Of course, Ty did retain some of that silent angry man, but he never became the antihero I expected him to be, though he did do a few non-heroic things in dealing with his intense issues. And I reckon one day I'll have my antihero set on a course of vengeance who finds a woman who has a heart of ice. Those concepts never go away. They just have to come to me naturally.

But I had to give Ty and Lexie their story as it came to me naturally.

And I loved every second of it.

Kristen Ashley

♥ ♥ ♥ ♥ ♥ ♥ ♥ ♥ ♥ ♥ ♥ ♥ ♥ ♥ ♥

From the desk of Anna Sullivan

Dear Reader,

There's a lot more to being a writer than sitting at a computer and turning my imagination into reality. Of course I love creating characters, deciding on their personal foibles, inventing a series of events to not only test their character but also to help them grow. And that's where everything begins: with the story.

But every writer does her share of book signings and interviews. As with every profession, there are some questions that crop up more often than others. Here are some examples—and the answers that run through my mind in my more irreverent moments:

Q: Why did you become a writer?
A: Because I like to control the people in my life and the only way I can do that is to invent them. (And

unfortunately, I still don't have much control; it's regrettable how often they don't listen to me and get into trouble anyway.)

Q: Those sex scenes, huh? (This invariably comes along with a smirk, waggling eyebrows, or a wink.)
A: I have three kids, you do the math. And please don't wink; it's almost never cute.

Q: Where do you get these ideas?
A: I used to ask my children that after they did something...unexpected. They'd usually come up blank. So do I, so I'll just say I don't know where the characters come from, but they won't leave me alone until I write them. I think there may be a clinical diagnosis and prescription meds for my affliction, but what kind of fun would that be?

But seriously, I hope you enjoy my second Windfall Island novel, HIDEAWAY COVE, as the search for Eugenia Stanhope, kidnapped almost a century before, continues.

Now Holden Abbot is joining the quest for truth, justice, and the American way...Wait, that's Superman. Well, Holden Abbot may not be the man of steel, but he's tall and handsome, and his smooth Southern accent doesn't hurt either. And even if he can't leap tall buildings in a single bound, Jessi Randal is falling head over heels in love with him. She may be Eugenia Stanhope's long-lost descendant, though, and that puts her life in danger, along with her seven year-old son, Benji. Holden may have to do the superhero thing after all. Or he may only be able to save one of them.

I had a great time finding out how this story ended. I hope you do, too.

Anna Sullivan

www.AnnaSulivanBooks.com
Twitter @ASullivanBooks
Facebook.com/AnnaSullivanBooks

♥ ♥ ♥ ♥ ♥ ♥ ♥ ♥ ♥ ♥ ♥ ♥ ♥ ♥ ♥

From the desk of Rochelle Alers

Dear Reader,

Writers hear it over and over again: Write about what you know. I believe I adhered to this rule when continuing the Cavanaugh Island series with MAGNOLIA DRIVE. This time you get to read about a young Gullah woman and her gift to discern the future. As I completed the character dossier for the heroine, I could hear my dearly departed mother whisper in my ear not to tell too much, because like her, my mother also had the gift of sight.

Growing up in New York City didn't lend itself to connecting with my Gullah roots until I was old enough to understand why my mother and other Gullah held to certain traditions that were a litany of don'ts: Don't put your hat on the bed, don't throw out what you sweep up after dark, don't put up a new calendar before the beginning of a new year, et cetera, et cetera, et cetera. The don'ts go on and on, too numerous to list here.

I'd believed the superstitions were silly until as an adult

I wanted to know why my grandfather, although born in Savannah, spoke English with a distinctive accent. However, it was the womenfolk in my family who taught me what it meant to be Gullah and the significance of the traditions passed down through generations of griots.

In MAGNOLIA DRIVE, red-haired, green-eyed Francine Tanner is Gullah and a modern-day griot and psychic. She is able to see everyone's future, though not her own. But when a handsome stranger sits in her chair at the Beauty Box asking for a haircut and a shave, the former actress turned hairstylist could never have predicted the effect he would have on her life and her future.

The first time Keaton Grace saw up-and-coming actress Francine Tanner perform in an off-Broadway show he found himself spellbound by her incredible talent. So much so that he wrote a movie script with her in mind. Then it was as if she dropped off the earth when she abruptly left the stage. The independent filmmaker didn't know their paths would cross again when he made plans to set up his movie studio, Grace Lowcountry Productions, on Cavanaugh Island. Keaton believes they were destined to meet again, while Francine fears reopening a chapter in her life she closed eight years ago.

MAGNOLIA DRIVE returns to Sanctuary Cove, where the customers at the Beauty Box will keep you laughing and wanting more, while the residents of the Cove are in rare form once they take sides in an upcoming local election. Many of the familiar characters are back to give you a glimpse into what has been going on in their lives. And for those of you who've asked if David Sullivan will ever find a love that promises forever—the answer is yes. Look for David and the woman who will tug at his heart and make him reassess his priorities in *Cherry Lane.*

Happy Reading!

Rochelle Alers

ralersbooks@aol.com
www.rochellealers.org

♥ ♥ ♥ ♥ ♥ ♥ ♥ ♥ ♥ ♥ ♥ ♥ ♥ ♥ ♥

From the desk of Jessica Scott

Dear Reader,

The first time I got the idea for my hero and heroine in BACK TO YOU, Trent and Laura, I was a brand-new lieutenant with no idea what deployment would entail. I remember sitting in my office, listening to one of the captains telling his wife he'd be home as soon as he could—and right after he hung up the phone, he promptly went back to work. He always talked about how much he loved her, and I wondered how he could tell her one thing and do something so different. And even more so, I was deeply curious about what his wife was like.

I was curious about the kind of woman who would love a man no matter how much war changed him. About the kind of woman with so much strength that she could hold their family together no matter what. But also, a woman who was *tired*. Who was starting to lose her faith in the man she'd married.

Having been the spouse left at home to hold the family together, I know intimately the struggles Laura has faced. I also know what it feels like to deploy and leave my family, and how hard it is to come home.

I absolutely love writing stories of redemption, and at the heart of it, this is a story of redemption. It takes a strong love to make it through the dark times.

I hope you enjoy reading Trent and Laura's story in BACK TO YOU as much as I enjoyed bringing their story to life.

Xoxo

Jessica Scott

www.JessicaScott.net
Twitter @JessicaScott09
Facebook.com/JessicaScottAuthor

♥ ♥ ♥ ♥ ♥ ♥ ♥ ♥ ♥ ♥ ♥ ♥ ♥ ♥ ♥

From the desk of Shannon Richard

Dear Reader,

So UNSTOPPABLE had originally been planned for the fourth book, but after certain plot developments, Bennett and Mel's story needed to be moved in the lineup to third place. When I dove into their story I knew very little about where I was going, but once I started there was no turning back.

Bennett Hart was another character who walked onto the page out of nowhere and the second I met him I knew he *needed* to have his story told. I mean, how could he not when he's named after one of my favorite heroines? Yup, Bennett is named after Elizabeth Bennett from Jane Austen's *Pride and Prejudice*. Don't scoff, she's awesome and I love her dearly. And *hello*, she ends up with a certain Mr. Fitzwilliam Darcy...he's my ultimate literary crush. I mean really, I swoon just thinking about him.

And I'm not the only one swooning over here. A certain Ms. Melanie O'Bryan is hard-core dreaming/fantasizing/drooling (just a little bit) over Bennett. Mel was definitely an unexpected character for me. It took me a little while to see that she had a story to tell, and I always like to say it was Bennett who realized her potential before I did.

Both characters have their guards up at the beginning of UNSTOPPABLE. Bennett is still dealing with the trauma he experienced when he was in Afghanistan, and Mel is dealing with getting shot a couple of months ago. Mel is a very sweet girl and she appears to be just a little bit unassuming...to those who don't know her, that is. As it turns out, she has a wild side and she lets Bennett see it in full force. Bennett and Mel were a different writing experience for me. I was discovering them as they discovered each other, and sometimes they surprised me beyond words. They taught me a lot about myself and I will be forever grateful that they shared their story with me.

Cheers,

Shannon Richard

♥ ♥ ♥ ♥ ♥ ♥ ♥ ♥ ♥ ♥ ♥ ♥ ♥ ♥ ♥

From the desk of Lauren Layne

Dear Reader,

I am a hopeless romantic. For as long as I can remember, I've been stalking happy endings. It started with skimming Nancy Drew and Sweet Valley Twins books for the parts about boys. From there, it was sneaking into the Young Adult section of the library way before my time to get at the Sweet Valley High books—because there was kissing in those.

By my mid-teens, I'd discovered that there was an entire genre of books devoted to giving romantics like me a guaranteed happily ever after. It was the start of a lifetime affair with romance novels.

So it shouldn't come as a surprise that as I was stockpiling my book boyfriends, I also did a fair amount of thinking about the future hero of my own love story. I had it all figured out by junior high. My future husband would have brown hair. He'd be a lawyer. Maybe a doctor, but probably a lawyer. He'd be the strong, silent type. Very stoic. He'd be a conservative dresser, and it would be strange to see him out of his classic black suit, except on weekends when he'd wear khakis and pressed polos. We'd meet when I was in my mid-to-late twenties, and he'd realize instantly that my power suits and classic pumps were his perfect match. Did I mention that in this vision I, too, was a lawyer?

Fast forward a few (okay, many) years. How'd I do?

Well...my husband has brown hair. *That's the only part I got right.* He's an extroverted charmer and wouldn't be caught dead in a standard-issue suit. He's not a lawyer, and I've never seen him wear khakis. Oh, and we started dating in high school, and were married by twenty-three.

I couldn't have been more wrong, and yet...I couldn't be more happy. Although I am a "planner" in every sense of the word, I've learned that love doesn't care one bit about the person you *think* is your perfect mate.

In my Best Mistake series, the heroines learn exactly that. They have a pretty clear idea of the type of person they're supposed to be with. And they couldn't be more wrong.

Whether it's the cocktail waitress falling for the uptight CEO, or the rigid perfectionist who wins the heart of a dedicated playboy, these women learn that being wrong has never felt so right.

I had a wonderful time wreaking havoc on the lives of Sophie and Brynn Dalton, and I hope you have as much fun reading about the best mistakes these women ever made.

Here's to the best of plans going awry—because that's when the fun starts.

Lauren Layne

www.laurenlayne.com

3103